THE ITALIAN PARTY

This Large Print Book carries the
Seal of Approval of N.A.V.H.

THE ITALIAN PARTY

CHRISTINA LYNCH

THORNDIKE PRESS

A part of Gale, a Cengage Company

GALE
A Cengage Company

Farmington Hills, Mich • San Francisco • New York • Waterville, Maine
Meriden, Conn • Mason, Ohio • Chicago

LIBRARY OF CONGRESS CIP DATA ON FILE.
CATALOGUING IN PUBLICATION FOR THIS BOOK
IS AVAILABLE FROM THE LIBRARY OF CONGRESS

ISBN-13: 978-1-4328-5490-4 (hardcover)

Published in 2018 by arrangement with Macmillan Publishing Group,LLC/St. Martin's Press

Printed in the United States of America
1 2 3 4 5 6 7 22 21 20 19 18

Edward T. Hall, the cultural anthropologist who advised members of the State Department in the '50s, wrote that you can live in another culture all your life and you will never completely understand it, but you will come to understand your own.

— HOLLY BRUBACH, "Dislocation, Italian Style," *The New York Times,* July 18, 2014

■ ■ ■ ■

PART ONE:
TERZO DI CAMOLLIA

■ ■ ■ ■

Whoever steps into a *Ristorante* or *Trattoria* is expected to have at least a full hour's time and a three-course appetite.
— "Eating in Italy: The Sacred Canons of Gastronomy Prevail Despite Innovations," *The New York Times,* March 4, 1956

ONE:
LA LUPA, THE WOLF

"FROM ROME THE COAT OF ARMS,
FROM SIENA THE HONOR"

Tuscany, April 25, 1956

1.

Newlyweds Mr. and Mrs. Michael Messina drove down the Via Cassia from Florence, he at the wheel, she with the map. The car was brand-new, a two-tone Ford Fairlane in canary yellow and white, headlights gazing into the future, the only car of its kind in all of Italy. It was twice the size of the tiny, drab little Italian matchboxes they were passing, like an eagle amidst starlings.

A young girl bicycling home from school along the side of the road, a woman selling wild asparagus at the pullout, a man tying down grapevines who was stretching his back as they sailed past — they could do nothing but stare, mouths agape, then shake their heads. *Americani.* It was like they came from another planet.

It had been eleven years since the end of war in Europe. Most Italians just wanted to forget and move on. Rebuilding was well under way, yet the scars of war were still evident everywhere, in every sense, if you knew where to look. Milan, for example, had been nearly leveled, but with great practicality the Milanese had bulldozed all of the debris into a neat, enormous pile on the outskirts of the city, covered it with dirt, nicknamed it "the Little Mountain," and built a new city center. Naples distracted itself with Sophia Loren. In central Italy, the scene of much heavy fighting as the Germans reluctantly retreated up the peninsula, many chose to leave rather than rebuild, so that ghostly ruins were being slowly swallowed by nature, half an ivy-covered arch here, a fig tree growing through a cracked tile roof there, stone walls crumbling under the claws of rampant, unruly caper bushes.

"Don't you wish," the wife said, tracing her finger along the edge of the car window, "that when you met someone, you could see the story of his or her life? Fast, like a quick little movie, you know?"

"That sounds awful," said her husband,

teasing. "I don't want people to see me picking my nose in fourth grade."

"No," she insisted, "it would be just the most important events, the ones that have shaped who they are. So you could really *know* them."

"Still not signing up," he said. They passed a dilapidated blue bus, every face inside turned to watch them, wide-eyed.

"Really? Don't you think it would help us all get along better? Understand each other better?"

"Like if I saw Stalin's childhood puppy getting run over I would have liked him better? Don't think so."

She blushed. "I guess you're right."

As the car zoomed down the road, Scottie took it all in, her eyes hungry for a new landscape, a fresh start. She reminded herself that it was better that Michael couldn't see the story of her life. He would never have married her. But she would like to see his — there was so much about him she didn't know. In fact, she really didn't know much about him at all. Where to even begin?

"Did you have your teeth straightened?" she asked.

2.

Michael and Scottie stood out from the moment they strolled down the gangplank of the sleek ocean liner that carried them and their possessions to Italy. They seemed to have stepped right out of an advertisement for Betty Crocker, Wonder Bread or capitalism itself. He was twenty-four, handsome, always in a nicely cut suit, camera around his neck. She, barely twenty, was a knockout. Blond, pretty, quick to laugh, always in an elegant hat and pearl choker. She had what the Italians call *raffinatezza,* a word that covers everything that is the opposite of vulgar — a quality Italians deeply aspired to, while at the same time remaining powerless to resist anything gilded, mirrored, shiny or bejeweled. This spring the papers were full of the marriage of Grace Kelly and Prince Rainier, and it was as if Siena's own version of the royal couple had arrived. Even though there were other Americans coming and going in Siena, those two would become *the* Americans. *Gli americani.* Both of them so young, healthy, wealthy and in love. They seemed so *free.* That was how they seemed.

They were arriving in Siena as part of a wave of missionaries bringing the American way of life to what they were certain would be a grateful populace.

Michael felt like he'd won the lottery. This beautiful creature had agreed to marry him and come on a foreign adventure. A Vassar girl, from a good family out in California! Him just a boy from the Bronx! And the best part was, she wasn't that smart. Because that's what Michael wanted. What he needed. Someone who wasn't too curious. Someone who would mistake his version of things for the truth.

The Italians would take them at face value, see only what they were meant to see. As a culture the Italians valued *furbizia* — slyness — more than honesty, but they would not expect to find it in Americans, who were generally seen as genial idiots ripe for the plucking. It was only natural for Michael and Scottie to make assumptions about each other, too. They had known each other just a short time, and no courtship is entirely honest. It was convenient for Michael that Scottie had been taught that asking questions — as long as they were not too personal, or impertinent — rather than offering opinions made a man feel like he was being listened to, and supported. She had been taught that a woman likes to feel beautiful, and a man likes to feel superior.

That was what she had been taught.

That was what he believed she had learned.

3.

The Fairlane leapt over potholes that threatened to eat the smaller Italian cars.

"You know, this road's been here since Julius Caesar's time," said Michael.

"Tell me about Caesar," said Scottie. "Would he get along with Eisenhower, you think?"

He stretched his arm along the seatback and tickled her neck, as if she were a small dog. "Well, they could sure swap ideas about building highways," said Michael, who enjoyed retreating into history when the present felt too threatening, which was much of the time. Behind the movie-star-handsome dark brows, strong, masculine nose and square chin, he was a nervous fellow, still the schoolboy who had compensated for his social insecurity by doing well in school. The classroom, in fact, was the only place he had ever felt at home. "Caesar had his legions lay these stones by hand to a depth of four feet, which is deeper than Ike's crews are building the new interstates." Michael had told her that within a few years, Americans would be able to drive from the Atlantic to the Pacific without

14

waiting at a single stoplight. Michael had told her that the Italians were using some of the billion dollars that America had given them to rebuild after the war for high-speed roads here, too. Michael had told her a lot of things. She hoped there wasn't going to be a quiz. The classroom was the last place Scottie ever felt comfortable. Letters and words on a page were a jumbled code she struggled to decipher. No one had ever told her that she had dyslexia. Her teachers assumed she was stupid, and so did she, unable to see that her ability to adapt to almost any situation with good humor was a greater asset than any PhD.

"A new highway's going to come right through here. It'll put this place on the map. No more donkey carts," he said as he swerved around one.

"I love the donkeys." She waved to the lop-eared donkey and the woman leading it, who glared at her and made a gesture. Michael didn't see it, so Scottie said, "What does this mean?" and Michael looked at her, a little shocked, and laughed nervously.

"Where did you see that?" he asked.

"Is it rude?"

"Very. I wouldn't do that again."

She laughed, and he laughed with her. Neither of them would ever sink so low as to make rude gestures!

The car rat-a-tatted over the old basalt stones underneath its mighty wheels. The green fields they passed were dotted with red poppies. Scottie spotted distant villas tucked into greenery, her eye drawn to the occasional gray or pair of bays grazing in an olive grove.

"Nice," she said. "Not thoroughbreds, but well put together, though." She looked over at Michael. "We should go riding sometime." She pictured them galloping along side by side over these lovely green hills. That was what she would do if her best friend, Leona, were here with her. She and Leona always had fun together. Couldn't marriage be like that?

4.

As they came around a curve, Siena suddenly appeared above them, a walled fortress city perched on a leafy green hilltop, terraces of tan brick and stone buildings with dark red terra-cotta roofs underneath an immense cupola, and the black and white Cheshire cat stripes of the Duomo's prickly bell tower jutting up into a clear blue sky.

"I think you're going to like it here," Michael said. "Siena's a very interesting place. It was on an ancient religious route, so it became wealthy, cultured and powerful, thanks to all those foreigners and their money passing through. The world's first bank was born here — Monte dei Paschi di Siena, in 1472. Before Columbus even set sail!"

"You know everything," she teased.

"You'll like this," he said. "The stripes symbolize the black and white horses of the legendary founders of the city, Senius and his brother Aschius."

Michael did not mind that Scottie was obsessed with horses. He had no intention of ever trusting his own life to a thousand-pound animal with a brain the size of a walnut. But it was a charming, aristocratic quality in her. An expensive habit for sure, but she came with enough money to support it.

"It looks so old, like something from a fairy tale."

Yes, he thought, childlike. She's childlike. He saw that as a good thing. It made him even fonder of her. She needed to be taken care of. "I don't want to pry," he said. "But it may be difficult to manage your money from overseas. Did you make arrangements with your bank? It can be complicated, and I'm happy to help."

Scottie blushed and turned wide blue eyes

on him. "I don't have any money," she said. She blinked, and there was an awkward moment of silence. "Did you think I did?"

5.

Now he knows, she thought. He stared back at her for a moment, his sleek sealskin eyebrows raised, then looked out the windshield and laughed to himself in a way she found hard to interpret.

The road narrowed as it zigzagged steeply up to the city.

The beauty of their marriage was that she, too, at the moment of saying "I do" felt like she had won the lottery. A Yale man. Handsome. And not some frat-boy bruiser either — Michael was sensitive, with an artistic soul. He was compassionate, having endured the tragedy of losing his brother in the war. True, he was not wealthy — yet. But he was ambitious and hardworking, so success was sure to follow. He had a good job with Ford, that most solid of companies. This was the age when every American family was for the first time buying a car or two, and as Michael had told her, Eisenhower was building interstates so that Americans could go see this land their loved ones had laid down their lives defending. Scottie felt that with Michael, she was literally going places. And fortunately, those places were across the Atlantic, where no one would ask too many questions.

6.

"With the plague came depopulation and poverty, poverty led to military weakness, military weakness led to the city being conquered by its loathed rival city-state Florence, which led to humiliation and more poverty." They were climbing through olive groves toward the city now. He steered around another donkey cart, this one piled high with firewood.

"That little guy could sure use a pedicure," she said, craning her head to study the poor beast's hoofs in the rearview mirror.

So she didn't have money. He had to admit that was a surprise. He ran over their conversations in his head. Had she lied to him? No. He had made assumptions. Father in oranges in California. Vassar. Nice clothes. Friends with the DuPont girl. She must mean she didn't have money *yet*. There would be a trust fund for her. Perhaps it came later, when she turned twenty-five or thirty. It was fine — she was still perfect. Nearly perfect.

Michael felt an urgent need to make her

understand the *importance* of everything they were seeing. How it got this way. How bad things were, but how much better they would soon be. He wanted her to share his love of history.

"Except for the bank, which did fine, Siena pretty much limped into the twentieth century as a market town for poor share-croppers growing subsistence crops in a not particularly fertile zone of heavy clay soil, vicious mosquitoes and baking summer heat."

"Baking summer heat. Got it." She smiled at a little girl on a red bicycle, who stared back at her wide-eyed, as if she were watching a spaceship float past.

"The rest of Italy refers to Tuscans as *maledetti,* damned, trapped here as if in hell." He pointed off to the left. "Other than the train station over there, which was decimated, even the Allies pretty much ignored Siena as they bombed their way north, chasing the Germans out of Tuscany."

She glanced over at him. On the roof at Vassar the night he proposed he told her that his brother Marco had been killed at Monte Cassino in 1944. Michael, the youngest of their parents' six children, was only twelve at the time. He didn't seem to want to say more about it then. She wondered if he would now, but he went on blithely. "I saw a picture in an old issue of *Life*. The Allies paused their tanks in Piazza del Campo just long enough for a photo op before they moved on to more important targets."

"But they like us, right? The Italians?"

"Oh yes," he said. "They love us."

They came to a stop at an intersection with about twenty signs pointing in all different directions. "It says to enter the city at Porta Camollia," she said, deciphering the directions.

"*Sì, signora,*" he said with a confident smile. He piloted the Ford Fairlane under the arched gate in the massive city walls, and they motored slowly down Via Banchi di Sopra, a crowd of curious and excited children gathering behind them as if they were movie stars. Scottie looked up at the laundry festooning the narrow streets and said, "These women are going to be so happy when they have dryers."

"And televisions," said Michael. "I heard everyone goes to the corner bar when they want to watch something, and there's only one channel."

"I can't believe they still breastfeed their children," said Scottie.

They shook their heads at how sadly

backward things were here. But help was on the way!

7.

"Left here," Scottie said, squinting at the property manager's foreign scrawl. There was something about the city being divided into three parts, *terzi,* but which part were they in now?

They turned, she believed, onto Via di Città, but it wasn't. It was some other street, which led to an alley. There were no signs. Suddenly her map seemed all wrong, a threatening labyrinth. They turned around, barely, Michael red-faced, the tendons in his neck standing out. She shrank down in her seat, ashamed and a little frightened, as he roared up the narrow street past a laughing old man in a tattered black hat and took a sharp right onto —

"Wait," Scottie yelped, madly searching the map. "I'm not sure that's —"

"It must go *somewhere,*" Michael snarled. Her genial husband was gone, replaced by — who was this man?

Scottie looked up from the map to see brick walls narrowing and arching over them. The sky disappeared and they were plunged into semidarkness. She couldn't understand how he thought the car was going to fit.

"I think it's the other way, Prince," she said gaily.

"Well, I can't back up," he snapped, and she was quiet. They inched forward, the web of laundry lines seeming to get lower and lower over them, and the walls closer and closer, until . . . *crunch.*

The eagle was firmly lodged between two brick walls.

Michael hit the accelerator hard, but only produced a horrible noise and a smell of burning rubber. He put it in reverse, but got the same result. He smacked the steering wheel with his palms. His formerly beautiful mouth was set in an angry, ugly line.

We're strangers, she realized.

They couldn't get out of the car. They had to sit there, avoiding each other's eyes, waiting for help.

Two:
Il Bruco, The Caterpillar

"THE REVOLUTION SOUNDS MY NAME"

1.

Scottie was no stranger to adventures gone wrong. When she was a child in California her pony had regularly bolted on her and carried her under guillotine-like tree limbs. Like a trick rider, she simply dropped her head and torso down one side of the evil beast and spurred him harder. She had often gotten lost while hiking in the mountains above Los Angeles and come home after dark, always lying to her father about having "visited a friend" so that he would not be worried about her. And after her father had decided his little tomboy needed "polishing" and sent her to Miss Porter's, a fancy boarding school back east, she and Leona had snuck out of their dorm when they were thirteen and gone into New York City to see a shirtless Kirk Douglas in

24

Champion. Spotting a teacher attending the same matinee, they hid under the seats, Scottie pretending to Leona that she was licking the sticky floor, Leona tying an unsuspecting man's shoelaces together. Scottie had come to believe that an adventure really wasn't an adventure until something went wrong and you had to rise to the occasion. She reached for the radio, but thought better of it. She thumbed through her Berlitz phrase book, looking for the word for "stuck." *La macchina è . . .*

Michael stared straight ahead. He looked as if he were in some kind of trance. She felt a new kind of worry bloom inside her like a fungus. Why wasn't he doing anything? His hands were still on the steering wheel, as if somehow the crushing jaws of this unfriendly place were going to suddenly open up and free them and he could race forward. Even though it was silly, she couldn't help but feel it was all her fault — in *Roman Holiday* Audrey Hepburn had stuck her fingers into the Bocca della Verità, an ancient carving. It bit you if you were lying.

It made perfect sense that the jaws of Siena had snapped shut on her.

2.

As he sat in the stuck car, feeling the persona he had presented to his new bosses and to Scottie disintegrate, Michael remembered something his literature professor had said, that in Dante's *Inferno* the worst, Ninth Circle of Hell was reserved for those guilty of treachery. Because they had made a mockery of love of family, of country, of friends, of God, they were exiled to a place where they were frozen, their screams rendered immobile and eternal. While Scottie's natural instinct was to defuse tension and laugh at complications, Michael had a more operatic temperament. He was hearing the clashing cymbals that foreshadow the hero's agonizing death, already seeing the coffin with his body being unloaded at the pier in New York, his mother weeping over it. But not, a voice crept into his thoughts, weeping as much as she had wept for his war-hero brother. He sighed. It was truly a bad day when even thoughts of death were not a consolation.

Trapped in the car and deeply unsure what to do about it, he found himself staring at an election poster plastered to the wall next to the car. A man's enormous face stared back at them. VOTARE GIANNI MANGANELLI, it shouted in huge type. A single word was scrawled over it in red paint: mai.

"I would vote for him," said Scottie brightly, as if they were stuck in a traffic jam instead of between two walls. "Looks like a friendly type. What's he running for?"

"Mayor," said Michael. He pretended to study the party shield in the corner of the poster, as if he didn't already know it by heart. "Looks like he's the Christian Democratic candidate. That's the Catholic party. They're pro-American."

"Oh. Well, that's good. And what's *mai* mean?"

"Never."

"Oh," she said again. "So a Communist wrote that?"

"Yes," he said, his fear deepening.

"That's not very nice."

"No," said Michael. "It is not. The Communists are trying to take over Italy."

"Oh dear," she said. "But not here, right?"

"Yes. Here," he said, trying to sound casual. "This is the heart of Italian communism." *The blood red heart,* was what he had been told. *And you must cut out its aorta.*

Michael did not actually work for Ford. That is, he *was* coming to Siena to open a Ford office there to convince the Tuscans that a fine American tractor was the way to prosperity. But that was not his real job; it was only his cover. His real job was to secretly make sure Gianni Manganelli, Catholic party candidate, won the Siena mayoral election. Michael was, unbeknownst to Scottie, working for the CIA. Being a secret agent was not what he had originally planned to do with his life. He had planned to teach art history at a small boarding school — green fields, quiet libraries, sherry — but somehow, he had shocked even himself, and now he, the person his classmates would have voted least likely to do anything more heroic than rescue a kitten from a tree, was on a top secret mission. He had been told by none other than Clare Boothe Luce, the American ambassador to Italy, that the fate of the world might well depend on him. "Half the planet is enslaved by communism," she had intoned. "Do you want the entire globe in chains?" As if suspecting his doubts about his abilities, she added, "This is a new kind of war. Men who have the talent of being invisible are the ones who will win this one."

All he had to do was single-handedly sway one small election, so all of Western civilization didn't come tumbling down.

Thus far he had bluffed his way along, pretending to be confident, competent. But he was scared out of his mind. His father was right. The world would be better off if his brother Marco had lived instead of him.

"Well, gosh," said Scottie, who of course knew none of this. "Getting our car stuck doesn't really set a good example for our side, then, does it?"

The children who had been following them started climbing all over the car. They were laughing and pounding and putting their faces up against the glass. Scottie was making monkey faces at them when Michael began shouting, "Off! Get off!"

3.

I hate Italians, he thought. He had always despised the way his parents, who had emigrated from Sicily in 1914, clung to their traditions even as they were at each other's throats, so proud. Proud of what? Coming from a place that was stuck in the Middle Ages? A country that had sided with the Nazis until it was no longer convenient? That was now flirting with the Kremlin?

His family had managed to embarrass him even at the minimalist city hall wedding he and Scottie had agreed on. He was relieved when his sisters refused to come at all, claiming a wedding not held in a church was not a wedding in the eyes of God. He told Scottie they were ill. Scottie's Aunt Ida

29

was there, clearly disapproving of the match, which was bad enough. Then there was Scottie's roommate and best friend, Leona, who had mistaken him for the elevator operator even though they had met several times before. But his parents were the worst. He cringed as they embraced Scottie, and his mother cried and told her in broken English that this was the happiest day of her life. His father handed her a small paper bag.

"Candy-coated almonds," he said. "Tradition. To remind you that life ahead will be both bitter and sweet." Then his mother had given her a piece of iron to ward off evil spirits.

Scottie seemed charmed by all the superstition, but Michael saw Leona and Aunt Ida exchanging a look. He knew that look. All he wanted was to get away from anyone who would embarrass him or turn Scottie against him. But now he was in an entire country of people just like his own family.

4.

He's frightened, she realized. And ashamed of it, because of course men weren't supposed to ever be frightened. Maybe Michael was right to be scared. What did she know? They must be in real danger. They were trapped, and the place was full of Communists. But even Communists wouldn't actually let them die here, would they? And they wouldn't hurt them? They could rob them, she supposed, and redistribute their wealth, but they'd have to get inside the car first.

Scottie tried to summon fear, but she couldn't. Really, small twinges of guilt aside, she was having fun. She was already planning what she would write to Leona about this. *And then we got the car stuck!* She reached into the backseat, picked up the copy of *Footloose in Italy* Leona had given her and hid her smile in it. She ran her finger slowly over the words: "When they are happy Italians will sing, and when they are sad they are sour. They have a rather low boiling point, and when they get angry it is best to stand clear of flying gesticulations."

As if on cue, Michael shouted, *"Via! Via!,"* making shooing motions with his hands. The children laughed and slapped their palms on the car hood.

Finally, a woman with a broom — *a real broom, Leona, like in a fairy tale, a collection of long twigs bound together* — came and shouted at the children and chased them away.

Eventually Scottie would come to know Signora Beatrice Mulinari, known in the *contrada,* or neighborhood, as Nonna Bea, whose ancestor had first made panforte, a fruitcake, for the barefoot monks of the Chiostro del Carmine back in 1205, and whose recipe Nonna Bea still used when making panforte for the current generation of monks. She was the only bad cook in all of Italy, operating on the theory that tasteless food brings us closer to God. Her panforte, in fact, was so hard as to be almost inedible, but the monks didn't complain, perhaps also feeling that suffering through it was a form of penance. Toothless and subsisting herself on a diet of thin broth, she had never in her life been farther than Colle di Val d'Elsa, ten miles from Siena. She was expecting her seventy-five-year-old son home for lunch — he did not dare resist her watery *pappa al pomodoro* — but how could he get through with this thing blocking the road? She stood in front of the car and shouted and gestured at it, as if it were a recalcitrant goose.

"Incastrato!" Scottie shouted. Michael looked at her in surprise. "It means 'stuck' . . . right?" she said, suddenly unsure. It did have an odd sound to it that was awfully close to . . . She hoped she

hadn't just announced that they were castrated, or wanted to be castrated, or that someone else should be castrated.

The old witch jabbered at them. It was unclear whether she was angry about the stuck car, or sympathetic, or insulted by the suggestion that castration was imminent, but at last a *carabiniere* arrived to point out that they were blocking the road.

Leona, who had traveled to Italy the previous summer, had described the *carabinieri* — military police — in glowing terms. *Long capes and ridiculous Napoleonic hats. Tall black leather boots and crisp uniforms and black horses. Every last one handsome and dark-eyed. Dreamy!*

5.

Tenente Bruno Pisano had fought alongside the Allied Forces after the *carabinieri* arrested Mussolini and was not ill-disposed toward Americans, but he was deeply irritated because he had been on his way home for lunch and now had to deal with this idiocy. His *pici con le briciole* was getting cold. He stared at the car and at the foreigners trapped inside. He threw up his white-gloved hands in disgust and shouted at them.

"What's he saying?" asked Scottie.

"It's illegal to block the road," said Michael.

Scottie laughed and said, "Well, he'll have to get us out in order to arrest us, won't he?"

Michael looked at her, then, to her relief, also laughed. He put his hands in the air. "We give up!" he said.

Scottie heard a bellow and turned around in her seat. She could see two gigantic white animals through the rear window of the car. She gasped at their size.

"Oh my God," groaned Michael. "What next?"

"Oxen! I've only seen them in books."

"Neutro! Neutro!" shouted the *carabiniere.*

"Neutered?" Scottie asked, flipping through her book.

Michael sighed and put the car in neutral.

An old man in a tattered sweater put a chain around the frame of the car, or at least that's what Scottie imagined from the clanking and the little she could see through the rear window of the Fairlane. She slid into the backseat to get a better angle. The man whistled to a boy who sat astride one of the oxen, barefoot and in short pants. At the old man's command, the boy backed the yoked oxen up slowly, talking to them. The beasts loomed over the old man, their massive shoulders rippling with muscle extending way above his head, their chests as wide as a doorway. The boy sat so high up that Scottie thought of illustrations in children's books of elephant boys in India, tapping their charges with sticks. She had never seen such huge animals — they had to weigh three thousand pounds each. They looked prehistoric. They tossed their horned heads and their wet black noses glistened.

"Ciao," she called through the window to the boy atop the ox. He had thick curly blond hair, and when he looked down to wave to her, she saw a flash of blue eyes. His thin legs, outgrowing the short pants, hung down the animal's rib cage.

"Hello, missus," he called down. "I speak English good."

"Are you learning in school?" she called out.

"Andiamo, Robertino," called the old man, interrupting them. The boy kicked the sides of the ox, which bellowed and began to pull forward, its mate holding back for a moment, then, resigned, leaning into the collar.

7.

"Tirate, ragazzi," urged the old man, Bernardo Banchi, who had been growing wheat just outside the walls of the city for sixty years, as before him his father, grandfather and a long series of nearly identical Banchis going back to medieval times had grown wheat and sold it to breadmakers who made bread for the inhabitants of Siena. He had just received an offer for his farm from an American hotel chain. He had told the impatient man he would have to think about it. He was raising his grandson, Robertino, who was fourteen. Banchi had always imagined that Robertino would grow wheat, too, but he spoke English now and wanted to go live in Rome someday. Though it was only a half day's train ride away, Banchi had never been to Rome, nor had he any desire to go, as it was no doubt full of Romans. He lit his cigar and watched his animals work.

8.

Scottie felt the car lurch, and then there was a terrible scraping sound and it began to slowly roll backward. The boy cheered and patted the oxen. The crowd that had gathered to watch also moved backward, as if they were extras in an opera.

"Ruined," said Michael.

They could have started the car at that point and slunk off under their own power, but the old man continued to placidly tow them backward with his oxen.

As soon as the street was wide enough, Michael kicked open the jammed door and jumped out onto the cobblestones as they rolled slowly along. He tried to talk to the old man, but Banchi just nodded and waved and kept the oxen walking. Michael fell in meekly beside him.

Scottie watched her new city reveal itself outside the window as the car moved backward through the streets at the pace of a slow walk. The *carabiniere* was silent, marching along and frowning, no doubt calculating the fines he would levy, but the old man seemed to be narrating the story of their rescue to everyone they passed. People laughed and shrugged and pointed to the scraped-up car. Michael was red-faced, staring at the ground.

The Italian boy stood up atop the moving ox, showing off, swaying like a hula dancer.

Women wearing thin housecoats and hairnets over curlers peered out at them from darkened doorways. Scottie waved and smiled, the way Grace Kelly had from the deck of the *Constitution,* not too vigorously, as if she were halfheartedly hailing a cab.

The women stared at her.

"*Americani*," they said to each other, and people began calling it out to each other. "*Americani, gli americani si sono incastrati con la macchina.*" They were laughing, yet it almost sounded like a threat.

"I thought you said today was the anniversary of when we liberated them from the Germans? Eleven years isn't that long," Scottie whispered through the lowered side window to Michael.

"The French liberated Siena. And the partisans, who were . . . Communists."

"Jeepers," said Scottie, an adorable expression Michael felt he would soon come to loathe.

I don't want to save the world, he thought. *I want to go home. What have I done?* As the *carabiniere* in his black uniform and shiny black boots demanded his papers, Michael felt as if he were about to be shot. He pretended to look through his wallet for the missing documents. He had visions of them being locked in some disease-ridden jail. Not a jail — a dungeon. They had those here. What if something happened to Scottie? *My God,* he thought. *This poor innocent girl. Forgive me.*

9.

"Documenti, per favore," snapped Tenente Pisano again. He wanted to get these tourists out of his hair immediately, but certain procedures must be followed.

Scottie unsnapped her large square purse and handed their passports out from the slowly moving car.

"You . . . is . . . American?" said the old man in halting but proud English, as the blue passports changed hands.

The boy began singing "You Ain't Nothin' but a Hound Dog" and gyrating atop the ox. Michael ignored them both. Scottie wondered if she would ever again see the confident, suave man she thought she had married.

"My husband has come from America to sell tractors," she called to the old man.

"In quale albergo alloggiate?" demanded the *tenente.*

"We're not staying in a hotel," said Michael in Italian. "We've come here to live. I'm opening a tractor business."

10.

Tenente Pisano's brow darkened. His prospects for consuming even tepid *pici* were fading.

"You cannot just arrive here and open a

business. Where is your *permesso di soggiorno*? Where is your *Modulo Vanoni*? Has the Guardia di Finanza been advised? Who has authorized this? I must see the proper documents immediately, and make sure they have the proper signatures and *bolli*."

These Americans think because they saved us from the Nazis, they can do whatever they want.

11.

As Michael looked through his wallet, the old man turned to Scottie. *"Trattori?"* He laughed. "I like the beasts instead. More, how you say . . . reliable. The old ways, still good."

"You'll be able to plow twice the land in half the time," she said.

"And then what I do with the rest of the day? I'll get into trouble. I stick with the *buoi*!"

The boy was attempting a handstand atop the ox as they turned into Via di Città. A child with a toy drum and several stray dogs now in tow, they passed a woman leaning against a building under an ad for Lucky Strikes plastered to the wall. She was about thirty, Scottie guessed, a little heavy, dressed simply in a knee-length pale pink dress and flat shoes, her large breasts sagging under-

40

neath the thin fabric. She was smoking. *She could use a better bra,* Scottie thought, but then noticed something strange: The entire procession in front of them — the old man, the men and women laughing and joking at the impromptu parade — fell silent at the sight of the woman and turned away, as if to look at her would burn their eyes. The woman smiled slightly as she met Scottie's eye and blew a plume of smoke, as if they were sharing a private joke.

"*Via,* Gina," said the *carabiniere,* falling back to address the woman as the car passed and the procession moved on. Through the windshield Scottie saw him shooing her away up the street.

12.

Finally, the oxen stopped. Scottie quickly pulled up the emergency brake so the car didn't roll backward and bump the heels of the poor beasts.

She stepped out of the car and smiled at the crowd. The men smiled back, but the women frowned and pulled away, ambivalent about this latest invasion of foreigners, and the group dissolved into the doorways and alleys of the medieval city.

"Piazza del Campo," announced Signor

Banchi, doffing his battered fedora and grinning with a sparse array of yellowed teeth, eager himself to get home to a bowl of *ribollita.*

As Michael continued to look through his wallet for documents Scottie was fairly certain were not there, one of the oxen lifted its tail and a stream of liquid excrement came out, splashing onto the paving stones. Michael gasped as his shoes and trousers were spattered. Scottie covered her mouth to make her laughter look like sympathetic shock. *Oh, Leona, the look on his face.* Michael caught the edge of her smile and frowned, hurt by her mockery. She was, she thought, really not a nice person, and now he knew it. She had an urge to tell him everything, but quelled it. *Maintain the façade,* she told herself.

Tenente Pisano decided the foreigners had been suitably punished and no judicial action was immediately necessary.

"You will present yourselves at the Questura with your documents," he said, and strode purposefully off toward his plate of *pici.*

Scottie pulled a huge colorful wad of lire

out of her purse. She couldn't remember what the exchange rate was — 1,300 lire to the dollar? Or was it 130? So confusing, and the money looked like something in a board game.

"Where is the nearest riding stable?" she asked the old man as she tried to figure out what to offer him. "Horses?"

"Horses! I love horses!" said Robertino. "You know Palio? I am *barbaresco* for Istrice in July! I will be *fantino* in August!"

Scottie had no idea what he was talking about. "What's a *barbaresco*?"

"Groom," said Banchi, shooting Robertino a look. "The Palio is a horse race run in July and August. I know some nice horses for sale. Come to farm outside *le mura*. Ask for Banchi."

"Sì," she said eagerly.

Michael blanched. "Darling," he said, the term no longer affectionate. "Slow down. I haven't sold a single tractor yet."

"Oh, but you will, darling," she said. "You'll sell hundreds of them, I know you will. Italians love everything from America." She wasn't sure if she was saying it to convince herself or him.

She finally just offered Signor Banchi the whole wad of money.

Signor Banchi, offended, frowned and

waved the money off. *"Di niente, di niente,"* he said, and disappeared around a corner with his massive beasts, after saying, "No more *incastrati."*

Abandoning their defeated car, Scottie and Michael turned to find they were gazing out at a huge, shell-shaped stone piazza that sloped down to a squat building with a tall, slender brick bell tower. The space was alive with activity — people strode purposefully across and around the piazza, the tables in front of the bars and restaurants that lined the square were full of gawkers enjoying the continuous spectacle while attacking elaborate ice creams, and everywhere scooters buzzed to and fro. Tiny delivery trucks like toys honked, and women shook rugs out of second- and third-story windows. Rows of windows of every shape — arched, square, rectangular, columned — lined the square, and Scottie's eye found the ones the property manager had circled in the photo, a series of six tall brown shutters looking out over the piazza.

She wasn't sure what to say, so she said, "There!" brightly and pointed.

Michael seemed to be of the same mind, that it was best to pretend none of this had happened. "Yes," he said, nearly matching

her fake enthusiasm. "Number 5. There it
is."

13.

Her heart ached as she realized that they
had entered a new phase of their marriage.
From now on they would be cautious of
each other. She had smelled his weakness
and fear, and he had caught a glimpse of
her cruelty. She felt nostalgic for a time only
fifteen minutes earlier, but she remembered
that she had not been honest with him then,
either. She had never been honest with Michael. She had not told him that she was
pregnant with another man's child when
they met. That she had married Michael so
that she would not be "ruined." Any day
now, she would tell him she was pregnant,
and would pretend it was his.

When she looked at Michael she had the
sense there was something she was forgetting, like in dreams where she realized she
had a dog she hadn't fed in months and
woke up shouting.

14.

Scottie and Michael made their way toward
a massive wooden doorway set between a
souvenir shop and a restaurant. It was
blocked by a short, dark-haired, dark-jawed

45

man in a blue sport jacket, blue tie loosened, with a bullhorn, who was addressing a small crowd standing in front of an ornate marble fountain just under Scottie and Michael's future apartment. He looked like a soccer star about to launch into an unlikely discourse upon the beauty of the Fontana Gaia, with its snow white marble friezes of Adam and Eve being tossed out of Eden.

There was, Scottie thought, a very *animal* appeal about the man. He was the sort that she and Leona would have giggled over, back when they were schoolgirls together — in other words, a month ago.

Michael ducked into the *tabacchi,* a small store with racks of newspapers outside.

"Impedite la truffa elettorale," the man with the bullhorn shouted over the din of the scooters, his *basso* voice echoing around the square and causing a flock of pigeons to rise up and circle above them. *"Votate Comunista."*

The people nodded, and some of them clapped. The man made eye contact with Scottie and smiled for longer than seemed quite right. Michael reappeared at her side, a pair of gigantic antique keys in his hand, each six inches long.

"That man just said . . . ," whispered Scottie.

15.

Having endured the mortification of the Ford being rescued by oxen, Michael found himself in Piazza del Campo staring at the squat man with the bullhorn. Ugo Rosini, mayor of Siena. Communist. The man at the center of his mission. The man he needed to bring down. He had never seen a real live Commie before in the flesh. This guy looked physically strong, which was unnerving, and confident, which was worse. The man's eyes landed on his, and Michael felt a cool sweat and his heart raced, as if he were facing a bear about to charge.

His heart raced out of more than just fear — Ugo was, as Scottie noticed, a very masculine man, and Michael had a terrible secret. He wanted to kiss some men, touch them and be held by them. He found certain men beautiful, exciting, wonderful, but also terrifying, the way that small children felt about airplanes and dinosaurs. It was awful. There were many names for this, scientific and less so, but no matter how you sliced it, it was forbidden. He could see that in the eyes of his father, who had yelled at him when he was a child not to swing his hips when he walked. At Yale any man who wasn't utterly hearty and manly in every way was taunted for being a fairy. Sometimes it was much worse than that. It was illegal for homosexuals to work for the United States government. If his truth were known he would go to jail for it. So Michael had kept his tastes a secret from everyone except one person.

And that person lived in Rome.

16.

"Mayor Rosini said we are tired of being mired in corruption, tired of back-room deals, tired of foreigners interfering with our elections," a woman in a peacock blue suit and a pearl pin standing next to them said politely in English, smiling and handing them each a red leaflet with a hammer and sickle in the corner. She had a boxer dog on a leather leash studded with brass cows.

"Well, I would be, too," said Scottie. "That's just not right, is it? Lovely boxer."

The dog bounced up and down happily as Scottie petted her.

"We're new here," Scottie started to say to the woman, but Michael cut her off.

"Darling," he said, then with a quick and elegant movement lifted her in his arms, his eyes locked on those of Mayor Rosini, as if they were in some sort of Old West duel. She was shocked and also quite pleased by the gesture.

"Permesso." His voice was low, as his father had demanded. He nodded to the door the mayor was blocking.

"Ah, *scusate*," said the mayor, politely stepping aside with a courteous wave and a smile so that Michael could carry his beautiful American bride across the threshold of their new home, accompanied by the cheers of Siena's Communist Party.

"Viva l'amore!" they cried.

Love, she thought, looking into her new husband's face. *That's what I'm forgetting.*

THREE:
IL DRAGO, THE DRAGON

"MY BURNING HEART BECOMES
A MOUTH OF FLAMES"

1.

Michael unlocked the apartment's heavy wooden front door, and they found themselves in a dark and narrow hallway with a series of closed doors off it on the right. There was no overhead light, so they left the door to the stairwell open behind them. Scottie followed Michael as he threw open door after door in turn. She was startled to discover each room was just an equally sized, dark, empty box — no closets, no bathroom or lighting fixtures, no tub, no toilet, no kitchen appliances or cabinets. Five large echoing rooms end to end, all with two windows on the far wall, heavy brown shutters closed.

"It's like an empty dollhouse," she said. She threw open the shutters in the last room, half expecting to discover a giant little girl kneeling in the piazza, peering in at her.

"This is the best address in the whole city," Michael huffed, and she realized she had offended him. "The building is owned by a marchese. It was their family palace."

"What's a marchese?"

"A nobleman. Marquis. Techically they don't exist anymore, but old habits die hard."

She wondered if Michael would mind if she took her bra off. It was feeling pinchy. She wanted out of the girdle, too. How long did she have to be this perfectly put together person for him?

2.

Scottie was critical of the apartment, which bothered him. He so badly wanted to please her, to make her happy, to not replicate his parents' awful yoke of mutual hatred. He had no idea how to do this, except to do what he had always done, to excel at whatever was in front of him — school then, career now — in the hopes that being good at something would make him lovable. He wanted to loosen his tie, undo his shirt collar, but it felt strange to do that in front of her, disrespectful. He stared out the window at the Communists gathered in the square below. He lifted the camera slung around his neck and began taking pictures.

"The light will be prettier at sunset," Scottie said.

He could file a report tonight, a coded telegram from the main office in Siena. Luce and the CIA would be pleased.

He snapped another photo of the square and the crowd of Communists gathered below. He would go to Rome tomorrow and deliver the report himself. Better.

3.

"It's beautiful," she said. And it was — the sunlight streaming in revealed high-beamed ceilings, white walls and shiny white terrazzo floors speckled with sandy browns and golds. It still had the feel of "palace."

"It's perfect for dancing," she said, holding up her arms in waltz position. "Nothing to bump into."

He looked pained. "I'm a terrible dancer," he said apologetically. "Two left feet."

She was disappointed, but chose to make light of it. "So that's why you kept me trapped at the punch bowl at that mixer."

"You've discovered my secret." They both laughed lightly and made themselves busy.

One of the rooms, it turned out, did have a distinguishing feature: two short pipes sticking out of the wall. "Is this a bathroom?" she asked.

Michael looked at the two water pipes sticking out of the wall. "I guess so," he said. "Or the kitchen. Or the mad chemist's laboratory." They smiled at the absurdity of it.

He followed her back through the rooms as she threw open the shutters, discovering another room with two pipes in it.

"Which one do you want as the kitchen, and which as the bathroom?" she asked. "Or we could be very New York and have two bathrooms and no kitchen, and just eat out all the time." Since she wasn't much of a cook, it was a more than a half-serious suggestion.

He was staring out the window at the people gathered in the square below. He lifted the camera slung around his neck and began taking pictures.

"Might have to go to Rome tomorrow," he said. "Ford Italia's head office."

"Ooh, Rome. I've always wanted to see the Pantheon."

"Better if you stay here and get us set up, isn't it?"

It was her turn to feel hurt, and a little embarrassed. "Of course, of course," she said. "I'm going to make us a real home here."

She had forgotten she was a wife and not a friend, and that they were not here to have adventures. Michael had a job to do, and so did she. Her job was to love him and take care of him and have his children. For now she was ignoring the child she was already carrying, though her body was making its presence known. She pushed it all away, and told herself it would be fine. She was already into the happy ending part of her story. There was nothing to worry about.

4.

They stayed overnight in a genteel but run-down old hotel a few hundred yards from the piazza. The bathroom was tiny and the plumbing whistled and groaned, though neither of them was so impolite as to mention it. They laughed apologetically when they got into the canoe-like bed and rolled toward each other. In the morning they returned to the apartment, where Scottie would await the movers.

Michael left on the early train. Scottie felt alone and a little frightened when she heard the heavy front door shut behind him, but also pleased that he trusted her to deal with the movers. Two weeks ago she was living in a dorm with a cafeteria and a chaperone, and now she was alone in a foreign country, a grown-up in charge of setting up a household. *Leona, I'm playing house for real!*

Somehow, the drivers made it to Piazza Mercato without getting stuck, and the heavy crates of their belongings were shuttled one by one up the slope of Piazza del Campo and into their apartment building, up the stairs and into the rooms. Scottie learned some Italian curse words, and had to laugh at the herd of little boys who gathered to watch the ant trail of boxes make its way across the piazza on creaking handcarts.

She was moving boxes around, sweaty, dirty, her hair pulled up in an old handkerchief, when she heard a new voice in the hallway: *"Permesso?"*

"Come in," she called, adding in her best boarding school French (that had earned her a C from Madame Soubrette), *"Entrez, s'il vous plaît."* She really must learn some basic words in Italian.

A slim man in his forties appeared, wearing a tweed suit and a brown fedora and carrying a calfskin case. His dark eyebrows, lightly flecked with gray like his short hair, danced above deep brown eyes. He had round glasses and a slightly formal air. "You

55

must be Mrs. Messina?"

"Mr. Barco?" she asked. She was expecting the property manager. She had a lot of questions for him about fuses, trash collection and a broken shutter.

"I am Carlo Chigi Piccolomini," he said, as if the name should mean something to her. It didn't.

"Are you a salesman?" she asked cautiously. He did have something of the Fuller Brush Man about him: neat, efficient, friendly.

"I am" — he gave an embarrassed smile — "the landlord."

"Oh!" she said, blushing. "I'm so sorry. You're the marquis. Do I call you Signor Marchese or — ?"

"Please call me Carlo."

He was so elegant, and mature — she felt embarrassed about her plain dress, her imperfect makeup, a chipped nail.

"I'm Scottie," she said, shaking his hand. "Your English is perfect."

Oh God, she thought. *I'm such an idiot.*

"I went to school in England, but my wife was educated in America, so I'm terrified of pronouncing the word 'schedule,' " he said. The left side of his mouth twisted upward in a sly smile, and the light glinted off his glasses. She liked him right away — the

European aristocrats she had met at Vassar and Ivy League dances were snobs who pulled rank, but Carlo seemed funny and self-deprecating, like Cary Grant in *Philadelphia Story,* if it were set in Siena. There was something dashing yet familiar about him.

"I would ask you to sit down, but —" She looked around the apartment, filled with boxes and packing crates. Scottie and Carlo had to step aside as two sweating deliverymen hauled a giant crate up the stairs.

"Cucina, grazie," she said to them, pointing, then to Carlo, "I'm afraid that's the extent of my Italian." One of the men used a crowbar to uncrate the Hardwick aqua blue gas range.

"My husband and I went on a mad shopping spree in New York when we found out what 'unfurnished' meant in Italy. It was like we had just won a game show." It had been a truly joyous day, running around with cash from Ford. More fun than their actual wedding day, when Michael had seemed tense, ashamed of his sweet parents, and she had had to deal with Aunt Ida and Leona, neither of whom understood why she was marrying a stranger. But that shopping day she and Michael had genuinely had fun together, choosing the blue fridge, the matching stove, the elegant fixtures.

"It's so modern," said Carlo, running a hand over it.

The range looked so wonderfully, re-assuringly American that she felt like hugging it, as if she had run into a friend from back home. The moving man maneuvered it into place, but when he went to plug it in, the plug was the wrong size. Carlo called down to one of the little boys below to go get the electrician. A few minutes later, a man wearing gray coveralls and carrying a gray metal case arrived. He doffed his hat and got to work, but soon shook his head. Scottie could not understand the words, but she got the gist of it. None of the appliances worked. It was something to do with the voltage, or the wiring, or the kind of gas, or the plumbing. More little men in jumpsuits were called in as the day progressed. Scottie got dirtier and dustier and sweatier, while Carlo, who to her horror not only went to retrieve a tool chest but took off his jacket and rolled up his elegantly monogrammed sleeves and pitched in, seemed as clean and crisp as when he walked through the door. The only sense that he was exerting any ef-fort at all came from a faint smell of bleach that wafted off his white shirt now and then. It reminded Scottie of childhood, of run-ning through sheets on the line in the backyard of their house on Alden Drive in Beverly Hills.

"What do you think of Siena so far?" he asked.

"I think it's lovely. My Aunt Ida thinks all Italians are savages. She's terribly worried about me." She wasn't quite sure why she said this — it was the opposite of what she intended to say.

Carlo laughed. "And your mother? Did she tell you to be worried about Italians?"

Scottie blushed. "My mother died when I was a baby. I don't remember her."

"I'm so sorry," he said, pausing in his work to look at her, wrench in hand.

"They told me it was a car accident, but I used to make up more romantic stories than that."

Carlo gave her a quizzical smile. "Such as — ?"

"That she was shot down while flying her own plane on a secret mission to stop the Nazis. Silly, I know."

"Sometimes stories are comforting."

"Yes. I found out the truth when my father died last summer. My mother was his housemaid. They . . . well . . . He had to marry her. Also, she drank." She gasped a little as she laughed. "I haven't told anyone that, not even my best friend. I don't know why I'm telling you, and you a marchese."

Carlo laughed. "You think we don't have plenty of housemaids in our family line? And alcoholics — they are the virtuous ones. The popes are the worst. We have a pope in our family who had six children."

"Really? I thought they weren't supposed to —"

"They aren't. Strictly forbidden." He put down the wrench. "Well, you will have hot water. That is something, at least. But this stove — hmmm."

By late afternoon there had been a lot of gesticulating and raised voices when handyman after handyman threw up his hands and said he had never seen such things before, and had no idea how to make them operate.

"I've stolen your whole day," Scottie said to Carlo, although she would have been totally lost without him.

"I'm happy to help, and I'm so sorry," said Carlo, gesturing to the appliances. "I feel terrible about this."

He seemed so troubled that Scottie felt the need to reassure him. "I'm sure we'll figure something out," she said, then added in a whisper, "I'm not much of a cook anyway. This way my husband won't find out."

Husband. She said it as a sort of talisman, a way of warding off the attraction she felt for Carlo.

His eyes behind the glasses were large and liquid, like her horse Sonny Boy's. "I'd love to meet your wife," she said. "It would be lovely to have a friend who knows America. Where did she go to school?"

"Smith." She expected him to say more, but he didn't. Scottie tried to picture the four of them out together, having fun. The older couple would mentor her and Michael, like the parents they wished they'd had. Maybe Michael would absorb some of Carlo's charm. Was it disloyal to think that way, to want him to be different?

From an open crate Carlo picked up the lasso Scottie had brought with her from California when she was sent to boarding school at age fourteen. "Ah, you are a cowgirl?"

"Hardly. I've never actually gotten that over the head of a steer. But I love to ride," she said.

"I raise cows and horses. You know Persani?"

"The breed that the D'Inzeo brothers ride?" Raimondo and Piero D'Inzeo were famous Italian show jumpers, contenders to win the Olympics this year. Scottie had followed their stellar careers in the sports pages and in *Chronicle of the Horse,* and she and Leona had swooned over their aquiline profiles and military bearing.

Carlo brightened in surprise that she knew them. "Yes," he said, obviously pleased. "You must come to the farm sometime and see the mares and foals."

She wanted to say yes very badly, but something about Carlo felt dangerous to her. Not him, but the way he made her think about Michael. The contrast between them. "I would love to. But I've made a promise to myself that I'll get us all set up here before I go horse-crazy." She squinted, the sun in her eyes. "By the way, what's with all the shutters?" Each window had wooden inside panels that closed out the light and fitted over the glass. Then there were the slatted outdoor shutters. She'd noticed that, all day long, every window on the piazza but hers had been shuttered. "Are you Italians vampires so you have to live in total darkness?" Later on she would wonder if she had overstepped, being so casual with an actual marchese. Who knew why she said the things she said? Half of them she regretted later. But Carlo was so easy to be around, so quick to laugh. It was a cliché, that thing about feeling like you had always known someone, but here it was. In a land of strangers, she had found a friend. That was all it was.

"Yes," he said. "Those of us who are not werewolves. But the shutters are for the heat. During the day you close these" — he showed her, closing the outdoor shutters — "but leave these open." He opened the glass window wide.

"It's so dark." She had grown up with sunlight and fresh air filling the house day and night.

"But cool," said Carlo. "Then at night, you leave the outside ones open but close the indoor wood panels, so your neighbors can't see you. There is nothing to do in Siena but gossip, I'm afraid, and we Italians love to spy."

He rolled down his sleeves, put his cuff links back in, donned his tweed jacket and replaced the fedora he had left sitting on a moving crate.

His eyes lingered on her for just longer than they should have, and she ran her hand self-consciously over her hair, loose, messy, unsprayed. There was something about the way he was looking at her. A wistfulness.

"I'm so happy to have a young couple in the house. I hope you and your husband are very happy here," he said. "My grandfather was born in this room, I think."

"What was his name?"

"Giuseppe."

"I'll talk to him now and then," she said. "In case he's listening. Oh, I need to give you the rent."

She went for the envelope that Michael had left her, but Carlo waved her away, suddenly quite formal, the nobleman again. "You may drop it off at Signor Barco's office in Via Garibaldi. He handles all of my business here. I am rarely in Siena these days." A shadow passed over his eyes, and his hand on the doorknob tightened. She fought the urge to put her own hand over it, to ask him what was wrong.

"I hope we'll see you again," she said.

"Perhaps we will," he said. *"Arrivederci, signora."* And the heavy door shut behind him.

She saw that he had left his tool chest behind, and ran over to the window to call to him, but she could not find him in the crowd below. He had vanished.

5.

As darkness settled on the piazza, the beautiful, gleaming, cutting-edge appliances that had traveled four thousand miles across the ocean stood, unplugged and unplumbed, in the shiny-floored kitchen, while Scottie heated a can of Campbell's soup on an East German hotplate that had magically appeared in the midst of the chaos.

"The toilet works," she said cheerily to herself. It was pink, with a black seat, although the plumber (another little man in gray overalls) kept asking where the bidet was, and was rather openly disgusted when she said she didn't have one. On the other hand, he had no idea what the shower attachment to the bathtub was for, and seemed genuinely frightened when she said that it poured water over one's head.

"Water over the head?" he kept repeating, as if something had been lost in translation. She was sorry Carlo had left, and missed his comforting, capable presence.

When the plumber finally abandoned her and she was alone, she wanted to join the crowd in the piazza, but found that she felt shy, afraid to talk to anyone, and afraid of getting lost. She was standing there, feeling awkward, when the mayor crossed in front of her. She smiled at him out of politeness, and to her horror, he stopped.

"You are American?" he asked in English.

"Yes," she said.

"Welcome to Siena. I am Ugo Rosini." He shook her hand, and held it just a second

65

longer than an American would. And twice as long as ultrapolite and correct Carlo had.

"Yes, I know," she said. "Your face is on a lot of posters."

"I'm running for reelection." His smile was confident, and more than a little flirtatious, which surprised her, though Leona had warned her about Italians. Well, not warned her. Encouraged her. "The men aren't rude like people say," she had said when she returned from Rome. "They make you feel like the sexiest woman on the planet. Like you're Elizabeth Taylor or something, even if you don't have any makeup on and your hair's a fright. They eat you up with their eyes."

Scottie did in fact feel like she was being consumed. It was not unpleasant, since she felt the ring on her hand made her invulnerable. Ugo asked, "Have you been to the top of the Museo dell'Opera Metropolitana?"

"I haven't been anywhere," she said.

"Not to the Duomo?" His tone was a mix of surprise and reproach.

She shook her head.

"We must go immediately," he said. He offered her his arm.

She hesitated. Was this kind of spontaneous invitation normal in this culture? Would it be offensive to refuse? Was there anything to fear here?

"*Signora,*" he said in a tone of reproach, "I am the mayor. It is not only perfectly safe, it is my job to show off my beautiful city."

Even in flats, she was taller than he was, though he had the athlete's bulky strength she had noticed earlier. He led her through the streets, giving her thumbnail sketches of the city's long history. "First we will see where St. Catherine lived. She was very crazy woman."

"That's not a very nice thing to say."

"Well, she refused to marry her dead sister's husband like her parents wanted and stopped eating and cut off all her hair to make her point."

"That sounds reasonable to me."

"She had visions of Christ, and decided to dedicate her life to helping the sick."

"Not crazy. Selfless."

"Then she got into politics, trying to achieve peace in the world."

"Now she sounds crazy."

Ugo laughed. "You're right."

"Are you really a Communist?" she asked.

"Yes," he said.

"You're the first one I've ever met. You're not what I expected."

"Let me guess. Two heads, red eyes and a plan to overthrow America." He gave her arm a little squeeze, pulling her against him more closely as three men in suits and fedoras passed them heading in the other direction on the narrow brick street, stepping aside to make room for them. They knew Ugo, clearly, but just nodded. Their eyes lingered on Scottie, and she could hear them talking and laughing as soon as they passed them.

"They think we're lovers," he laughed. "Maybe we should be."

He meant it in jest, and she answered in jest. "Sounds like a good way to end the Cold War to me. We might win the Nobel Peace Prize."

But as they entered the stairwell to climb up to the top of the half-finished Duomo, he paused. She had taken one look at the metal stairs and kicked off her shoes and climbed eagerly, reminded of New York City fire escapes where you could see the ground below your feet the whole way up. She had always liked that feeling of vertigo you got when you looked at the spaces between the stairs. She paused on the landing above him, pigeons disturbed from their roost fluttering overhead. A floodlamp lit the stairwell from below. When she looked down, there was a pained look on Ugo's face.

"What's the matter?" she called.

68

He grinned. "Stop there, just for a moment," he said. She did, and he walked up two stairs until he was right under her. "I just want to look at heaven," he said.

She froze, horrified. He was looking up her dress. She wanted to scream. It was happening again. Just like at Vassar. There it had begun innocently, like this, and then things had gotten out of control. And then she had missed her period.

She had so badly wanted to tell Leona, to beg for her help and advice, but only a few months earlier they had both made fun of a girl who had had to leave school because of a "mistake." Scottie, ever eager to make the glamorous Leona laugh, to distinguish the two of them as smarter than the sheeplike, well-behaved, white-gloved hordes, had casually referred to the girl as a slut.

No, she had decided that she could not tell Leona, could not risk losing the friendship at the center of her world, so instead, when she met Michael at a mixer and he paid attention to her, she let him court her, and married him. She left Vassar before graduation, a smashing success who had landed her "Mrs." degree.

It was all a lie, and now this man could seem to see that.

She pulled her skirt around her.

"Wait," he whispered, laughing a little. "Don't you see that this is your power? You are doing nothing wrong. It is I who am looking, that is all."

She stared at his face, aghast. He was looking into her eyes. Laughing, but also asking to be tortured. *For goodness' sake,* she thought. *Really?* She was confused, and angry, and a little frightened.

He lifted one eyebrow playfully, put his hands together in prayer. She gave an involuntary laugh.

"I thought Communists didn't believe in God."

"I'm praying to you," he said. "Tease me."

Was he right? Was this her power? Did she have power? She moved one foot, slowly, across the metal bars. *This is so wrong.*

She heard him sigh. She slid her foot a little farther. Daring, testing, she lifted her dress away from her legs a little. He gave a low moan. It scared her, to think she was doing this. Yes, it was all in good fun, and yes, she was wearing underwear and a slip, but still. This was a respected man in Siena! The mayor!

It was a joke, it was playful, but you weren't supposed to play these games. These games led to women being ruined, to babies being abandoned, unwanted. Men never seemed to suffer from these games, but women . . .

It was Vassar all over again, hands on her body. She felt nausea rising, panic.

Stop, she told herself. *Stop. You're not there, you're not that girl anymore. You're here.* He was right, she had the power.

She walked down the stairs.

"I'm so sorry, I've forgotten something at home," she said. "I should go." He made no move to stop her as she passed him, but he said, "Please, *signora,* I have offended you and I'm sorry. I only wished to pay you a compliment, to make you laugh."

She stopped a few feet below him on the stairs. "You were very kind to offer to show me the city, but I have to go."

"It was lovely to meet you," he said with a big grin. "And I think even though you are shocked, you enjoyed meeting me, too. Siena is a small place. I will see you again."

She felt how flushed her face was, and was suddenly mortified. She ran back down the narrow street and into the Campo, then walked briskly back to number 5, letting the heavy wooden door slam behind her.

FOUR:
L'ISTRICE, THE PORCUPINE

"I ONLY STAB IN SELF-DEFENSE"

1.

Scottie threw herself on the couch in despair. She had very conflicting ideas about sex, all of which were based on very little information and almost no experience. She had had no mother to talk to, no sisters. Only Leona, who knew as little as she did. Sex with Michael was quick, and they both kept their eyes closed.

You were not supposed to like it.

You were not supposed to long for it.

You were not supposed to think about it.

You were not supposed to dream about it.

It was not supposed to be fun.

It was not supposed to be about power.

Was it?

Women who did these things were homewreckers, whores.

Weren't they?

2.

Michael was looking forward to celebrating the fact that he and Duncan were living in the same country, that Michael had improbably, impossibly managed to make that happen. Duncan, the blueblooded scion of an old railroad family, the consummate Yale man, was the only person other than Ambassador Luce he knew in Rome, and was the entire reason he had come to Italy at all. They had arranged to meet after work at a noisy bar near the Spanish Steps. It was full of expatriates, women in fur stoles and men in sharply tapering trousers that made them look like bandleaders. Duncan, jovial, easygoing, with the quasi-British locution of his class, seemed to know everyone, and to Michael's annoyance they all came over to greet him with shrieks and hearty *ciao*s and air kisses and said the same boring things: "Where did you get that suit?" "Have you been to that new club on Via Veneto?" "The ambassador is doing a damn fine job, no matter what they say." The bar was decorated with large oil paintings of sad clown faces. Michael was impatient as the minutes ticked by. It was Yale all over again, Duncan the big man on campus, Michael the dog under the table waiting for scraps.

They had met at a bar in New Haven. Michael had finally worked up the courage to enter, then lost his nerve at the sight of men in eye makeup. He was leaving when Duncan, who was in his "Masterworks of the Renaissance" course, had spoken to him. Michael had tried to pretend it was a mistake, that he had only come in to make a phone call, but Duncan had pursued him around campus, invited him to meal after meal. Michael felt like Cinderella, and how could he not give in to such an insistent prince?

Though Duncan was the initial pursuer, Michael had always feared that Duncan's attachment was not as deep as his. He was resigned to this. He repeated to himself lines from Auden: *If equal affection cannot be, let the more loving one be me.* At each milestone — when Duncan graduated and moved to Scarsdale to work in his father's firm while he went to Columbia Law — Michael had assumed it was the end, that they would never see each other again. Instead, though there were sometimes silent gaps lasting weeks or months, Duncan always eventually called, inviting him to New York for stolen weekends at the Waldorf-Astoria, or gossipy lunches at 21 where Duncan did wicked imitations of his colleagues. They always ended up in bed.

Then Duncan had gone to work for the State Department in Rome, while Michael pursued a master's, aiming for that green-lawned boarding school job, and a quiet, chaste life where he could continue his monkish isolation from the "real" world. He had always been a nervous child, and his wartime fears of Nazis, fears that came true when Marco was killed, had morphed easily into fear of a Communist takeover of the United States. Every news report and every political speech fed that fear until, like most other Americans, he was frightened of strangers, terrified about the Soviets' plans for world domination and anxious about the bomb. He worried about mind control — what if the Soviets were brainwashing Americans right now, via subliminal messages inserted into TV broadcasts? Having loved Duncan, he did not need to ever risk another love affair. If he could spend his days immersed in centuries whose events had been safely corralled into books, he would, he thought, be safe.

Except that when he was actually offered a teaching job at a school so exactly out of his imagination it was uncanny, he had declined it. Instead he had spoken to a rather shadowy fellow who was known on campus as a CIA recruiter. "I speak Italian, so you must send me to Rome, where I can be useful," he had insisted with a new forcefulness. He had sailed through training, and here he was. He and Duncan could never be together, he knew that, but he would make sure they were never truly apart.

He grabbed a bottle of champagne and leaned into Duncan as he poured it, slipping a hotel key into his pocket. "Room 114," Michael whispered.

"Darling," said Duncan as his wife, Julie, walked into the bar wearing a black and white Dior gown and an ermine cape with matching hat. She stretched out her long neck and allowed Duncan to graze her cheek with his lips.

"I didn't realize you were in Rome," she said to Michael, reaching out a gloved hand to take the glass from Duncan. "How many of these do I have to have to catch up?"

"It's Julie's birthday," said Duncan.

"Many happy returns," Michael said.

'We're late, I'm afraid, and must run, but it's lovely to see you. Always nice to see friends from back home." Her affect was perfectly flat. Her face painted on, her eyes elongated, her lips blood red. A vampire. A snob.

"Michael's living in Siena," said Duncan.

"He and his wife. An heiress from California."

Julie's painted eyebrows rose. "Well, we must make a foursome sometime," she said. "Does she play bridge?"

"I don't know. I'll ask her."

Duncan and Julie disappeared into the crowds on Via Condotti, and Michael hailed a cab. On his way back to his hotel, a gang of thugs surrounded the cab and tried to force the door open. Michael was terrified, certain that he was about to be killed. It would have been such a dramatic death, but the taxi driver yelled at the men and ran a red light to get away, then apologized to Michael. He seemed used to this.

"We boast we are saints, poets and navigators," he said, "but also we are criminals. You, *signore*. You're Italian, too, aren't you? Or am I wrong?"

Michael had lain awake all night, but Duncan had not come to his room.

3.

Scottie was terribly anxious about what to tell Michael. She had to tell him something, in case they ran into Ugo when they were together and he acted strangely. But she couldn't say, "He made a pass at me," because then Michael might feel called to

77

defend her honor.

Perhaps it was best just to stick to a close version of the truth.

She burst into genuine tears when he walked through the door from Rome the next day.

"I just wanted to see the city, but then I got embarrassed about whether I was doing something wrong or not, so I ran off, but he must have thought I was very rude, or crazy . . ." She left out the rest. "I don't know the rules," she said. "But I'll learn them."

Michael was clearly mystified by this. "You don't have to," he said, as if it were obvious. "You're American." He held her in his arms. "It's my fault. I should never have left you."

"But I think I've made an ass of myself with the mayor. And you're opening a business here. I'm so sorry."

"I don't care what that Commie thinks," he said. "We don't answer to him. Do you play bridge, by the way?"

"No," she said, wondering why he was asking at this moment. "Don't leave me alone again, okay? I missed you." She kissed him, and pulled him close to feel the warmth of his body. He smelled good, and she sank her face into his neck. "What did you think of Rome?" she asked. "Was it beautiful? What did you do?"

"Just work things," he said. "It was pretty horrible, actually. I brought you this." He produced a small replica of the Colosseum in white stone. "Many fewer pickpockets than at the real thing. You wouldn't like Rome."

She wished she'd had the chance to decide for herself. She told him about the appliances, and the plumbing, and Carlo Chigi Piccolomini.

"He came himself?" Michael explained that the Chigis and the Piccolominis were two of Siena's oldest families, with buildings and libraries named after their various illustrious members, which included bankers, generals, astronomers and popes.

"Yes, he mentioned the popes. He was very charming," she said lightly. "And his wife went to Smith. He raises horses."

"Oh no."

Scottie laughed. "I've sworn off them," she said. "For you."

4.

Scottie was distraught when he came home, told him a confusing story about going sightseeing with Ugo Rosini. She was worried that she had embarrassed him. That was sweet. His tone as he reassured her was light, but he was genuinely alarmed by the story. He had been warned about this in training. Did Rosini know why he was really there? Was he trying to get information out of her? Get into their home so he could plant a listening device? This was what they did, they went after those who were close to you.

For the millionth time he wished he could tell her why they were really there. But he had been sworn to secrecy, taken an oath, and they had stressed over and over that it wasn't safe.

He studied her as she got ready for bed. The courtship and marriage had been a bit of a blur for him, with everything else that was on his mind. The CIA encouraged intelligence agents to marry. And Clare Boothe Luce, no less, had suggested he marry a Vassar girl. "They know how to keep secrets," she said as he sat on a silk-striped chair in her New York apartment when he went to discuss his mission with her, already in way over his head with these glamorous people, yet determined to impress them all. Scottie was a set of very appealing labels: beautiful, Vassar, California, money (or so he'd thought), horses. And no parents to disapprove of him, to point out that he was not in her class. He couldn't believe his luck. It was while shopping for appliances that he had felt his awe of Scottie turning to affection, that he began to see her as a human being. She wasn't well read, but she was game, and game was something he himself was short on, especially when he ran low on the Benzedrine his CIA trainers had introduced him to and supplied him with so generously. "Takes the edge off," they had said. He tried on the boat over to educate her a little bit about Italy, about the history of the place and its current state, but he could see she wasn't much interested. Her eyes would glaze over the way the undergraduates' did when he was teaching a section of art history. Maybe it was better that he hadn't become a high school teacher, he thought. He didn't have the charisma for it, which disappointed him, because history was so real to him, so fascinating, so alive.

But now he was here to ensure Italy's future would be as a non-Communist country. And he would do it. He would sway the election in the way they had trained him to, by meeting "opinion molders" in the press and government, by showing local business owners that prosperity lay in ties with America, not the Soviet Union, and by a little under-the-table, illegal campaign funding where needed.

Or he would fail, Italy would go Communist, and nuclear war would annihilate them all.

And it would be all his fault.

Oh God, he thought, reaching for the Bennies.

5.

When she was brushing her teeth that night she said shyly, "If we want to, we can, you know."

He took her in his arms and kissed her forehead. "I'm awfully tired after the trip," he said. "Rain check?"

They had hardly had sex since their marriage, and they hadn't even talked about starting a family. She chalked this up to him being Catholic — they left family planning up to God. Would he believe her when in a few weeks she announced that she was pregnant with their child? She had tried to give him no reason to doubt her honesty. When he turned his back she ran a hand over her breasts. They were growing, and her belly wasn't quite perfectly flat anymore. Mornings were queasy, but by lunch she was always ravenous. For now she could blame the pasta for her changing shape . . .

Michael and Scottie made their mandated appearance at the Questura di Siena, the police station located under an elaborate marble arch striped in black and white.

"This would have been part of the new Duomo, but it was left unfinished when the plague hit in 1348," said Michael in docent mode as he held the door of the police station open for her. "The workmen dropped their hammers and ran home. Within a few weeks, most of the city was dead."

"The medieval equivalent of a nuclear blast," said Scottie. Michael paled.

Tenente Pisano did not look particularly pleased to see them again. He became even less pleased when it became clear that they did not have their documents in order.

"You must go back to America," announced Pisano. "America dumps on us Lucky Luciano, I send back you." It was a sensitive subject with the Italians, that the U.S. had deported several top Mafia figures back to Italy.

Michael shut himself in the only room in their apartment with a telephone jack and placed lengthy, operator-assisted calls to Rome and dictated cables to Detroit.

As Scottie unpacked their dishes, she

could hear muffled yelling coming from the next room. At last Michael emerged, red-faced and angry, and poured himself a bourbon.

"Maybe I could help," she said.

"You?" he snapped. There was the man she liked least, back again. Michael in a state of fear and frustration. Michael feeling trapped.

She thought of Ugo talking about her "power." Maybe she should use it. Not, she told herself, in *that* way, but for good. "Why don't I talk to Mayor Rosini? It will allow me a chance to apologize for running out on him the other day."

"We can't have a Communist pulling strings for us!"

"He's the mayor. You're opening a business here that will be good for the community. What does it matter what party he belongs to?"

"It matters."

"Oh, pooh," she said, went into the bedroom and picked up the phone. Five minutes later, out she came and found Michael having a second bourbon in the living room.

"I can't believe they don't have ice in this country," he fumed.

"You can stop worrying. It's all been taken care of," she said. "We won't be deported."

Michael brightened, surprised. "What did you say to him?"

"I said it was absurd. The police are acting like we're criminals. We're here to *help*. I reminded him we're the good guys."

Michael laughed. "And what did he say to that?"

"Nothing."

Michael threw his arms around her, lifted her off the ground and spun her around. "You're amazing!"

But Ugo hadn't said nothing. He had said, "I would love to show you San Galgano the next time your husband is out of town."

7.

Under Italian rules, Ugo Rosini would have made a perfect lover for Scottie. He was physically under her spell, which meant she could have made all the decisions. She was not especially attracted to him, which meant she would not lose her head. He was a man of importance in the city, so he would have willingly done things for her — as an Italian, he would have felt it to be his duty. He liked to make women laugh. She would have become the effective First Mistress of Siena, and wielded considerable power of her own.

And he was a Communist, which would have, for the Sienese, lent the whole thing such a *delicious* irony.

An Italian husband would have looked the other way and enjoyed the fringe benefits, but an American — perhaps not. Perhaps Michael would have found a pistol and righted the slight by shooting him, or her, or himself. Such things happened even in the expatriate community.

Americans and the British have their famous "sense of honor," while Italians have *figura* instead. *Bella figura* is when you've done something notable, admirable, something that provokes a little envy. *Brutta figura* is terrible — you've done something wrong, been caught at it, and you feel shame. *Figura* is an outward thing, about how you are perceived, rather than how you feel inside, as honor is. The Italians are always about appearances. If you are not caught doing something unpleasant, then there is no need to feel bad about it.

8.

Scottie took a break from unpacking and sat on the windowsill, quite wide since the building's walls were at least two feet thick. She drew up her knees and stared out at the fan-shaped piazza. It was a hive of deliveries and waiters setting up tables and chairs for the bars and restaurants that buffered the contours of the space.

It was like a television, she thought, luring her to the windows to watch the show. At midday, when she paused in unpacking plates and glasses, men in hats crossed quickly on their way to lunch, then returned slowly a couple of hours later. At three, when she was cutting shelf paper for the bookshelf that would have to serve as a linen closet until they could buy an armoire, children made their way home from school in noisy flocks.

By four p.m., it was roasting inside the apartment. Michael had been in and out all day on business. As she went to close the shutters, she spotted a slim figure darting across the square.

"There's the ox boy again," she said, pointing down as Michael joined her at the window. The boy was carrying suitcases for two obvious tourists, who hurried to keep up with him. The wife, hobbled by a narrow skirt, placed a precautionary hand atop her straw hat.

"I saw him earlier, too," she said. "He was dashing in and out of buildings. He's out there every day. What was his name again?"

Michael stared down at the boy. "Robertino Banchi," he said.

In the evening, when the whole population of Siena emerged from the brick labyrinth for the *passeggiata,* which looked from Scottie's vantage point like the swirling but deliberate movement of a corps de ballet, she saw the boy again, this time carrying a box for an older lady. Around him, swarms of teenagers flirted, little children broke and ran, and everyone moved arm in arm around the piazza in a huge counter-clockwise gyre of pleasantries, gossip and ogling.

"Robertino reminds me of a bellhop," she said. "Knows everyone's business."

9.

Michael sat at a café table in the piazza, having a bourbon and soda and writing up his report on Rosini. He left out all mention of Scottie, but suggested he had "initiated contact through an intermediary to determine Rosini's openness to American ideals."

Robertino appeared at his side, all flattering eagerness. *"Buongiorno, Signor Americano,"* he said. "What I can do for you? Take you to Duomo? Show you good jazz bar? Find girl for you?"

Michael looked into the boy's piercing blue eyes. Could this boy be useful in meeting people who would help him sway the election? He went everywhere in the city, unnoticed. Another invisible, like him.

"Well. I do need someone I can trust to do some work for me. Very important work. Too important for a boy, I think."

"Can trust me. No one but me. I American like you."

"You are?"

"*Sì, sì,* my father was American GI. You no see my eyes and hair? I American!"

"You wouldn't lie to me?"

"No, *signore!*"

"I would need this to be a secret between us. You mustn't tell anyone that you're working for me."

"Top secret!" The boy grinned. "Like Il Pipistrello!"

"Yes," said Michael. "Just like Batman. You'll pass my house every morning at eight. If I need to meet you, I'll be in the window. If I'm holding a newspaper, I'll be feeding pigeons by the Duomo at nine. If I'm holding a cup of coffee, I'll meet you on the road near Sovicille at three. If one of us doesn't show, we meet at the Fortezza at nine in the evening. Got it?"

The boy nodded.

He hoped he hadn't made a huge mistake in using the boy as an asset. There was no handbook for this. In training they had said,

"Be friendly but not too friendly when recruiting an asset. Set up a relationship of trust, but never actually trust him. Try to get information on him that you can use against him in case he becomes untrust-worthy."

He ordered another bourbon and soda. He had an asset!

10.

Scottie was in the stairwell carrying empty boxes, in search of a trash bin. She had forgotten to ask Carlo where it was. The front door of the building opened, and Robertino came in with a package.

"Buongiorno, signora," he said.

Scottie, shy, echoed the greeting, then followed it up with *"Dov'è la spazzatura?"* — a phrase she had spent several minutes memorizing.

"Oh, you speak Italian now," said Robertino.

"No, no," laughed Scottie. "All I know is how to ask where the trash goes!"

He was delivering a package to the *primo piano* (first floor) and explained for the confused Scottie why the first floor wasn't the second floor, because there was a ground floor.

"Why don't you just call the ground floor

the first floor?" Scottie asked.

"Because is on the ground."

There was more to living in a foreign culture than just learning the language, it turned out.

"I can teach you," he said.

11.

After the incident with Rosini, Michael was worried about Scottie. He sent Robertino to offer to teach her Italian, and told him to make sure it seemed like it was the boy's own idea. He didn't want Scottie to realize he was spying on her.

In his weekly encoded report to Luce and his unnamed, shadowy CIA handlers, Michael listed Robertino as a newly recruited "mid-level civil servant," forty-four years old. One of the rules was that he was supposed to give his contacts aliases, so that reports could be circulated without compromising sources. The first two letters were related to the station's location, and the names were always in all caps, to signify they were aliases. To Robertino he gave the alias IS OXBLOOD1, meaning he was the first paid source whom Michael (whose own cryp for internal purposes was Geoffrey Sneedle) had recruited.

A cable arrived from the Rome station the

next day praising him for recruiting a paid asset. It seemed the vast majority of clandestine officers never recruited any. He would celebrate by taking Scottie out to dinner. He had read a few chapters of a book called *How to Have a Happy Marriage,* and it mentioned that sharing successes over a nice meal out made a woman feel like a real partner.

"I'm taking Italian lessons," Scottie announced when he got home, handing him a stinger. "From the ox boy, Robertino."

"Really? What a great idea," he said. The brandy and crème de menthe felt heavy on his tongue. "Let's celebrate. I'm taking you out."

She clapped her hands and kissed his cheek.

It's working, he thought. *I'm good at this.*

It was a perfect arrangement: Robertino chaperoned Scottie every afternoon, and reported to Michael where they went and who they talked to. Michael was impressed by how Scottie took to life as a foreigner — she quickly became much more comfortable in the city than he was. But of course she had no mission other than to keep house for him. He envied her naïveté, her unsullied innocence, her lack of secrets. She was the American ideal he was sent there to promote. She was like Dale Evans, he thought: a beautiful, pure, faithful, true cowgirl. She was the only one *not* there with an ulterior motive.

12.

Michael was a much quieter person than she'd thought when she met him at the mixer at Vassar. In Scottie's experience, people who were shy often turned out to be very talkative when you got to know them, but Michael didn't seem to fit that mold. He was gone every day now, setting up the new Ford showroom in the *zona industriale* just outside the city walls. She'd thought that he'd sell tractors all day, then be home for the dinner that she'd cook up on the beautiful American appliances. Some days, he was, and he would regale her with stories of Italian farmers making the transition from mules and oxen to tractors, and she would tell him stories of domestic life among the "savages." But often he was out with potential clients until late, and came home so tired he could barely fall into bed.

Instead, it was mostly Robertino with whom she shared stories. Over the next few weeks, as Scottie took welcome breaks from setting up the apartment, the Italian lessons with Robertino slowly unwrapped and revealed the local culture that had been hidden from her when she arrived. Robertino would come in the afternoons when he was done exercising horses at the stable where he worked. She loved that he brought the smell of horse with him. She would think of questions for him, things that she needed to do, or buy, or wondered about, and have them ready when he arrived. Then they would go out into the city and get what she needed, learning as she went. As they walked through the city, Robertino solemnly explained that cappuccino was never drunk after lunch, because that much milk was considered too heavy late in the day. *Tisana* was a healing tea. You must never grate cheese on a dish containing seafood — considered a disgusting combination. Ice in a drink would cause a heart attack. Stepping in dog doo was good luck; seeing nuns behind the wheel was bad. Thirteen was fine, but seventeen was unlucky. All stores closed from one to three p.m., or sometimes four, so that everyone could go home for lunch. Lunch was at one, never at two or three, and dinner no earlier than eight p.m.

"For a seemingly anarchist culture," Scottie pointed out, "you have a lot of rules, and most of them seem to be related to digestion."

"Nothing is more important than eating," said Robertino, and Scottie felt as if an important piece of her Italian education had just fallen into place.

13.

Michael was surprised how much he learned about Scottie from Robertino's reports. The kid was always telling him about something funny Scottie had said, or done, or something she had noticed about the Sienese.

"She got very sad when I showed her where they leave the babies," Robertino said when they met one morning out near Sovicille. They could not be seen together in Siena, as per agency protocols.

"Leave the babies? What are you talking about?"

"At the door of the nunnery, the revolving wheel. If you have a baby you don't want, you put it there and turn the wheel to send it inside without them seeing you. The nuns give the babies funny last names like 'Gift from God' and 'Little Toy,' and they find them homes. The *signora,* she's an orphan, too."

"Yes, I know," said Michael, but he realized he didn't, really. He had seen it as convenient that Scottie did not have family ties, but now he thought she must be very

95

lonely. But perhaps asking her about it would make her sad. He wished he knew more about what happy marriages were made of. If only he had time to make a study of them — he needed to finish reading *How to Have a Happy Marriage,* he thought. His own parents were only a model of what *not* to do. He wished there was someone he could ask. But he had so much to do, and so little time. The election was coming up, and he had reports to file, and tractors to sell to keep his cover intact. He would make time for that later, once the election was over. She would understand. Plus, she was so down-to-earth — she would know he adored her because he worked so hard to take care of them.

14.

Scottie and Robertino stopped by his grandfather's house just outside the city walls one afternoon so Signor Banchi could teach her the names of the plants in the garden. He pointed out *rosmarino* and *timo* and *lavanda,* rubbing the leaves between his fingers to release the fragrant perfume of each.

Scottie knew she should probably get a textbook to learn Italian, but she had always had difficulty reading, and Robertino wasn't really that kind of teacher. He simply talked to her in Italian and expected her to catch on. He began by going around the apartment and naming everything. It was pure poetry.

"Tappeto, caffettiera, rubinetto, divano, fazzoletto, asciugamano . . . ," he said. Then he named actions like walking, standing, sitting, cooking: *"camminare, stare, sedere, cucinare."* From there they were off — she often begged him to slow down, but he rarely did, so she just made him repeat things over and over.

"Andiamo a camminare. Andiamo a fare la spesa."

Scottie didn't know what the phrases meant at first, but she discovered as she went. Let's go for a walk. Let's go shopping. Robertino explained that she must address him with the *tu* form of verbs, while he addressed her as the formal *Lei.*

"It is correct," he said, as if it were also very important, so she obeyed. She felt safe as she followed Robertino around the city, echoing him — *"Vorrei due chili di pomodori, per cortesia."* Because of the way her brain learned, she didn't think "the word for tomatoes is *pomodori*"; she just looked at the display and said *"pomodori."* It was more like the way a child accumulates language, in large experiential verbal waves. She began to realize that most of what we say in life follows predictable patterns. We use the same phrasings for asking for things, for talking about the weather, for expressing sympathy, for expressing affection. There are scripts we follow without even thinking about it. She wasn't learning the language word by word; she was learning it by living it. With her difficulty reading, she had always felt a little dumb, even though she had gone to the best girls' schools in America. Every B-minus had been a hard-fought struggle. Here in Italy she felt like a different person altogether — more expressive, more curious, more open. The only problem was how bothered she felt by the way the men looked at her, something she could not bring up with Robertino, of course, who was still a boy.

"*Buongiorno,* Signor Sindaco," Robertino said as they crossed paths with Ugo Rosini one day in Via di Città. Scottie now knew that *sindaco* was the Italian term for mayor.

Ugo smiled broadly at both of them and tipped his hat. "Beware of the most beautiful woman in Siena," he told Robertino. Scottie felt herself blush so hard her face burned. Robertino, fortunately, didn't notice, and launched into a discussion of the latest car he wanted to buy. As he chattered about the merits of Alfas versus Fiats, she thought of something Leona used to say. "A man liking you doesn't make you special. It just means you have something he wants."

15.

"Do you ever see my husband?" she asked Robertino one day as they were visiting the Duomo. They were admiring the floors, which depicted classical figures. Scottie was peering down at the Roman goddess Fortuna, who had one foot on the sphere and the other on a ship, holding her sail aloft. She often felt that same precarious thrill.

He looked straight at her. "See him?"

"Yes, you know, around Siena." She blushed a little, despite having promised herself she wouldn't. "I'm not spying on him or anything. He just works a lot, and I miss him."

"If I see him, I will tell you," he said.

Two days later he arrived at the apartment and announced, "He had lunch with the priest, Father Giovanni, at Trattoria Pepe. They both had lamb."

She laughed. "And for dessert?"

"Torta della nonna."

"I'll have to learn to make that. I didn't

know he liked it."

"He also likes spaghetti with clams. The waiter at Trattoria Il Bosco told me that. He orders it all the time, when he has lunch with the people who are shopping for tractors. You should make that for him."

"I will. Thank you."

He tipped an imaginary hat at her. "Anything for you, *signora.*"

16.

From what Michael could gather, most of what Robertino and Scottie talked about was horses. Robertino was proud to have taught Scottie all of the terms: *cavallo, cavaliere, salto, scuderia, zoccolo, pelo* . . . In preparing his cover as a tractor expert, Michael had read that before the war, horses in Tuscany were fairly rare — cart horses, mostly — and even the horses in the famous Palio horse race were just farm beasts drafted for the event. During the war, horses were primarily a source of food. He had tried to hide from Scottie the fact that there was still an equine butcher only a block from their apartment.

"I can't look," she said when she finally discovered what the horse sign over the door meant.

"They think it's a cure for anemia," he said.

Now, with incomes growing and a new prosperity in the air, there was a class of Tuscan entrepreneurs who were embracing the horse as a sign of status and building flashy places like the stable where Robertino worked in the mornings. Michael had learned the names of the newly rich Sienese who kept horses there, and included them in his reports. Anyone attracted to that kind of lifestyle would be more interested in capitalism than communism, he reasoned.

Scottie could be useful there, too. She seemed quite observant, and intuitive. She had made him spaghetti with clams the other night, even though he had never told her it was his favorite. She was a terrible cook, but he appreciated the gesture. He should buy her something nice. That was in the book, too — *buy her presents even when it's not her birthday, so she knows you care.* He would ask Robertino what to buy her.

17.

"I love that the Italian word for a female rider is *amazzone,*" she said to Robertino as they walked along the wall of the city near Porta Romana. "Like we're Amazons." She bought them both *gelati* — *cioccolato*

101

for him and *limone* for her — and they sat on a bench overlooking the distant hills.

He admired her bracelet. "Mr. Messina bought it for me," she said, twisting her wrist to admire the pearls. "Do you think it's too flashy?"

"No," said Robertino. "I think it's perfect."

"I do miss riding," she said with a sigh.

"A woman on a horse," said Robertino, "is to be feared."

She told him about the horses she'd had — starting with Shorty the pony, who bit and kicked and had to wear an anti-grazing strap, put in place after he had yanked many little girls down his neck and over his head in search of green grass. Shorty had taught her to have a good seat and be a decisive rider, transmitting confidence to her mounts. And he had taught her patience — hard-earned, since she had started riding as a tempestuous little six-year-old who would pound her fists on the unimpressed pony's sides when he disobeyed.

Her voice caught as she told Robertino about her beloved Sonny Boy.

"He was magnificent," she said, licking the small wooden spoon. *"Era un cavallo magnifico."* She told Robertino the story of buying him at Saratoga, saving him from slaughter, how she brought him along slowly, encouraging him and bringing out his best.

"He loves to jump," she said. "He just loves it."

"Why did you sell him? Because you came here?"

She sighed. "I had to when my father died," she said. "Last summer."

"You have no brothers and sisters?"

"No. There's an aunt, but that's it."

"So you inherited everything? Like I will inherit my grandfather's farm?"

"I thought so," she said, thinking of the Spanish-style mansion on Alden Street — the twisted wrought iron, the cool painted tiles, the fountain in the courtyard. "But no. I found out something secret about my father when he died." Robertino, she knew, loved secrets and gossip.

"A secret?"

"He had no money after all."

18.

"She thought her father was rich," Robertino said, "but he wasn't."

So there is no trust fund coming her way, thought Michael. "I thought he was in oranges."

"That's what he told her, but it wasn't true. He worked for a man who owned many, many orange groves."

They were near the heavy, huge walls of the Fortezza. Michael didn't like to meet in the city, but he was having lunch with a local winemaker later who seemed like a prospect on two fronts: buying tractors and finding out what Rosini's weaknesses were that could be exploited to make him look bad and lose the election. The kid had signaled him that he had information, so here they were — except the information wasn't about one of Siena's power brokers, it was about his own wife.

"He was stealing from the man, a little bit here, a little bit there. For a long time the rich man didn't notice."

Michael pictured Scottie's father raising a daughter alone, a daughter who liked horses. An expensive habit. He would never steal himself, but he could see how it could happen, that you would skim a bit just to make your little girl smile. "And then?"

"He got caught. He was going to go to jail, so he killed himself."

"Oh my God. I didn't know that. She said he . . . died." Michael realized he had never asked how.

"Her aunt told her, 'You know what a mirage is? Think of it as a mirage. It was a beautiful mirage, but now it's gone. It's all gone.' She never told anyone, Mrs. Messina. Not at school, not her friends. She only tell me."

Michael pondered this. How awful for Scottie. How lonely.

"She had to sell her horse to pay for her last year of school. Me, I hate school," Robertino said. "I would keep the horse and quit!"

She had lost everything. Her father, her money, her beloved horse. A doubt crept into his mind. Was that why she married him? Did girls marry for love, really, or was that just in the movies? Didn't they marry for security? Did it matter? Men needed wives, and women needed husbands. If you also loved each other, it would be an amazing bonus, but you couldn't count on it. It would be nice, he thought, if she loved him, but at the same time the idea made him nervous. Too much closeness — that could be dangerous for both of them. To really be safe, he needed to keep her in the dark.

19.

She hoped she hadn't been stupid to confide in Robertino. It was just that he was the only person she had to really talk to. And he confided in her, too. He told her about a horse he was exercising at the stable, a mare named Camelia who was evil to everyone, but whom he adored. He described the way she shied at ducks and bikes and children, flying into the air sideways.

Scottie thought about Sonny Boy, remembering saying good-bye in the horse trailer, sitting down on the ground and sobbing as the truck pulled away.

"We can go to the stable where I work," Robertino said as they chose ripe peaches — *pesche,* not to be confused with fish, *pesci* — from a display outside the fruit store. "I will show you all the horses. You must meet Camelia."

She shook her head. That grief had not yet dissipated. "I can't," she said.

20.

They were of course *both* children, Scottie and Robertino, Michael thought as he walked across the beautiful intarsia floor of the Duomo, stopping as he always did to admire the figure of Fortuna. It wasn't surprising that they got along so well, though he was startled at how much Robertino had learned about her. The bond of horses knit them together. That made sense. For both of them the horse was a way to bound upward across class lines, though neither of them would have seen their hippophilia — he loved that word, and made a note to himself to look up what the word was for people who love hippos — as anything so socioeconomic. For them it was just a deeply rooted passion, profound and inexplicable. He envied them that.

He had never had that kind of friend. Even as a child he had been guarded, already aware that he was different in a way that others found distasteful. When he allowed himself to be excited about something, like when he shouted with joy as he unwrapped a Christmas present from Marco, a picture book of castles, his father had frowned and his sisters had teased him, fake shouting as they opened their own gifts of socks and pickled olives. Marco had tried to help, telling him not to be "such a girl about everything." He dragged him over to meet the boy next door, but the boy had a bike and other friends, and ignored him. Michael had not felt hurt for long — when that same boy sat next to him in math class, he had reveled in watching him fail.

He kneeled to pray and, as he had been instructed since childhood, reviewed what his sins were, both mortal and venial, made sure he felt sorrow and resolved not to sin again. Then he stood, crossed himself, passed under the gaze of winged cherubs, pushed aside the curtain and entered the ornately carved confessional. He had a lot to say today.

FIVE:
LA GIRAFFA, THE GIRAFFE

"THE HIGHER THE HEAD,
THE GREATER THE GLORY"

1.

On a beautiful day in June when the last of the scarlet poppies were like a sea of fading valentines in the fields, Michael drove the repaired Ford through Porta Camollia and down the hill to the outskirts of town, through the gates of the new *zona industriale,* and parked in front of his Ford Tractors office, which was attached to a warehouse, perhaps the only unattractive building in all of Siena. The car showed no signs of its brush with the walls of the city. Michael was impressed with the care the mechanic had taken. The man had made sure every single dent was perfectly hammered out, taking hours more than he was paid for. *"Tutt' a posto,"* he announced when the job was done. Gelso Brunetti was his name. He was grateful for Michael's appreciation of his work, and they had shared an espresso together and talked cars.

Though Michael had learned what he assumed was Italian from his parents, it turned out it wasn't the same Italian as that spoken here in Siena, which Brunetti emphasized was the Italian spoken by Dante. Michael's accent and vocabulary marked him not as an American but as a southerner, *un Siciliano,* and the Sienese were incredibly snobbish about people from anywhere below mid-calf on Italy's boot.

The industrial zone was home to several businesses hoping to capitalize on Italy's rapidly mechanizing landscape. Michael's main competition was Macchinari Agricoli di Siena, run by the clever and industrious Signor Brigante from Milan, who favored shiny green suits that reminded Michael of beetle carapaces.

"Buongiorno, Americano," called Signor Brigante. "A good day to sell tractors to the damned Tuscans, eh?"

With the Italians' legendary distrust of anyone born more than ten miles from themselves, it was a toss-up whether farmers would buy from Signor Brigante or *l'Americano,* though "neither" seemed to be the case at present. Though Michael felt uncomfortable when Signor Brigante sidled into his showroom to rail against the stingy, balky, truculent Sienese, he could hardly disagree with him. Everyone around here seemed to have a nemesis, and when he and Brigante squeezed into the local bar after work one night to watch the enormously popular game show *Lascia o Raddoppia* (*Double or Nothing*), the men were all slapping each other's backs and calling each other "Maremma Pig," "Ball-less Prick," "Mother-loving Fool" and "Sainted Idiot." It was the kind of testosterone-laden jocular aggression that had made Michael deeply uncomfortable at Yale, and even Brigante, from uptight Milan, looked startled. They had not repeated the outing.

Signor Brigante stocked gas-powered tractors made by Landini, Fiat and Pietro Orsi, plus a new model from a family-owned firm in Padua, Antonio Carraro, that had been making carts and farm equipment since the 1600s and had wisely come up with a compact tractor well suited for the Mediterranean landscape. Heavy-duty diesels based on tank technology were the wave of the future, though, and Signor Brigante had foreign models, too, including the DT-54, a bright blue tread design from the Stalingrad Tractor Company.

"This is the tractor that built the glorious USSR," he boasted.

Just the acronym triggered another of Michael's many visions of mushroom clouds and radiation levels, of how unpleasant it would be to have one's flesh burned off.

Inside the warehouse Michael rented sat a row of shiny new Ford tractors that had been shipped from the company's factory in England, arranged in increasing size like a display of dinosaurs at the Museum of Natural History in New York. They looked honest and hardworking, but also large and ungainly compared to the small Italian models. Michael ran through the product numbers and key features in his mind, as he did every morning. He had spent several weeks at Ford headquarters in Dearborn, Michigan, training. The other reps in his training group there had seen through him, he thought, had sensed he wasn't one of them, so he had worked doubly hard to learn everything he could. They were the sons of Ford dealers, and had spent their whole lives immersed in the world of engines, carburetors, tires and spark plugs. This was their college, their transition to their adult lives, which would be spent patrolling remote asphalt lots in Spokane and Des Moines and Jacksonville. They would do battle with Chrysler and Dodge, while he would fight other enemies.

Benzedrine came to the rescue, as it was doing frequently these days. He popped the small white pill and instantly felt mental clarity returning.

Fordson New Major 45 horsepower. Hydraulics. Disc brakes. Locking differential. He had painstakingly translated all of the information into Italian. The brochures were being printed up in Rome.

Rome. He could justify taking the train down tomorrow, maybe. Maybe he and Duncan would have some time alone.

Except for a few curious lookyloos, he had not had many customers come to the warehouse yet, but that was okay. The ads had only just begun to run in the local papers. And besides, that left more time for his real work.

The best case officers melted neatly into their posting. They had a knack for talking to people, lending a sympathetic ear. Some officers never paid any of their assets, which made the Agency nervous about the validity of the information. HQ was always pressing officers to get signed contracts, information in exchange for this many dollars every month, but that was a very American-centric point of view. In most places in the world, including Italy, it would be insulting if not dangerous to offer someone money and a contract with the CIA. It was much more acceptable to get a little, give a little.

He dropped an armload of newspapers on his desk, then unlocked a filing cabinet. He removed a file, sat down at his desk and stared at the list of names. Finally, he circled one. He then took out a clean index card, removed the cover from his typewriter and typed on the card.

Brunetti, Gelso
Via Pia di Sopra, 22
Born 1930 (approx.). Mechanic. Married to Maria, born 1930 (approx.). Father of Ilaria (1950) and Gianluca (1952).
Communist.

He put the card into a box in the filing cabinet that also contained the names of Tenente Pisano (Monarchist), Signor Barco the property manager (Catholic) and Signor Brigante (Socialist), along with many others. Robertino had turned out to be very useful. In exchange for some American comic books, he had innocently divulged the party affiliations and kinship relationships of virtually everyone in his *contrada,* including his grandfather, Signor Banchi

114

(Communist).

That was the good news, the news he had included in his reports to Rome. The bad news was that in the weeks since he had arrived in Siena, Michael had continually tried to locate and talk to the so-called opinion molders, but had found the Sienese distant and snobbish, especially to someone with a Sicilian accent. He had gathered lots of information, but Robertino was his only asset. He was getting a little panicky. If he got lucky, the election would go his way and he could take the credit. But if it didn't . . . He didn't want to think about that.

He wanted to be a hero. To show his father that he was someone worthy of — what, love? No, he really just wanted his father to feel bad about not having loved him. He wanted to make his father feel small, and mean, which is what he was. That would never happen, he knew, but it was pleasant to imagine it. Michael told himself he wanted to honor Marco, whom he missed, but really he wanted to be a bigger hero than Marco was. *You saved Europe. I saved the world!* He really hoped there was an afterlife in which he could affectionately, eternally lord that over Marco. He also wanted, right now, to make Scottie glad that she had married him. The problem was that, because it was all top secret, no one would ever know what he had done. Though if he pulled it off, he would definitely tell Duncan.

2.

One day Robertino and Scottie passed the busty woman Scottie had seen the day of their arrival. She was smoking, and had a pile of cigarette butts at her feet. Robertino averted his eyes as they passed, just as everyone else had.

"Eh, Robertino," the woman called to him, laughing, grinding out another cigarette.

"Who is that?" Scottie asked.

"Nessuno," he said. No one.

"Come on, she knows your name. I think she's a pros— prosti—"

"Prostituta," whispered Robertino, mortified.

Scottie thought of the hookers she had seen in New York, women with painted faces and tarted-up fashions.

"She looks like everyone else. How do they know?"

"They know her. We all know Signora Gina. Please, missus, is not nice to talk about." He was squirming.

3.

Michael opened the top newspaper, *La Nazione,* and began reading. He sent Luce weekly summaries of how events were covered in the local press, whether stories seemed to be slanted against the U.S., and if so, who wrote them. There was a reporter named Rodolfo Marchetti who bashed America on a regular basis, ridiculing its films as treacle, its products as flimsy and its presence in Europe as imperialist. The worst part was, he was an excellent satirical writer, and the pieces were nothing short of brilliant. Michael had a wild longing to flip him, to get him to write a lengthy piece about the joys of Mickey Mouse, or Superman, or NATO. But it seemed impossible.

The front page today was about the uprisings in Poland, where a hundred thousand workers had taken to the streets to protest the policies of the Communist leadership. They called on their fellow Poles to be loyal to their sovereign nation, while the Soviets saw them as disloyal to the empire. *La Nazione* took the Poles' side, and the Communist daily *L'Unita* took the Soviet side, no surprise. Last week the shocking news had hit the world press that Khrushchev had denounced Stalin in a four-hour tirade at the Party Congress, openly criticizing his cult of personality, mass executions and military and agricultural blunders. What did it mean, the papers kept asking, and everyone had a contradictory answer. Some said it was the beginning of a loosening of Soviet control over the Eastern Bloc. Others said it was a consolidation of power in new hands. Things had begun to shift and change in ways that Michael found unnerving. It felt to him like the entire world was having a migraine.

He turned the page to "News of Siena": Ugo Rosini, the Communist mayor, was predicted to win an easy reelection. Siena would go to the polls in four days.

Damn it.

He reached for the book to encode a telegram to Rome.

"Permesso?" called a quavering voice that startled him. He slammed the code book back into the drawer and went to the door. A small man in a battered black hat was standing just back from the doorway. Robertino was in front of him, bouncing up and down on his heels.

"You remember my grandfather?" he said. "He wants to see the tractors." Robertino seemed almost embarrassed by the old man's presence.

Michael greeted Banchi, who doffed his

hat and spoke nervously and formally to Michael. The old man stood in awe in front of the gleaming line of tractors.

"Troppo belli," he said, as if looking at a line of cancan dancers. He ran a rough hand over the grille of the Ford 600.

"Can I see it go?"

Michael liked putting the tractors through their paces — they were so loud and huge and strong — and he did get a nice cut of each sale.

"Certo," he said, and removed his jacket, leaving his tie on. He rolled open the large warehouse doors, retrieved the keys from the box in his desk and climbed up on the blue tractor, careful not to get dirt on his trousers or his freshly polished oxblood wingtips, and settled himself into its metal seat. He pushed in the clutch and turned the key, and (thank goodness) the tractor started up. "It has a pressurized cooling system, so it stays cool even during the hardest jobs."

"I told you," said Robertino to his grandfather. The old man looked delighted as Michael put the tractor in gear and drove it out of the warehouse into the sun, across the parking lot and up and over the curb into the adjacent empty field. He was distressed to see that Brigante was out there, too, showing a buyer a shiny red trac-tor.

The old man shaded his eyes as he watched. "I do like red," he said.

Robertino squinted as he looked at the red tractor. "How fast is that one?"

"Ford's live-action hydraulic system sends five gallons of oil pumping through the system at all times, making implement response time immediate."

The old man continued gazing dreamily at Brigante's shiny red model, and Rober-tino went over to look at it. Michael saw it was a Belarus MTZ-2, made by the Minsk Tractor Works. A piece of Commie crap if he ever saw one.

"The headlights on that tractor are all the way back by the steering wheel," Michael pointed out. "And it has half the engine power."

Brigante putted past, dropping a disc harrow into the soil. *Bello, eh? Forte!* he called, lifting his hat in salute as the machine churned up the soil.

Robertino and Banchi whispered to each other. The boy was obsessed with speed, but Michael wanted to prove to him that strength was what mattered. American strength.

"Hey, Brigante," Michael called, and

waved him over. When the red Soviet tractor rumbled up, Michael waved to a chain on the rear of his tractor and threw down a challenge. "How about a duel? Strongest tractor wins."

Robertino whooped, and Michael saw that he had gone up several notches in the boy's estimation. It was absurd to feel happy about that, but he did.

Brigante immediately agreed. He jumped down, and the chain was used to affix one tractor to the other, rear to rear. Robertino drew a line in the dirt. The two men jumped back into their seats.

"Ready?" called Michael.

"Prontissimo," called Brigante.

Robertino dropped his arm, and they both hit the gas. The two tractors, red and blue, strained at each other. The huge rear wheels began to cut deep into the earth. Engines roared, and black smoke filled the air. Michael looked down and saw the gauges on his instrument panel all at maximum. The front wheels of his tractor began to rise up under the strain. Then, with a boom, the Ford lurched forward, towing its prey behind it. *I am defeating communism,* he thought, elated. *I am defeating communism.* Just before he crossed the line of victory, the chain broke with a hideous snap and both tractors shot forward. Michael was thrown off the tractor and landed facedown in the dirt, the wind knocked out of him. Brigante, who narrowly missed being decapitated by the broken chain, lay bruised and bloodied on his side of the line in the sand.

Michael finally caught his breath and saw that he and Brigante were alone, Robertino and Banchi nowhere in sight.

"Toscani di merda," growled Brigante, wiping the blood off his face. "Let them go back to their oxen."

Back in his office, brushing the mud off his clothes, Michael remembered the telegram he had been encoding. It was still sitting on the desk. *It's going to take a miracle to get our guy to win this election. He's going to have to rescue a baby from a burning building or something.* With a heavy sigh, he sent it off to Luce.

4.

Scottie loved the little donkeys that the local people used to transport almost anything. One day as she and Robertino were going down to Fontebranda so he could show her Siena's oldest fountain, in use for washing since 1081, a donkey was coming up the steep, narrow street, led by a woman who seemed old, but whose face was age-

122

less. She might have been forty or eighty; Scottie could not guess. She had curly copper hair pulled into a bun. She was beautiful, elegant, tall — not the typical tiny tradeswoman with the shy smile and the black cardigan.

The donkey was old, with white hairs around its muzzle and eyes. Both it and the woman were panting. The baskets on either side of the beast's spine were full, though the contents appeared to be dried herbs, so perhaps the load was not so heavy after all.

"Che carino," she said. "How cute." She reached out to rub the donkey's face between its eyes, and a hand grabbed hers. She found herself staring into the dark eyes of a very angry woman, face twisted in a grimace.

"Non si tocca!" shouted the woman. Don't touch!

"Eh, eh!" shouted Robertino, coming between them. Scottie pulled her hand away. It stung where the woman had clenched it.

"Via, via," shouted Robertino to the woman, shooing her off.

"Americani di merda," said the woman, spitting on the ground.

"Via!" shouted Robertino once again, slapping the donkey on the rump. The woman

continued up the road, not looking back, but Scottie heard her muttering something about Robertino.

"What is *traditore*?" she asked.

"Very bad word," he said. "When you are not royal to your country."

"Loyal," said Scottie.

"Yes, right, loyal."

"Traitor. Why did she call you a traitor?"

He blushed. "She does not like Americans," he said. "She is crazy."

There was something he was not telling her. Why wouldn't she like Americans? The U.S. had pumped endless cash into Italy since the war ended. Her country was helping to modernize life here. Make things easier for everyone.

Scottie had a funny feeling it was the same woman who had made the rude gesture at her in the street on the day they arrived.

"Who is she?"

Robertino looked evasive. "The witch," he said. It was a simple, weird, yet apt description.

Her heart was pounding and she felt shaky as she watched the woman climb up the steep road with the donkey and disappear.

"I'm so sorry," said Robertino. He seemed to feel he should have protected Scottie.

She quickly said, "It was my fault. I

shouldn't have touched her . . . ass." She started to laugh. The pun was not the same in Italian, and Robertino looked confused. "*Asino* is 'ass,' " she said. "Which is . . ." She pointed to her own. "It's not the nice way to say it."

"What is the nice way?"

She thought for a moment. "There isn't one."

5.

"Buongiorno, Americano!" called Brigante, smoking a cigar and lounging in his doorway. Michael was not in the mood to talk this morning, and tried to wave and keep going, but Brigante was quick.

"You heard about the fire?" he said. He dropped a newspaper on Michael's desk. MANGANELLI SAVES GIRL FROM FIRE IN AQUILA: TRAGEDY AVERTED. Michael picked up the paper and skimmed the story, hiding his shock and confusion. A house fire had broken out in the Aquila *contrada,* next door to Catholic mayoral candidate Manganelli's home. He had rushed in and saved a little girl of six. Manganelli's hands had been burned, but the girl was safe.

A TRUE HERO AND MAN OF THE PEOPLE, read the sub-headline. BY RODOLFO MARCHETTI.

125

"Manganelli's front door in Via Casato di Sotto is covered in flowers," said Brigante. "I walked by there myself this morning. Lucky bastard. He's sure to win the election now, and what did it cost him? Nothing but a few charred fingers."

Michael would write a memo to Rome today, happily reversing his prediction.

As Brigante chattered on about the latest gossip in the industrial zone ("I hear there's a plumbing supply warehouse going in next door — you know what they say about plumbers, their pipe is in every house"), Michael couldn't shake off the feeling, no matter how absurd it seemed, that somehow he had made this happen.

6.

Michael and Clare Boothe Luce celebrated Manganelli's victory in Siena's mayoral election with huge sirloins at the Grand Hotel Plaza, and an array of cocktails that had Michael's head spinning.

"Mission accomplished," said Luce, raising her glass. "To you."

"There are still plenty of Communists in the city, I'm afraid," said Michael, who feared that he would now be transferred elsewhere, possibly out of Italy altogether.

"How's your lovely little Vassar girl?"

asked Luce, looking a little pale in pink chiffon. She snapped open a cloissoné pillbox and downed a few somethings. Michael was longing to ask her for one, but didn't.

"Terrific," said Michael. "She's dying to come to Rome, actually." Rome would be a great post for them, he thought.

"Oh dear, no," said Luce. "Don't let her come here. You'll never get her back to Siena. In fact, I'd like to keep you there for another few months. You're my most solid, reliable intelligence officer. You have no idea what we're dealing with elsewhere."

Luce then complained to him about other intelligence officers who had "gone native." She was furious about the reports coming out of Florence. "They sound like they were written poolside at Bernard Berenson's villa in Settignano," she said, "which I'm sure they were. People act as if life in Italy is one long party. I read the riot act to the entire Florence consular office. You know what I told them?"

"What?"

"Lay off the cocktails and sex and take your mission seriously!" She laughed and signaled to the waiter for another martini.

Sometimes Michael felt like he was not an intelligence officer for a superpower locked in a cold war that could lead to nuclear destruction, but instead had written himself into a screwball comedy about rich people's hijinks, like *My Man Godfrey* or *Bringing Up Baby.*

The Italian Party.

"Keep your eyes open," she said as the waiter poured from a chilled silver shaker. "A Soviet invasion is not out of the question."

7.

At last, he had time alone with Duncan. Today was just for the two of them, a picnic on the Palatine Hill — grilled quail wrapped in pancetta and a bottle of Frascati. Julie had left for London with the twins to attend Wimbledon. Michael had always borne an irrational dislike — really anger and jealousy — toward Julie. She had never liked Michael, and he knew it. He told himself there was no way she could suspect anything; he and Duncan had always been extremely cautious and discreet.

Now he felt nothing but gratitude toward her.

He had so much to tell Duncan. He filled him in on everything that he had done to get Manganelli elected, which in truth wasn't much, but who else was around to take the credit from him? He felt a little guilty that when he boasted to Duncan about having made an "asset" in Siena, he didn't tell him (as he hadn't told the CIA) that Robertino was only fourteen. He said that Luce wanted to keep him on in Siena.

"The CIA — so glamorous," said Duncan, gnawing on a quail leg.

"I wish you were in the Agency, too." In truth, it was nice to be in the power position for a change, the one with the better job. Duncan was undersecretary for U.S. Information Services, whose mission was to present a good face for America overseas. USIS was in effect a large-scale public relations firm, never to be referred to as "propaganda." Duncan's job seemed so innocent compared to his, just to show Italians how happy Americans were, and how wonderful American products were.

"You turned out to be a master of cloak and dagger, of course," Duncan teased.

"Not dagger," Michael protested with false humility. "It was strange, though, how I cabled that thing to Luce about how Manganelli's only chance of winning was saving a baby, and then he did save a little girl."

Duncan refilled his wineglass. "To fortuitous coincidences," he said. "And to you."

I am the happiest I have ever been, Michael thought. Umbrella pines spread overhead, bits of columns were scattered every-where, and everything felt leafy and green and ancient. Settled, and safe. History and the present, finally allied.

Last night Michael had stayed over at Duncan's apartment on Via del Babuino. This morning they had slept in, an almost unimaginable luxury, watching the sun make the shutters glow. Because even straight Italian men strolled arm in arm, Rome was a place where they could pretend that they lived in a world where their kind of love was tolerated. At home in the U.S., they had to be constantly aware of who was watching them, listening to them. Last night after dinner on the Via Veneto, they had made their way to the Pantheon, and in a shadowy niche within arm's reach of the mortal remains of Raphael, they had kissed, the only time ever in public during the six years they had been lovers.

"I bet Luce thinks you're a hero," Duncan said, leaning over the picnic basket to toss a quail bone to a stray dog.

"That's the Flavian Palace over there," said Michael. "And down there is where Julius Caesar was stabbed."

"Oh God, not another history lesson," said Duncan, groaning. "Please, Professor, tell me more."

Michael lay back and looked at the clouds, white, fluffy and innocuous. He felt relaxed for the first time in years.

Tonight is the beginning of always. His literature professor had written it on the board, and then explained how it was attributed to Dante, but he never said it. The man had raged about inaccuracy, equating it to treachery, but Michael had stared at the phrase and thought it didn't matter who said it, it was beautiful.

"You know what I would do if I were a spy?" Duncan said, uncorking another bottle of wine. "I would try to get my hands on the Communist Party membership rolls."

"Too dangerous," said Michael. "What if I were caught? My cover would be blown."

"I'd have my asset get them," Duncan said. "Make it look like a regular break-in. Take the cash, too."

"I could do that," said Michael, thinking, *How the hell would I do that?*

Six:
Oca, The Goose

"A CALL TO ARMS"

June 24, 1956

Scottie awakened and looked around with satisfaction. She had worked hard over the past two months to make their apartment into a home. Finally, the boxes were unpacked and pictures were on the walls and it was done. And almost without effort, from doorknob (*maniglia*) to coat hanger (*gruccia*), Scottie's Italian had progressed fairly quickly, too, and she could now make herself understood in most situations, and follow the general lines of a conversation as long as the person didn't speak too quickly. Robertino was a natural teacher, and she looked forward to their afternoons together. He was outgoing, peppy, always in a good mood, and perfectly confident of everything in his life.

In contrast, Scottie felt confused. She

wondered if there was something wrong with her marriage to Michael, or if this was what marriage actually was. In the movies she liked, *Holiday* with Katharine Hepburn and Cary Grant, and *The Awful Truth* with Irene Dunne and Grant, couples teased and bantered and gave each other a hard time as a sign of affection. She and Michael were polite strangers. He did everything a good husband was supposed to do — he was kind, attentive, bought her presents, flowers, took her out to dinner, made love to her. But there was something missing. Maybe it was just that he worked so hard. He was often out late, and had to get up early. She had begun to suspect he didn't really enjoy sex with her. Was that her fault? Should she be doing something different? Was she a nymphomaniac if she wanted it and he didn't? Was he getting it from someone else, like the prostitute Gina down the road? These were questions she could not ask Robertino, or anyone, in any language.

She wanted to be an excellent wife. She applied herself in the same way she had applied herself to riding — with attention to detail, research, creativity, ingenuity and passion. She had become an excellent rider, but she felt that as a wife she was still a rank beginner, suitable for leadline only.

She was three months along. Soon she would have to tell him she was pregnant. She hoped he would be so happy that he wouldn't suspect the truth. She felt that an engine of deception was always running inside her, a projector showing a film of how she needed things to be. She wished she could just tell him everything, apologize, throw herself on his mercy — but she feared it would ruin the fragile bond they had formed. What if he refused to love the child? In any case he would think less of her — he who was so good to her, and who worked so hard to support her. It would hurt him to think she had lied to him. He would never love her after that, and she so badly wanted him to.

Passion. *That is what's missing,* she thought. Was that even something real, something to hope for?

She hoped having a child would bring them closer. She pictured a little boy, like Robertino, growing up confident and full of fun. Certainly Michael would like that.

If only Leona were here. Except Leona didn't approve of Michael, and Scottie didn't know how to explain everything she was learning about Italy to Leona. Their letters to each other had petered out. She felt an ache of nostalgia for her days at Vassar, and yet at the same time she saw that Scottie as young and shallow.

She moved the aqua sofa slightly to the left, then back to the right. She fluffed the throw pillows, yellow on the right, pink on the left. She stood back to assess the room.

And then she started to cry. She sat down, telling herself it was the pregnancy, that women were especially emotional during these months. For a moment it seemed like it was okay to cry; then she got irritated with herself for even wanting to. Was she living on the street? Was she starving to death? She was bored — hardly something worth crying over. In the midst of this back-and-forth, the doorbell rang.

"I hope I'm not disturbing." It was Carlo Chigi Piccolomini, looking calm, cool, crisp. She wanted to hug him.

"Not at all," she said. "Come in." He looked closely at her face.

"You've been crying," he said as he took his hat off, his face full of concern.

"I —"

"I'm sorry, it's none of my business. The apartment looks beautiful — so different with all the furniture."

"Thank you," she said. "I spent about an hour deciding how to arrange those throw pillows, so please notice them. I'll get us a drink."

He wandered around as she went to the kitchen to pour them lemonades.

"Looks like your big day of shopping in New York paid off," he called out.

"Yes, but it was fun to buy the rest here. Siena has wonderful little shops." She returned to the living room, but it was empty. She set the tray down.

She found him in the bedroom, where she watched as he ran his hand over the nubbly pink chenille bedspread.

"You don't mind that I snoop? It's just fun for me to see what you have done with it. I remember my grandparents' moldy old furniture. Here was an *armadio* we used to hide in as children. There is where I was slapped for saying *'va fanculo'* to the nanny when I was six." He rubbed the fabric of the aqua and pink striped curtains between his fingers. "Lovely," he said. "Venetian silk."

She glowed. No one had been here other than Michael, and he had seemed put off by all of the beautiful Italian things she'd found, as if he'd rather she just order from the Sears catalog.

"I found the armoire around the corner," she told Carlo. "At that little store."

136

"Yes, you have discovered that Italians do not believe in closets."

"It took four men to carry it up the stairs in pieces. I think they're still cursing me."

"I doubt it," he said, pausing by a stylish cylindrical table with a mirror top. She reached past him and clicked a button to reveal a hidden bar inside. He gave a whoop. *"Che carino!"*

"Fully stocked, of course. Unless you like vodka. My husband won't have it in the house."

"I see," Carlo said. "No Russian liquor in an American house. What is your favorite drink?"

"Mine? I don't know. I like gin martinis, and Scotch, and Kentucky bourbon."

He nodded at her lasso from California on the wall. "You are ready to catch any stray cows that wander into Piazza del Campo."

"Ready at all times."

They returned to the living room, and he sat on the sofa, she on the chair. "It is a beautiful home," he said.

"Well, that's the problem, I think," said Scottie. "Is it a home? I mean, it looks like something from a magazine because it is from a magazine. I read a lot of them and copied the pictures. It's like a stage set."

He frowned, looking around.

"You think I'm crazy?"

"No, I understand. It reminds me of those rooms at the Metropolitan Museum of Art in New York, where you stand in a doorway behind a velvet rope, trying to imagine people laughing, dancing, playing cards in those silent, gloomy spaces."

"Yes, exactly!" She mimicked a docent, "Bedroom, from the Sagredo Palace in Venice, eighteenth century. The Croome Court Tapestry Room, Worcestershire, 1700s. Apartment of Americans in Siena, 1956."

He smiled. "I can see that you are tired of objects, of things."

"Yes. I am." She stood and threw open the shutters, leaned out the window and sniffed, catching, amidst the scent of coffee, bread, fish, exhaust and garbage, a sweet and lovely familiar aroma.

"Horses," she said. "I can smell horses."

He joined her at the window. "Yes. You know that in a few days, the Palio horse race will be run here, right under your windows. You will have the best seat in the piazza."

"I can't wait. Robertino, my Italian teacher, explained it all to me. He's the groom for Porcupine." Robertino had been talking nonstop about the race for weeks, the endless details, rules and traditions, the trivia: "In 1858, the Goose secretly switched out a bad horse for a good one in the dead of night and no one noticed," or "There are six *contrade* that are still part of the *Corteo Storico,* the traditional parade, even though they were officially abolished in 1729 for breaking the rules. They are called the *contrade soppresse.*"

"He's hoping to be a jockey in the August Palio," she said.

"That will be an enormous honor for him. You know that a few nights before the Palio, you can stay up late and watch from here as every farmer and breeder with a cart horse comes to the *prova di notte.*"

"Yes, Robertino told me. It's so the horses can learn the turns, and how to run on tufa." Tufa was the ochre-colored earth laid down over the stones. Already, young boys in medieval regalia had begun marching up and down the streets beating drums. On July 2, horses representing ten of the seventeen *contrade,* would run. On August 16, the other seven would run, plus three more drawn by lot. Robertino had explained you didn't pick your *contrada* — you were born into it, depending on where your parents were living at the time. That meant family members were often from different *con-*

trade, leading to intra-household conflicting loyalties. No one took it lightly.

"What *contrada* are you?" she asked Carlo.

"Tower," he said.

"It's all a bit hard to understand, the loyalties."

"That's because it makes no sense. In Siena during the Palio, you feel more loyal to the neighborhood where you were born than to your spouse, if he is from another. It's *pazzo,* crazy."

"I kind of get it, though," she said. "Where you're from, that's deep."

"Is primal."

"Robertino said that in time of war, which is what the Palio is, you stick with your tribe. Always."

Carlo looked away, and she saw a shadow on his face. "That kind of loyalty — blind, based not on reason but on fate — I find it very frightening." He was speaking quietly but intensely, as if he needed her to understand. "So many times I have asked myself why do people draw these arbitrary distinctions, why do they separate themselves this way? Countries are no different — just arbitrary lines drawn on maps. This is mine, that's yours. What makes sense for a boy like Robertino — 'my soccer team, my school' — it becomes grotesque and fright-

140

ening in the mouths of adults."

"So you're not coming to the Palio?"

He shook his head and stood. "I must go. I just thought I would stop by and make sure everything was all right with the apartment. You're okay?" He peered at her.

"I'm fine. We love the apartment," she said, wishing he could stay, that they could go out and have lunch. The apartment felt better with him in it.

I wish I were married to Carlo . . . Stop it, she told herself. *Jesus.* She remembered the vision of a happy foursome she'd had. "I would love to meet your wife sometime."

"Yes, sometime," he said. Then, with a tip of his hat, he was gone.

Robertino was busy with Palio preparations in his *contrada* and had said he couldn't meet her this afternoon, so the day stretched ahead of Scottie, empty. The loneliness she had felt before Carlo's visit was amplified by the sight of the indentation he had left in the sofa cushion. She was filled with a longing, a yearning that she could not express. A yearning for what? She wished there was one person she could tell everything to, someone who would love her despite her background, her flaws, her mistakes. Wasn't that what all the novels and movies had promised? A one true love?

She washed the lemonade glasses and went out to see what was happening in the streets. Even after two months of walking through the piazza every day, and gazing out over it at night, the spectacle still fascinated her. Today, she saw a teenage boy with a green tie holding hands with a shy girl in white tulle, a small wine-stain birthmark on her face. Two men in hats walked arm in arm, smoking short cigars. Six women standing near the fountain were clearly gossiping about each other's waistlines and dresses. There was nothing like this in America, she thought as she walked past. Times Square was busy in a commercial way, with its huge colored billboards, but during the day it was full of hordes of people in dark suits hurrying to work, eyes down. Piazza del Campo was Technicolor.

She left the piazza and walked up Via di Città. Because she was tall and blond and clearly not Italian, everyone she passed on the narrow street stared openly at her. She had one label here, as if she were a character in an allegory, or a tarot card: La Straniera, the Foreigner. She had gotten used to this odd form of celebrity, and accepted that it meant she had to be careful of her appearance, since she was effectively stepping onto a stage every time she left the apartment. Today she was wearing a pale pink cardigan over a white full-skirted dress embroidered with a row of large strawberries, small hoop earrings, a pearl choker, white gloves and a simple hat. Gone were the plaid Bermuda shorts and kneesocks that were practically a uniform at Vassar.

Michael had laughed when she'd said she was tired of being a foreigner. She didn't bother explaining to him her dislike of people noticing differences rather than similarities. He just wouldn't get it. She wanted to meet Italians, be immersed in Italian culture the way Robertino was. Everything about it fascinated her — the way food was revered, treasured rather than seen as an inconvenience to be packaged in a way that made it as easy as possible to prepare and consume. Nothing in Italy was "instant" or "new and improved." There were no tray tables to eat off of while you were doing something else, or diners with lunch counters so you could eat in a hurry, and though you could get a *panino* in a bar, they were new and strange and filled with things like a veal cutlet or just boiled spinach, and if you didn't sit at a table to eat it, it was considered barbaric. She had explained to Robertino about carhops and drive-ins in California.

"You eat dinner *in your car?*" he asked, as if she had suggested eating in the manure pile behind the barn. "With your *hands?*"

She strolled through little Piazza Postierla. She could hear drums somewhere close by, and remembered that Michael had told her to stay in today. The warlike Palio energy worried him, she could see. A militia of nine-year-olds was waving snail flags and chanting as she walked down the Via della Diana toward Porta San Marco, passing women getting their water from a well, bucket by bucket. She decided to stop in and see Signor Banchi.

She had never gone there alone before, and it felt very adventurous to make her way solo through the streets. When she went there with Robertino, Banchi was always delighted to explain the calendar of Italian country life, in which every month had its labors and rewards. He had a saying for every situation, from *"A cavallo giovane, cavaliere vecchio"* (A young horse needs an old rider) to *"A goccia a goccia si scava la roccia"* (Drop by drop the rock is carved).

His small, verdant farm was just outside the walls of the city, walls that sharply delineated urban from rural. In fact, the

144

caper plants colonizing the ancient gate made it look like the country was slowly ambushing the city. Banchi had taught her how sheets and tarps were set out in November to collect olives, nasty to taste unless cured in brine, and most of which were then crushed under a huge stone at the communal press. He explained that the oil must be protected from light and heat or it would go rancid. He had shown her the tiny grapes now growing into pale green orbs, beginning to blush, and explained how you tasted for sugar when deciding when to pick. He showed her how to find wild asparagus and *borragine,* and promised her that in the fall he would show her where to find truffles, which she had never tasted, and which mushrooms in the surrounding forests were edible ("Mushrooms and poets: One in ten is good"). In his garden he showed her how to tend artichokes, tomatoes, basil, potatoes and arugula ("Who doesn't labor reaps nettles"), leaving enough for the wild creatures and insects who would do their tithing no matter what measures you took to stop them.

"You could spray the bugs and poison the moles," Scottie had said helpfully.

"Plant enough for everyone," he said. "And no one has to be greedy."

Yes, a visit to Banchi was just what she needed.

Scottie pushed open the gate and walked down the stone path toward Banchi's front door, which was at the top of a flight of stairs. Before heading up, she peered through an archway into the cool darkness of the ground floor, where a milk cow named Lodovica lived alongside the two enormous oxen who had rescued their car. Their names were Lapo and Cecco, two poets who were friends of Dante; Banchi could quote long stretches of all three writers' works by heart. Utterly good-tempered beasts, the oxen let her lean against them and inhale their sweet smell as they ate fresh hay. When Banchi had made fun of her for tickling their ears and spoiling them, she gave him a proverb in return: "Who pets the mule doesn't get kicked."

"Ciao, ragazzi," she said, then climbed the stairs to the front door of the farmhouse, open but with a striped cloth hanging in the doorway to deter flies.

"Signor Banchi?" she called. *"Permesso?"* She saw comic books on the kitchen table, some in Italian, some American. Batman. Tex Willer. Lash Lightning.

From the back room came Robertino, a

scrap of bread in his mouth, pulling a straw cap onto his mop of blond curls. His azure eyes in olive skin startled her, even though she saw him nearly every day.

"What are you doing here?" he said. "We have no lesson?"

"I know," she said. "It's stupid, I was lonely and bored, and I thought . . ."

"You were lonely? You missed me?"

"Yes. It's silly, I know."

She was about to say that she'd come to see Banchi when Robertino took a quick step toward her, grabbed her arm and kissed her on the mouth.

"No!" she said, pulling away. He was just a boy! But when she looked at him, she saw that he wasn't just a boy, that she had misread everything.

He was confused, and angry. "You said you missed me. You came here to find me."

"No, I meant . . . No, Robertino, I do miss you, but not in that way. I miss our lessons."

"Oh. I am just a boy to you." He was sulky, put out. Everything was ruined, just like that, in an instant. She was an idiot.

"It's not that. You know I'm married," she said, hoping to save his pride at least. "In America, we're faithful to our husbands."

"Always?" He seemed mystified by this.

"Always. And," she added, the words

tumbling out of her mouth even before she had thought them through, "I'm pregnant." *Sono incinta.*

"Oh!" he said, his manner changing, brightening a little. She had saved his pride. And something else, she saw — she was no longer an object of sexual desire. She had transformed in his eyes, with those two words, from a woman to a mother. Whore to Madonna. It angered her to see how quickly his attitude changed.

"*Auguri!* Congratulations!" he pumped her hand in a chaste handshake. "Mr. Messina is delighted, I'm sure."

"He doesn't know yet," she said. "It's a surprise."

"Of course, of course, I will keep your secret."

"Do you think — do you think he'll be happy?"

"Of course he'll be happy," Robertino said. "Nonno is with the rabbits." He grabbed a peach from a bowl on the table and was out the door and down the stairs before she could even ask what the latest Palio gossip was. She followed him out, feeling relieved but also stupid. He disappeared, then reappeared from behind the house atop a bay mare with two socks.

Scottie had seen the occasional cart horse

in the city, but this was the first saddle horse she had seen up close since arriving in Italy. Her eyes traveled over the mare's legs, seeing how her pasterns angled into her fetlocks, gauging the angles of her croup. She was beautifully put together. Her head wasn't classic Arab — too straight a nose — but Scottie guessed she was an Arab-Thoroughbred cross. Short, strong back, balanced neck, good bone and big round feet. A real athlete. She had white lines on her front legs where someone had clearly hobbled her with something thin and painful, like wire. She had more white irregular marks right across the most sensitive part of her nose, which Scottie guessed was from a nail-studded noseband. All the scars were old and long healed, but still Scottie felt rage rise in her. She pointed to the scars. "What happened?"

"Only she knows," said Robertino. "She came from Sicily. They are hard on horses there."

Scottie sighed. At least the horse was well taken care of now. "She's fast, isn't she, and springy?" she called out. "Is this the famous Camelia?"

"Yes," he said, obviously proud.

"Where are you training today?"

"Near San Galgano."

149

She reacted to the name — that was where Ugo Rosini had offered to take her.

"Is it *bella*?" she asked.

"Bello," he corrected, his power restored. *"Un bel posto."*

He loosened the reins, sending the horse into motion. She watched him ride off. He floated above the ground, bareback, his small body seemingly an extension of the horse, itself a liquid, fiery phantasm. Formally trained riders would have scoffed at the half-out-of-control riding style, but it reminded Scottie of Indians she had seen in California whose barely broke horses retained their feral energy, all the more beautiful for their high heads and wild eyes.

He would be all right. He would find a girl, many girls, and forget he had ever had a crush on her. She, on the other hand, felt earthbound and jealous, but not of love, just of riding. She was a wife now, and soon to be a mother. Horses would have to come later, if ever. She fought back tears again. She walked over to the rabbit hutch, but didn't find Banchi.

She was filled with a terrible despair, a sense that, as in a board game, she had landed on the wrong square, and would never find her way home again.

Maybe she would go surprise Michael at work.

Michael was not in the office, which was all locked up. She had only been down to the industrial zone once before. A man from across the way was staring at her, leaning in the doorway of a warehouse, smoking a cigarette.

"Buongiorno, signora," he called out. "You want to buy a tractor from me instead?" He leered at her.

What an awful man, she thought. She hurried off, wondering, if Michael was not at work, where was he?

By one o'clock, she was back in Piazza del Campo, where in preparation for the Palio a corps of twelve-year-olds was tossing orange and green Selva flags featuring a rhinoceros high into the sky. They jeered a boy who missed his catch and called him a *coglione,* which meant both "stupid" and "testicle."

Nothing was making any sense to her. She decided to subdue her emotions with a giant bowl of pasta. Having been raised to think Italian food was all baked ziti and overcooked spaghetti with watery red sauce, she had been happily exploring the menu of

Ristorante Il Campo every day for lunch before her afternoon lessons with Robertino. The headwaiter, Signor Tommaso, had taken to always giving her the same table, so she had a good view of the goings-on in the piazza.

"You are dining alone, *signora*?" he asked her today as he did every day, pouring her *acqua frizzante.* He loved to share all the local gossip about the Palio, as well as Italy's headline news, usually about gruesome deaths — MAN FIGHTS WITH WIFE, THROWS SELF IN WELL — and which American movie stars were visiting Capri and Rome.

"Have you seen the paper today?" Signor Tommaso asked. "Vivien Leigh and Laurence Olivier are having a baby."

"How lovely," she said, her hand going to her own belly.

"An enormous quantity of diamonds was stolen in London."

"I'll be on the lookout."

"In Lucca, a woman ran over her husband with a tractor."

"Oh dear. Bad for business. Or good for it."

He suggested the specials — *penne arrabbiata,* and a trout with almonds, but they sounded light, and she wanted weight to tamp down her emotions. *"Pici cacio e pepe,"* she said, longing for the heavy hand-cut pasta dripping with cheese. "And figs with prosciutto." The figs — black and sweet — went so well with the salty prosciutto. "And cake," she added. *"Torta della nonna."*

She watched Signor Tommaso work. Waiting tables in America was a student's job, a stepping-stone on the way to another career. Here, being a waiter — a job for men only, never women or mere boys — was a career, a profession elevated to an art form. Orders were never forgotten, and diners all felt pampered. Dishes were recommended, but whisked away if an ingredient was less than perfect.

"You will have a good view of the *tratta* two days from now," he said, bringing her a glass of cool Vernaccia. "Everyone wants a window on the piazza for the week of the Palio."

Scottie was taking a forkful of cake when she saw the woman again. The mean, angry woman with the donkey who had yelled at her and called Robertino a traitor. The woman was across the piazza, staring at her, eyes blazing. Scottie, feeling bold, waved. The woman turned away and disappeared into the crowd.

Scottie stopped in Via Salaria to pick up a

loaf of bread for dinner. She had walked around the city all day, but had barely spoken to anyone. She missed female company. Italian women were polite but did not seek to make friends. Maybe her baby would be a girl.

At first it had been annoying not to be able to buy everything she needed in one place, but now she was enjoying the daily routine, chatting with the owners, buying only what she and Michael would eat that night. Turned out she didn't need that large American refrigerator, which was fortunate since it still didn't work, and the power went out regularly. What was the point of storing food when you could buy it fresh? *Due etti di mortadella, un mezzo pane, un po' di insalata, grazie, e un chilo di pomodori.*

At the *panetteria,* she waited her turn, looming head and shoulders over the crowd of tiny Italian women, who pulled away from her instinctively, leaving a circle of space around her like a demilitarized zone. She stared at the huge, thick, crusty loaves. When she first saw them, she had laughed out loud. Unsliced bread! So old-fashioned. The store did smell good, though. The bread, when she managed to hack through the thick crust, narrowly avoiding cutting her arm off, was chewy. It had a funny taste, too.

"Bread of Tuscany have no salt," explained the lady who owned the store.

"Why?" Scottie asked.

The woman shrugged as if the question were absurd.

Today the steady military rat-a-tat of the Palio drums in the street outside was beginning to give her a headache. A woman standing near her nudged another and whispered. Scottie pretended they weren't talking about her. This happened all the time.

Suddenly she felt a terrible tightening in her belly, an agonizing twisting sensation. She dropped the bread she was holding, and her purse, and gave an involuntary groan.

None of the women spoke English, but Scottie felt well looked after, as if a troop of strong-armed dwarves from a fairy tale had taken her under their wing. They had surrounded her, held her up, and she had been led by several of the women through the back room of the bakery into an adjacent apartment. Small, dark, warm, it felt like a bread oven itself. As she started to vomit, a woman held her dress back so it did not get soiled, while another quickly mopped up the floor.

"Troppo bello per rovinarlo," the woman said, smoothing the dress, and the others clucked in agreement.

They led her to a small bathroom, but didn't close the door. *"C'è sangue, sangue?"* They pointed to her private area.

Blood. They were asking if there was blood.

I've lost the baby, she thought.

It was like having six mothers at once — she didn't feel embarrassed to be in the midst of these women. She felt the terrible cramping again.

A hush fell over the room as, in front of all of them, she checked her underwear.

"No sangue," she said.

A cheer went up in the room. The women beamed and held their hands together in joy.

She had not lost the baby.

"Medico?" she asked. She hadn't seen a doctor since arriving in Siena. They must have them. She'd heard ambulances now and then.

One of the women pulled in a little girl of about ten, with huge brown eyes, her blue flowered dress way too large for her, who was apparently studying English in school.

"You have . . . cramp," she said to Scottie,

156

after the women had shouted at her for a while, gesticulating. Scottie was sitting at a tiny table on a rickety little chair. A single lightbulb swung over her head, dressed up with a frilly pink halo of paper. A hunk of bread was in front of her, and a glass of water. She felt drained and still crampy.

Just a cramp, she thought. The women were trying to tell her something about a muscle, that her uterus was a muscle, that it had a cramp because it was growing. *Incinta, incinta,* they said.

"Pregnant," said the little girl.

"Yes," said Scottie.

"They say you should eat, get strong again," said the little girl.

"What is the address of the doctor?" asked Scottie.

"No need for doctor. Mamma send for herbs."

Scottie was worried, suddenly guilty that she hadn't seen a doctor yet. "But when you're pregnant, the doctor?"

They all shook their heads. "The doctor is for when you're sick."

"You take the herbs," the girl translated for a sensible-looking woman in a simple blue maternity dress. "She has seven *bambini,* I mean children," said the girl.

"Herbs?"

"Yes. You must —" Here the girl paused, her "Dick and Jane" vocabulary exceeded. "You must drink the tea to calm the cramps, so they do not get worse and you do not lose the baby. And you must eat."

The women talked over each other in their eagerness to get the girl to transmit their messages. Scottie could tell they were derisive about the doctor, a man. Clearly the women felt they knew their bodies better than he did.

"This happens many times. No need for doctor. You eat. You drink tea. It will help, but the baby is coming when it's coming," they said with a glorious obviousness that flew in the face of all the conflicting articles in American women's magazines obsessing about pregnancy. She had read one in *McCall's* that said a woman should hardly gain any weight during her term at all. She doubted this group would agree.

A slump-shouldered woman came in, eyes down, with a small packet wrapped in white paper and handed it to Scottie. "Tea," she whispered. *"Buono."*

"Where did you get this tea? What is it?" Scottie asked in Italian.

The woman, not understanding her, nodded and said, *"Sì, té."* Scottie recognized

158

her, suppressing a gasp — it was the prostitute.

"Thank you," Scottie said. The woman blushed and rushed out again.

"Ah, Gina," murmured the women, as if they were a Greek chorus. There was much eye rolling and sighing.

The little girl filled the awkward silence. "Herbs come from mountain. Monte Amiata. Woman there, how you say, healer. Better than doctor."

She drank the tea, felt it wash down inside her. After a couple of minutes she stood up. The cramps were gone.

"Thank you, *grazie, grazie*," she said. She took out her wallet and tried to hand the bakery owner some money, but the woman staunchly refused it.

"*Fa niente,*" she said over and over. It's nothing.

The tribe ushered her back through the room behind the store, past flour sacks and mixing bowls. A light snow of flour was on every surface. There were glass French doors standing open with a beaded curtain drifting slightly in the breeze. Beyond was a courtyard where a large domed brick structure stood, a huge pile of slim pieces of wood next to it, a wooden paddle leaning nearby.

"That's where the bread is made?" Scottie asked.

"Sì sì, forno a legna." A wood-fired oven. Scottie thought of the field trip her fourth-grade class had made to the Helms Bread Factory on Venice Boulevard in Los Angeles. All gleaming stainless steel, huge industrial ovens, workers in white paper hats and hair-nets, laboratories and conveyor belts. The latest in modern technology.

They passed back through the store, and the woman unlocked the door and turned the sign from *CHIUSO* to *APERTO,* and Scottie was back on the street, a loaf of bread under her arm.

A baby. It was no longer just an idea. It was real. It was coming, like a hurricane bearing down on her.

If she had lost the baby, she could have left. Women did this, and sometimes it wasn't the end of the world. Clare Boothe herself had been divorced, and Henry Luce had still married her.

Would she leave Michael, if she could? He was a good man. Did a husband have to be more than that?

Intermezzo

The mayor of Siena was driving his new pale yellow Fiat 600 along Via Roma. In the narrow street he passed close to a tall blond woman in a pink sweater over a full-skirted white dress. The dress was embroidered all over with a pattern. What were those little red things? Cherries? Tomatoes? Roses? He recognized her. The American. These foreigners. They were full of smiles, their perfect white teeth gleaming. They were so open, so friendly, so young, so rich.

And so dangerous.

He believed in growth — things could not stay the same forever. But a cautious, careful growth that would preserve the best of Siena, while modernizing the less desirable aspects, like the filth running through the streets of some neighborhoods, the crime, the poverty.

This put him in opposition to some who wanted to tear down everything that was old and make it new. He was an honest man, but he saw it would be hard to avoid being corrupted by this power he now had. He was already being courted by every wealthy and powerful man in the city. It made him a little giddy, these back-to-back conversations, meetings, conferences, lunches, dinners. He would never be hungry again, he realized, until he was out of office. He might end up with gout if he wasn't careful. Or worse.

He passed the *zona industriale,* saw the sign for the new Ford Tractors dealership. He had mixed feelings about these American businesses opening here. It was all well and good to be able to buy these American products, but that was Italian money leaving the country at a moment when they needed to hold on to every lira they could. No, he was not a fan of such moves — if foreigners wanted to invest in Italian business, that was one thing, but American-owned hotels and businesses would strip them of their . . . The car made a funny noise. He paused, wondering if he should pull over.

But he was running late to meet his favorite prostitute. She didn't like it when he was late. She berated him with every curse she knew. *Porca miseria, quanto sei stronzo* was her favorite. Pig's misery, what a jerk.

He rounded the curve and headed down the hill through Porta Romana. A donkey cart piled with yellow squash was ahead of him on the curving road. The stone walls on either side were close — and he couldn't see who was coming from the other direction. He braked and went to downshift, but the stick moved loosely in his hands. He pumped the clutch, not understanding what was happening . . . Why was the car not responding? It was a brand-new car! *Porca miseria.*

He made it around the donkey cart, practically on two wheels, yet taking the time to notice and compliment himself on how skillfully he was driving. Then he saw a Bee ahead — Piaggio's tiny pickup — right in the middle of the road. He hit the brakes harder, but nothing happened. In a panic, he swerved to avoid the Bee and crashed head-on into a stone wall. His last thought was a clear picture of the pattern on the beautiful American woman's perfect white dress. *Strawberries.*

■ ■ ■ ■

Part Two:
Terzo Di Città

■ ■ ■ ■

Italy has the largest Communist party outside the Iron Curtain. She is the only country in Europe where the Socialists are allied to the Communists. This is what explains the intense interest everywhere in the crisis through which Italian "social communism" is going.

— "Italy's Big Left Bloc Is Shaken," *The New York Times,* July 1, 1956

SEVEN:
L'ONDA, THE WAVE

"THE COLOR OF THE SKY, THE STRENGTH
OF THE SEA"

1.

Scottie had been too worried about conceal-
ing her pregnancy when she left America to
bring any books on childbirth with her, and
now she wouldn't find any in English, and
probably not in Italian, either. She couldn't
see Italian women turning to Dr. Spock for
advice. Plus, she wasn't the type to learn
from books anyway. Almost any woman in
Siena could tell her what she needed to
know.

The baby was real now, to her, in a way
that it had not been before. She had never
thought of it as something that would leave
her body and take up its life in the world. It
was just a Problem. She had a brief thought
about what would happen if she had a girl,
and together they went to look at Vassar . . .

She pushed the memory out of her head — Michael was this child's father. If she said it often enough, it would become true.

She went home and made a nice dinner for the two of them — the three of them, really. Chicken marsala. It took her hours, and it came out perfectly.

Except Michael did not come home by seven, or eight, or nine. She finally dumped the dinner in the trash and did the dishes and went to bed.

It was after ten by the time she heard his key in the lock. He came in complaining about Palio drummers blocking his way.

Instead of saying, "I'm pregnant," she said, "I have a headache."

She pretended to be asleep while he went off to work the next morning, still furious with him, and the more furious for knowing he had no idea she was angry at all.

At lunch she polished off a plate of the most exquisitely delightful *tagliatelle ai funghi porcini* at the restaurant downstairs, on the excuse she was following the orders of the local women. Signor Tommaso, obviously pleased by her appetite, explained that fresh porcini mushrooms would not come for another few months, and that when they did the woods would be full of eager hunters. This dish, made from the dried version, would be a "foreshadowing." She skeptically sniffed the shriveled tan and brown mushroom that Signor Tommaso brought out on a plate to illustrate, but each bite when the actual dish arrived was a miracle — the hand-rolled noodles put up a slight resistance to her teeth, then surrendered in a cloud of velvety flavor so intense she felt she would swoon.

After lunch she returned to the bakery, feeling a bit shy but wanting to thank the women who had been so kind. The owner had simply nodded and taken her money for the bread. The other women had once again given *La Straniera* a wide berth.

Scottie was ironing Michael's shirt as he lifted pots on the stove. "Mmm, smells good," he said.

She would tell him now. Earlier that day she practiced in front of the mirror. "I'm having a baby," she had said out loud, turning sideways, studying her body. She would tell him now. Now. Now.

What if he figured it out? What if he realized the baby was not his? What if he threw her out onto the street, like she deserved?

She felt her resolve weakening. She could tell him another time.

Then a boxed ad on the back page of the newspaper on the table caught her eye. *Cuccioli.* Robertino had taught her that word. Puppies. A puppy would be good training for both of them. And an instant friend for her. It would warm Michael up to the idea of having a little one around.

She opened a can of Del Monte peaches, topped them with whipped cream and popped a maraschino cherry on top like she had seen in the June issue of *Life* Michael had brought up from Rome. Michael ate the peaches in silence, reading the paper as she hung up the freshly ironed shirt.

Next she served him a Salisbury steak with a side of mashed potatoes and a perfect pool of gravy, while deftly removing the plate that had held the peaches. The meat for the steak had required quite a bit of wrangling with the butcher, who found it upsetting to have to grind up perfectly good beef. She tried to say she was making a *ragù alla bolognese,* but this didn't help — why was she not then buying veal, and a chicken liver? The butcher's mother was from Bologna, and this was how it was to be made, he insisted.

She sat down opposite Michael and spoke to the newspaper. "Do you like our home?"

He gave her a quizzical look over the top

of the paper. "Of course I do. It's the best address in the city."

"But . . . does it feel like a home to you?"

"Of course it does. You've done a beautiful job. Oh honey, don't you know that?" His voice was warm, kind but also . . .

"No," she said.

"Come here." He pulled her onto his lap, brushed her hair back with his hand. "You know what I love about it? It's a showplace of all that's best about America."

"You don't think it's — cold?"

"Not at all. I love it. And you're a wonderful cook."

At this she laughed. "And you're a great liar."

"I love that you cook American."

This was one of Michael's odd quirks, that he wanted her to cook American food. "It's not easy. I found those Del Monte canned peaches in the back of a dusty old dry goods store. They're probably left over from World War II."

"They were delicious. And so was the burger."

She removed the plate with the crusty remains of the Salisbury steak and topped off Michael's glass of milk. "Hey, what do you think about getting a dog?"

"Would be nice, but we don't have a yard

for it." He wiped his mouth with a chintz napkin she realized she'd have to wash and iron again tomorrow. She must find some paper napkins somewhere. The Italians were really behind the times on disposable products.

"I'm out walking all day anyway," she said, keeping her tone cheery. "And I'm lonely when you're away, you know." She smiled at him as she rearranged the flowers as she had been taught in homemaking class at Miss Porter's. She hated the class, felt flowers looked prettiest in the fields where they grew wild, but she did remember some of it, taller flowers in the middle.

"I know you're lonely," he said. "I mean, I can see it, and of course, you're thousands of miles from your friends. You're brave to have taken this on."

"So it's okay if I get the dog?" she pressed, putting a fresh plate of brownies on the table. They were a little burned — she had made them in a tiny electric countertop mini-oven she'd bought at the hardware store, and all of the gauges were in Celsius.

"Oh no," he said. He was staring down at the "News of Siena" page.

"What?"

"The mayor's been killed in a car crash."

"The mayor of Siena?"

"Yes." He was reading the story intently.

"Ugo Rosini is dead?"

"No," said Michael. "You were so caught up in making the house pretty that you missed that there was an election."

"I — I guess I did," she said. "So it's not Rosini?"

"It's Manganelli who's dead." He sounded upset. "The guy who beat Rosini. He only took office a few days ago. He was pro-business, the Christian Democratic Party. Bad blow for us businessmen."

She hadn't even bothered to try to understand the complexity of Italian politics. There were about forty political parties. It was like when a British boy had taken her on a date to a cricket match and then tried to explain the rules to her, both dull and complicated.

Ugo was alive. She felt a sudden desire to run into him, to see him in the flesh. To feel desired.

"Let's go down and have an ice cream in the piazza," Scottie said.

Michael put down the paper and sighed. "I'm sorry. I have to go out. Work." He stood up and put his napkin on the dirty plate, adding, "I just don't think getting a dog is a good idea. I'm sorry. I'll make it up to you. I'll ask Ford for a trip home at

Christmas."

She blinked at him, a rage rising in her that she had not felt since her pony Shorty had dumped her in the water obstacle at a horse show. She followed him toward the door, twisting her apron in her hands.

"I'm pregnant," she said as he took his hat off the rack.

He looked at her in surprise, then frowned. "We can't start a family now."

"Well, we are. I'm having a baby."

"Here?" He was incredulous.

"People have children in Italy."

"Yes, and they get diseases and worms and run over. It's filthy and dangerous here. Run by Communists, for God's sake. Who knows where Italy will be in five years? Six months, even. The whole place could be at war."

"At war?"

"With us. You can't raise a child under those conditions. It's not safe."

She was so confused. What was he talking about? What was he actually afraid of?

"Well. It's too late. I — I'm having a baby," she said. She was racked with guilt. Part of her wanted to tell him, to throw herself on his mercy, to live honestly.

She said nothing.

"I assumed you were . . . being careful," he said. "Because we didn't talk about starting a family."

"But . . . you're Catholic."

"You're not." They stared at each other, realizing the things they had both taken for granted.

"I just assumed you'd want children . . . It's normal for a man to —"

He flinched as if she had struck him. "This is terrible timing." He turned away, and she went into the bedroom and shut the door. She heard the front door close.

Who bought tractors after dinner, she wondered.

2.

The political situation in Siena had just been upended again. Michael read the article in the evening paper with growing dismay as Scottie served him a hideous piece of ground something. He noticed she didn't eat it. She must think he was crazy for asking her to cook this stuff. The truth was he hated this kind of crappy American cooking, but the rules were very clear that agents were not supposed to "go native." Their homes were supposed to be as American as possible. The Agency actually preferred if their people didn't speak the language. *This kind of immersion in the local culture can lead to ambiguous loyalties,* one

175

urgent notice had warned. Not all of the rules made sense to him, he had to admit. Most of them seemed to have been made by people who had never left America. But he was here to do a job, so he followed them. And that job had just gotten harder.

Only four days into his tenure, Mayor Manganelli had lost control of his brand-new Fiat 600 and slammed it into a wall near Porta Romana, the latest of a million victims of car accidents in Europe this year. He was taken to Ospedale Santa Maria della Scala, but had died within the hour, and the vice mayor, an odious tax lawyer named Vestri, had been sworn in. New elections would be called for November 4. His mission was not over.

The article, by Rodolfo Marchetti, went on to complain that the Italian love affair with *la macchina* was turning deadly, especially since traffic lights, speed limits and rules of the road were basically nonexistent. "We're killing each other and bankrupting ourselves for gasoline," Marchetti wrote. "Trying to live like Americans."

Scottie chose this moment to announce they were starting a family. Was she insane? The idea of bringing a poor innocent child into this terrible world, bombs pointed right at them, two empires on the verge of World

War III! But later, he felt terrible about the way he had shut her down. She didn't know. She didn't live in the world he lived in. She thought life was buying tomatoes and waxing the floor. She was lonely — terribly lonely — and of course wanted to start a family, since she had none. He would make it up to her. The idea of being a father terrified him, but he couldn't say that. He would get her a dog after all. It would be a good distraction.

He sent Luce an encoded telegram from the central Siena post office in Piazza Matteotti using his Geoffrey Sneedle alias, since they had told him never to trust the phone lines. He hoped she'd get it — he had heard she was ill. The rumor was that she had been poisoned by the KGB. He had laughed when Duncan told him about it, pointing out that it was more likely that she was suffering from the side effects of the steady stream of Dexedrine and Benzedrine she swallowed to get through the day, and almost certainly sleeping pills at night, but Duncan was serious. "I think it's true," he had said, sipping a pear grappa from a handblown Venetian glass during one of their evenings out in Rome. "It's very serious, Michael. They're combing the palazzo for signs of poison. These Russians are everywhere, and they will take down anyone who stands in their way."

He gathered up all the evening newspapers and went to write up a detailed report about Manganelli's death and what this would mean for politics in Siena.

3.

The next morning Scottie dressed quickly and slipped out while Michael was still asleep. He had come in very late and gone to bed in the guest room. So now they were giving each other the silent treatment. Other women had talked about this. She had never thought it would happen to her. Out of habit or perhaps malice she left him a bowl of Cheerios — the dregs of the last box from the shipment that came with them from America — and turned on the percolator, putting in the last scoop of the Maxwell House they'd brought. How he could drink that stuff was beyond her, but he claimed to love it.

She walked across the Campo and into Via della Galluzza. She lingered, looking into the window of a dress shop, admiring a blue and white striped belted cotton dress in the full-skirted Dior style. Soon she would not be able to wear dresses like that.

"Signora Messina?" It was Carlo Chigi

Piccolomini.

The sight of him was, as her father would say, like a cold beer on a hot day. He was smiling at her with his lopsided grin, his eyes flashing behind his glasses. He was holding the hand of a little girl with a headful of reddish ringlets. She had his eyes, almond-shaped and sly. Carlo gave Scottie a toothy smile as he locked the front door behind them, turning the huge key slowly — crank, crank, crank. The way he moved drew her eye to his forearms, the nape of his neck, the tilt of his fedora.

"What a pleasant surprise," she said.

"This is my niece, Ilaria."

Scottie greeted the little girl, who said, "I live in the Tartuca."

"I live in the Selva," said Scottie. "But I wasn't born there, so I can't actually be a member of the *contrada.*"

"Like Mommy," said the little girl. "She was born in Roccastrada. Uncle Carlo is a Tower."

"Yes, when the Palio starts next week we will be archenemies, won't we, *cara mia?*"

"*Sì,*" the little girl giggled. Carlo swept her up and kissed her cheek, and she squealed with delight. It was such an uncontrolled sound of joy that Scottie reached out and put her hand on Carlo's arm.

179

"I'm pregnant," she said, beaming.

His face lit up, his mouth open in joy. *"Auguri!"* he said. "Did you hear that, our friend is having a baby. That is why she looks especially beautiful."

Ilaria clapped her hands. Scottie felt that finally, finally, her child had been welcomed and celebrated. And Carlo had called her beautiful. She felt warm and happy.

Carlo put Ilaria down and smiled at Scottie. "We are walking the same way, no? We go together?"

He took Scottie's arm, which she did not admit to herself she had been longing for him to do, and steered her and Ilaria around puddles and dogs' land mines. He was such a gentleman.

"Is it far to San Galgano?" The words were out of her mouth, planned or unplanned, she could not be sure.

"About an hour to the southwest. Just past Monticiano. You haven't been there before?"

"No. I might drive out there," she said. "I've heard it's worth seeing."

Carlo thought for a moment. "The road is not well marked. I will take you myself if you don't mind stopping in Monticiano first." There was a hesitation in his voice, and she assumed he was just being polite.

"I wouldn't want to take your time."

"No, no, I'd like to show it to you." There was something else he was saying; she didn't know what it was, but she saw that it was important to him that she go.

Ilaria looked up at her. "I'll show you the ducks." The girl's sweet face made her heart ache.

"Well, if it's really not too much trouble —"

"It would be my pleasure, Mrs. Messina. My car is parked near the Fortezza." He was suddenly quite formal, as if to banish any sense of impropriety.

She felt as if things were getting slightly out of her control, but at the same time that was like the best part of riding. You used the bit and your legs to direct the horse, but there was always a moment when the animal, at speed, was immune to your commands. Some riders only rode in fenced arenas because they were terrified of being run away with. Scottie lived for that moment when you knew you might not be able to stop the horse, so you didn't try, you just rode it out and trusted the horse not to kill you both.

4.

Michael got a cable from Rome saying that he needed to provide more information on the Communists in Siena, so that "measures could be taken" to prevent Ugo Rosini from being elected mayor again in November, "a potentially disastrous outcome."

The thought that he was going to be a father kept slipping into his consciousness, distracting him from his work. What kind of a father would he be? His own father was cold to him while at the same time doting on his four sisters. His father even liked his sisters' husbands, whom Michael saw as monosyllabic and sports-obsessed. He could have had better conversations with Banchi's oxen. Scottie had pointed out it was "normal" for men to want children. He picked up a copy of *Life* magazine. They sent him *Life* and *Look* with orders to leave them on café tables so that the Sienese would see how wonderful life in America was. He flipped through the pages, looking at pictures of normal men. Normal men bought life insurance so their children would be taken care of when they died. A normal man read the paper while his wife was in the delivery room having their first child. Normal men had heartburn, and no wonder: A Union Oil ad featured a veteran enjoying the amazing comforts of modern life but warned that "eternal vigilance — historically the price of liberty — may in our time be the price of prosperity, too."

A survey reported that American women's ideal man was six feet tall, with black wavy hair and blue eyes. He was a business executive, sincere and honest, but also polite, sporting, helpful, communicative, well read, and enjoyed dancing and woodworking.

Woodworking?

Michael sighed. He would rather fight Communists.

5.

Carlo had one of the super-popular, tiny new Fiat 600s in robin's egg blue. She looked at his hand on the gearshift, how the thin hair climbed down his arms possessively, like a single strand of ivy taking over a column. His hands were broad with long fingers, and his nails short and clean. Michael's hands were quick and nervous, always in motion. *Stop that,* she told herself. *Stop comparing them.*

Just outside the city walls, they turned off the pavement into a narrow, bumpy driveway that led through a dense group of trees up a hill. At the top, the view opened up and there was a beautiful gray stone farmhouse next to a crumbling tower. Before they drove down the road, Carlo paused for a moment.

"This is where my wife lives," he said simply.

They got out, and a tall woman with a cloud of curly copper hair shot through with gray came out of the house and hugged Ilaria.

Scottie half recognized her, but thought she must be wrong. It couldn't be. She was wearing tan trousers covered, Scottie noticed, in white dust, like powdered sugar. The woman stared at her down a long aristocratic nose, expressionless, and then, after a glance at Carlo, broke into a wide smile.

"Signora Scottie Messina, my wife, Franca." Carlo was speaking English.

Franca looked an awful lot like the woman with the donkey.

"I recognize you, I think," Scottie said carefully.

Franca smiled. "You must be mistaken."

Scottie shook Franca's hand, feeling the strength in her thin, callused hand. She paused, never sure when the *tu* form, or informal "you," was appropriate, and decided to stick to English, although it felt like a form of defeat.

"My husband and I live in the apartment you own, in the Campo," said Scottie. "We love it."

"Ah, yes. One of Carlo's family properties."

"Are you a baker?" asked Scottie, nodding at the white dust.

"Sculptor," said Franca. "I'm finishing a piece in marble." Franca's hands moved nervously when she wasn't holding something.

"Wonderful," said Scottie. "I'd love to see it."

"Where is Ciucco?" asked Ilaria.

"In the barn," said Franca, and Carlo explained, "Franca has a dear old donkey that Ilaria is in love with."

A donkey. Franca *was* the woman with the donkey who had hissed at her in the street. She felt cold, and a little afraid, but kept her face pleasant.

"There are new ducklings in the pond," Franca told Ilaria. Ilaria ran around the back of the house, and a barking dog, some sort of little beagle mix, followed.

"Carlo said you went to Smith," said Scottie.

"Yes," said Franca. "I left in 1937." Scottie expected her to say more, but Franca didn't, instead moving into the house. Carlo waved his hand for them to follow. As she glanced at his face, Scottie saw a tension there under the polite smile.

Franca had turned the ground floor, which used to house the animals, into a studio. There were small chalk and clay models around the space, which was littered with bits of wood, wire and the clay and chalk that had been chipped away. Bunches of herbs hung from the ceiling; Scottie recognized lavender and rosemary, but couldn't name the myriad of other dried flowers and plants hanging there. The smell was amazing — a garden, condensed. There were shelves lined with jars containing more herbs and what looked like stones suspended in cloudy water.

"Franca is an herbalist and a brilliant sculptor," said Carlo, running his hand over a marble column that reminded Scottie of a cypress tree. Franca smiled at him and tossed her hair.

"Carlo knows nothing about art," she said. "But I love him anyway."

Carlo smiled at her and said a simple "Me, too, *amore.*"

Scottie admired the flowing, sensuous, abstract shapes. They were a strange couple, she thought, yet Franca seemed happy when she looked at Carlo. He seemed to make her relax, and in those moments she became beautiful, Scottie thought, despite the fact that she wore no makeup and sloppy clothing. And yet, behind the eyes . . . what was it? A hardness. Pain. They must have been married a long time, been through so much together, including the war.

Franca handed them both a glass of wine, which had appeared out of nowhere. "It's not great," she said, "but it's from my own grapes."

There was a piercing scream, and as they ran outside, the beagle arrived carrying a duckling in his mouth, followed by sobbing, horrified Ilaria.

Scottie looked at the limp little bloody body and felt suddenly very ill. She saw Franca watching her carefully.

Carlo tried to get the duckling away from the dog, but he ran circles around them, the little beaked head bobbing out of his mouth making the girl scream even louder. Scottie sank onto the stairs, feeling the blood drain from her face. The nausea she had felt in the bakery was back.

"You're pregnant," said Franca quietly.

Carlo was hugging the sobbing little girl. He said, "The duck has been transformed into an angel."

"An angel with little yellow wings?" Ilaria asked, her eyes brimming with tears.

"Exactly," said Carlo.

With a cool glance at Scottie, Franca

herded Ilaria into the house, promising her sweets. Carlo turned to Scottie.

"Are you all right?"

"Yes, sorry," she said quickly.

"Ilarietta," he called. "We have to go now." Franca came out, and he added, "Franca, come with us to San Galgano. You can show Scottie around."

"No, I'm working. Leave Ilaria here. I'll bring her back to her parents tomorrow."

"Are you sure?"

"Yes. *Ciao, amore.*"

Carlo and Franca kissed each other on both cheeks. "I'll see you soon. *Ciao.*"

Scottie went to shake Franca's hand, but the thin, birdlike woman pulled her close and kissed her cheeks. It felt more like malice than affection.

As they got back in the car, Scottie felt awkward and unsettled.

"We don't have to go to San Galgano," she said.

Carlo put a hand on her back and the electricity hit her. "It's not far," he said, turning onto the main road heading away from Siena.

Carlo drove in silence for a while. "There is something I wish to tell you," he said. "About me. About Franca."

188

"It's none of my business," she said quickly.

He nodded. "It's true. But in you I feel I have found a friend. May I think that way?"

She looked at him. "Yes," she said.

"Siena is a difficult place for me. I do not have many friends. Perhaps none. It is my own fault."

She waited.

"Franca and I have always known each other. Our families . . . We were always together, like it was fate."

"She was from a noble family, too?"

"Yes. We were so different but still so close, best friends. I wish you could have known her then. She was so funny, so wild. I was, I don't know, a dreamer. When we were sixteen, well, there was a mistake. We were in love, and things went too far. She became pregnant."

"Oh."

"Our families were very angry, of course, but this happens. So we got married, and we lived with my parents. It was important to them that we be educated, so I was sent to England and Franca to America. The child was kept at home, a secret from our lives as students."

"Boy or a girl?"

"A boy."

"You must have missed him."

"I did, but to be truthful, also I didn't. I was too young to be a father. My parents were right to send me away."

"And Franca?"

"She was unhappy in America. She missed Raimondo. She did not finish at Smith, but came home."

The landscape outside the window shifted, as if in response to Carlo's story. The forest became darker and denser, and a fog settled over them.

"I came back from England, and for a while we were happy, actually."

She waited, knowing he was deep in the past. She imagined Franca and a little boy in sunlight, in vineyards.

"And then . . . I don't know. I wanted to have more children, but she became very nervous."

"During the war?"

"I was stationed near Poggibonsi, north of here. We had an apartment there so she and Raimondo could be close to me. I thought it was safe. I was wrong. A bomb hit our apartment building. Raimondo was killed. It was his fourteenth birthday."

"Oh. I'm so sorry." It was a deeply inadequate response, but to say more would have been worse. Everything she had sensed

190

about Carlo but not understood made sense now.

They drove along in silence for a while.

"It was hard for us to be together after that. I moved into the *castello* after my parents died, and she chose the farmhouse you saw."

"You've been apart a long time. But you're still married?"

"It's Italy. There are no divorces, or at least it's not worth the time and effort it would take. And I would not do that to her."

"You both didn't want to start over? Try again?"

Carlo shrugged. "Me, yes. But Franca . . . she is stuck in the past."

"I'm so sorry."

"I try to help her. She loves the visits from Ilaria. And she sells her herbs. She is wise in these things. Her grandmother was, too. It's good for her, to help people, to feel useful. But it's hard not to see the woman she was, hard not to miss her. And I think she must hate me a little. I wasn't there when it happened."

They drove on into the countryside. "This is a volcanic zone like Amiata," Carlo said as they climbed again, leaving the farms behind them and heading into a wilder zone. She found the beauty outside the car window almost unreal, mesmerizing. "The Etruscans had mines and quarries here. Cinnabar and alabaster." He seemed relieved to have told his story. *This is who he is,* she thought. *He is someone who moves forward. But poor Franca.*

"It feels very remote," she said. "When we drove through Chianti in April, it reminded me of a patchwork quilt. This is more like a scratchy wool blanket at summer camp." Carlo nodded and smiled at her, and as their eyes met she felt something inside her release.

Carlo had lived through so much. "You must hate seeing the German tourists," she said.

Carlo looked confused. "The Germans?"

"They killed your son."

Carlo was silent for a moment, then spoke quietly. "Italy changed sides in October 1943, and declared war on Germany, but the Germans were all over Italy and would not give up easily. The planes that bombed Poggibonsi were American planes, cutting off the German retreat."

"Americans?"

"They missed the railyard and hit the center of the city."

Scottie felt faint. "Oh my God." Hot tears

streamed down her face. "I'm so sorry," she said.

Carlo put a hand on her arm. "The past is past," he said.

Not for everyone, she thought.

Raindrops started spattering the windshield as they turned up a small unmarked road. Scottie could see a perfectly cylindrical little building at the top, horizontally striped like the Duomo in Siena, except if the Duomo were the teapot, this would be the matching sugar bowl.

"How strange and beautiful," she said. "What's it doing here?"

They got out of the car. The scattered drops had turned to a light, steady rain, but it was still warm. "Wait one second," said Carlo. He pushed open the wooden door and disappeared inside. The wind had picked up, and the views from the hilltop were spectacular, made even more so by the storm clouds massing overhead. When Carlo called, "Come now," Scottie went in.

Carlo had lit four tall candles in sconces on the walls, illuminating the striped, perfectly round interior of the chapel. She looked around, admiring the dome over-head, which carried on with the stripes all the way to a small disc in the center of the ceiling.

"It's amazing," she said. "Like being inside a snail."

"Here," said Carlo. He motioned her to the center of the room. Iron railings surrounded a large rock that emerged from a break in the floor, jutting up from the earth below.

In the rock was a black iron sword, only its hilt showing.

Scottie wasn't sure what to make of it. It couldn't be real, could it?

"Galgano was a knight from Chiusdino," said Carlo. "He was a good swordsman and quite the brawler and womanizer, too. But one day in 1180 an angel appeared to him and told him to change his life. His horse ran away with him and brought him here to Montesiepi. He plunged his sword into the rock and became a man of God."

"Like King Arthur."

"It predates the Arthur legend. This is the real thing."

Scottie reached down and touched the hilt of the sword. It felt cool to the touch, but also electric.

She stood up. "What a magical place," she said. "Thank you."

"Ah, but that is not all," he said with a

twinkle in his eye.

When they got outside the rain was falling harder. Scottie wasn't sure she wanted to go tramping around more of the countryside in her sandals.

"Close your eyes," said Carlo.

She did, and he led her a few steps around the back of the chapel.

"Okay, open them."

She was looking down a grassy hillside at one of the strangest things she had ever seen. A huge roofless Gothic cathedral lay below her, sitting in the middle of a field of yellow and green sunflowers.

"It's like something out of a ghost story," she said.

"Yes. I wanted you to see it before we left. I am sorry about the rain. We should probably go back. There is nothing inside except grass."

She couldn't stop herself. She ran down the hill toward it, the gray stones of the cathedral looming larger and larger. All of the latticework of the rose windows was intact, but there was no glass. It was the most arresting sight she had ever seen.

Carlo came panting up behind her.

"What happened to it?" she asked, looking up at the ominous sky above the church.

"Churches from this era often have lead

roof tiles. Heavy, durable and expensive, they were supposed to protect them forever, and many of them have. But here, a corrupt abbot sold the lead, probably to someone who melted it down to make weapons, and took the money. Shortly after that, a bolt of lightning struck the exposed timbers and burned the place down."

"That sounds like the definition of 'smiting' to me."

She walked through the portal where tall wooden doors would have been. Inside was a carpet of wildflowers growing up through the stones. The rain slowed, and a ray of sunlight cracked through the black cloud overhead and shone down into the space.

"I half think angels with duck wings are about to talk to us, too," she said.

He nodded. "It's my favorite place on earth." She looked over at him. His shirt was wet, and his hair slick. He was smiling at her, happy to share this wonderful place. He was standing at a distance, fifty feet or so away from her, looking at her, deeply, without hesitation, drinking her in.

"I thought I lost the baby the other day," she said. "But I didn't."

"A baby is a miracle," he said.

She put her hands on her belly and left them there, staring down at it. Her insides were churning, her heart in her mouth, pounding.

"I have a story, too," she said. "But I can't tell it. I want to, but I can't."

"Then don't," he said, staying where he was. They were talking across a wide expanse of space, as if through a wall. "You are unhappy. I don't want you to be unhappy. I brought you here so you could be happy for one day. Let's be happy together for one day."

She saw him about to take a step back, to turn, to head toward the car. She saw the day ending with a squeeze of her hand, with the acknowledgment of friendship.

She went quickly over to him. Put her hands on his shoulders. Stared into his eyes. He knelt in front of her and put his hands on her belly.

Her dress was wet, and she was conscious that it clung to her. He was looking up at her, the raindrops dripping from the rim of his fedora, his eyes once more on hers. She could not look away from him. What was she looking at, for, into? She could never have put it into words, but whatever she had been looking for, she was now looking at it. She took one hand off her belly and put it over her breast, which was aching with desire. But it wasn't her own hand that she wanted there. She reached down, keeping her eyes on his, and took his hand off her belly and put it on her breast, and it was as if a giant void in her had been filled. She sighed deeply.

He gently rubbed the wet fabric. She inhaled, but didn't move.

He stood, and she thought again of what Ugo had said about power, and she decided, *This time I will not be taken, I will take,* and she moved into his body, feeling the warmth of it through her dress. She raised her face and kissed his mouth.

He kissed her with such certainty it made her knees nearly buckle. His arms closed around her and she felt the whole cockeyed, askew world suddenly slide into place.

"Cara," he said. *"Carissima."*

The sun came out, and it was suddenly warm. From the trunk of his car he produced a bottle of wine, and a blanket he spread out on the dry ground under a huge tree. Laughing, he removed what remained of their clothes and hung them from the branches of the tree to dry. He was lean, and pale, and had dark brown moles. His toes were long and sensuous. They gazed at each other in the dappled sunlight under the tree, touching what was new and unfamiliar, as if each was blind and the other was a sculpture. Then she lay naked in his arms and he caressed her hair and kissed her and she climbed on top and put her hands in the air as she rode him until they shouted with joy, and then lay still again. She wanted to lie like that forever, the only two people on earth.

"Are you sorry at all?" she asked. "Because I'm not."

He laughed. "Not sorry."

"Even though it's a sin? Even though we're both married, and I'm pregnant?"

"Passion is not a sin," he said. "Not in such a beautiful place. Are you sorry you have made love to an old man?"

"An older man," she corrected. "A knowledgeable man." He kissed her and ran his hand up her leg, and as they rolled over, she wrapped it around him, hearing thunder in her ears, but as the thunder grew she realized she heard something else.

Drums? No. Hoofbeats.

No, she thought. *No.* She sat up and saw that Robertino was cantering toward them. She grabbed Carlo's hand and he sat up, too. They pulled the blanket around them. Robertino pulled up the horse when he saw them, looming over them, the horse's hoofs churning in the dirt, inches from them.

Robertino's face was a traffic jam of emotions.

"*Buongiorno, signori,*" he said formally, coldly. The horse, feeling his anxiety, danced under him, tossing its head.

"*Ciao,* Robertino, listen," she said, trembling.

Robertino nodded curtly and rode off. Scottie put her face in her hands. Why did the birds keep singing in the trees? She wanted to scream at them to shut up so she could think.

"He won't say anything," said Carlo, standing and handing over her dress.

"How do you know?" She thought she was shouting, but it came out as a whisper.

6.

Michael parked along a gravel road under an oak tree, set up a folding chair and an easel, placed his half-finished watercolor on it and settled in to wait. Anyone who came along would find just another foreign artist, in love with Tuscany's famous light, though the light was in short supply today, and it smelled like rain. Squalls were visible in the distance. He looked out over the misty overlapping, undulating hills, the vineyards, the olive groves. It reminded him of the fresco by Lorenzetti he had mentioned to

Luce during his job interview. Its title was *Effects of Good Government on the Country-side,* and it was part of a series of frescoes on the subject of leadership. Painted in 1339, this particular panel showed hunters, farmers, livestock and travelers all peace-fully coexisting just outside the walls of recognizable Siena. Since he had moved to Siena the fresco had taken on a deeper significance. Lorenzetti's allegory sought to illustrate for anyone passing through Siena's city hall — citizens and politicians — the risks of tyranny and corruption and the rewards of justice and virtuous leadership, that the Common Good trumped personal advancement.

Unfortunately, it was a short leap from Common Good to Communism.

It was hard to believe he shared DNA with these people, and spoke their language. They didn't just live differently, they *thought* differently. Backward.

But it was still a beautiful painting.

Robertino should be coming by soon. He had said he was riding to San Galgano today. Michael dipped his brush in water and put a tiny dab of Winsor Green in the corner, where a beech tree should go. The color immediately spread and began to pol-lute that entire area of the painting, turning a distant castle a sickly hue. He cursed and dabbed at it. Michael had always felt Winsor Green was like Sunday dinners with his entire extended Italian family — vile but necessary, and highly invasive. And now he would be a father himself. He would do it all differently.

He heard hoofbeats and stood up. Robertino appeared, atop a charging brown horse. Michael felt a little nervous. He was asking a lot of the kid. Asking him to break the law, betray his people. He thought again of that Ninth Circle in Dante. Traitors, frozen forever. Would the kid feel loyal to his father, the American GI, or to his grandfather's political party? Or would sheer greed, a sort of loyalty to his own survival, win out over all of it?

"Do you know where Communist Party headquarters is, in Via Cavour?"

"Sure," said the kid.

"Do you think you can get me the list of party members without getting caught?"

He held his breath. The kid might say no, or threaten to tell someone.

"Sure." The kid gave a mean smile, his blue eyes sparking with the challenge.

Michael blinked, startled. It was that easy? "You won't tell Rosini?"

The kid's lower lip twisted. "I'll squeeze

in the back window. How much you pay me?"

Michael hesitated. The whole thing was risky. What if the kid were caught, and told someone who he was working for? Using him at all was foolish, but he was such a good source of information, and could slip so easily into any situation. He was already known around Siena as nosy, talkative, a pest. Any questions Robertino asked would be interpreted as only serving his own interests. As part of the kid's campaign to ride for the Porcupine *contrada* in the August Palio he had powerful locals to sway, and so did Michael.

"I've got the first issue of *Matt Slade, Gunfighter,*" Michael said, producing the comic book from under a block of paper in his watercolor case. "Just arrived."

Robertino looked unconvinced. "How about a tractor for my grandfather? He liked the blue one."

"I can't give you a tractor. They cost millions of lire. How about *World of Fantasy? Devil-Dog Dugan? Yellow Claw?* Pretty choice stuff."

"I want the tractor."

"I told you, I can't give away tractors. How about tickets to the movies? You can go with Mrs. Messina."

Robertino gave a small snort that Michael could not understand. The kid seemed to be in some kind of foul mood, but he was fourteen, so it was to be expected. "A thousand dollars," Robertino said, his eyes narrowing.

"That's a lot of money."

"Less than a tractor."

There was something feral about the kid that scared him a little. The ease with which he had agreed to treachery and theft. It was wrong to entrust Scottie to him. Maybe wrong to trust him at all.

"Okay," he said. "A thousand." Michael sometimes had the feeling it was he who worked for Robertino, not the other way around.

The boy reached into his pants and pulled out a small brown paper package, then dropped it on the ground in front of Michael. Dust rose from where it landed.

"For you," he said, then sank his heels into the horse's side. The beast shot forward.

Michael picked up the package off the ground and unwrapped it. It was a magazine called *Physique Pictorial.* He dropped it again and his stomach came up into his mouth, and he retched. He stood there for a moment, panicked, panting, staring at the thing on the ground as if it were a snake.

He had seen it before, though not this issue. On the cover was a very muscular man in a Greek statue pose wearing nothing but a tiny pouch. The scrap of fabric was like something a little girl would carry to church with a quarter inside for the collection plate. Though this pouch contained more than a quarter. He knew that inside the magazine, there would be very few articles but lots of photos of men in very tight pants or even showing their bare buttocks, splashing in water troughs, demonstrating how to administer a shot, or performing wrestling moves on each other.

Michael calmly packed up his Winsor Green and the rest of the watercolor set. He put them back in the car; then, almost as an afterthought, he picked up the magazine and put it in his briefcase and locked it. He got in the car and drove back through the narrow gate in the walls at Porta Camollia, under the inscription that read in Latin COR MAGIS TIBI SENA PANDIT. Siena opens its heart to you.

The boy knows.

7.

Scottie was silent in the car on the way back to Siena. The landmarks they passed were a rebuke. The turnoff for Franca's. The bridge of La Pia, the scene of one of Siena's favorite gruesome stories of infidelity and death. What if Robertino told Michael? Or told anyone? Siena was, according to everyone, a small, gossipy place. She would be branded a whore, like Gina. Maybe she was like Gina. She had taken Carlo, as much as he had taken her. She felt deeply ashamed and more than a little shocked and angry with herself. At Vassar Leona had a mare that went into heat at every horse show. The poor beast would stand in her show stall or tied to the trailer, tail up, legs spread, juice running down her hind legs. People would avert their eyes, distract their children. Leona had called the horse a "nympho" and sold her.

The rain beat down on the little car, and Carlo had to concentrate on the road, leaning forward to see the few inches that the wipers cleaned. He parked back near the Fortezza.

"I can't ever see you again," she said.

He looked like she had spat on him. "Don't be a child," he said slowly.

She walked away, furious with the entire world.

She took a hot bath when she got home and tried to scrub away her guilt. She was making meatloaf when she heard Michael's key turning in the heavy lock — thunk, thunk, thunk. She had it all planned out. She would greet him as if nothing had happened between them. She would be a perfect, faithful, adoring wife, like the women in the ads. *My husband loves Crest!*

"I'm sorry I was such an ass about the baby," he said, coming up behind her and putting his arms around her, around her belly. She could feel him trembling with emotion. "Please forgive me. You caught me off guard, is all."

"I understand," she said. "It was a surprise for me, too." She turned and hugged him hard, and they stayed that way for a moment.

"Well, I have another surprise. Guess where we're going on Saturday?"

She really, really hoped he wouldn't say San Galgano.

"Rome?"

"Better. I called the number in the paper. Let's go get you a puppy!"

Eight:
La Selva, The Forest

"TALLEST FOREST IN THE FIELD"

June 29–31, 1956

1.

She was watching the *tratta* from her window, trying to find Robertino's face in the crowd, hoping that this dream come true for him did not fall flat. He had not shown up for her lesson the day after he had caught her and Carlo in San Galgano, or the next day.

The horses were sleek and shiny, blacks, chestnuts, bays and grays, and the *fantini* (jockeys) all wore identical tunics in the black and white of Siena for this selection heat. The crowds were gigantic, seething, and the *barbareschi* (grooms) were all gathered inside the courtyard of the Torre del Mangia, so that was probably why she couldn't spot him. A mare named Ondina

208

was picked for the Porcupine. Knowing that Robertino would lead the mare from the Campo to the *contrada* stables and stay with her twenty-four hours a day for the next four days, until the Palio was run on the evening of July 2, Scottie decided to go see Signor Banchi and leave the money for the last two lessons for Robertino.

As the sun rose, the city was a churning mass of noise and warm flesh. When she got to Banchi's, there were three men in suits there, agitated, talking to him out front. Banchi looked upset. She hesitated, but he saw her at the gate.

"Signora," he said. "Maybe the *signora* knows something."

She walked down between the rows of lavender to the front door, bees buzzing around her.

"Have you seen Robertino?" Banchi asked urgently.

"No. He didn't come for the lesson yesterday or today. I assumed he was busy in the *contrada.*"

Banchi looked at the men, worried. "These are the officers from the *contrada.* Robertino did not show up at the *sorta* this morning. The *contrada* was given the horse Ondina, but he's not there to take care of her."

Didn't show up? Robertino would never

209

miss the Palio. He'd been talking about it pretty much nonstop since the day she'd met him.

The men from the *contrada* left, and Scottie put a kettle of hot water on to make some chamomile tea for Signor Banchi.

"Maybe we should talk to the police," she said.

Banchi frowned. "I'm not sure. My grandson . . ." His voice trailed off.

"Is there someone you want me to talk to?" she said, setting the tea down in front of the old man, noting his trembling hands. "Someone he might have gone to see?"

"Perhaps his mother," said Signor Banchi, frowning, his fear becoming anger as Scottie watched. "His mother destroys everything. She has probably asked him to do something for her. I tell him to say no, but he never does." He slammed his open palm down on the table, making the bread crumbs jump. "And now she's lost him his job as a Palio groom. They'll never pick him as a jockey for the August race now!"

Scottie was confused. "I thought his mother was dead?"

"God forgive me, but I wish she were dead." His watery eyes turned to meet hers. "Her name is Gina," he said. "She is a prostitute."

She thought about the way she had asked Robertino about Gina, how uncomfortable he must have been. The poor kid. But Gina was so young — she must have been a teenager when Robertino was born. Scottie did the math in her head: It was during the war. He must have been born in 1942, when German and Italian troops had been fighting side by side in North Africa and Russia.

Scottie left the money she owed Robertino with the old man and went to the corner where Gina could usually be found. She was not there. Scottie looked for the telltale pile of cigarette butts, but there were none.

It was time to meet Michael to go get the puppy. What should have been a happy event now felt like an unwelcome distraction. She met Michael by the Fortezza, where they now always parked the Ford, safely outside the city's car-eating center. Michael backed the giant vehicle out of the lot, dodging the merchants setting up for today's outdoor market. They zigzagged down from the city to Pian del Lago, a vast flat green expanse where cattle grazed here and there. She felt grateful for the space between them in the Ford, so sharply in contrast to the dangerous intimacy of

Carlo's little breadbox on wheels.

She told Michael about Robertino's disappearance, but he seemed unconcerned. "That kid is like a cat," he said. "Always lands on his feet. I wouldn't worry about him." She did not reveal the secret of his parentage. She felt protective of Robertino, or perhaps ashamed for him.

Michael was talking about the people who owned the puppies. "Apparently they're leaving their farm and moving up to Turin. The husband has taken a job at a factory there. Common story these days. Huge migration going on. High time. This country's only hope for the future is to industrialize." He reached across and put his hand on her knee. "Let me do the talking. They'll probably claim they're purebreds, ask for a lot of money, but they'll be mutts for sure and left behind if they don't sell."

"Leave them behind? To starve? That's horrible."

The road climbed again, and they picked up the Monte Maggio road. They drove for about a half hour, then turned off and chugged up an unmarked rutted gravel road in low gear, passing through a chestnut forest full of shadows.

When they turned off the gravel road and she saw the state of the farm, she understood that perhaps leaving a dog behind was the least of these people's worries. Though the family had not moved out yet, the place already had an abandoned air. Grass grew in the gutters of the old stone house, and the roof was falling in, one huge timber already collapsed, a cascade of handmade bricks and roof-tiles around it. A couple of skinny sheep and an angry goose followed them across the terra-cotta *aia* to the steps that led upstairs to the front door, complaining loudly. As at Banchi's, the farm animals lived on the ground floor, but here the air was full of the acrid odor of manure, and there was a sense of disorder and hopelessness, of defeat. The roots of a large fig tree were pushing up the bricks. Six skinny barefoot children skulked around, staring at Scottie, and a baby cried somewhere inside. One of the thousands of flies flew into Scottie's mouth, choking her.

Michael called out and went up the stairs and knocked, but no one answered, and finally a white fox terrier with black and brown spots and fabulously furry eyebrows came tearing around a corner, barking like mad, preceding a very tired-looking woman carrying a basket of wet laundry on her hip.

"Mi scusate," she said. "I'm sorry — I was down at the stream. *Basta,* Ecco," she said.

213

The woman smiled shyly at Scottie, a smile that revealed much warmth but a distinct lack of teeth. *She's not much older than I am,* Scottie realized. She did her laundry in a stream. At least the women in the city had fountains of clean water nearly on their doorsteps. You could read statistics about how almost no rural Italian homes had running water, but seeing it written on a woman's face was another thing.

"The puppies are gone," she said. "Someone came this morning and bought them. But you can have this one. He's a good dog."

Michael, disappointed, began to say that they only wanted a puppy, that they had driven a long way, but Scottie put her hand on his sleeve. "Tell us about the dog," she said to the woman. "What's his name?"

"Ecco," she said. Scottie knew it meant "here," as in "here he is."

They sat down in the kitchen, which had a huge open fireplace, soot stains on the ceiling, and just a simple table with a couple of stools. The woman offered them some wine, which they accepted to be polite, Scottie trying not to stare at the three mismatched chipped cups. The woman proudly explained the dog's family tree, the barefoot children lurking in the shadowy corners of the room. Scottie got the feeling the dog had been a splurge in happier times, now regretted. The dog's great-great-grandmother apparently belonged to an Italian who used airships to discover the hidden landscape of the North Pole in the 1920s. Titina was the first dog to circle the Pole. On a later voyage there had been a crash, but both the explorer and Titina had survived.

"Are you talking about Umberto Nobile?" Michael asked.

"*Sì, sì,*" the woman said, brightening. "This dog is the grandson of his dog!"

"I'm sorry, but we can't take this dog," said Michael, standing up.

Scottie looked at him questioningly, asked in English, "Why? He's a cute dog, and yes I wanted a puppy, but I won't have to house-train him. No chewing, either."

Michael nodded toward the outside. The woman waved a hand to excuse them, and Scottie followed Michael out.

"Umberto Nobile is a famous Commie!" he whispered. "Notorious!"

"Michael," she said. "It's a dog."

"I don't want us to have anything to do with Communists."

"I know you hate Communists, but isn't there some big thaw going on? Maybe the

Cold War is over."

"Who's been telling you that?" he demanded, grabbing her arm. The goose squawked, hearing his tone. She looked into his eyes and saw raw fear. "Banchi? Did you know he's a Communist, too? I don't want you to see him anymore. Those lessons with Robertino are over. I'll get you a real teacher."

"I think you're overreacting," she said.

"They *want* you to think that things are loosening up. It's a lie, all part of a move by the Soviets to consolidate their power overseas. To bring together the Communists and the Socialists all over Europe. In Italy the left coalition is only two percent behind in the polls. Two percent! This is their big push," he said. "They want Western Europe. They want bases, and tanks, and nuclear missiles pointed at America. It's the domino theory coming true. And the next domino is Italy."

Scottie sighed in frustration. The things Michael was worried about seemed so far away from where they were standing right now, where this poor woman struggled to put food on the table. His blindness made her seethe.

"Fine," she said, not caring that she was loud. "Let's go home."

216

Michael grabbed her hand. "We'll take the dog. But I think it's best if you don't try to understand politics, okay?"

Michael was quiet in the car. The dog sat on the backseat and stared out the window.

"*Ciao,* Ecco," she said to him. She liked the way he looked at her, appraisingly, before he jumped over into the front and sat next to her, his paws on her lap. He was thin and ribby, but his fur was a soft curly fleece, and his ears neatly folded over like her father's heavy stationery. When she offered him a wafer cookie she'd stuck in her purse, Ecco sniffed suspiciously, then refused it. The dog had an aloofness about him, almost a snobbery, like the Sienese themselves. What was he hiding? She realized she was not thinking of him as a dog, but as an Italian. He would be her ambassador. She gathered him in her arms and hugged him, feeling his little heart beating under her palm. *My Communist dog,* she thought.

They took a different road back to Siena, which annoyed her. "I want to get back in time for the evening *prova,*" she said. Each of the three nights before the Palio, the horses would run morning and evening test heats, or *prove.* They didn't count for anything, but gave the jockeys, the horses and the crowds a taste of what was to come on the big day. She hoped she would see Robertino in the crowd with Ondina.

"Forget the horses for one minute," Michael said, pointing out the simple stone arch of the Ponte della Pia. "I want to show you something beautiful. It's got a famous tragic story to it."

She didn't have the heart to tell him she knew it already.

"In the 1200s a doomed noblewoman named Pia Tolomei left the city over that exact bridge with her husband, who thought she was cheating on him. He locked her in his castle in Maremma," Michael said. "And she either starved to death or jumped out the window. It got her literary immortality, though. She's mentioned in Dante." He had taken out a camera, was snapping a picture of her.

"I'm sorry I'm a disappointment to you," she said.

"Oh! Oh no!" he said quickly, putting down the camera, genuinely surprised by this. "Why would you say such a thing? Did I make you feel that way?" He looked so tortured by this thought she had to say something to reassure him.

"I'm . . . a terrible cook. I didn't mean to

get pregnant."

He laughed, and took her hand and kissed it tenderly. "You're a wonderful wife," he said. "Way better than I deserve." He took her in his arms and held her. "You're the best thing in my life right now."

2.

Scottie was bathing the dog as Michael slipped out of the apartment. He stood in the shadows of the Fortezza Medicea. Although transformed during the Fascist era into a lovely public space with tall shade trees, the massive fortress was in fact a bitter symbol for the Sienese of their defeat by the odious Florentines under the leadership of Cosimo de' Medici in 1555, marking the end of the Republic of Siena.

There is plenty of animosity to this day between the two cities, he had written in his last report.

He shifted anxiously in the darkness, listening for Robertino's footsteps. The fortress's almost absurdly massive walls had been built with no sense of refinement or decoration, just intimidation. Michael could imagine the Florentines pouring boiling oil off of them onto obstreperous Sienese below.

The morning after they met on the road,

Robertino had passed him in Via di Città and slipped him a note that the break-in had gone smoothly and he had the Communist Party membership list.

Then Robertino had not shown up for the handoff.

What the hell was going on? Did it have to do with *Physique Pictorial*? There was no way the kid could know he was gay. It had to be a stab in the dark, didn't it? There was nothing, no trace. It was a scare tactic. That was what being gay meant, that even straight men feared being accused of it. Robertino had to be testing him. Maybe he just wanted more money.

Michael had stood in the window with a newspaper at eight this morning as the crowds filed into the piazza for the damn test race, but the kid had not shown up again. So now he was waiting for him at the Fortezza, their backup meeting point. He hoped the kid had gotten distracted by all this Palio hullabaloo and would reappear. Still. If anyone found the list of party members on him, if they forced him to tell who he was working for . . . Michael would be at the center of a very ugly scandal, found to be interfering in Italian politics. He would be cut loose without pity. Michael had learned in training that four years earlier, two CIA officers had been captured while trying to remove an agent from China and jailed. Secretary of State John Foster Dulles refused either to acknowledge they were in fact Agency men or negotiate for their release. If Michael went to jail, no one was coming to get him out. What would happen to Scottie, and their child? He felt sick at the thought.

He checked his watch again. He would give the kid fifteen more minutes.

The moon was coming up over the old fortress. It was a warm summer night, with fireflies hovering around the bushes. Michael was reminded of evenings back home, watching movies outdoors in Van Cortlandt Park with his older brother. *Marco, I hope you're watching over me. I hope you're proud. I hope you're jealous.*

But he wouldn't be. Marco had teased him mercilessly when he was little, stabbed Michael's teddy bear with a pencil and called him a fag when he cried. Michael was too little to know what the word meant, but the sense of it was clear. At those movies in the park Marco had threatened Michael if he sat too close, and at the same time protected him, chasing off boys who teased and threw popcorn.

A cloud slid over the moon, deepening

the darkness outside the Medici Fortress. Somewhere a radio played "The Great Pretender."

And then someone grabbed him from behind.

He woke up in the trunk of a car.

I'm dead, he thought. The idea was something of a relief, as he had imagined it so many times, except he wanted to know what exactly he was being killed for. Was this the KGB? Or just run-of-the-mill thugs like the ones who had attacked the taxi in Rome? It seemed important to know. *Oh fuck,* he thought, remembering what else was in his briefcase. *Physique Pictorial.* Could he get rid of it before they killed him? He did not want that mentioned in the eulogies.

They drove for what seemed like a long while. He dug deep into his memories of training and went through all the hand-to-hand combat moves in his mind.

Finally, after ten or twenty minutes of bumping and gear grinding, the trunk opened. There were two men, older than he and very strong. One of them had a bushy mustache that looked fake.

Michael started to yell and raised his fists to strike.

"Relax, it's a drill."

"A drill? I nearly pissed myself."

The two men looked at each other. "Come inside," they said.

In the darkness it was hard to get the lay of the land, but this was clearly an abandoned farmhouse deep in a forest. Michael could hear insects and saw fireflies. Water was running somewhere. It would have been charming under other circumstances.

The interior of the stone building had a dirt floor and piles of ancient animal dung, some broken glass in the corner and a table and chairs that had seen better centuries. One of the men lit a kerosene lantern.

This was a CIA safe house, they explained. They showed him a map of how to get to it, which he had to memorize, and then they burned it in front of him. Michael could sense that they were skeptical of him, that they didn't think he was a "real" spy.

"I'm very close to getting my hands on a membership list for the Communists in Siena," he blurted, wanting to impress them.

"An enemies list. Excellent," Mustache said.

Michael thought of Signor Banchi and the mechanic Brunetti. "I wouldn't say they're all enemies," he said. "What are you going to do with the list?"

Mustache said this meeting was about the

new elections that Michael had cabled Luce about. The Catholic, pro-America candidate, the slimy tax lawyer and now acting mayor Vestri, *must* beat Ugo Rosini, who, if he won again, might never be shaken out of office.

"It's going to be tough. He's very popular," said Michael cautiously.

Mustache sighed impatiently, as if Michael were a tiresome child. Just in case their man didn't win, he said, and things degenerated on a national level, an arms cache would be delivered soon.

"Guns?" He was glad Robertino hadn't given him the list. What would they do to the people on it? Jail them? Kill them? Poor old Banchi.

The man was still talking, saying something about Operation Gladio. Michael must generate a "friends list" of those who could be counted on to take power by force if the Communists took over the government. He would be in charge of arming them.

"You must connect with a network of those friendly to our cause. Create a stay-behind net."

War. Michael felt slightly faint. The safe house must have been a mill at some point. Suddenly rushing water was all that Michael could hear, the voices diminishing beneath the roar.

"It could come any day."

"What?" Frogs were bellowing some-where, and a flurry of moths circled the lightbulb. His heart was racing erratically.

"The coup. The Soviets have tanks in Yugoslavia. They could be here in a day. We have to be ready to fight at the ground level." Mustache was growing more impa-tient with him, and swatted angrily at a mosquito. The other guy, large and muscled, had no expression.

"It's a matter of loyalties," said Mustache.

Mussolini drained the saltwater swamps and eradicated malaria in Italy, Michael remembered. But now the disease was back again. Couldn't America just help with that? Send some DDT, build some highways, buy a ton of olive oil and shoes, and stop push-ing Coca-Cola down their throats? Trust that true friendship would win them over?

Mustache told him what he had to do in the wake of Manganelli's death, what would ensure a Catholic victory in the next elec-tion.

Blame the left.

A whisper campaign. These were the "Dark Arts" from his training at the Farm. He was to start the rumor that Manganelli's accident was no accident. That he had been taken down by a bitter left angry at the results of last month's elections. That the left — headed by Ugo Rosini — intended instability, fear, the end of democracy. Everything, in other words, that was the opposite of Wonder Bread, and *I Love Lucy,* and Perry Como. He was, in short, to create in others the fear and anxiety he already felt. He was to foment a right-wing revolution.

He thought of that green-lawned boarding school where he would, right now, be teaching wide-eyed adolescents about long-dead artists like Duccio di Buoninsegna and Simone Martini. Instead he had chosen *this.* The reasons why were suddenly rather obscure to him. To impress Duncan? To prove to the people who made it illegal to be gay that they were wrong? That he was just as good an American as anyone? He had come to Italy to promote American ideals. And, yes, okay, to sway an election by bribery. But it was all in the service of good. Now he had to arrange a pro-American resistance movement? Maintain an arms cache? Run a psy-ops campaign single-handed? Start a war?

If he didn't, they made it clear, Michael would be transferred not to Rome or Paris, but to some distant snake-infested jungle nation or the front lines of a South American civil war.

3.

She watched the *prova* through binoculars, but it was not Robertino who had led the bay mare Ondina into the piazza the evening they brought Ecco home, or the next morning. She was trying not to think about Robertino's disappearance, telling herself he would turn up, that it had nothing to do with her, that he was fine. She took the dog out for a walk and passed Gina's corner, but there was no one there. Perhaps the police had swept the street of prostitutes before the tourists arrived for the Palio. She bought a nice new collar and leash for the dog, and bathed him. Michael had come in late, tossed and turned all night, and then this morning packed and left for Rome again.

They were both exhausted and preoccupied, she thought. She couldn't share with him, and it was useless to ask what was bothering him. Other than his outburst at the farm about Communists, he never talked about what was upsetting him. Tractors must not be selling well, but because of male pride he couldn't talk about it. She tried to think of something she could do for him. She had discovered a book on dating and marriage on his shelf, which she found charming. If he was studying, she could, too. *Make your husband's life better every day!* That was how a good wife thought. *What can I iron? What can I cook? How can I make our home more comfortable?* Why couldn't she be more like that? Despite Michael's reassurances, she was a terrible wife, and who knew what kind of a mother she would make.

Her mood slid downhill like an avalanche. Thanks to her stupidity, she couldn't call Carlo, couldn't tell him that Robertino had disappeared or ask what he thought. She wandered around the tumultuous, noisy city with the dog, tossed on a turbulent sea of emotions. She stopped again at the place where Gina usually stood, but she wasn't there.

She dared to go across the street into the *ferramenta* — hardware store — and ask the thin man at the counter if he had seen Gina lately. He frowned, and she said quickly, "In America we try to find these women other forms of employment — I thought I might help her." Her lie did not erase his frown, but he said, "She has moved her business elsewhere." So her suspicions about a pre-

Palio sweep were correct. Scottie waited as he served a man who came in to buy one three-centimeter nail, and another who wanted his scythe sharpened. Finally the hardware store owner, clearly eager to get her out of his store, told her that when the police harassed Gina in Siena, she often moved to a pullout on the road from Siena to Grosseto. He described the place not far from there where she took her clients. Scottie was careful not to ask how he had come by this information.

"Better than threatening her, I suggest you tell your husband to stay away from her," he said. "She's trouble."

4.

Michael sat on the train to Rome, trying to keep his hands from shaking as he pretended to be just another man in a hat reading a newspaper. The smoke-filled car was choking him, but the windows wouldn't open. He had slept badly. The safe house adventure had angered and terrified him. And where was the damn kid?

This was a disaster.

He popped another Benzedrine and tried to focus on the newspaper as the train clicked along.

Arthur Miller and Marilyn Monroe elope, U.S.

revokes his passport.

Red Cross will distribute food in Poland if it carries a label that says "Gift of the American people."

At the Excelsior: James Stewart in "The Man Who Knew Too Much."

He had sent a telegram last night after the CIA thugs had dropped him off, asking to meet his CIA contact in person. This sort of sticky situation could not be handled remotely. He needed face-to-face contact, whether it was protocol or not. He had received a message to meet his handler today at the bottom of the Spanish Steps. Someone would ask him if he could recommend a restaurant with a view of the Tiber. That was the code.

He made his way from the train station on foot, passing Santa Maria degli Angeli e dei Martiri. People were streaming in and out, women with their heads covered, all of whom reminded him of his mother. He went to mass regularly, but didn't get comfort from faith the way she did. He felt trapped by sin and guilt. It had begun when he was a child, with the idea that as soon as you received communion and were pure again, the sins began accumulating immediately. He had tried to talk to a priest once about it, but the man's brows had knitted into one glaring pelt and he had said that Michael was not trying hard enough to be good. "God loathes weakness," he said.

Michael checked his watch and trotted through Piazza Barberini and down Via Sistina toward the Spanish Steps. It was a sunny afternoon, and the piazza was crowded with tourists snapping photos with their Kodaks and Leicas. Michael was facing the Via Condotti when he heard a voice behind him. "Excuse me, I don't suppose you could recommend a restaurant with a really *excellent* view of the Tiber?"

It was Duncan.

"Wars are waged on many levels," Duncan said. "Isn't this better than tanks and bombs?"

They stood in the Borghese Gardens. All around them children were playing, dogs frolicking and people eating gelato. A little girl in a blue dress passed them carrying a red balloon. She smelled like poop. Michael had a sense that none of it was real, that Duncan had hired these people to play these roles, like extras in a film.

"You're not just a USIS librarian," Michael said. He had thought he was impressing Duncan by being a big man in the CIA, a veritable James Bond, when in reality

Duncan was his superior. Always his superior.

"Could have knocked me over with a feather when you signed up with the Agency. I was delighted, of course."

"You lied to me. Now I don't know who to trust."

"No one, of course."

He had planned to ask for his superior's help in extricating himself from the CIA. He needed to confess how he had recruited a fourteen-year-old, how the kid had gone to get the Communist membership rolls, how he had disappeared. How he might have been involved in the disappearance of a prostitute. How Michael was now in way over his head and wanted out before the Italians unmasked him.

"Are you really the Agency's top man in Rome?" Michael asked.

"Let's say I have more of an oversight role."

Duncan must have sent the two men who had grabbed Michael at the Fortezza. What kind of power did Duncan have in the Agency? Michael had heard rumors in training that counterintelligence chief James Angleton often put in place individual, handpicked agents, who reported only to him, to shadow the CIA's own agents.

Moles to ferret out moles. Whatever Duncan was up to certainly seemed to go beyond clandestine officer, or even station chief. There was something he wasn't telling him, a connection he had (Someone from Yale? His family? Some sailing school buddy from summers on Nantucket?) that would probably boggle Michael's mind.

It was like back at Yale, when Duncan hadn't told him he had joined a secret society. Duncan was always drawn to the elite of the elite, the more secret the better.

"I don't want to arm a militia," Michael said.

Duncan slapped his back and whispered, "We can't stop now. You've exceeded our expectations. You have a man inside the Communist Party!" It was the kind of approval Michael had longed for, but now it made him nervous.

"I don't understand what we're really doing here," he said.

"You're living in the Red center of the entire country," said Duncan in the tones one would use to explain the mechanics of a seesaw to a child. "It just makes sense to have a resistance movement in place should the Communists seize power or the Soviets invade."

Michael stared at a plane passing overhead.

"Eisenhower's not entirely happy about counterintelligence, either," Duncan admitted. "David K. E. Bruce just sent in his report on Operation Mockingbird. I managed to take a peek." He giggled like a naughty schoolboy, then rattled on, while for Michael all the ramifications of the truth spread out like a stain. He had not kept secrets from Duncan, but Duncan had kept them from him. What he had taken for love was a power game.

He would not give in, not show weakness. "When you say things like that, 'managed to take a peek,' what do you mean, exactly? Did you steal a copy? Did you use your invisible ink decoder? Did you pretend to be dusting someone's office and read it while wearing a French maid's outfit?"

"Why are you in such a mood?"

"Because you act like this is all a game. We're planning a coup in case of a democratically elected Communist government."

Duncan gave a superior smile. "Want to know a secret? We've already done it in Iran." To Michael's shock, Duncan told him how the CIA had spread anti-Mossadegh propaganda, including outright lies about Iran's democratically elected prime minister, and had toppled that regime in 1953 so that the pro-American shah could be installed. "And then we did it again in Guatemala. Really, the same tactic could work anywhere," Duncan said gleefully.

"Does Eisenhower know about this?"

Duncan shrugged. "We tell him what he needs to know."

"But . . . that just seems so wrong," Michael said. "We say we want democracies and then we overthrow them?"

"Look, they think they're voting for a better way of life, but we know they're safer if they stay tied to the U.S. The way I see it, the ends justify the means. Would you rather have World War III?"

"By saying that, you could justify almost anything."

Duncan was quiet as they passed a bench of nuns eating ice cream cones.

"It's not like the Soviets aren't doing the same thing," he said at last. "We're just keeping up. Can't back down now. Can't blink. Let's go visit Pauline."

The statue of Pauline Borghese in the Borghese Gallery was Michael's favorite. Life-size in snow-white marble, she lay on one hip, topless, a drapery discreetly covering her from the waist down. As tourists milled around them in the still summer air,

Michael stared at Pauline, taking in her bold but emotionless stare, the casual way she hefted an apple in her hand, as if she might throw it at a servant who was slow with her coffee. She had been so poor as a child she'd been forced to work as a laundress, but eventually her brother, Napoleon, had married her off to a general, and she had traveled to Haiti, where her husband suppressed a slave rebellion. There both of them came down with yellow fever, which killed him but didn't stop her from sleeping with anything that breathed. She returned to Europe and married a member of the noble Borghese family and continued her wild and wanton ways until her death at forty-four. She was, Michael thought, utterly disloyal, amoral and without any merit beyond beauty.

A man in a pinstriped suit and derby hat walked past, a furled umbrella in his gloved hand. He nodded at them as he moved on to Bernini's *Apollo and Daphne.*

"Who's that?" Michael asked.

"Lord Sebastian Gordon. Nothing to worry about. Works in fashion. Friend of Clare's from her days at *Vogue.*"

Michael sighed. He thought about Scottie, about the baby that was coming. About the normal side of his life. Maybe he was taking everything too seriously. In the grand scheme of things, he was working for the good guys. Michael popped a Benzedrine and pointed to Pauline's toes. "Her feet are almost as beautiful as mine."

It was a joke between them, Michael's absurd vanity about his feet, his pride in the prominent bones and long toes. Duncan was smiling. He was so handsome, eyes you could swim in. The worst part was that even though Duncan had lied to him, Michael still longed to make him proud, to earn the love of this wonderful creature who had singled him out for notice in this huge, cruel world.

"Let's go get a drink," Duncan said. "There's a new bar across the street from the embassy."

"What if we run into someone? Aren't CIA men never supposed to be seen together?"

"You take the rules too seriously. The whole staff of the *Rome Daily American* will be there, half of whom are CIA. Here." Duncan passed him the briefcase he had been carrying all day. Michael had wondered what was in it.

"Fifty thousand dollars. That was all I could get for now, but don't worry, there's more where that came from."

"What the hell — what's this for?" He stared at the plain brown leather case with ridiculously flimsy gold combination locks on top.

"For whatever you need. To organize your stay-behind militia. To buy the articles in the local papers about how great Manganelli's temporary replacement is and why he should be — what's his name?"

"Vestri. He's a corrupt weasel."

"Yes, well, we didn't all like Ike, either. If you have a discreet way to funnel the cash directly to the campaign, that's best, but we can't be seen buying elections."

"Of course not," said Michael. "That would be wrong. And illegal."

"We usually work through journalists. Get them to say something about his plans for the city, how he's going to make everyone rich. And to say something negative about the other guy."

"Ugo Rosini. Like he ran over Manganelli?"

"Good idea. You can use your man inside the Party to help discredit him from within. Nothing overt, just watercooler rumors. What kind of a civil servant is your man?"

He thought of Robertino dancing on top of the ox. "He's in the agriculture department. Livestock inspector." It was giving him pleasure to lie to Duncan, he realized with dismay.

"Perfect. He can gossip with the cattlemen at the stockyards."

Michael did not know if there were cattlemen or stockyards in Siena, but he nodded.

"You know journalists, right?"

Michael did not want to admit that though he had met a lot of people, he didn't really *know* anyone, except his own wife and a fourteen-year-old "livestock inspector" who'd disappeared.

"Yes," he lied, the Benzedrine giving him courage. "I'm in the process of flipping a journalist named Rodolfo Marchetti." In truth he had never met the man. "Been very Red, but he's ripe for a change, I think."

"Use this to reward him for positive articles. It's just like they taught you in training. Be positive, discreet and friendly, never insulting. It's a gift for a job well done, not a bribe. And have someone write something nice about Clare, would you?" Duncan added, slowing as they turned on the Via Veneto, pulling his straw hat down slightly and putting on what Michael thought of as his public face. Affable, but closed.

"The ambassador?"

"She's feeling very down lately. Turns out

239

it's arsenic poisoning."

"She *was* poisoned?" Michael was alarmed.

"We thought it was the KGB, but it seems it's from paint flaking off her bedroom ceiling falling on her while she slept. Her gums are bleeding, teeth falling out. She's a mess. But she's determined to make it through the embassy Fourth of July party. She will hand a hot dog to every person in line, or die trying. Then the poor lamb will go to her newly painted lead-free room and collapse."

The thought crossed Michael's mind that Duncan might be having an affair with La Luce.

"Say that she's coming for the Palio in August," Duncan said.

"Is she?"

"God no. She'll be on Niarchos's yacht in August. She's very disappointed in the Italians. Calls them 'impossible.' She'd love to cut off all aid to the damn place entirely. Win this election, would you? It will really cheer her up."

"Hearts, minds and wallets, huh?"

Duncan frowned at him. "You do love your country, don't you, Michael? You haven't developed sympathy for the Italians because of your heritage?"

At first Michael thought he must be joking. His *heritage*? "Of course I love *our* country." Michael stared Duncan down impatiently. "America is the greatest nation in the world, and I would do anything to protect it."

Duncan smiled, then frowned again. "Oh, and keep your eyes open. Word is that the Soviets have a new man in Siena, too."

5.

The heat seemed to begin even before the sun rose. Scottie's limbs felt weighted. Ecco, who was supposed to sleep on a small towel near the front door, had clearly spent the night on the new sofa. She kissed his head and made him half a fried egg on toast. She would have to find out what Italian dogs ate, since they didn't have Alpo or Thrivo here. After watching the already slick-with-sweat horses run the morning *prova* — still no Robertino — she closed the heavy shutters, but she couldn't bear to sit inside in the dark all day. She wanted to go down to Banchi's and see if Robertino had reappeared or sent word, but probably Michael was right. She, *La Straniera,* would just be in the way.

It was, after all, none of her business. She had paid Banchi for the last lessons. What right did she think she had to pry deeper?

The right of someone who cares, she thought.

She and Ecco walked as quickly as they could through the choked streets to Signor Banchi's, but he wasn't home. On her way back into the city she stopped at the Porcupine *contrada* office in Via Camollia, but it was locked. As she passed the Church of Saints Vincenzo and Atanasio, she heard voices inside. She hesitated — Catholic churches made her a little nervous, as if lightning were going to strike her the moment she set foot inside. Even though she knew your head and shoulders had to be covered, she felt like there were more secret rules she didn't know, and like somehow her very presence there was offensive. This was one of the older churches in Siena — low, squat and plain on the outside, in the twelfth-century style. She looped Ecco's leash over an iron dragon head outside, pulled her straw hat down securely, pushed open the door and stepped into the cool, dark interior. As her eyes adjusted to the light, she saw baroque flourishes, gold, a carved wooden altar, candlelight reflecting off huge canvases. Two men were talking in a corner. They looked at her in annoyance as she came in, and one of them, the priest, said, "No tours today," in English. The other man was one of the men she had seen at Banchi's, an official from the *contrada*.

"*Buongiorno*," she said, continuing in Italian, "I'm wondering if there is news of Robertino Banchi."

They shook their heads, and waited for her to leave before resuming their hushed conversation. It was probably about the Palio, but then again maybe it was about something else. Someone else.

She didn't have an Italian driver's license, but as she left the church, she passed a small mechanic's garage where a very dark-eyed man with a sinewy body in oil-stained coveralls was lying on the ground working on a Vespa. There was a row of similar Vespas along one wall. He looked up at her and saw, she knew, a tourist ripe for the plucking.

"Do you by chance rent these machines?" she asked in English.

NINE:
L'AQUILA, THE EAGLE

"THE EAGLE'S BEAK, TALON AND WING —
UNGUIBUS ET ROSTRIS"

1.

The old farm buildings of Centro Ippico ai Lecci were surrounded by huge, spooky oaks that must have been hundreds of years old. Scottie parked the Vespa she had rented from the young mechanic in Via Camollia, who was, she knew full well, making a small fortune on the deal. It suited her to be seen as just a tourist out for a jaunt. It was in truth a slightly impractical mode of transportation for outside the city, putt-putting slowly up hills and threatening to stall at any moment, but Scottie enjoyed the ride out to the stable, Ecco balancing on the seat in front of her. When they arrived, she kept Ecco on his short leather leash and stood by the rail of the riding arena, watching a swaggering man do a very bad job lunging a young horse.

You have no patience, she wanted to tell him. The horse was irritated, jaw clamped, neck muscles rigid, learning nothing except to hate humans. The man greeted her and said he'd be done in a minute. Tommaso Gatti, he said his name was. Tom Cats, it would be in English. He was wearing a beautifully cut tweed jacket and tall brown boots, and was in his thirties, she guessed. Arrogant. Definitely condescending to her, the stupid American, telling her how difficult the horse was, but how he would "win." She disliked him immediately, but when he finished and came over to the rail, she inquired about the price of stabling and whether trails were available.

"*Sì,*" he said. "From here you can ride all over la Toscana," adding, of course, a weaselly "I can show you myself. It's dangerous to ride alone." The poor chestnut, sides heaving, wet with sweat and foam, needed to be walked out.

She asked for Robertino. "He's my Italian teacher," she said, "and he's just disappeared on me." She acted annoyed rather than concerned.

"An unreliable boy," said Tom Cats. "Uneducated, you know. He is probably off somewhere having the time of his life. I sup-

245

pose he owes you money?"

Scottie was offended on Robertino's behalf, and on her own, as if her interest in the boy could be nothing more than financial. "Does he have friends who might know where he is?"

"A boy like that? No."

"What does that mean?"

He lifted his shoulders.

She turned to leave, frustrated, but then felt a wave of courage and turned back to him.

"Did a woman named Gina ever come here?"

Tom Cats tilted his face up under his hat and stuck his chin out. "Gina? How do you know Gina?" He stared at her. "I don't know her." And with that, he finally went to walk the poor sweating horse out.

Scottie and Ecco remounted the trusty scooter. She tried to remember exactly what the hardware store owner had said about where Gina's new "workplace" was. She followed the Via Cassia from Siena toward Grosseto, views of mountains opening up all around her, looking for a pullout that matched his description. Finally, she saw a woman sitting on an overturned bucket by the side of the road, no vehicle in sight. The woman stood as she pulled up, a hopeful look in her eyes until she saw Scottie was a woman. Scottie saw she was older than Gina — in her forties perhaps, though it was hard to tell. She was wearing a yellow dress trimmed with pink lace, and smoking.

"Buongiorno," said Scottie. The woman glanced at her but said nothing.

"Have you seen Gina?"

The woman shook her head, trying, like the riding stable owner, to figure out why an American woman with a dog was looking for a whore.

She said something that Scottie couldn't understand in what sounded like Arabic.

"Sorry, again?" said Scottie.

"Naples, today," the woman said slowly, pointing down the road. Scottie realized the woman didn't speak Italian, only the Neapolitan dialect.

Scottie nodded and looked around. Cicadas hummed in the air, and she could smell fresh-cut hay. In the distance a broad purple pyramid loomed over the softer green hills, the colors in sharp contrast to the verdant patchwork below. That must be Monte Amiata.

Across the Cassia was a one-lane dirt road that curved up the hillside. This was, she knew, the direction Carlo lived in. She should not go that way. Scottie fired up the scooter again and headed up the road. After a couple of miles she passed several unmarked forks in the road and eventually an old cemetery. She couldn't see any farms, just a vast expanse of undulating hills, cypresses and low dense brush spotted with bright yellow blooms. She parked the scooter at a crossroads to get her bearings and to let Ecco stretch his legs. With an excited growling bark, the fox terrier darted into some deep brush along the dusty roadside.

Twenty minutes later, he had not reappeared. She could barely hear him barking in the distance. Was he in danger, or just on a scent? Robertino's disappearance made everything else in this landscape feel sinister. The sun dropped closer to a row of cypresses on the horizon, and she looked at her watch again. Nearly seven. Michael would be back from Rome tonight. She was meeting him at Bar Nannini at eight after the evening *prova*. She'd have to change first — driving a scooter on a dusty road turned out to be a messy proposition, despite the crisp ads filling the papers and magazines showing beautiful women zooming around, newly liberated from mere foot travel.

The minutes ticked on, and anxiety settled over her hot brain like a wool blanket. If she had to choose between her husband and her dog . . . Some loyalties were better left un-examined.

Robertino was like her, looking for adventure. When she went over their conversations together, his collection of small jobs — exercising horses, delivering his grandfather's eggs to the hotels and running errands for tourists — seemed so innocent, but Banchi's revelation that Gina was his mother meant that there were aspects of his life she knew nothing about. Working at the stable would have exposed him to money, and perhaps also corruption, and crime. Robertino, a naïf, could easily have gotten in over his head.

He's the sort of boy I'll have, she thought. *He thinks the best of people, and then they disappoint him. I did.*

He's like Michael, she realized.

She turned away from the view and faced the dense brush — *macchia,* they called it — on the other side of the Vespa. The heavy scent of the yellow broom flowers was worsening her headache.

She looked down and saw marks in the dust. Little oblongs and sharp round holes. She remembered the first time she had ever seen footprints like that, at Grauman's Chinese Theatre with her father. "High heels," he had said, pointing to Betty Grable's prints in the cement.

They led to the small opening in the *macchia* Ecco had disappeared into, then stopped. She got down on her hands and knees and started to climb into the thicket. Branches grabbed at her hair.

She continued down the tunnel Ecco had taken, wondering if she was going to have to back out of it. After she had gone about fifty yards, she saw sunlight ahead. She came to a small clearing in the brush and stood up. Her hands were caked with red mud. It was all over her knees as well, staining her pants. The buzz of flies filled her ears, and she gagged at the smell.

She was in a sort of room — a small cot with an ancient thin mattress half rotted away, the ring where many fires had been made. There was a body on the cot. From the flies and the smell she knew it was no longer alive. She couldn't see the face, but she recognized the thin dress, saw red high heels lying on the ground next to the cot. Steeling herself, she took a step closer, saw a syringe on the ground next to the shoes.

There was a rustling in the brush, and she jumped as an animal ran past her, something strange and shapeless, followed by Ecco. There was a terrible snarl, then yelping. Then silence.

Her heart was pounding and she felt herself starting to retch. She had to go back the way she'd come. She dropped to her knees and crawled toward the road, getting even more filthy. When she emerged once again into daylight, a man was standing there.

Carlo. Of course.

2.

Michael sat on the train, realizing that he was looking forward to seeing Scottie. He was craving her smile, longing to hear about the mundane details of her day. He would ask her about the shopping. About whether she might like a new summer dress. She was like Central Park, beautiful and quiet and manicured and safe. They would have a nice dinner, and he could briefly pretend to himself that he was what she saw, a straight man whose only job was to sell big, beautiful blue tractors.

Art Buchwald's column, "Europe's Lighter Side," was a humorous look at how American businessmen could write off a trip to Europe on their taxes. Michael smiled at the portrait of Americans abroad, spending their money, having a good time, leaving nothing but good feelings in their wake.

3.

For a moment they stared at each other, as if trying to make sense of what they were seeing.

"There's a dead woman," said Scottie. "In there. I think it's Gina."

"Dio mio," said Carlo. "Sit down." She sat on the scooter seat.

"There's a syringe," she said.

"Drugs. But how did you — ?"

Why were you crawling through my property? would have been a very logical question. "Robertino is missing. I thought maybe Gina would know where he was. I found out, well, anyway, I found her."

Carlo was in khaki pants, jacket and vest, white shirt, tie, fedora and short boots with leather *ghette,* or laced leggings, over them, not perfectly clean after a day of work but at least tidy. He had a long staff. He was dressed like a *buttero,* she recognized, an Italian cowboy. He had leaned his rifle against the scooter. A black horse with a large ugly head was standing nearby, swatting flies with its tail. "I must telephone the police," he said. "There's a farm nearby. I

252

will be right back. You are okay to wait here?"

She nodded. He mounted his horse and disappeared.

She called for Ecco, but got no response. What would she tell Michael about this?

Carlo returned after a few minutes. "They are coming," he said. They avoided each other's eyes, but shock was setting in, and she wanted to throw herself into his arms in a *really* undignified way.

"My dog," she said. "He ran off. Did you see him?" It was perfectly natural to keep her eyes moving over the landscape.

"No. But I heard him before. Don't be too hard on him. He probably saved Gina's body from . . . animals." They were quiet for a second, both listening, looking out over the *macchia,* and she could smell Carlo's scent — leather and horse and pipe tobacco and something else. There was nothing but silence, and the wind over the hills. Carlo let out a piercing whistle, and they stared and listened again. Nothing.

"She was covered in flies," she said. "I didn't have anything to put over her."

Still without looking at her, he took her hand as they stood side by side, and when she felt the warmth of his fingers, how strong and rough they were, her throat

253

closed up and she was overwhelmed with emotion, followed immediately by embarrassment.

"I'm sorry for what I said the other day," she wanted to say, but instead she said, "That's a lovely horse you have," even though the horse's head looked so heavy it seemed it would pitch forward any second. Her voice was high and unsteady.

"Sit down," he said, now finally looking at her, frowning, handing her a handkerchief.

She still couldn't meet his eyes, though she could feel them on her. He had seen many dead people. Had seen his own son dead. She sat down on the ground and tried to get her breathing under control. He crouched next to her, staring into the distance. Then he stood up and gave another whistle.

"I think I hear barking," he said. He whistled again.

She inhaled. His smell reminded her of her home in California, of evenings playing cards with her father when the winter rain battered the windows and the palm trees nearly bent double in the wind.

At that moment, Ecco came bursting out of the *macchia,* panting, his face a horror movie mask. She gasped.

"Un istrice," Carlo said calmly. "Porcu-

254

pine." He leaned down and picked up Ecco gently. The dog's face was filled with quills, some dangerously close to his eyes. He was oddly quiet, and looked like he, too, was in shock.

"Oh goodness! I need to get him to a veterinarian as soon as — the police."

He took a pair of pliers out of his jacket pocket. "Hold him," he said. Scottie winced as Carlo began to yank the quills out of Ecco's face one by one with a sharp flick of his wrist. Ecco stayed surprisingly quiet.

"You've done this a lot," she said.

He nodded. "The hunting dogs," he said. "They never learn." His hands moved with confidence, and his mouth curled in a frown as he continued working on the dog.

"Poor Gina," she said. "Signor Banchi didn't speak to her. But Robertino tried to help her. Banchi thinks maybe she got him involved in something, that that's why he's disappeared."

Carlo nodded, surprised, she could see, by how much she knew.

"Prostitution has always been somewhat tolerated," he said, continuing to remove the quills from the dog. "But now, with the tourists, people are angry. *Brutta figura.* Bad impression. That's not the Siena we want the world to see. So the police harass the prostitutes, and they come and work out here. They wait on the Cassia until a driver stops, and then they bring him to hidden places they know from . . ." He paused, not willing to tell her everything, she could see. "Places they know. Hiding places."

"What do you think happened to Robertino? Is he caught up in all this?"

"I don't know. People are on the move. It's all different now. Things are changing so fast."

They were silent for a moment.

"The stableman where Robertino works said he's unpopular. Is that why? Or because of his mother?"

"That and he has nine rival *contrade* breathing down his neck, and the *barbareschi* do sometimes sabotage each other."

"Really?"

"Palio madness. But I'm worried that it's more than that." His voice dropped, as if someone might be listening. "Did Banchi tell you about Robertino's father?"

"I thought he was an American GI."

"It's more convenient to say that. But there are people who remember the truth. He was a German. Even for a Nazi, he was not a good man. It's part of why Gina was tolerated, and not tolerated. She was so young. And why Robertino is . . . something of an outsider."

Scottie was furious. "But it's not his fault who his parents were!"

Carlo sighed, and she saw that there was a lot he wanted to say, but couldn't. "Your family, who you come from . . . It's not like in America. The Sienese are . . ." She remembered what he had said about not having friends in Siena. Instead of finishing the thought, he reached out and removed a twig from Scottie's hair. His eyes landed on hers at last. "If you're going to venture into the *macchia,* you should watch out for *cinghiali.*" *Cinghiali,* she knew, were the sharp-tusked local wild boar. Vicious. Ecco shifted in his arms and he broke their gaze, resumed the last of the quill pulling. "If you come face-to-face with the *cinghiale* you'll be sorry." But there was something more than that in his warning.

"Carlo." She was once again about to say, "I'm sorry for what I said the other day," but a plume of dust appeared along the road, and they turned and saw a black Alfa racing toward them.

"You didn't find her," Carlo said urgently. "I did."

Before she could protest, the cloud of dust enveloped them as the Alfa skidded to an unnecessarily dramatic stop.

Tenente Pisano got out of the car, his black boots shining.

"Signor Marchese," he said with great deference, then frowned at her. "Signora Messina?"

"Signora Messina is my tenant," said Carlo. "She's just come to talk about a problem with the apartment. She's not involved in . . . this. Gina is in there. There are drugs." He pointed to the tunnel in the *macchia*. "Any sign of Robertino in Siena?"

Pisano shook his head and looked reluctantly at the opening in the *macchia*. Scottie could see he did not want to sully his crisp uniform.

"Signor Tenente," Scottie said. "I'd like to help find Robertino in any way I can."

"How could you possibly help?" he snapped.

"I don't know. I was hoping you could tell me. I was *offering*."

"It's your fault we have drugs in Italy."

"My fault?"

"Yes. The Americans freed all the Mafiosi, and now they are making heroin. It's an abomination."

"Well, you can't possibly blame *me* for that!"

Attempting to maintain his dignity, Tenente Pisano crawled into the brush muttering an array of curses.

Carlo took the reins of his horse and moved off down the road. Scottie pushed the scooter alongside him.

"We grew up together," said Carlo, nodding over his shoulder at where the *tenente* had diappeared. "He's gotten very full of himself, but I believe he's still a good man. I would offer you a cup of tea, but I think you said something the other day about never wanting to see me again."

She blushed, but when she looked at him, he was laughing.

Oh God, she thought, feeling all her resolve start to disappear.

"I'm sorry," she said. "It's just . . ."

"I understand," he said quietly. "So I won't invite you. Unless . . ." He pointed to a cluster of tall pines. "Castello delle Castagne."

"A castle?"

"An exaggeration."

She very, very badly wanted to see Carlo's house. But she knew it would not stop there. And so did he. Carlo was handsome, kind, charming, intelligent, funny, tragic . . . and very romantic.

"I would love to, but I have to get back to Siena," she said.

Carlo gave a slight bow of acknowledgment. "Another time, then," he said. "Enjoy the Palio."

"I'll try, but I'm so worried about Robertino. If he knows who was giving her drugs . . ."

Carlo nodded. "That is why you saw nothing. Better to stay out of it."

She put Ecco safely onto the scooter.

"Thank you," she said, trying to put as much meaning into it as possible.

"Il piacere è stato tutto mio, gentile Signora Messina" — The pleasure was all mine — he said with grinning faux formality, then leaned down and picked up the largest of the quills, about eight inches long, striped in black and white like the town's cathedral, with a vicious point.

"Like the Sienese," he said with a grim smile, handing it to her carefully.

There was no time to change. With poor punctured Ecco on the seat in front of her like the figurehead on a ship, his ears pinned back in the wind, she buzzed back into Siena through Porta Tufi. She threaded her way through the narrow streets under festoons of laundry, and created a parking place by moving a trash bin in Piazza Mercato behind the Campo as the crowds came pouring out of the piazza. The evening *prova* was over, and the restaurants would be setting up as fast as magicians could make a rabbit appear. She pulled on gloves, rearranged her scarf and brushed the twigs out of her hair using the rearview mirror. She'd have to return the scooter tomorrow morning. There was nothing to do about the mud stains on the formerly crisp knees of her trousers. She sighed, snapped on Ecco's leash and walked up the stairs and into the piazza under the disapproving gaze of the saints on the Torre del Mangia.

I saw a dead body, she thought. *I saw a dead body, but I can't tell anyone. I mustn't get involved.*

As they crossed the piazza, Ecco stopped to be petted by an adoring trio of girls in white dresses and perfect little hats. She could feel the stares and hear the pointed chatter as she and Ecco arrived at Bar Nannini. Nothing in Siena went unnoticed by anyone. Would Tenente Pisano spread the word that *La Straniera* was hanging out roadside with *il marchese? Che figura,* she imagined they were whispering about her. She tried to stand tall. The scarf did a poor job of covering the dried mud, Ecco's blood and dog hair. She felt ashamed and at the same time resentful that she was supposed to be perfectly pressed all the time. She wanted to bark at the people at the surrounding tables.

Poor Michael was stepping out of the crowd to greet her, clearly alarmed. "What happened to you?"

She wished she could tell him everything. Why couldn't she? Because he would be even more worried than he already was. He would probably put her on the next ship back to America.

"I . . . I rented a scooter to take a drive in the country and I skidded out," she said.

"Oh, Scottie. The baby . . . You need to be careful. Are you okay?"

"I'm fine. And then Ecco ran off and came back with a faceful of porcupine quills. I'm sorry I'm late. It was kind of a terrible day."

The sad part was that she felt empowered by not telling him. Perhaps that was how he felt when describing his Rome trips simply as "boring." He listened to her highly edited story as the waiter, Paolo, showed them to a coveted table outside, Michael sipping his gin martini, his eyes on the parade of people passing their table. There was something a little thrilling about not telling, she realized. The power of secrets. But this thought also depressed her, with all its implications for her marriage, and the rest of her life with

262

this person.

A pack of young *contradaioli* in Snail neckerchiefs marched past chanting. Their energy made her feel flat in comparison.

"I brought you this," he said, handing her a large black box. "I went to Nina Ricci. If you don't like it, I'll exchange it."

She opened the box. It was the most absurd, fabulous little hat she had ever seen, a little cap of white feathers that came up to a saucy question point curl on top.

"It reminded me of Ecco's tail," said Michael.

"I love it," she said, thinking it was not something she would ever wear.

4.

Scottie was late and, when she arrived, a mess. She told him some crazy story about having rented a scooter and taken a drive outside the city. Not that he could blame her for wanting to escape — the drumming alone could drive a person to madness.

He wished he could tell her about the bizarre meeting with Duncan — secrets were so corrosive, he thought.

At least she seemed to like the hat.

5.

"I think I'd better have a vet look at Ecco," she said, sipping her Campari and soda, hoping it would change her mood. The dog was lying on the tufa-covered paving stones under their table, subdued at last, faint droplets of dried blood on his muzzle.

"Where's your bracelet?" Michael asked suddenly, staring at her wrist. "Oh, Scottie, you haven't lost it?"

"It must have fallen off when I crashed," she said. She realized Pisano would find it when he removed Gina's body. There would be questions. Would Carlo cover for her? She knew somehow that he would, that he would be her friend above all. That he was loyal.

The waiter arrived with a plate of crostini, an appetizer of little toasts.

Michael sighed and covered her hand with his. "I'll buy you another one," he said. "On the Ponte Vecchio. We'll go up to Florence soon and have lunch. Make a day of it. We'll get some baby things, too."

"How are tractor sales?" she asked as Paolo brought her another Campari and soda and another gin martini for Michael.

He shook his head. "Not great."

6.

Scottie said something in Italian to the dog about bones. When had she learned to speak Italian so well? It was highly impressive, though the Agency would not approve. It would be good for her to meet some other English-speaking wives. This mixing with the locals was not the norm for Agency spouses, but then Scottie did not know she was an Agency spouse. He felt guilty about all the nights he left her alone. Always, but especially when he was coming back to Siena from Rome, the taste of Duncan on his lips, he was ashamed of what he was, and angry that he had to hide behind her.

"Maybe you should invite Leona to come over, and you two could go down to Capri," he said. "Get out of the heat for a couple of weeks."

Leona. Only a few months ago they were so close, and now she felt like her former best friend would hardly know her, and Scottie wouldn't know what to say to her.

"I can't leave now. Not while we don't know what's happened to Robertino."

7.

Michael was trying so hard to be nice. He was right, of course, that she should get out of Siena for a bit. She was trying hard to find the one person besides Carlo who could ruin her marriage. If Robertino told Michael — or anyone — what he had seen at San Galgano . . . and yet she couldn't bear the idea that the boy might be in danger. He might not want to be her friend anymore, but she would continue to be his.

"Look," Michael said. "I know I've been away a lot, and you've been lonely. When we're in Florence, we'll sign you up for the American Women's Club, okay?"

She laughed a little, surprised. "Do you really see me as one of those corporate wives who lives in an English-only bubble and looks down on the 'natives'? Bridge, shopping, tea, art history lectures, a barbecue on the Fourth of July and a turkey at Thanksgiving to keep the American spirit alive?"

"Yes," he said, looking confused. "What's wrong with that?"

"Nothing," she said. *Everything,* she thought. "You're right," she said, lying.

She watched two rival squads of chanting *contradaioli* meet in the center of the square. It had been a strange, discombobulated day, yet she didn't want it to end.

"Let's get some dinner," he said.

"One more drink." Without waiting for Michael to agree, she waved to the waiter and ordered another Campari. She had no taste for it, had barely touched the second one, but she ordered it anyway, to keep them there. She moved her chair around so that she and Michael were sitting side by side, the piazza spread out before them like a stage.

The evening air felt good on her skin. She watched the *passeggiata* of people moving around the Campo, wishing she were one of them. She thought of Robertino, of Ugo, of Carlo, each so alive in his own way, and poor Gina, dead.

"I'd like to ride in the Palio," she said.

Michael smiled at her, confused. "It's not for women," he said.

The café lights were coming on, and the chairs around them were filling up with older people who preferred to sit and watch. Scottie could hear someone talking about Gaudenzia, a gray mare who had won three Palios in '54, when besides the traditional July and August races, the town had added a September event as part of the Pope's yearlong celebration of the Virgin.

"I know," she said. "But I want to do it anyway."

To her surprise, he didn't protest or condescend. He nodded.

Around a potted lemon came a waiter leading a petite woman in a pink dress, arm in arm with an older man with a short white beard who was wearing a pale blue plaid sports shirt tucked into olive green trousers. They were sharing a joke, the woman giggling. Michael, visibly surprised, said, "Julie?" The woman dropped the man's arm and gave Michael a confused half smile, her cheeks flushing.

"Nice to see you again," she said.

"This is my wife, Scottie." Julie gave Scottie a longer look. Scottie offered her hand politely.

Michael said, "Julie's married to a friend of mine from Yale."

"Duncan sent me off to do some sightseeing," Julie said, a little stiffly. "He's always trying to get rid of me. Tuscany is so beautiful. We've come to see the Palio." Michael looked at the older man, and Julie jumped in. "This is my guide, Signor Giannelli. Duncan said it wasn't safe to travel alone."

"True," said Michael. "He was absolutely right."

"Maybe we could have a table with a view of the tower," said Signor Giannelli smoothly to the waiter, who led them away to a farther table as Michael and Scottie gave a polite wave.

"Is this Duncan a close friend of yours?"

asked Scottie when they were out of earshot. Michael never talked about friends.

"He works at the embassy in Rome."

"Oh. She seems nice."

"Yes, well," said Michael, preoccupied, "I don't know her well. Look," he added. "You've had a long day and probably want a bath. Let's get a quick dinner and make it an early night."

As they stood up and left, Scottie could feel Julie's eyes on her.

8.

The sight of Julie was a shock. What was she of all people doing in Siena? Who was that Italian she was with? Could snooty little Julie have a lover? An older man, no less? He wondered if he should tell Duncan he had seen her, or let her tell him. It felt good to know something Duncan didn't.

If Duncan had sent Julie away now, why hadn't he invited Michael to stay longer? Why was he sitting here in Siena when they could have been dining now in a little place in Piazza del Popolo? Heading back for a night together, perhaps pulling the bed out onto the huge terrace with the potted lemon trees. Was Duncan lying there now, looking over the lights of the city? Was he alone? A flame of jealousy rose in him.

"She and her husband are terrible snobs," he told Scottie.

"I could tell," she said, and he loved her for it.

9.

They moved over to Ristorante Il Campo, where Signor Tommaso had saved a table for them with an excellent view of the milling crowds. Again she sat side by side with Michael rather than across from him, so that she could people-watch. At the table next to her, an older couple were also sitting side by side, arguing in a friendly way. She tried to eavesdrop, only to practice her Italian, she told herself. *Barbaresco, quattordici anni. Rapinato.* They were talking about Robertino, she realized in amazement. She tried to remember what *rapinato* meant — kidnapped?

She leaned closer, as if she were just resting on an arm of her chair. The couple did not seem to notice her listening. The man was owlish-looking, with sandy hair, thick glasses and a light plaid sport jacket. The woman had dark hair in a swinging bob and was dressed stylishly in what looked like Balmain.

"Scottie," said Michael.

She looked at him.

"Don't," he whispered.

She covered her mouth with her hand. "They're talking about Robertino."

"I heard they received one of his ears in the mail," said the woman to the man.

Scottie gasped. The couple turned and looked at her in surprise.

"I'm sorry," she said in Italian. "It's just that I hadn't heard that. Did that happen today?"

She could see that Michael was tongue-tied and embarrassed by her eavesdropping. How did he hope to succeed as a salesman if he was so shy?

The couple nodded at Scottie, visibly adjusting their expectations of the woman they had assumed was a tourist. "You speak Italian," they said approvingly. "But you are not Italian?"

"Siamo americani," she said, with a sigh. "I'm learning Italian from the missing boy, Robertino Banchi."

"Oh!" they said.

The waiter brought plates of velvety *pappardelle col sugo di lepre.* Ecco sat up, his nose twitching.

"You said *rapinato,"* Scottie said. "What makes you think he was kidnapped?"

"I heard that there was a ransom note," said the man, "but it may be a false rumor."

"Is that really true about the ear?" Scottie asked.

"Well . . . ," said the woman, her earrings dangling in the candlelight. "It's something I heard."

"He's not just my teacher, he's my friend. I went to the stable where he worked. I can't seem to get any information at all. I heard his mother . . . died."

Michael looked at her sharply.

"Drugs," she added.

Michael again shot her a look.

"Oh," said the woman. "Very sad."

"Probably a client gave them to her," said Scottie. "Or a pimp. Out there on the Cassia. Apparently the Mafia is making heroin." Michael's eyes widened.

The Italian man went on as Scottie listened, leaning forward in her chair.

"There have been other kidnappings," he said. "Sardi." He was referring to the new crop of immigrants from Sardinia who had moved in to fill positions as shepherds when local Tuscans like Ecco's previous owner fled to factory jobs in the northern cities of Milan and Turin. The Sienese looked with mistrust on the newcomers, and suspected them of every crime.

"Someone should talk to the Englishman," said the woman knowingly, adding sotto voce to Scottie, "The boy posed for an artist, an English lord. Sebastian Gordon."

"I didn't know that," said Scottie, also whispering. "Someone *should* talk to him."

"Listen, we're going for a *digestivo,*" said the man as he paid their bill. "Over in the Istrice *contrada.* Would you like to join us?"

Scottie looked at the swirl of people in the piazza. The noise was growing, and the drums had accelerated. Ecco had awakened and was staring up at her. Every *contrada* was known by a symbol — eagle, caterpillar, seashell, dragon. The Istrice, or porcupine, was Robertino's *contrada.* This couple were sophisticated and stylish and Italian, and they were talking to her, not talking down to her. They could be friends. They could help her find the boy.

All of Scottie's training told her to defer to her husband. But she knew he'd say no.

"We'd love to," she said. She didn't look at Michael, just rose up with a smile, leaving him to pay the bill and follow.

10.

As if running into Julie wasn't bad enough for one night, who was sitting at the table next to them at dinner? Rodolfo Marchetti, the Red journalist who was always bashing

273

all things American. Scottie, to Michael's shock, struck up a goddamn *conversation* with Marchetti and his wife. Then, to put a cherry on the sundae of his week, Scottie revealed to Marchetti she was actively looking for Robertino. And it was worse than that. Marchetti was writing a story on the disappearance of Robertino. He talked about Lord Sebastian Gordon, Luce's pal that Duncan had pointed out at the Borghese. Michael was terrified Marchetti would discover a connection between himself and Robertino and print something. Wild rumors were flying, and all he needed was a journalist sniffing around his door, with the arms shipment arriving any minute. Michael watched Scottie talk to Marchetti and his wife about Robertino as if she were goddamn Myrna Loy in the goddamn *Thin Man. How does she know all this?* was Michael's first thought, followed by *I recruited the son of a Nazi. His mother is a dead prostitute. Mafia. Drugs. Shit. Shit. Shit.*

11.

The couple's names were Rodolfo and Fiammetta. Fiammetta was from Milan, but Rodolfo was born here, in Siena, and the Istrice was his *contrada.* Scottie found them utterly charming.

They walked up Via Banchi di Sopra until they came upon an amazingly beautiful scene, like something out of a dream, she thought. The red, white, blue and black arabesques of the Porcupine *contrada*'s flags were draped from the buildings along the narrow street, barely wide enough for four people to stand shoulder to shoulder. Striped sconces on either side of every doorway held candles. A long, long table had been set up, an uninterrupted length of white tablecloth and a mixed assortment of chairs apparently borrowed from every kitchen in the area. It seemed to stretch for blocks. More candles in huge candelabras lit the table, and abundant wine bottles with the porcupine logo were interspersed with large baskets of bread. People were just beginning to sit down, greeting each other with boisterous *ciao*s and pouring the wine. They all wore neckerchiefs with the Istrice logo on them.

Scottie hesitated, feeling they were intruding, but Rodolfo cheerily towed them all forward.

"He loves showing it all off," said Fiammetta. "Sienese pride, you know."

"Venite, venite," said a woman Scottie recognized as the old woman with the broom they had seen the day they arrived in

Siena. She had seen her since then, scurrying around Signor Banchi's house, though she would never look at or talk to Scottie. Banchi called her Nonna Bea, and so, it seemed, did everyone else. For the special occasion Nonna Bea had donned a slighter lighter shade of black.

"Is Signor Banchi coming tonight?" Scottie asked her.

The old woman shook her head as if the idea were absurd.

"We have American guests," said Rodolfo to a huge burly man in a spattered chef's apron, the *capitano* of the *contrada*. People were staring at them.

The man gave them a broad smile. "Welcome to Istrice!" Immediately they found themselves seated near the head of the table. As women began to appear out of arched doorways carrying huge steaming plates of tortelli with butter and sage, the captain of the *contrada* took his place at the head of the table. Scottie tried to say they had already eaten, but the women with the trays of pasta were unstoppable, and she found herself digging into a second dinner as the toasts began. First there was a long, laughing discussion of the benefits of being a porcupine, which ended with a ribald joke about sex. Scottie felt herself blush.

"Can you follow all this?" asked Michael.
"Yes," she said. "Most of it."

There followed some more in-jokes about the *contrada*'s alliances with Bruco (Caterpillar), Chiocciola (Snail) and Civetta (Owl), and their arch rivalry with Lupa (Wolf), with whom they shared a boundary. As if on cue, some wolf howls from a distant rooftop could be heard. The Istriciani booed them merrily.

Drummers marched through, the percussion almost unbearable in the enclosed space, and then flag wavers, all teenage boys in bright medieval costume. A rather uncomfortable-looking man in a suit of armor accepted a plate of pasta from Nonna Bea but could not sit down.

The voices of the noisy diners echoed off the stone streets and brick buildings, and Scottie felt the wine going to her head. The candles seemed brighter and the laughter louder. She hoped Michael wasn't too angry she had dragged him here.

At a seemingly preappointed and highly anticipated moment, the captain of the *contrada* stood up and banged his glass for silence. Amazingly, the crowd quieted. A dog barked somewhere in the distance. Ecco, at her feet, pricked his ears. The crowd seemed to hold its breath, and then the captain opened his arms and began to sing. *"Nessun dorma! Nessun dorma . . ."* A woman with long black ringlets appeared behind him, playing the violin.

His voice was perfect, and Scottie felt the hairs on her neck and arms go up.

"Tu pure, o Principessa, nella tua fredda stanza, guardi le stelle che tremano d'amore, e di speranza!"

It felt like he was singing to her: "Oh princess, in your cold room, look at the stars that tremble with love and hope!"

Michael, too, seemed enraptured by the man's voice and by his words. She was oddly moved to see him caught up in the music, as if she had found something deeply human in him at last. A way in. She took his hand, and he squeezed hers.

"Ma il mio mistero è chiuso in me; il nome mio nessun saprà! No, no! Sulla tua bocca lo dirò quando la luce splenderà!" My secret is locked inside me; no one knows my name. No, no! To your mouth I will tell it when the light shines!

I've never been more alive in my entire life, thought Scottie.

"All'alba vincerò . . . vincerò . . . vin- ceeeeeeeerò!"

The crowed erupted in screams of ecstasy. Children pounded the table with their fists.

Men leapt up and surrounded the captain, thumping him on the back.

"That was something," said Michael. Scottie laughed at the understatement.

Next up was an entire roast pig, carried out by four men and carved to great cheers, followed by a speech by a man introduced as Acting Mayor Vestri. He must be the one who had stepped in when the other mayor, Manganelli, had his fatal car accident. Scottie studied the man as he delivered a paean to honor and glory. He was a sharp contrast to Ugo — in his sixties, she guessed, thin and bent slightly like a shrimp, wearing a black suit and red tie. He had jowls, a short straight line of a mouth, large, thick glasses and a high-pitched, nasal voice. There was something oily about him. He looked corrupt.

"I'd love to meet the mayor," Michael said to Rodolfo.

Rodolfo called Vestri over after his speech, and Michael introduced himself. "I have a Ford tractor business here in town," he said.

Vestri studied Michael with his little eyes. "You are Sicilian?" he asked cautiously.

"My parents," said Michael. "I'm from New York."

"New York!" crowed the man, and grasped his hand. "We are always excited about doing business with America. Come see me sometime."

"I'll see you tomorrow morning," Michael said. Vestri smiled, his hooded eyes dancing with what Scottie realized was greed. *This is how men work,* she thought. *It's deals and handshakes. Backscratching.* Of course, on some level she had always known it, but she had never imagined Michael in this world. It impressed her to see this new side of him.

Each member of the Palio team was introduced except for the horse, who they said was sleeping, which Scottie doubted since he was stabled only a few doors down from the ruckus. The jockey was hailed as a gift from God, and his praises sung. He was cautioned against taking bribes, which he solemnly swore to ignore on the soul of his mother. He was guarded by three men who let no one get near him.

"They're serious, aren't they," said Michael, leaning across to Rodolfo. "A rival *contrada* might get to him? Hurt him?"

"They're not as much afraid of him being hurt as being bribed," said Rodolfo. "It's all part of the game. Secret emissaries sneak around all night, tossing messages tied to rocks, sending cash hidden in women's bras, all in order to throw the race."

"Isn't it more fun just to let the best horse

win?" asked Scottie.

They all shook their heads at that.

"Oh, honey," said Michael.

12.

Michael felt off balance all night, trapped in a funhouse mirror. He stared at the acting mayor, Vestri. This was the man he had to give fifty thousand dollars to. And Marchetti — the journalist he had to either flip for real or hide from in plain sight. He hadn't had to find them, befriend them, because Scottie had done it all for him, without even meaning to.

13.

A small, wiry red-haired kid was at last produced. *Il barbaresco,* they announced. The groom. Rather than universal cheers, there was some grumbling. Scottie thought he looked a little devious. Had he somehow gotten Robertino out of the picture?

"I know we are all praying for the safe return of Robertino Banchi," said the captain, quieting the unruly crowd. "But in the meantime, we must support the boy who has volunteered to take his place." The groom smiled and waved and slunk off to chat with the men standing and smoking off to the side, clearly not sorry at all to be in this honored position at the expense of the missing boy.

Scottie's eye caught Nonna Bea on the edge of the crowd. She was staring at the groom. She lurched forward and limped up to him and started screaming in his face.

"Vergognati! Vergognati!" For shame! She jabbed a bony finger into his chest. At first the crowd was surprised into silence, then started laughing. Embarrassed, the groom shouted back at Nonna Bea, who was not letting up.

"Shut up! Shut up! *Zitta!*" he screamed.

Scottie felt Michael stiffen next to her. She gathered Ecco under her arm.

The crowd found the groom's shouting disrespectful, but the boy took their silence for approval and raised his fist to strike Nonna Bea. At this, a mass of men went for him, then started punching each other. Chairs were overturned. Women screamed, but also egged on their men.

"Let's go," said Michael, grabbing Scottie's arm.

Scottie shook him off and grabbed Nonna Bea with her free hand and pulled her out of the mix as she tried to kick at the groom.

"Signora, stop," said Scottie. Ecco was barking and squirming.

"Never!" shouted the old woman. "He was

jealous of Robertino! What have you done?"
she shouted at the boy.

Someone lurched toward Scottie, and Michael reacted with a move so quick she couldn't quite figure out what he did. The other man was suddenly lying on his back, breathless.

Again Michael pulled at Scottie. "For God's sake," he said. "Let's go."

There were whistles and more shouting, and a trio of *carabinieri,* led by Tenente Pisano, arrived at a run.

He unholstered his pistol and fired into the air.

"I hate the Palio," Scottie heard him mutter as she slunk past him, avoiding his eye.

14.

"Tractor parts?" asked Brigante, startling Michael. The rain was pounding on the metal roof of the warehouse. What was he doing here? Wasn't Palio Day a local goddamn holiday for everyone? Except, of course, Brigante wasn't Sienese; he was from Milan. He wouldn't give a hoot about the Palio. The arms cache had been delivered last night while the city drank and sang, six crates stenciled ATTREZZATURA AGRICOLA — agricultural equipment. Under a layer of radiators and carburetors were disassembled machine guns and packets of explosives that looked like innocent modeling clay of the type he had made his mother a crèche from as a child.

Michael had no idea how the crates had gotten through customs, or if some boat had just unloaded them at night. Someone was certainly bribed, he thought. Even though he knew a disassembled gun could not shoot, they still felt dangerous to him.

"Yes," said Michael. "Tractor parts."

"So you're a mechanic, too?"

"No. I'll sell these to mechanics."

"Oh. Have you ever visited a prostitute?" asked Brigante, leaning in the doorway and lighting a cigarette. Italians smoked incessantly, even more than Americans.

"What? No," said Michael.

"That's what I thought. But if you decide to try it, there's a new girl who stands in a pullout on the road to Grosseto who is fantastic. She's from Naples. They know things down there."

"Aren't you worried about diseases?"

"I dip my dick in grappa afterwards. There are boys, too."

"What?"

"I'm not saying you like boys, or I like boys. Heaven forbid. But there are boys."

"Don't the police do anything?"

Brigante laughed. "Of course not," he said. "The police and the politicians are the best customers." He ducked back out into the rain, protecting his cigarette with his hand.

Michael wondered if Brigante knew something. Was Brigante a spy himself? He had a flash of hitting Brigante over the head with the butt of a machine gun, burying his body.

Jesus, he thought. *Making the world safe for democracy is a goddamn hard job.*

He planned to bury the arms cache in a forest, making sure no one was around and marking the spot on his map with an X, like the pirate's treasure maps in the books his brother had read him when he was little. Marco was both unbearably kind and unbearably cruel to the point where Michael, even looking back, could not distinguish between the two.

"You and me, we're going to get out of here and have adventures," his brother had said, sitting on the edge of his bed, seeming so grown up, sixteen to Michael's four. The rumble of the Third Avenue El made the water in Michael's glass shake. "Like Jim Hawkins."

"I can really come, too?" Michael said.

"Sure. Somebody's gotta swab the decks

and clean the parrot cage." Marco laughed.

Marco joined the army the morning after Pearl Harbor, and sent vivid letters home until a German bullet ripped through him on January 20, 1944, about two hundred miles south of where Michael was now standing, shovel in hand, crates of guns and explosives under his feet, cached in preparation for the next war.

He wished his brother were here now, so he could ask him if he had ever questioned his orders, if he ever had a moment's doubt. Though, Michael thought with a smile, he would probably dunk his head in the toilet for asking.

Intermezzo

Thunderstorms turned the sky shades of gray so dark it looked black and blue, as if bruised. In the stormy wet chaos and sodden, steaming crowds of Palio Day, no one — or so he thought — noticed an American with a briefcase joining the acting mayor briefly in the window of a building overlooking Piazza del Campo owned by Monte dei Paschi, the venerable bank. All the Catholic dignitaries of the city were there, enjoying the seven-hundred-year-old race held in honor of the Virgin Mary. Tradition, religion, celebration. The semblance of "always." Had the American's wife looked across the piazza at that moment, she might have recognized her husband in his aviator sunglasses, pale linen suit and white Borsalino. As the mayor and the American stared out at the jubilant crowds enduring the hours-long *Corteo Storico,* a parade of drummers, archers, flag bearers, trumpeters, *contrada* floats, and the *carroccio* pulled by oxen carrying the Palio banner, a bolt of lightning cracked above the Torre del Mangia. At that moment, a briefcase changed hands. It was that simple.

After that, the American left the gates of the city and, in pouring rain, drove to the abandoned *zona industriale.* He backed his Ford Fairlane through the large doors into the showroom of his office. He waited until no one — or so he thought — would notice him loading large wooden crates into the spacious trunk. No tractors would be sold today.

The American drove out into the countryside. When the rain stopped and the sky turned blue again, he pulled off the road in a secluded spot. Removing his pale linen suit and hat, he donned coveralls and took a shovel from the trunk. He dug a deep hole in the rain-softened earth, sweating in the summer heat and swatting at mosquitoes and small biting flies. He carefully placed the crates in the hole, covered it up, washed his hands and face with two bottles of Acqua Panna he had brought with him, and changed back into his suit.

The Palio went to Aquila, the Eagle.

Ten:
La Tartuca, The Tortoise

"STRENGTH AND CONSTANCY ENJOINED"

July 3, 1956

1.

Scottie made toast and eggs for Michael, who was reading his newspaper in silence. *Why do girls swoon over the idea of marriage?* she thought. *Because they're fed a pack of lies about what it is.* She was worried about him, but had no idea how to say that without compromising his masculinity, making him feel like she had seen weakness. At the Palio dinner he had thrown that man down like a rag doll, but then tossed and turned all night. He had spent the day at his office, even though she pointed out that it was very unlikely anyone would buy a tractor on Palio Day. Maybe he was furious about the brawl the night before. But how would she know, if he never said anything? She wished

289

she could pry open his head and see inside.

"That English lord that Rodolfo and Fiammetta mentioned — he might know where Robertino is."

Michael put his paper down. "I know you're worried about him, but I don't think it's a good idea for you to be looking for Robertino," he said. "Look at what happened the other night. It's the job of the police."

Another plank in the corral he was building around her. But she was a jumper.

"I just wish I could help," she said.

He looked down at the butter on his plate. "You're so kind. Like Elsie," he said. "Beautiful, sweet and kind."

"Are you comparing me to a cow on a milk bottle?"

The phone rang, and Michael answered it. He brightened up, told someone he couldn't make it but he knew Scottie would love to go. He hung up and turned to her, his face bright and uncomplicated for once.

"That was Carlo Chigi Piccolomini. He's going to Florence for the day and invited us along."

Scottie tried to control her expression. "You told him I would go?"

"Yes. You need a day away. It will be fun."

She turned so he couldn't see her face,

and said, "Yes. Maybe I'll sign up for that American Women's Club while I'm there."

2.

A telegram had been delivered for him, and he was eager to get her out the door so he could decode it. He needed to keep her busy. And safe from everything that was happening.

And then Marchese Carlo Chigi Piccolomini telephoned and invited them to Florence for the day. It was perfect. Scottie would be safely out of Siena, off the Robertino trail, and would strengthen their friendship with a nobleman known to be friendly to the American cause. She was proving incredibly useful to him, without even meaning to. He wished he was better at telling her that. He felt a sort of grateful relief to Scottie for being so . . . prosaic. With everything that was happening, he'd so much rather be in her head, thinking about Gucci's new bamboo bag or the eighteen-carat gold rope sandals Ferragamo had just custom-made for a special client. *She is like that cow in the ads,* he thought — *beautiful, sweet, reliable and uncomplicated.* When he had tried to tell her that, she had taken it completely the wrong way. He was sorry now he'd ever doubted his decision to marry her. It would be lonely here without a wife. He had grown fond of her. The way she had tried to save the old woman during that horrible, terrifying melee. It was sweet that she was worried about the boy. Of course she was — it was the right thing to do. His beautiful wife, the mother of his child. He handed her a small stack of bills he had taken from the briefcase. *That's not stealing,* he told himself. *That's hardship pay.*

"Replace the bracelet you lost," he said. "And get to know the marchese," he added, heading out the door. "He sounds like a very good sort."

3.

Michael went off to work, and she went out to do some food shopping to fill the time before Carlo arrived, to make it go faster. A day with Carlo. She tried to stay calm, tell herself it meant nothing.

It was the morning after the Palio, and the entire city felt subdued and slightly hungover. She had watched the hours-long parade and the minute-and-a-half race from her window, feeling almost guilty about having such amazing front-row seats when there were thousands and thousands of people packed into the square below. She did love seeing the horses snorting and tossing their heads, and her tears flowed as they raced three times around the square, lean and beautiful and out of control, but the whole event felt slightly anticlimactic after the riot of the *contrada* dinner.

Robertino should be here, she thought. Without him, the whole thing felt muted and pointless.

The famous gray mare Gaudenzia had run for the Giraffe, coming a close second to the Eagle *contrada.* Scottie admired the rough beauty of the cranky mare, who kept her ears back and took care of herself on the slick, dangerous track. She seemed to know her job and, except for a slight jostling on the last turn, could have won with or without her jockey.

Now it was all over until August 16, when the second and final Palio of the year would be run. She hoped Robertino would be back by then. She hoped he was alive.

"Ci sono notizie del barbaresco scomparso?" Scottie asked the owner of the fruit and vegetable store — an unusually tall woman with a long nose and sharp eyes, married to a short, round man, neither of whom ever spoke to Scottie beyond the most basic pleasantries — for news of the missing groom.

The woman shook her head but, to Scottie's surprise, took her hand. "You are American," she said. "You have connections. Make the police do something for a change."

Scottie nodded. "I'll try," she said, feeling a slight thrill.

"Grazie, signora," said the woman. "Such a kind and lovely woman you are."

Ecco dragged her toward the *macelleria,* where the butcher tossed him chunks of raw meat as he served the customers ahead of her.

The lord was the piece that didn't fit for her. How would Robertino have met an English lord? It was true that the Brits had been coming on the Grand Tour since the late 1800s, and now they were beginning to buy up property that was being abandoned by people like Ecco's former owners. There was a large and ever-growing colony of the English in Tuscany, but she didn't see them stopping by Signor Banchi's farmhouse. At a hotel?

Ecco sat and stared as Scottie looked over the cuts of beef. Whatever she chose would be beautifully wrapped in brown paper and tied with a string, as if it were a gift — this was the routine in every shop, even if you bought a box of aspirin at the *farmacia.* At first she had thought of it as wasteful —

why not just toss it in a bag, like at home? — but now she found the whole thing quite charming, a sign of the pride Italians took in what they sold.

"Buongiorno, Signor Gracci," she said to the owner, keeping her eyes on his face and not on his bloodstained apron. *"Vorrei due bistecche di vitello."*

"Certo, signora," he said. *"Subito."* He showed her some lovely veal. *"Chianina,"* he said. "I hear you are looking for Robertino," he added. *"Che brava donna.* What a good woman. The police, they have already forgotten about him. His *contrada* has replaced him. But you Americans, you do not turn your backs on a child so easily."

Word was traveling fast, Scottie thought with a slight chill.

4.

As soon as he got to the office, he opened his briefcase and took out the telegram to decode.

Rosini has reported break-in and theft of membership list to Siena police, who have notified Italian Secret Service. Destroy any connection and cease all contact with your asset. Maximum deniability essential. If asset's loyalty in doubt, eliminate.

Robertino was the asset. They were asking

him to eliminate Robertino? But why had it taken Rosini so long to notice the theft? There was something else going on here that he couldn't understand, something in this masquerade he wasn't seeing.

If asset's loyalty in doubt, eliminate.

Kill Robertino? He couldn't imagine actually killing a man, much less a boy. Yes, his Agency training had covered both self-defense and assassinations, but there was a difference between reading about something and . . . doing it.

On the other hand, if Robertino were gone for good it would solve a lot of problems for him. And he was now in for a pound, as it were.

5.

A day with Carlo. She had put her hair in pink plastic curlers held in place with sharp metal clips to get the wave just right, and now she sprayed it into place with Helene Curtis Spray Net and covered it with a polka-dot-patterned scarf for the car ride. She shaved her legs and armpits after putting a new blade in her heavy metal Lady Gillette razor, plucked and penciled her eyebrows using an eyebrow stencil, curled her lashes and waxed her upper lip. Painted her nails and toes with two coats of Peggy

Sage Spice Pink. Applied Revlon's thick, creamy ivory liquid foundation, Michel flesh-colored powder that came in a huge pink can with a large pouf, brushed on a light shimmer of Max Factor eyeshadow, drew on the latest "wing" effect with her eyeliner, applied Maybelline mascara to her upper lashes, and brushed on very light rose rouge to the "apple" of her cheek. Coty Dahlia Pink creamy lipstick from a golden case, finessed into a "smile" shape. Joy by Jean Patou eau de toilette. Taylor-Woods fifty-four-gauge stockings, Warners garters, underwear, cinch brassiere and the hated girdle. Just another day being female, she thought.

Up until age twelve, life had been simple. She had tumbled out of bed in the mornings, thrown on dungarees and a T-shirt, gathered her hair into a ponytail, pulled on paddock boots and been on her way to the stable within ten minutes of waking.

Because her mother was gone, it had been her Aunt Ida who'd intervened on a Christmas visit. "You have to wear these now," she'd said, dropping onto the bed a set of stiff, scratchy, reinforced garments made of thick white padding covered with white nylon lace. There were braces and straps and snaps, like the pony's cart harness.

"Why?" Scottie had asked.

"Because you've started to jiggle," she said. "And we can't have that. Only whores jiggle." She pronounced it "hewers."

As Ecco slept on the bath mat, Scottie pulled on dress shields to protect against perspiration, then two petticoat half-slips, and the short-sleeved ivy-patterned cotton dress she'd bought at Bendel's before leaving New York. She added rose earrings, a daisy-pattern necklace, a bracelet made of coins and another of laughing Buddhas, and her gold snaffle-bit Duval watch, slipped into the Dolcis red high heels that bit into her toes, and pulled on summer-weight white cotton gloves and a light duster and sunglasses.

She did not stop to ask herself if she was dressing up to make herself look good for Carlo, or if this was all a layer of protection from him, a way of hiding her true, vulnerable self under an armor of makeup and layers of clothing and hard metal jewelry. She simply grabbed her purse, traded the scarf for the new white feather hat Michael had given her, and left.

6.

I am trained to kill. Michael studied his face in the mirror. The bathroom attached to his office was small, but at least it was private — he didn't have to worry about Brigante barging in, unzipping and unleashing a prodigious manly stream into some ghastly urinal while chitchatting about a soccer team. *Though I am also trained to affect a French accent and wiretap a houseplant, neither of which I do very well.*

He ran a hand over his cheek. He had shaved carefully, as he did every morning, with a new blade, but even now his inexorable, irrepressible beard was forcing its way to the surface again. He hated the way his face darkened as the day wore on — by five p.m. each day he did look like a killer, or at least someone shady enough to rob your grandmother. He sighed and turned to the shelf where he kept a spare Dopp kit. He washed his face carefully to remove the grit that ruined the blade. Then he dampened a washcloth with water as hot as he could stand and held it to his face for three minutes, as the latest issue of *Esquire* had advised. When his beard was softened, he lathered up and shaved again, stripping off the criminal shadow and restoring the appearance of youth and innocence.

Some days he shaved four times. Occasionally he wondered what it would be like to simply give in and let his beard grow.

But even at Yale, where some slovenly types had advertised their commitment to their studies with bristled cheeks during finals, he had shaved every day, feeling that even a minor crack in the façade he presented to the world might lead to skipping naked across the quad reciting nursery rhymes, as an unstable classmate had done after a difficult semester.

He took a step back and admired the clothes he had chosen today, and composed a brief description of his look in the louche, knowing style that *Esquire* had defined as the male voice of the era: *This dashing spy sports a lustrous chestnut-over-sand windowpane plaid silk shantung jacket with a contrasting sapphire lining and pocket square, just the thing for a day of espionage and intrigue. The caramel Dacron boxy sport shirt has short sleeves to stay cool in the most torrid of climes, while the generous cut of the charcoal slacks could hide any number of weapons. His two-tone loafers are perfect for a quick escape, while his jaunty black straw Trilby is enlivened with a peacock-pattern grosgrain band and secret listening device that lets him foil dastardly plans while still looking sharp.*

Whatever happened, at least he would look good.

She and Ecco found the robin's egg blue Fiat parked just outside Porta Camollia. Carlo was leaning against it, smoking a cigar. He was wearing a stylish blue suit and a crisp white shirt with a red tie. Though in his playful moments Carlo could look like a little boy, he definitely looked like a man now.

"Carlo," she called. He looked up and smiled. He greeted her in the Italian fashion, a kiss on each cheek. She could smell his wonderful mix of horse and tobacco and tweed.

"I didn't recognize you two," he said, laughing, opening the car door for her and for Ecco, who jumped in. "That hat!" She blushed, self-conscious.

"Do you have business in Florence?" she asked, settling into the passenger seat.

"Bookstores. I'm desperate for something fresh to read."

"Why not shop here?"

Again that shadow on his face. "I prefer Florence," he said. "Better selection. Any sign of Robertino?"

"No. He would never have missed the Palio."

Carlo nodded, looking worried.

They drove down the winding road to the

301

valley floor, then picked up the Via Cassia heading north. They passed the hilltop cluster of buildings that comprised the walled town of Monteriggioni, and then Scottie saw the turnoff for Poggibonsi, where Carlo's son had died. She glanced at him, but his face displayed nothing. They passed Barberino Val d'Elsa, and Casole d'Elsa, huge towers and castles and imposing ancient stone.

"Do you know Lord Sebastian Gordon?" she asked.

"Not well, but yes. He's taking credit for getting Italian luxury brands recognition overseas. He does public relations for Gucci, I think."

"Robertino posed for him. Do you think he might know where Robertino is?"

Carlo considered this. "He might."

Carlo was not flirting, which was a relief. Maybe they could just spend the day together as friends. That was what Carlo had wanted, after all. A friend.

Florence was crowded — it felt like everyone in the world had decided to spend the summer of '56 there. Colorful flocks of laughing young men in loose, boxy shirts and women wearing scarves and big sunglasses swooped over the cobblestones on

Vespas past Scottie and Ecco and Carlo, and at least half of the people they passed were speaking something other than Italian — French, American English, English English, with the majority speaking German. Carlo joked about the latest "German invasion," but there was an undertone of slight alarm among the Italians, she thought — though this onslaught of West Germans came to soak up sun and spend, not to conquer.

"Neither Italians nor Germans ever seem to mention the war," Scottie said cautiously as they strolled along the Arno. She didn't want to bring up his painful past, but it seemed awkward to ignore it, too.

Carlo sighed. "Yes. Perhaps we all pretend that it never happened."

"That's understandable."

"Everyone wants to forget the bad years and embrace the *benessere,*" he said. "You know that phrase?"

"Yes. Well-being."

"We want to be like your hat. Stylish, amusing, light as air. I have some banking to do. I will meet you in front of David in an hour, okay?"

She nodded. It was all very innocent, just two friends having a day in the city.

Ecco was enjoying the Florentine smells

as she made her way to the Ponte Vecchio to look for a new bracelet. She remembered how Michael had told her this was the only bridge the Germans didn't detonate as they retreated from the advancing Allies. Now that she knew what the Americans had done, she saw it all in a different light. *They should hate us,* she thought. *But then we liberated them, too. And now we're rebuilding their country. It's all so complicated.* She studied the fabulous old covered span and its row of shops jutting improbably over the Arno. She chose the first bracelet that was hawked at her and headed back into the city center, feeling like the *Queen Mary* being towed by tiny tugboat Ecco through dense crowds.

As she passed a medieval palace adorned with heavy iron dragons, she glanced up at the sign: GUCCI. Carlo had said that Lord Sebastian Gordon did public relations for Gucci. Before going in she paused to gather her nerve. Fancy stores had always intimidated her.

She stood in the massive doorway. Something about the way the dark-haired, chicly coiffed saleswomen looked at her made her feel like they knew she was faking it. She had felt so right, so strong leaving the apartment this morning, but now she saw that her gloves already had a stain on them, and her stockings had a run starting. The veneer was chipping away and the real her poking through. Still, she and Ecco made their way into the store.

"Excuse me," she said to a woman in a chignon and pencil skirt folding scarves under a ceiling frescoed with angels. "Is Lord Sebastian Gordon here today?"

"He does not work in the *shop,* madam." The woman feigned horror at how inappropriate the very idea was. "He has a studio of his own in Via dei Cimatori. Number 6."

And then Ecco began to make that horrible whomp-whomp-whomp sound . . .

"No no no!" shouted the enraged saleswomen, rushing toward them. Scottie tried to drag Ecco away, but he retched up a pile of grass-flecked chunky yellow vomit on Gucci's pristine white marble floor. Scottie spotted last night's peas and bread crusts in the mess.

"Mi dispiace," she shouted in apology as the saleslady cursed her roundly. Her face was red as she escaped and clomped away, dragging poor Ecco behind her, nearly twisting an ankle on the cobblestones in her precarious, painful red heels.

The wave of shame was followed by anger.

Go to hell, she thought. The poor dog was just being sick.

She stalked off in a rage, unaware of where she was going. Florence suddenly felt hot and dark and ominous, all appearance and deception, omnipresent laundry strung between iron balconies that hung from bullet–riddled façades. A group of young men leaning up against a Cinzano ad papered to the wall catcalled at her, making rude gestures. Ecco growled and strained at his leash, and the men sneered and laughed. She and Ecco turned abruptly into a narrow side street. She looked up and saw she was in Via dei Cimatori. She took a deep breath. She would steel herself and hunt down Gordon. She would have something to tell Carlo when she met him in a few minutes.

She rang the bell at number 6, admiring the heavy iron door handle shaped like a horse head. No one answered.

Disappointed, Scottie walked slowly back toward Piazza della Signoria. Everything felt like a dead end.

Under the statue of David, pigeons circling overhead, Carlo's face lit up when he saw her, and she suddenly felt right again. An old woman selling scarves held an armful out to them as Scottie wordlessly took

Carlo's offered arm. *"Per sua bella ragazza."* For your beautiful girl.

Memories of their afternoon at San Galgano flitted across her consciousness. The feel of his hands on her body. His mouth on hers. It was as if her belly and breasts were not swelling with the child, but with something else that was growing inside her.

8.

Michael sat in his office, reading the paper and writing a report to send to Rome. He hoped Scottie was having a good day in Florence. On one of his visits to Rome, Duncan had pressed him, and Michael had confessed that he was not exactly "doing his duty" with regard to Scottie.

"She's pregnant!" Michael protested, glancing around the bar to make sure no one was listening. "You're not supposed to be in . . . there . . . when they're pregnant, are you?" He hated these conversations — they felt so disloyal to Scottie, and God knows they were embarrassing — but Duncan loved them. He loved to tease Michael.

"You have seen Klimt's *Beethoven Frieze* illustrating the *Ode to Joy* in Vienna? One of the figures is a pregnant woman in a beautiful skirt, her naked breasts distended and her naked belly huge, her wrists in golden jeweled cuffs. She is surrounded by red-haired sexualized sirens who seem to be in a state of perpetual orgasm, and she gazes at a comical huge brown hairy beast with buttons for eyes."

"And? What does Klimt have to do with us?"

Duncan laughed and sipped his martini. "They say she is meant to symbolize wantonness. Back in 1902, it was one of the most scandalous images ever exhibited. Can't you picture the nice Viennese ladies fainting at the sight of it?"

"Yes. I feel faint myself."

"No one wants to see a pregnant woman as a sexual being. It violates something primal in us. But there's something you should know. They want sex when they're pregnant. They crave it."

Michael realized he had no idea whether Duncan was lying to him or not. Sex was the part of marriage that was hardest for him. He felt terrible about this, wondered if Scottie noticed anything wrong.

He hoped she was buying herself something nice in Florence.

9.

"I went to Gordon's office, but he wasn't there." Scottie and Carlo were walking across another bridge toward the Oltr'arno side of the city, one bridge down from the Ponte Vecchio, scooters zooming past them. The river was broad and placid, with several fishermen down in the current, and shorebirds wading in the shallows.

"I know where he lives. You could stalk your prey to ground."

"He doesn't have a telephone?"

"Out in the country? I doubt it."

Scottie considered this. "Would it be terribly rude to just show up there?"

"I don't think so," he said. "Why don't we stop on our way home?"

Home. She didn't want this day to end. They'd been avoiding each other's eyes all day, pretending to be people who did not think the things they were thinking. They were good people who loved their spouses no matter what their flaws were. That was what marriage was. Loyalty. Absolute loyalty to someone else.

"One thing I want to do before we go," he said. They strolled arm in arm, and she could feel the heat of his skin through the jacket sleeve. He pointed out the Pitti Palace and the Boboli Gardens with wry asides about Savonarola and Dante and the Medicis. But he wasn't a lecturer like Michael — he asked her about things. "Do you find that building harmonious? What do you think that woman thinks she looks like? Where in America is your favorite place of all?" She was laughing, chatting, relaxed, telling him about her evil childhood pony, and her father's addiction to baby lamb chops. But always, there was an undercurrent of electricity.

"Sometimes I wonder if my memories are even memories at all, or just things I wish happened," she said.

Carlo told her about something called *Sehnsucht.* It was a German word that he said had no real equivalent in English or Italian. "A pervasive sense of longing," he said to her. "A yearning for something lost, but something you never really had."

"Like white Christmases?"

"Yes. And it can be cultural as well as personal. England between the wars. America's longing for a West where cowboys kept you safe."

He led her through a warren of narrow streets to a small doorway that led to an even smaller upholstery shop that also had every size and shape of lamp shade, from tiny to enormous. She slipped Ecco's leash over the iron hook outside the door, and he drank from the small dish beneath it. Carlo dropped her arm and talked to the owner

310

while she wandered the aisles, admiring beautifully fringed pillows and bolts of brocade and striped silks, tassels and braid. She wandered all the way to the back of the shop.

Carlo found her there. "Ready?" he asked.

"No," she said softly, and took his hand. She pulled him close, and they kissed. She could hear the shopkeeper moving about up front. *Just one more kiss,* she thought, leaning into him, her knees weak.

She heard the front door jingle, and a voice call out, "Carlo, I'm running out to get a coffee. Watch the shop, would you?"

Carlo's *sì* was hoarse.

He engulfed her with his arms, his chest. She floated on a wave, higher, higher, higher, hoping the crest never came.

10.

Trying to sniff out if the theft had been tied to Robertino, and if Robertino had been tied to him beyond just his lessons with Scottie, Michael called Rodolfo and invited him to lunch on the pretext of asking him to explain the current agricultural situation. If things went well, he would bring out the contract in his briefcase offering Rodolfo a few thousand dollars a month in exchange for articles that were pro-Catholic and pro-

311

America. Just a little PR, he would say. Laying the groundwork for doing business here.

"I don't really understand what this strike is about," Michael confessed in complete honesty as they sat down outdoors at Ristorante Papei in Piazza del Mercato. Though the fish market had ended by ten, a faint whiff of *pesce* floated on the hot air, reminding him of Fridays at home with his parents and making him slightly nauseated. The papers were full of news about an ongoing strike of agricultural workers. As the ostensible owner of a tractor franchise, Michael felt it was part of his cover to be fluent in farm issues, but instead of simple talk about weather and crop yields, as it was back home, the news here was all a mass of acronyms: CSIL, CGIL, UNI. Michael longed for an encyclopedia of Italian culture so that he would not have to ask stupid questions. On the other hand, in this case a stupid question was a way to get Rodolfo to open up to him.

Before they could proceed with lunch, there was the obligatory verbal sparring between Rodolfo and the waiter about yesterday's Palio and the next one. Michael saw it as very similar to the tiresome way college boys talked about football, a way for men to converse and show friendship without vulnerability. Since the *contrade* had begun as militias, the Palio was in essence a war game, a definition Michael applied to all organized sports, a way to convert the natural human desire to fight into play and pageantry. He had no patience for a fake war when he was fighting a real one.

Without looking at the menu, Rodolfo ordered a plate of *pici cacio e pepe* and a glass of red wine. Michael did the same.

"What is the Confagricoltura?" Michael asked as the waiter brought their wine.

"To understand this you must understand the history of farming in Italy," Rodolfo said.

This was not an uncommon way of beginning a conversation, Michael had learned. Italians always wanted to give you the big picture, and every single one of them, right down to the mechanic who had repaired the Fairlane and had knowledgeably discussed the Battle of Montaperti in 1260 and the origins of Siena's rivalry with Florence, seemed to have a passion for history and be able to quote Dante from memory. It was hard for Michael to picture a random gas station attendant in Missouri (or a university student in New Haven) describing the details of British bureaucracy in pre-Revolutionary America or quoting Chaucer at length. Rodolfo proceeded to give Michael an overview that touched lightly on the Etruscans and Romans, moved to the 1500s with Cosimo de Medici and the growth of cities, the expansion of feudalism into the surrounding countryside, the rise of *mezzadria,* or sharecropping, the *bonifica,* or improvements to the canals in the Maremma under Mussolini, and eventually, as they finished their pasta and the waiter poured them each a second glass of wine and brought out trays of eggplant and zucchini, as well as a pair of tender pork cutlets, outlined the postwar organization of unions and chambers of commerce that regulated the current agricultural system.

Michael was fairly sure he would remember none of this tomorrow, especially since the entire time Rodolfo was talking, Michael was trying to figure out how to genially convince him to write an article that would spread malicious rumors about Ugo Rosini, and also perhaps to say something nice about Ambassador Luce, to please Duncan.

"Sad about Mayor Manganelli," Michael said.

"This insanity with the cars," Rodolfo said. "Before the war you were happy if you had a bicycle. Now everyone has a car but no one is competent to drive one. We should stick with horses."

"Who do you think will be elected in November?"

Rodolfo shrugged. "The priests will encourage one side, and the unions the other. But probably people will vote for who their fathers voted for. What did you think of Vestri?"

Michael was cautious. "I don't know enough about him. But Siena's growing fast. We're having these same issues in American towns, the postwar boom. It's important to pick leaders who understand how to navigate expansion, who give business owners room to grow."

Rodolfo sighed and lit a cigarette. He leaned back in his chair.

"You must understand. Italians are resistant to being governed. Every invading force has thought 'these people do not even fight us.' But eventually we throw them off because we do fight, just not openly, because this is suicide. We subvert, we evade, we undermine. This is something that is frustrating, but is also beautiful, like the way insects consume a corpse. Unlike Americans, we believe that every politician is corrupt. Every law is to be circumvented. We are startled when we meet someone who is truly good. Like your wife."

"Scottie?"

"She is looking for this boy. The police made a show of it, but they have moved on to other things. She will not stop, will she?"

"I don't know about that. She's in Florence shopping today. The only thing she's hunting is a bamboo bag at Gucci." Michael rolled his eyes.

Rodolfo laughed and shook his head. "Gucci? I bet she's tracking down Gordon."

"Gordon?"

"I told her the other night that Robertino posed for Lord Sebastian Gordon. Gordon works for Gucci. She has probably gone to talk to him. Under cover of shopping." He laughed again, as Michael's stomach churned.

"And Robertino is of no benefit to her. He is not her child. But she devotes herself to this, because it is right, and because no one else is doing it. This shames us, because we all wish to be this way, like the heroes in comic books."

Somehow it didn't seem like the right moment to offer money in exchange for an article suggesting that the left had bumped off Manganelli.

"Yes," Michael said. "She is an innocent."

Rodolfo took a drag on his cigarette and looked at Michael. "No, I do not agree. Two nights ago she was practically throwing punches. She is very *vispa.*" While Michael smiled, agreeing that Scottie was "spirited," Rodolfo added, lowering his voice, "Listen, you mentioned Manganelli's death."

"Yes?"

"I heard something the other day. A rumor. It may explain why no one is buying your tractors."

It was true. No one had come to buy a tractor this week. Brigante, who was selling one a day, was crowing about it.

"What?"

"That Manganelli's death was not an accident. That the CIA was behind it."

Michael's jaw dropped.

"I know, it sounds crazy. But you would be surprised. It would not be the first time that a foreign power decided to intervene in Italian politics."

Michael blinked. "But . . . no offense, Siena is a very small town. As we say, there are bigger fish to fry."

"True. But if you wanted to decapitate the Communist Party, this would be the place to start."

Did he know? Michael told himself to breathe. "Manganelli wasn't a Communist."

"No, but he was friendly to them. He was talking about working with all of the parties

317

to move Siena forward in a way that honored the past but also advanced quality of life for all. He was friendly to the unions, and like Rosini was resistant to some key developers. American developers."

"American developers?" This was the first Michael had heard of it. "Who are they?"

"I don't know. But I know Vestri will practically suck their dicks. He's from the far right wing of the Catholics, one step away from fascism. Anyway, I know that probably you have not sold many tractors, and I thought you should know why, that it's not personal."

"Thank you for telling me. I can assure you the rumor is not true."

"Can you? How?"

"That's not how Americans behave," said Michael, amazed by his own flat tone. "Oh, I have a scoop for you," he added. "Heard it through the grapevine at Ford in Rome the other day. Ambassador Luce will attend the August Palio."

Rodolfo's eyebrows went up. "Really? That is news. What an honor for our little city." He downed a coffee that the waiter had brought without being asked and stood up to leave. *"Arrivederci,"* he said, and strode off.

Michael drank his coffee. He paid the bill

and was halfway across the piazza before he heard a yell.

"Signore!"

He turned, and the waiter was holding up his briefcase.

11.

They got lost on the winding gravel roads on the way to the villa. Carlo apologized profusely, said he felt all turned around. She nodded.

This spell they had over each other . . . What did it mean? Was it the kind of thing you tried to perpetuate? Or was it a dream they would wake from? They could never be together. Her confidence that she was doing the right thing by hunting down Gordon was evaporating, and she was hot and crabby and anxious. She no longer felt beautiful or sexual, but rather hot and bloated and uncomfortable. She was dying to get out of her girdle. Most of the makeup that she had carefully reapplied in a small dusty mirror in the shop seemed to have ended up on her gloves after wiping the sweat off her face. She felt slightly sickened at the memory of how she had wrenched her clothing aside in her haste to feel Carlo inside her, how frantic she was, grabbing him, desperate, clawing at him to pull him deeper and deeper inside herself, rubbing her breasts against him. She and Carlo had rutted like animals. That wasn't romance. There was something wrong with her, she thought. Michael's urges were so tidy, so controlled. They made love without even wrinkling the sheets.

She'd made Carlo pull over at one of the roadside gas stations so she could do some respackling on her cosmetics and relieve herself, but the toilet was just a hole in the floor, and the room was filled with the buzz of flies. God in heaven, what had she become? She stank of desire and betrayal, so she had sprayed herself with more perfume, which was now turning her stomach. Yet she wanted Carlo again.

Finally, after they had driven up a long, cypress-lined, rutted gravel road that switchbacked between fields of golden sunflowers closing tight for the night, what Carlo had described as "a pink monstrosity" had indeed appeared in their headlights: a large pink-and-mustard-colored villa with graceful arches revealing a loggia, a Grecian triangular pediment held up by columns, two stories of green shuttered windows lit up, and a row of darkened small barred circular windows just below a cornice guarded by Greek statues and topped with a shield bearing a huge crest of arms.

It was a far cry from the tumbledown farmhouses they'd passed on the way, a skinny dog or two growling beneath a laundry line, ageless blank-eyed women gazing from under headscarves as they pruned grapes in the waning daylight.

A wide drive of pea gravel took them up to the front of the villa. As she got closer, Scottie could see even in the fading daylight that the old building's glamour was a little tattered. Ivy was pulling at the stucco, which had crumbled away in places to reveal stones beneath. The paint was worn through and showed the many layers of color that had been applied over the years.

"Faded glory," said a very tall man with a long nose that seemed to precede him as he appeared around the corner. Unmistakably English. The man, in his late thirties she guessed, wore a perfectly cut white linen suit, a polka-dotted pale blue handkerchief in the breast pocket, and held a martini glass. With his slicked-back hair, he looked like a film star, Scottie decided. But there was something else. Something about him made her uncomfortable.

"Lord Sebastian Gordon," said Carlo as the man air-kissed him and her and kept talking as if they were continuing a conversation in midstream.

"I suppose decay happens to the best of us. The place was built by the Medicis in the 1400s, and made its way through the usual accidents of inheritance down to my dear departed mother," Gordon said. "I blame you for that," he said, turning to Scottie. Seeing her confused look, he pointed to the ivy. "It's called *vite americana*. An import from your neck of the woods. Virginia creeper. The Italians went mad for it in the last century before they realized it's beautiful but destructive. Gets into every crack and crevice. Someday it will tear the whole place down. Invasive species, you Yanks. We're all around back," he said. "By the pool. Follow me." He walked around the side of the villa through a gate in the hedge.

"He didn't even ask us why we were here," said Scottie. "And how did he know I was an American?"

Carlo shrugged. They followed Gordon into the garden, their feet crunching on the gravel. Ecco, on his leash, lunged ahead of Scottie.

The man was so . . . theatrical. She didn't know what to make of him.

"Just a few friends," Gordon said as they caught up to him, waving to a scattered group of forty or fifty people spread out around a pool and gardens.

Scottie heard a quick "Carlo! *Amore mio!*" and saw Franca coming toward them. *Oh God,* she thought. *How can I face her?* Franca was in a long pale green gown. Her red hair was undone, and wild. She swayed a little, drunk, and stared hard at Scottie in a way that chilled her, then put her arm through Carlo's. "I must speak with you," she said to him. "You don't mind?" she said to Scottie in English, her eyes dark and fiery. She seemed agitated.

"Of course not," said Scottie, backing away. It was all, all, all wrong.

As Scottie watched them go into the villa, Gordon took her hand and stared into her eyes. "Gorgeous," he went on. "Just stunning. My God, you're a Neroccio in the flesh."

"A what?"

"Neroccio di Bartolomeo de' Landi," said Lord Sebastian. "You must go straight to the Pinacoteca in Siena and see the *Madonna and Child Between St. Jerome and St. Bernard.* It will be like looking in a mirror, my dear. Now make yourself at home."

"Wait," said Scottie before he could disappear like the Cheshire Cat again. "I'm so sorry to bother you, but I understand you know the boy who's been teaching me Italian, Robertino Banchi."

"Very upsetting," he said smoothly. "I was in England and have just returned to hear how he's simply *disappeared* into thin air. This country is sinking into anarchy. I'm afraid it's up to us to find him. The police are hopeless."

"Yes," she said, surprised. "I completely agree." It was such a relief to meet someone who didn't tell her to back off or not to worry, even though this man was downright *odd.*

"Must mingle," he said. "Let's talk more later, shall we?"

12.

Michael debated with himself as he headed back to the office. He definitely didn't want Scottie embroiling Ambassador Luce's friends in this mess. It was unnerving to think Gordon knew the boy. But that was Italy. Everyone knew each other.

And then, out of the blue, Gordon himself called, introducing himself as a friend of Luce's. Michael was unnerved by the coincidence — in the Agency, they taught you there are no coincidences. The phone cord stretched as he reached for his box of Benzedrine.

To Michael's surprise, Gordon invited him to the villa for a party. "Lots of people you should meet," he said casually. "All the expats worth knowing. A very pretty girl I think you'll like." A good spy would go, Michael thought, though Gordon's unctuous tone gave him the creeps. He half wondered if the Brit had Robertino tied up with heavy velvet rope in some upstairs bedroom, drugged with opium perhaps, a party game gone wrong. These decadent Brits, he wouldn't put anything past them. At least the Americans saw other nations as potential markets to exploit. The Brits saw them as animals.

13.

Carlo had completely disappeared with Franca. Scottie felt stung and unreasonably angry. God, it was all so fraught, so tangled with the past. Italy was not carefree and sexy like they made it seem in *Roman Holiday*. It was dense and mysterious and dangerous and confusing. Scottie had dived into an azure sea on a sunny day, only to find her feet caught in a centuries-old fishing net that was pulling her down into cold, dark depths.

Cicadas hummed. She felt self-conscious at the sight of people talking and laughing in small groups around a long pool with floating candles in it. Even though the sun was down, the heat was still stifling, yet everyone looked crisp and cool and stylish. She was dripping with sweat. How did they do it, she wondered. There was some trick she had never learned. People turned to look at her as she wandered through the crowd with Ecco, but no one introduced themselves. She could hear English, and Spanish, and French.

A very handsome liveried waiter with huge dark eyes and curly black hair handed her a martini. Scottie took one sip and felt faint.

"Let's walk around a little," she said to Ecco.

What had once been formal gardens were overgrown. Stones were falling out of the walls, and large clusters of caper plants had filled the gaps. At the far end of the garden was an entrance to what looked like a cave. A grotto, she remembered they were called.

She rounded another corner and came upon a huge bronze fountain of a leering man. Neptune, she decided, from the ocean motif. Neptune was large and vulgar, covered with moss and waving his trident over carved little boys with fishtails who were spitting water. But the worst of it was a mermaid, sitting, her back against Neptune's leg, gazing down at herself as she cupped each breast in a firm hand, water spouting from the nipples. The statue was leaning back — her fishtail was split in two, and she sat astride a dolphin, a clamshell covering her private parts.

"Gives new meaning to the word 'brazen.' " She turned, and there was Gordon again, now followed by a waiter carrying a tray with glasses of Campari and soda. Gordon nodded at the mermaid. "The Medicis were a very naughty bunch. They shared the favors of poor little Simonetta Vespucci, then rewarded her by having her body paraded through the streets of Florence after her death, with a proclamation that read 'Beauty is dead.' And of course she was the model for Botticelli's Venus. I do prefer a natural beauty," he said, examining her much more closely than she would have liked. "It shows real confidence to face the world as you are, doesn't it?" Scottie could hardly absorb this before he was taking her by the arm. "I must introduce you to *everyone.*"

"Robertino —"

"Yes, utterly delightful young lad. Though hard to get him to sit still. My painting of him as Hermes is rather a *blur.*"

"You said you were away, but you do know

he's been missing for a week now? I'm very worried. His mother is dead."

"Worrisome indeed. I talked to the police myself this morning about the boy. They seemed to have no clue where he's gone. I dearly hope his disappearance is not connected to his mother's death. Her lifestyle was both risqué and risky, after all. And then there's all this business about the horse."

"What horse? From the *contrada*? Ondina?"

"No. Someone at the stable where he worked was mistreating a horse."

"Camelia?"

"I don't know the horse's name. Robertino didn't like it, and told the man off. The chap didn't take it very well, and continued to beat the horse, and now the horse has disappeared."

"Before or after Robertino did?"

"Same time, I think."

"But that's wonderful!" said Scottie, Ecco pricking his ears and wagging his tail at her change in tone. "He's not kidnapped or dead, he's run off with the horse!" She could see him in her mind, galloping across the countryside.

"I thought so, too. But if he's stolen the horse, he could go to jail. He might be wiser to stay hidden, or go somewhere else and start over."

"He wouldn't leave his grandfather," said Scottie. "And it's awfully strange that he'd miss the Palio. You'd think he'd have stashed the horse and reappeared, acting innocent. That's what I'd do."

Gordon smiled at her. "Yes. Well, he's a resourceful young fellow, and I'm hoping for the best."

"Have you seen Carlo Chigi Piccolomini?" she asked Gordon. "He's my ride and I've lost track of him." She didn't mention Franca, couldn't say her name out loud.

Instead of answering, Gordon waved over a woman. "Julie, darling, come meet a fellow American."

The elegantly dressed woman came closer. "Oh yes," she said. "I remember you. You're Michael Messina's wife."

The night before the Palio. "Of course," said Scottie. "I'm sorry. You're married to a friend of Michael's from Yale, right?"

"Yale. Hmmm." said Julie. "We do have a lot in common, don't we? Good-bye, Sebastian."

Scottie heard Gordon chuckle as he moved off.

"You came with Carlo Chigi Piccolomini," said Julie.

"He's our landlord," said Scottie.

"Quite the dark history there." Julie gave her a knowing smile as Gordon melted into the boxwood labyrinth.

"You mean about their son? Yes. So sad." Scottie was cautious.

"I don't know about you," Julie said, "but I've been shopping in Florence all day and I'm exhausted." She waved to a waiter and directed him to move a couple of chairs together. "I need a drink with ice, and I bet you do, too. *Due, per favore,*" she barked at the waiter. *"Con ghiaccio."*

"Ice, really? I haven't seen any since leaving New York," Scottie sighed, sinking down into the flamingo pink chair. "Are you visiting Italy? Your Italian is good."

"My husband and I live in Rome. We met Sebastian there. He's such a sweetie. I love those old queers, don't you?"

Scottie was a little shocked at this, but now that she thought about it, it made sense that Gordon was a homosexual. That would explain the theatrical behavior. She suspected her riding coach Mr. Perry was a homosexual, though she had never said that to anyone. Mostly it was based on the fact that unlike the other men she had met, he was not predatory, and his interest in her felt nonsexual. Occasionally at Vassar the

330

girls described certain men as "light in the loafers" or "fairies," and some of the female professors were, yes, rather exceptionally *close* friends, but despite her perspicuity about animals, Scottie was oddly uncurious about her fellow humans' private lives, and she disliked idle gossip of the sort this woman Julie clearly traded in. Still, it was nice to talk to an American.

"Gordon has blocks of ice delivered from Florence," Julie said, nimbly lighting a cigarette and offering Scottie one, which she declined. "I think a poor little donkey carries it the whole way."

"Is your husband here, too?"

"No," Julie laughed. "Though he'd fit right in. He's always working. Michael, too, I bet?"

"Yes."

"We learn to get by on our own, don't we? And to make friends." She gave the word a special emphasis that Scottie ignored.

"Yes."

Julie petted Ecco. "You're smart to have a dog. He's adorable. You should let him go. I'm sure he won't run off."

Scottie unleashed Ecco, who promptly dived into the pool, climbed out again, and shook himself, making two women standing near the steps screech.

"Oh goodness," said Scottie, cringing and sinking down in her chair, though really she enjoyed shaking things up a little, and seeing Ecco have fun. She hoped this wasn't the moment when Carlo reappeared, or Franca.

Julie laughed. "Being good gets you nowhere in Italy, and he knows it. In this culture they value *furbizia.*"

"*Furbo,* like 'sly'?"

"Very good. You've seen this already, I'm sure, or you will soon. Italians are always looking for the shortcut, and they admire the one who finds it, not the one who follows 'proper channels.' "

"Probably because things were so hard during the war."

"Maybe, but I think it goes back further than that. Don't you think it's their character?"

"I don't know."

"Don't get me wrong. I like Italians." The way she said it, she was saying more than that. "Italy has been ruled by so many people: the German tribes, the Bourbons, Napoleon, the Austrians, even before Il Duce and his pal Adolf came along. Someone is always trying to tell them what to do, so they find ways to smile and smile but also to do exactly as they please. And now they're the unofficial western front of the Cold War, a chessboard for two empires. Look," she said, pointing to where the dog was being petted and hand-fed shrimp by the same women he had just splashed. "All is forgiven."

"You know a lot about Italy."

"I have a lot of time on my hands."

Scottie nodded. "Me, too. Does your husband also work for Ford?"

Julie smiled. "He's at the State Department."

"Oh. How exciting. So he works with Ambassador Luce?"

"Yes. Clare's quite an interesting woman."

"I wish Michael would take me to Rome with him sometimes. He's always there and I'm stuck here. I like Siena, but . . . Rome."

"You really must press him harder on that. He and Duncan are such pals. They're always out together."

Scottie was surprised to hear this. Michael always said his trips to Rome were all business.

"I should probably look for Carlo. And Franca," she said.

"I hear he's such a nice man, for a Fascist."

Scottie paused. "What do you mean?"

"Well, people don't like to talk about the

war, but given his age and position you must have figured out that Carlo was in the army, of course."

"Of course. I wouldn't hold that against him."

"No, of course not. And what's done is done."

There were things Julie was not saying, and Scottie felt irritated with her. "Do you miss home?" she asked, changing the subject.

"Desperately," said Julie. "I can't wait to get pregnant again so I have an excuse to abandon Duncan and go home for a long stretch."

"You have children?"

"Yes. Two. And you —" Julie looked at her appraisingly. "You're pregnant?"

"Yes."

"You're not thinking of delivering here, I hope?"

"Children are born here every day."

"Yes, but it's such a good excuse to get away."

"I don't think I want to get away. I like it here. And Michael would miss me."

Julie looked at her, took a drag on her cigarette and put it out. "Yes, of course," she said.

"And there's a boy, a friend of mine who's

gone missing. I'm looking for him."

Julie raised her eyebrows and said nothing. Her makeup was done like Scottie's, in the latest style. Seeing it on another face, Scottie saw how hard and cruel it made her look, the black-edged eyes, the blood red lips. She looked around at the partygoers.

"You're watching everyone," said Julie at last.

Scottie laughed. "A bad habit." She had learned to evaluate people at age fourteen as an outsider from the West arriving at boarding school. Tonight she was watching for Carlo, of course, but also making a list in her head, assessing the party guests the way she did a paddock full of horses at an auction, imagining Robertino in their midst. Most people couldn't see more than the color of a horse, and barely noticed what sex it was. She had known a polo player who referred to his "gelding" for six months before Scottie pointed out it was a mare. Scottie could tell from the flick of an ear, the twitch of a shoulder muscle, the slant of a haunch exactly what a horse was thinking, and what it was capable of. Humans weren't all that different when you bothered to look closely. She pointed out for Julie the two screeching women, Americans, mid-twenties, insecure, standing up to show off their figures. "Actresses, don't you think?" Julie laughed and agreed. Three men smoking in the corner.

"Furtive," said Julie.

"Businessmen."

They spotted a couple of teens with greased-up hair, looking for sex. An older overweight couple in expensive clothing: Scottie described the woman as an "alpha mare," while Julie said her submissive husband was perhaps a poet. A small flock of blank-eyed, gazelle-like women: models, definitely models. A man in dark glasses smoking a cigar. Sex again, they both declared. A Frenchwoman and her younger escort, talking loudly. Artists.

They were giggling together like schoolgirls.

"I've missed this," Scottie said. "Having a girlfriend to talk to."

"Me, too," said Julie.

Scottie reached for another Campari from a passing tray and held the glass to her cheek. *I can't lose focus,* she thought.

She kicked off her shoes and rolled down her stockings. She sat on the edge of the pool and put her feet in the green water. No one seemed to care. Everyone was talking a little louder, leaning a little closer, smoking a little faster. Scottie saw the

Frenchwoman head toward the grotto. A cloud of cigarette smoke formed coils over the pool.

She felt a movement inside her belly. It startled her until she realized what it was.

"My baby just moved," she said in wonder.

Julie slid down next to her, put her hand on Scottie's belly. "A kicker," she said. "Fasten your seat belt."

A large orange carp surfaced and nibbled at Scottie's painted pink toes.

In that moment, she decided that whatever this was with Carlo, it should end before it went any further. The appearance of Franca, no matter how malevolent she acted toward Scottie, was a blessing. And Julie — an American breath of fresh air, of good sense, a reminder of who she was. What Scottie wanted wasn't an affair with Carlo, it was a happy marriage to Michael. She wanted Michael to love her. She wanted them to be a family, to love each other and raise the child together. Things had gone terribly astray, but she could put them right again.

"Come with me," Julie said, getting to her feet. "This might shock you. But I think you should see it anyway."

"I'm pretty unshockable," she said.

"That's what I thought. But I didn't have *me* there for moral support."

Both of them barefoot, Julie took Scottie's hand in hers and led her through the box-wood labyrinth to the grotto.

Scottie followed Julie down the steps into the darkness, where they found two men, their white sport shirts unbuttoned, their faces lit by a torch burning in an iron sconce shaped like a dragon's head. One man was on his knees, the other standing, facing him, leaning back against the stone wall. Scottie, behind Julie, stopped and stared, while Julie studied her face intently. The man on his knees had turned to look at the two women, the other man's large erect penis in his hand. In the torchlight, the chin of the kneeling man glistened, and so did the sweat on the chest of the other, whose eyes were closed. As they stood there, very still, the standing man moaned a little and thrust his hips forward.

14.

At least the villa was cool inside, the moon-light filtering between the uneven slats of the heavy green shutters. Gordon had strong-armed Michael into a lively poker game inside.

"Straight," said Gordon with a smirk, laying down his cards. "Have you seen my grotto?"

338

Michael disliked his type of queen. That kind of behavior made straight people uncomfortable and gave homosexuals a bad name. It smacked of decadence and libertinism. It was the kind of thing people laughed at on a movie screen — Edward Everett Horton playing with dollies, or Cary Grant in a frilly robe — but condemned in real life. The Brits — they all seemed a little gay to him. But why couldn't Gordon keep that kind of thing behind closed doors, like the rest of them did?

Still, Michael had always wanted to see a Renaissance-era grotto, so he followed Gordon's directions, past the pool, through the labyrinth and down a set of stairs. Two women were silhouetted in the flickering torchlight, partially blocking his view of . . .

"Scottie. Scottie?!" Scottie was here, *here*. standing on the steps of the grotto, watching . . . *watching*.

"She deserves to know," said a voice, and Michael focused on the other woman.

Julie walked past him up the stairs and disappeared.

15.

Michael grabbed Scottie's arm hard and dragged her out, up the stone stairs. Her feet slipped, but he roughly pulled her until they were back in the garden again.

"Wait," Scottie said.

"The car is this way," said Michael.

"I have to find my shoes. I have to tell Carlo I'm leaving with you. And Ecco — we can't leave the dog, Michael. Stop, you're hurting me." She pulled away from his grasp, and he turned on her.

"I thought you were — where is the marchese?"

"I don't know. He disappeared. His wife was . . . ill." She was furious with Carlo, she realized, but when Michael frowned, she added quickly, "I made him bring me here. I wanted information about Robertino." A flashing series of images coalesced in Scottie's mind, setting off a feeling of unease in her. "But Michael. Why are you here?"

"There's something I have to tell you," he said, casting his eyes downward. "I should have told you before, but I couldn't."

"What?"

He paused, glanced around, then said, "I work for the CIA." The words hung in the air before them, erasing ugly images from Scottie's mind.

"You do?"

"I'm here in Italy to get information on Communists. Information we can use against them to help our side."

And then she kissed him. She threw her arms around his neck and kissed him, deep and hard on the mouth. She held him tight, and then slipped a hand down and ran it over the front of his pants.

"A spy," she said. "You could have told me."

Eleven:
La Chiocciola, The Snail

"AT A SLOW AND STEADY PACE, THE SNAIL
DESCENDS INTO THE CAMPO TO TRIUMPH"

July 4, 1956

1.

Signor Banchi was grateful to the *americana* for coming to see him in the hospital, but it was hard to convey to her what he needed. He strained to say the name.

"Robertino."

"Yes," she said, spooning some cool lemon gelato into his mouth. "*Sì, sì,* we're all looking for him." He was lying in a group ward in the Ospedale Santa Maria della Scala, only a stone's throw from the Duomo, the hospital where sick travelers and plague victims had been brought since 1090. Italian hospitals did not provide food; your relatives brought it to you. A situation like his — widowed, no surviving children, grand-

342

son missing — was considered tragic. He would have to count on nuns and neighbors to take pity on him. Scottie's gelato was especially appreciated by the old man, who was mostly surviving on the nearly inedible creations of Nonna Bea, the only bad cook in all of Italy.

When Banchi looked at Nonna Bea he saw what Scottie could not — not a comic old crone, but a woman who gave selflessly to others, who had done so for nearly ninety years. Nonna Bea was part of an army of women who had kept Italy going through its darkest hours, which had lasted seemingly forever. During the invasions, the occupations, the wars, the famines, the plagues stretching back to the fall of Rome, Nonna Beas had nursed, fed and tended others in complete invisibility, never receiving a medal or a citation or having a statue erected in their names. Mammas and nonnas were loved but also teased and ignored. It was the way of things, that their sacrifice was expected, not honored. Sometimes the anger and resentment the women felt made them cruel and manipulative matriarchs, but for every Lucrezia Borgia or even Matilda of Tuscany, there were millions of nameless old women in black, always in mourning for someone, perhaps for their lost youth as much as any departed husband. Nonna Bea may have been provincial in her mind-set, negligent in her personal hygiene and inept in her cooking, but she was, in Banchi's mind, every bit as much a saint as Catherine herself.

His daughter would never grow old, never wear black. He had cast her out, which he was not sorry for, but he had not said goodbye to her, which he was sorry for. The last time he had seen her, the day the Americans arrived, he had averted his eyes. *I should have looked at her,* he thought.

He watched Scottie smooth his sheets and plump his pillows. So young and beautiful, like a spring day.

"I fed and watered Lapo and Cecco," Scottie said. Her voice sounded far away. "And the chickens and rabbits. It's a holiday today in America. Independence Day."

It would soon be time to harvest the wheat. He tried to tell her, tried to sit up —

"We are all here to help," she said. "You must concentrate on getting well. We will find Robertino."

He lay back in his hospital bed and looked up at the frescoes over his head, imagining his great-great-great-and-more-grandfather also staring up at them. The images were mundane, but chilling. A man in a black hat and cape examined a man who was wearing only underpants. Another physician looked as if he were preparing to bleed the healthy leg of a man with a gaping thigh wound. Faces stared impassively down from a blue ceiling dotted with black stars. The Black Death. An unimaginable pestilence. It was foreigners who had brought the disease. In 1453, three-fifths of the people died. From a thriving city-state Siena was reduced to a ghost town. Religious pilgrimages ceased, and without the revenue from travelers, the city lost the money to pay its army. His city, beloved Siena, was conquered by Florence, and slowly sank into five hundred years of poverty.

The newspaper said that the American ambassador, Clare Boothe Luce, was coming to Siena for the Palio in August. What an honor, everyone said.

Foreigners. This lady was nice enough, but the other American had come to see him, too. The man who wanted to buy his property and put a hotel on it. "You and your grandson will be rich," he said. He had held out the papers for Signor Banchi to sign, but Nonna Bea had come in and chased him away, threatened to sic the nuns on him.

Money felt like another form of plague to him, a dark force threatening them all. He had watched the rise of fascism, but found this more insidious somehow. There were no rallies or children dressed in black shirts. Instead, the children were wearing shiny shoes, pushing shiny bicycles. No one thought to question its hold on them. What was wrong with wanting nice things? "Wait," he wanted to tell them, "wait. It will never stop. It will drive us apart." Status had always been a part of Italian society; the sins of pride and greed were always rampant. The monuments they had built to themselves! On the backs of the poor! But at least lust for money and status were seen as sins. Now they were seen as virtues. He had fought with his grandson, yelled at him to stop denigrating their lifestyle. His last words to him were "If I put a knife through your chest, is there a heart in there for it to strike?" And now, with these horrible words burning on his tongue, with his daughter dead in a ditch, the boy missing, God had struck him down, rendered him a hostage inside a useless body.

"Where is that rascal grandson of yours?" Nonna Bea appeared in place of the American girl, put some soup to his lips. "Out cavorting with foreigners, no doubt, while his poor grandfather lies dying."

Signor Banchi coughed. He didn't feel like

he was dying. He was just very tired.

"The devil's got him. I'm going to take a switch to him when I see him," she said.

2.

Scottie woke up on the Fourth of July almost crying with relief at the revelation that her husband was a CIA officer — it explained all of his odd behavior. Of course he couldn't tell her anything about his work, but she guessed that he had been recruited at Yale. Half the CIA was from Yale, she'd heard. She wished she could write to Leona. Leona had found Michael "furtive." "See?" She could say. "He's furtive for a reason — he's a secret agent!" That would shut Leona up. It had shut Scottie up — she had felt her earlier doubts were disloyal.

"We're here to defeat communism," he had said in the car as they drove home from Sebastian Gordon's villa. "To get as many Italians as possible to see that our way of life is better. To sway hearts and minds."

"I can help you," she told him at breakfast, but he had refused, and motioned her to silence. Though they did not talk openly about it, they both knew that Scottie was the more gregarious by far. So why wouldn't he let her help?

"It's just not a good idea," he said. He

had made her come with him. They were walking outside the walls of the city. She noticed that Michael continually glanced around them. He had warned her that their apartment might be bugged by the KGB. She was never, ever, ever to say anything to anyone or even aloud to herself about who Michael worked for.

"It's so exciting," she said.

"It's dangerous. Very dangerous. There are bad people around."

"Please let me help you. I can move around the city, talk to people, much more easily than you can. I have every reason to chitchat. Plus, people talk in front of me all the time. They assume I don't speak Italian and have no idea what they're saying." She thought of Fiammetta and Rodolfo. "Like the other night — I can sit at a table next to someone and eavesdrop if you need me to. I'm just a dumb American girl," she said.

"You most certainly are not," he said, and kissed her cheek. He was leaving for the train station — he had to go to Rome again.

"Does your friend Duncan work for the CIA, too?"

"No," said Michael sharply. "Julie is a terrible gossip. I'd prefer it if you didn't pursue a friendship with her."

"What are you going to do in Rome?" she

348

whispered.

"I wish I could tell you," he said with a smile. "Look, I know you care for Robertino, but we can't help, and it's none of our business," he said.

"But . . . ," she said.

"What?"

"Hunting for Robertino, which everyone already knows I'm doing, is a great way to get to know people. I'll be friendly. That's good for the mission, right? You can't hate someone you're friends with, even if they're a capitalist and you're a Communist."

He considered this. "You're not trained," he said. "I don't want you to get hurt."

"I won't. I'll just ask questions about Robertino, and observe. I'll go to the stable where he works. Ask about the horse."

Michael reluctantly agreed. "Only to the stable. I already know you're better at this than I am," he said. "But I really can't stress enough that you have to be careful. It's not a game, Scottie."

"I understand," she said.

She used the *moka* to make an espresso, skipped the makeup, donned a pair of cropped, slim tan pants and a loose, sleeveless polka-dotted top that hid her growing belly, slipped on some sandals, put her hair under a blue-green scarf and added a pair of sunglasses. It wasn't a spy's traditional trenchcoat and fedora, but it would have to do.

After seeing Signor Banchi, she stopped by the scooter rental place.

"No charge," the young mechanic said. She stiffened, afraid it was some kind of sexual overture. But then the mechanic said, "Find him. Find the boy for poor Gina, God rest her soul." He crossed himself and kissed a crucifix that hung around his neck.

She installed Ecco in his usual spot, and the Kelly bag Michael bought her as a wedding present on the floor of the scooter in front of her. She zoomed out of the city through Porta San Marco, then sped down the long winding road to the farms on the valley floor. She picked up the gently curving road for Rosia, turned down a gravel lane for Sovicille. The landscape changed, the cheerful farms giving way to a steeper, rockier ground that she guessed took a lot more out of its inhabitants. Still, each little plot carved out of the forest had a small vineyard, a few olive trees and pigpens. Huge chestnuts arched over the road. The air was cooler here, and she could smell rain coming, hopefully after she made it back to Siena. She took the turnoff for Centro Ippico ai Lecci as a low rumble of thunder sounded in the distance.

A few people taking a lesson in the main ring looked at her curiously as she zipped into the stable yard and parked. There was a stout woman with short red hair like a halo of fire barking commands at them in heavily accented Italian. Scottie guessed she was British. She snapped on Ecco's leash to keep him from decimating the barn cat population and headed down the cool aisle of the main barn toward the manager's office.

The same man who'd been harassing the young horse last time was now sitting at a desk, looking at an agenda. Tom Cats. He looked very intent. This, Scottie knew, was par for the course at any stable — meticulous records were kept about which horse was on what medication and when, who signed up for riding lessons and when, and which horses needed to be exercised and for how long.

"I haven't seen the boy," he said, scowling when he saw her.

"I'm buying a horse, and I'd like to stable it here," she said, aiming for just the right mix of flirtatious and distant. "What are your rates and rules?"

He brightened considerably and first rattled off a long list of information in no particular order, from shoeing costs to extra straw, then handed her a piece of paper that duly spelled out everything he had just said.

"I can assist you in purchasing a horse, *signora,*" he said. "In fact I have several here for sale. All very lovely and well trained."

Scottie remembered how hard he'd been on the horse she saw, and how his poor technique ensured the horse would hate its job and all humans.

"I'd love to see what you have for sale," she said. "Though I can't buy today. My husband will come back with me for that." That would give her an out if he pressed too hard.

"Of course," he said with a patronizing smile.

He led her down the barn aisle to a stall where a huge chestnut gelding stood weaving back and forth.

"He's a dancer, see?" said Gatti. "Very special horse. I think he likes you."

Scottie knew that the horse weaved because he was bored, and that weaving was a form of obsessive behavior — like cribbing, in which a horse repeatedly sucked air while fastening its teeth on a stall door or anything else it could find. Both of these "vices" caused health issues. She immediately wanted to buy the big red and turn him out somewhere, but she reminded herself that she was not here today to save horses.

Next he showed her a small, fat bay mare with an utterly adorable face. "She's lovely," said Scottie, meaning it. The mare had large liquid eyes that showed no fear, just calm. If she had really been horse shopping today, she might have bought this mare on sight. She'd be perfect for Michael.

"You are the right size for her," Gatti said, giving Scottie a very long and appraising look. "She belongs to a man whose feet nearly drag on the ground when he rides her. I have convinced him it is not dignified."

You've convinced him to sell a good horse so you can make a commission, plus another commission on finding a new horse that will need expensive training, she thought. Stable managers were the same everywhere.

"Robertino Banchi spoke very highly of a horse he knew here," she said. "Though I'm not sure if it was a horse he exercised or just one he admired."

Gatti frowned. "He rode several horses," he said. "An excellent rider. I am having trouble finding someone as good as him."

"Perhaps he will return soon," she said.

"I hope so." Scottie could feel him not telling her something.

"Is there a horse he's particularly fond

of?" she asked. "I heard that a horse disappeared after he was gone."

Gatti frowned again, and then sighed in anger.

"You are speaking of Camelia," he said. "It has never happened before that a horse has been stolen from here. I myself sleep on the property to ensure the safety of all of our clients' horses."

"I'm sure it's not your fault," she said quickly. "Do you think Robertino stole the horse?"

"Possibly," he admitted. "He was very angry at the way she was treated. She is a difficult horse and he is a very softhearted boy who thinks he knows everything."

"Who owns her?"

"A fine man. An excellent rider. Robertino had no business sticking his nose in."

"Yes, he can be *impulsivo,*" she said. It was Robertino who had taught her that oh-so-easily translated word in Italian, but she did not feel guilty about using it against him. She would do whatever it took to find him. "What happened?"

"The mare came from Sicily, or so the dealer said. They are hard on horses there. There were signs she was beaten."

"How awful."

"Let me assure you we would never commit such barbarism here. She is a beautiful horse, so this man took a chance on her. But she bit and kicked, so he grew impatient."

"Did he hurt her?"

Gatti evaded. "She threw him off. It was a competition, and his father was present. It was an embarrassment. He sold the horse to Signor Barrico, the butcher. The butcher's truck was in the shop, but he was coming soon to get her. When I went to feed the horses the next morning, she was gone."

"Robertino knew she was being sold to the butcher?"

"Yes. He screamed at the man. He offered him everything he had for her. But the man refused. He wanted her dead."

"That's awful. If Robertino did take her, where could he hide her?"

Gatti threw up his hands. "Anywhere. In the forest, in an abandoned farmhouse. But this man, he will find his horse. He is not a man you should cross."

The British instructor was coming toward them, glowering. Signor Gatti looked like he wanted to run and hide. *"Ciao, amore,"* he said to her, and Scottie realized they were a couple.

"Who is this man?" Scottie asked quickly.

"Tenente Pisano."

355

3.

Tenente Pisano was staring at an ad on the wall in the passage above Piazza Mercato. Large notices were common all over Siena. Banns were published — to the *tenente*'s right, Guido Muzzi announced his intention to wed Elisa Sodi, and invited anyone objecting to step forward. A black-bordered poster with scrollwork announced the death of Annalisa Savini, aged 103. Then there were the posters for festivals — there was a *sagra,* or feast, in San Gimignano, a wild boar hunt in Buonconvento, and a *Festa delle Rane,* or Festival of Frogs, in Chiusi. The classic antique Palio posters were ubiquitous. But squeezed in the corner above a jutting brick was a square notice in blue announcing that the Palio was a tool of the Fascists. DON'T BE FOOLED, it read. TRADITION IS OPPRESSION. Minaccia Rossa, it was signed. Red Threat. What was this Red Threat? Tenente Pisano had never heard of this group, and he made it his business to know the names of every club, team, organization and society within the city. His first inclination was to laugh it off — attacking the Palio, a tradition beloved by all? This was political suicide. But Tenente Pisano did not like the implication that all was not as it should be in Siena, that there

356

were dark forces at work. He hated dark forces. Most irksome of all, the poster lacked the necessary stamp of the advertising division of the Questura. He reached up, tore it down and stalked off, already late for his mother's *trofie al pesto.*

4.

"I missed you," Michael said. It was the kind of thing Duncan hated, and he only dared to say this because he had been such a good, good spy, having planted an article about Luce coming to the Palio. The city was all excited about her visit, thanks to him. Yes, he had had to tell Scottie he was CIA, but she was already proving useful. He decided not to tell Duncan about running into Julie at the Palio, and again at Gordon's. He didn't want any mention of her to ruin what he imagined would be a jubilant visit of shared secrets. They were at St. Peter's, staring up at the ceiling of the Sistine Chapel. It was a veritable biblical cocktail party, with Noah at the bar; David slaying Goliath; Jesse, David and Solomon doing their thing; and of course God creating Adam with the touch of a lazy fingertip. Duncan was in a mood, which Michael assumed was because Michael's train had been two hours late.

But how could you not feel uplifted by the Sistine, Michael thought. He couldn't wait to tell Duncan about Minaccia Rossa. Michael had created the fake political movement after remembering his training at Camp Peary about "false flag attacks." Michael recalled the instructor explaining that it was a clever way of creating opposition to someone you didn't like. "Simply become one of them," he said. "And become the most extreme of all." Good, solid people in the middle didn't like extremists, didn't like violence. They would vote into office whomever they saw as being safely opposed to such acts, whoever would Keep Order.

So Michael had become Minaccia Rossa, the Red Threat. He had typeset the leaflets and posters himself, from the set of ink-stained metal hand type he had bought at a secondhand store in Rome. The small printing press came from a Florence bookbinder, paid for in cash. He had carefully incised the hammer and sickle on a block of wood. All of it was stored in the locked cabinet at the Ford office. He was inciting the Sienese to throw off tradition, wealth and foreign interference and vote Communist, or else. Hopefully people would be so outraged and frightened by the threats of Minaccia Rossa that they would vote the Catholic Vestri into office in a landslide, and the world would be safe for democracy, of a sort.

He knew Duncan would love the entire idea, but somehow the Sistine Chapel felt like the wrong place to reveal it. He'd rather tell him in bed. He stared out of the corner of his eye at Duncan's patrician profile, his sleek combed-back hair, his smooth cheek. A roommate of Michael's had once described Duncan as a tedious, balding snob, and he could not disagree, but in his warmer moments he reminded Michael of Dorothy Sayers's fictional detective, Lord Peter Wimsey. Aristocratic, intelligent and aloof. He longed to run his hand along Duncan's jawline, kiss his perfect pink ear. Desire was a sour taste in his mouth.

"Is it true that Michelangelo was gay?" Duncan asked.

"Don't you see how he's fetishizing the male body?" Michael pointed up. "And all his women, look at them, are Amazons. He sculpted both the Pietà and the David before he was thirty. Amazing. They called him Il Divino."

"Another talented fag."

Michael blinked, shocked. They didn't talk this way to each other. Duncan had always insisted that being homosexual made them elite, *better* than other people. It was Michael who wrestled with Catholic guilt and feelings of sin. Duncan had always been coldly dismissive of such weakness of mind, seeing his desire as a badge of status, membership in an elite secret sect of men who were smarter, more artistic, sensitive and sophisticated. "Of course they hate us," Duncan had argued. "Because we're so clearly superior in every way. Alexander the Great, Leonardo da Vinci, Shakespeare, Whitman, Wilde, Cole Porter."

"Liberace," Michael had teased. But he loved this confidence of Duncan's.

"What's the matter?" he asked Duncan now.

Duncan was silent, but in front of the Bernini altar, he turned to Michael.

"Julie's pregnant again."

Michael paused. "Congratulations."

"She's asked that we be more of a family."

He wanted to shout at Duncan that he had seen Julie at the goddamn *orgy* at Gordon's, and the baby probably wasn't even Duncan's, but he knew that if he humiliated him this way, Duncan would cut him out of his life forever. "Scottie's pregnant, too," he said.

Later, they stood on the bank of the Tiber in front of Castel Sant'Angelo. Duncan said nothing for what felt like an hour.

"Benvenuto Cellini was imprisoned in there," Michael said. "He was gay, too. And kind of an asshole."

It was meant to make Duncan laugh, but he didn't. Instead he looked up at the tiny windows of the cylindrical fortress, his hands sunk deep in his pockets, and said, "I hate this life. I don't want to be this way."

Twelve:
La Pantera, The Panther

"MY CHARGE STRIKES EVERY OBSTACLE"

Who decided that the best tree to line a driveway was the cypress? And who realized villas are prettiest when they're yellowish gold with green shutters? Who thought terra-cotta roofs looked best? Large urns of lemon trees? Clinging vines with orangey-pink trumpet flowers? In short, who was responsible for the stunningly beautiful cliché that is any Tuscan villa?

Scottie did not care. All she was thinking about was what attitude to take with Carlo. Only hours after their tryst in Florence, he had left her at the villa — completely forgotten about her, apparently, as if she were an umbrella. Yes, Franca was having some sort of breakdown, and as her husband he had to take care of her. It was all for the best, of course — but still. She had no car; if Michael had not arrived, she would have had no way to get home. Carlo's rudeness was shocking, and she felt angry and offended whenever she thought of it. The fact that she was going to see him at all was probably ill-advised, but . . . he was still their landlord, and he knew Pisano. It would be good to normalize things with him, make it clear that she did not care that he had bedded her and dropped her. Although "bedded" was a stretch, since that was the only place they hadn't actually made love. Really, she was so nervous that her hands on the scooter were clammy and her heart was thumping.

As she and Ecco putt-putted up a rutted driveway on the scooter, her gaze was stuck on a small herd of jet black horses inside a hand-hewn wooden pen. She spotted a heavy-headed stallion. Scottie didn't like stallions — they were bratty and often dangerous. She was riding a mare through public land once in California, unaware that the leaseholder had turned out a stallion along with his mares, and had ended up as the lettuce in a horse sandwich, her legs pinned under the stallion's forelegs as he mounted her mare. That adventure had been impossible to recount to her father that evening at dinner, or ever. Ladies didn't say such things.

A thunderstorm was hot on her heels as she rode past the stables and up the driveway to the castle. The sky behind her was nearly black, and lightning flashed in her rearview mirror, but she counted the seconds and calculated that the storm was still miles away. Ecco whined and looked up at her.

As her tires crunched to a stop on the gravel in front of what seemed to her a villa and not a castle, Carlo came out of the large front door, surprised to see her. He was dressed once again like a *buttero* in loose brown riding pants and a forest green vest and fedora.

"Cara," he said in surprise.

How dare he call her "dear." She feigned a cool detachment she did not feel. "So this is the castle?"

"Actually, that's the castle." He pointed to a short, stubby stone tower about fifty yards from the villa that seemed to have collapsed in on itself. Ivy grew over the piles of rocks, and doves sat in gaping holes in the masonry. "Built as a Saracen watchtower around the year 900," he said. "It stood tall until 1943. Someday my ship will come in and I'll rebuild it, but for now it's just a dream."

"You were going somewhere," she said.

"How is Franca?"

His face darkened. "Not good. I think she's gone up to the mountain, to a little house we have up there. She goes there when she needs to be alone. This is the worst I've ever seen her."

He was so sincere, so clearly worried, that she felt ashamed of her pique.

"I'm sorry I don't have much time. The weanlings are in the low pasture by the river. I want to move them before the storm comes. My *fattore*'s in Grosseto today buying fencing." He didn't ask her why she'd come. He seemed worried, preoccupied.

She was suddenly overwhelmed with the idea that she could get on a horse, right now, today.

"I can help you," she said.

"Are you sure?" he said. "In your condition?"

She had friends from Vassar who spent their entire pregnancies lying in front of the television watching soap operas, eating ice cream and growing as big as houses, but that wasn't her style. "My child may as well get used to riding horses now," she said.

"But your clothes — ?"

"I can ride in anything," she said quickly. "But boots would be better than sandals."

She tried not to inhale his scent as she

followed him into the entry hall, full of the daily detritus of living in the country — coats and hats hanging on pegs, seed packets, farm equipment catalogs, a jumble of ivory-handled walking sticks. Piles and piles of bills covered a small desk in the corner of the hall. So the marchese's life wasn't all champagne and fancy dress balls. She made Ecco wait outside.

Carlo said, *"È un casino."* She liked that word. It so perfectly conveyed a mess.

From a vast assortment lined up under a portrait of a man in a red uniform, she found a pair of boots that fit her. Carlo gave her some rough wool socks. As she sat down on the stairs to pull them on, he offered her coffee, which she agreed to, although she was already jumpy.

"So, is that your father?" she asked, pointing to a neat charcoal sketch of a man who looked like Carlo.

"Yes." She could hear caution in his voice.

"Is he alive?"

"No," said Carlo. He turned away, but then turned back, as if he had made a decision to face something. "He was shot, at the end of the war. He was close with Mussolini."

"Oh," she said. Was Carlo close with Mussolini, too? She didn't want to know the answer. "My father is dead, too. He was a thief."

Carlo laughed at this, and so did she, at the wild absurdity of it. "Like Billy the Kid?" he asked.

"If Billy were an accountant," she said, still laughing.

"You are constantly surprising me," he said, and her stomach flipped over, and not from the baby kicking her.

She should never have come.

"I'm glad you came," Carlo said as they headed out to the stable. "I've always wanted to ride with a cowgirl." He raised an eyebrow and a slow grin spread across his face. "To show her how much better riders the *butteri* are."

"Ah!" she laughed. "As I welcome the chance to show *you* how to ride."

"I have the perfect horse for you," he said. "*Vispa* like you."

The thunder was getting closer as they mounted their horses and headed through a swinging gate. The wind rolled around them. She had left Ecco inside the villa, and she hoped he wasn't chewing anything ancient or precious.

It felt so unbelievably good to be back in the saddle again, as if she had been holding her breath for months and could finally exhale. The only way she could pop her lowest vertebrae was by lifting both feet in the stirrups at the same time — she did, and all tension left her body. The smell of the leather, saddle soap and the ozone in the air put all her senses into play at once. She had wondered if being pregnant would make her feel awkward in the saddle, but for now at least it didn't. She smiled as she thought, *Baby's first ride.* She was finally bonding with this child inside her. What did it matter whose sperm this began with? This was *her* baby.

"What do you grow on your estate?" she asked as they skirted a large field of tall grass.

"Grapes, wheat, sunflowers. Plus Chianina cows, Cinta Senese pigs and Persani horses as well as the Maremmani."

"And you have a lot of houses."

He gave a little snort. "Yes. Most of them are falling down. Not every inheritance is a good thing. Probably they should all be sold, but I am sentimental."

She patted the shoulder of the black mare she was riding. Short but sturdy, she had sniffed Scottie's hand approvingly when Scottie offered it to her before mounting. She was a little heavy on the bit, but responded by arching her neck and using her back and hindquarters when Scottie gave her some leg.

"The Persani were used by the cavalry, right?"

"Yes. But they sold them all. They are becoming very rare now. No one wants them."

"Even though Raimondo D'Inzeo rides one?"

"It helps," he said, brightening. "Merano is a lovely horse, isn't he?"

She nodded.

"It is helping me sell them. A man from Belgium came the other day. Some people still remember the charge of Izbushensky in '42. The Italian cavalry, seven hundred men mounted on Persani, outflanked the Russian infantry. Hundreds of black horses flying at full gallop across a field of sunflowers a thousand miles from home. It was the end of five thousand years of history, the last battle on horseback that will ever be waged."

"Were you there?"

He turned and looked at her, his face strange. "Yes," he said. "Yes. You won't understand, but it was the most beautiful moment of my life. We carried sabers. *Sabers.*" He laughed and shook his head at this.

Sehnsucht, she thought. He's a man of

another era.

He jumped down to open a gate whose latch was stuck. "The horses have been leaning on it," he said. "Missing their mothers."

The raindrops were just starting to hit the dust.

"Let me help you." She jumped down and lifted the gate as he undid the rusty latch. They were side by side, and she could smell him again. Horses and sweat. Molasses and hay.

The gate swung open, but neither one of them moved. The rain began to pelt their faces. He was almost unbearably attractive. She felt like a moon being pulled into the orbit of a powerful planet.

A cow mooed somewhere, and it broke the spell. They remounted and rode along the treed edge of a plowed field.

"It's the next field," he said quietly.

She could hear the river in the distance.

I love my husband, she told herself.

They crested a rise, and a large grassy meadow spread before them, sloping down toward the fast-moving river.

"There they are." The weanlings — six of them, all bays and chestnuts — were running up and down in youthful giddy panic. They neighed when they saw Carlo and

Scottie's horses and came trotting toward them, tossing their heads.

Scottie watched as Carlo got behind them and drove them forward slowly, not panicking them, letting his adult horse's presence keep them calm and show them the way. So simple, and yet almost no one could do it.

She coaxed her mare into a canter and rode over to a gate in the hedge. This one was well oiled, and swung open when she shot the bolt. She backed her horse up, just away from the gate, and helped Carlo move the weanlings into the safety of the fenced lane.

"There's one missing," he said, locking the gate.

He galloped off, back across the field to the river. She followed him. He was a good rider, she saw, in tune with his horse.

They split up and rode in two directions along the riverfront. It was rocky and muddy, and she had to slow down, make sure her horse was looking where she put her feet.

She was circling a thicket of rushes when she heard a yell. She turned and saw Carlo. His horse was halfway out in the river, water up to the stirrups, and struggling on the rocks. Carlo had a rope around the weanling, who was swimming, but the colt's weight on the rope was throwing Carlo's gelding off balance. Disregarding the footing, she dug her heels into the mare and galloped as close as she could get. Carlo's horse was in danger of being pulled over. The weanling was already bobbing.

"Get out of there!"

She saw he wouldn't. *You're going to drown for a horse,* she thought.

"Drop the rope," she called. "I'll get the colt."

Carlo's horse staggered, not finding footing in the slippery rocks under water, and he let go of the rope as his horse dropped down underneath him.

Scottie watched them disappear into the roiling water.

She raced downstream, below the rapids, found a sandy spot and rode the mare as far out into the water as she could safely go. The colt appeared first, still dragging the rope. Seeing her horse, it swam toward her, wide-eyed.

She saw Carlo and his horse appear, swimming. Good. Carlo was holding the horse's tail, and they were heading for shore. When she looked back at the colt, it had stopped and was splashing, exhausted, in the middle of the river. She realized the rope had caught in some brush.

She had to get the rope off its head or it would drown. She rode out as far as her mare would go. The mare stopped, threw her head.

"I know," said Scottie to the mare. They were so close. She turned sideways in the saddle, pulled off her boots, tossed them to shore, jumped off the mare and swam.

Raised with the ugly currents of the Pacific Ocean and California's turbulent spring runoff, she knew the danger in what she was doing, and swam hard. She calculated the current right and landed against the stuck colt, barely avoiding its thrashing hoofs. She grabbed the half-submerged tree the rope was stuck on and slipped the rope over the colt's head.

"Swim!" she said. Its eyes were dull, and for a moment it did nothing but start to float away. Then instinct won out, and the colt swam to shore.

Carlo was now out of the river.

She was clinging to the half-submerged tree in the middle of the river, exhausted and getting colder by the minute. This was the danger. You lost your nerve, and fatigue set in.

"Rope!" he yelled, and threw it at her. She grabbed it, and he towed her to shore. They collapsed on the shore, exhausted, the horses standing nearby, all catching their breath.

"Scottie," he said. "My darling."

Ecco was leaping up and down and barking hysterically when they opened the front door to the villa, his pent-up energy a sharp contrast to their exhaustion. She thought he looked disapproving of her wet, muddy clothes. The horses were safely put away, and the rain was lessening. The sun had the temerity to peek through the clouds, as if it were innocently asking, "Did anything happen while I was gone?"

Carlo put water on to boil and handed her dry clothes. Men's pants. A shirt. She saw his monogram on the cuff.

Gordon had failed to deliver the message last night that Carlo had had to take Franca home. He had asked Gordon to arrange a ride for Scottie. Carlo was mortified, begging Scottie's pardon, asking how she made her way home.

"My husband came for me."

All we have in this life are the things we are true to, she thought.

"I had to help Franca. I will always love her." He was really saying something else, though, she knew, and it scared her. She wanted to run out the door. She went and sat on the other side of the kitchen table, a mass of books and papers safely between them.

"I love my husband, too."

He also sat down at the table, shifting so that a large ceramic candelabra didn't block his view of her. "We are both lucky, then. To have a great love, no matter the difficulties, no matter the heartbreak that comes, this is life's finest gift."

She couldn't think of a single American man who would have said that, or even agreed. Yes, she knew men who adored their wives, but their first loves were always their careers. "My husband is very hardworking."

"With the tractors."

"Yes. I'm very proud of him." Outside the French doors, a cat meowed to get in. Ecco stood on alert, nose to nose, the glass between them, but the cat did not back away.

"This is modern life," said Carlo. "Trying to make the world a better place. Progress."

She nodded.

"Sometimes I dream that Franca finds the right herb that will erase her memory and that she is healed, that she comes back to me happy as she once was. I dream that we grow old together, side by side."

Sunlight streamed through the windows.

She smiled and sipped her tea.

"I need to ask you about Tenente Pisano."

"Piccione? That's what we called him at school. His fondest wish is to see Umberto back on the throne as king of Italy. What about him?"

"He owns a horse that disappeared from the stable just after Robertino did. Apparently they fought about the way Pisano treated the horse. I can't help but worry that he's not the man to be looking for Robertino. He may be the reason the boy's on the run."

Carlo frowned and squeezed more lemon into his tea. A clock ticked in the next room. "If Piccione has a sin it's pride. That's how he got his nickname, Pigeon — from having a puffed-up chest. He had a thing with that horse. I saw him ride her. He came by here once and made an excuse about not getting off to say hello. I knew it was because he was fairly sure he'd never get her to stand still to mount again. I reached up to straighten his saddle pad where it was slipping, and — bam!" Carlo's fist shot out. "She whirled around and tried to kick me. *Bestiaccia di merda.*"

"It was a warning," Scottie said. "If she had intended to hit you, you'd be dead."

He shook his head, reliving the memory.

376

"I don't like dangerous horses. Here we have a job to do. No time for trouble. Life sends us enough of that already."

For a moment a lump rose in her throat and she couldn't speak. "Yes," she said at last. "Pisano must have known, before he bought her. Why did he?"

"I told you, she was beautiful. He thought he could save her."

"Save her?"

"Anyone else had bought that horse, she'd be dead in a week."

Hmm. She tried not to soften her view of Pisano. "But he gave up on the mare? I heard he called the butcher."

"She wore out his patience, I guess. I wasn't there when he fell off in the show. I heard she sent him headfirst into the water jump."

"Sounds like his pride got the better of his compassion."

Carlo frowned. "I'd like to know the whole story."

"Why don't you ask him? He's a friend, isn't he?"

He smiled a sad smile. "I don't have friends in Siena."

"Why?" She was prying, but she wanted to know.

"I was in the cavalry, as I told you. My

377

father was a high-ranking Fascist. That put me on the wrong side of history."

"But you were just doing your duty."

"Yes. But just by wearing that uniform, I was a part of something . . . very ugly."

It hit her suddenly, what it would mean to be with a man like Carlo. He would never lie to her. Would she lie to him? She had always lied: to her father about riding without a helmet, about how high the jumps she jumped were; to Leona about her parents, her *class,* about why she was marrying Michael; to Michael about nearly everything. She couldn't tell whether it would be a relief to finally tell someone the truth, or a loss of power. Her secrets were woven into the fabric of her being, protection against an unfriendly, unjust world. Maybe she and Michael were meant to be together.

"I think you should try again with Franca," she said. "I think . . ." She looked outside. It was once again a beautiful afternoon. "I think you should try."

"Thank you," he said. "For the horses. That colt would be dead without you, and maybe me, too."

"Sometimes it's better to let go of the rope," she said, then, remembering that he had in turn saved her, "And sometimes it's better to grab it."

She didn't kiss him good-bye, or even shake his hand, because she was afraid that if she did, she would never leave.

■ ■ ■ ■

PART THREE:
TERZO DI SAN MARTINO

■ ■ ■ ■

The State Department has discharged 126 homosexuals since Jan. 1, 1951, and is determined to remove any others from the department . . . "There is no doubt in our minds that homosexuals are security risks," and "we have resolved that we are going to clean them up."
— "126 Perverts Discharged," *The New York Times,* March 26, 1952, quoting Carlisle H. Humelsine, Deputy Under Secretary of State for Administration, U.S. Department of State

Thirteen:
Il Leocorno, The Unicorn

"IT SMITES AND HEALS, THE HORN I WEAR
ON MY FOREHEAD."

1.

"Congratulations. You've been hired," Michael told her as she came through the front door of their apartment in rolled-up men's pants and an ex-Fascist's dress shirt.

"Hired?" She was holding her wet, muddy clothes, poised to give a nervous explanation, but he didn't seem to notice. "Are you okay?" she asked. "I thought you were going to stay over in Rome."

He pointed at the light fixture overhead. He was always worried about bugs. "I'll explain it to you over dinner," he said. "I'm taking you out."

She nodded and went into the bedroom. Put her dirty clothes in the hamper. Picked something nice to wear — the white dress with the strawberries, she decided. She ran

383

a few inches of water in the bath. There didn't seem to be any hot water, but she sat in it anyway, shivering and scrubbing.

No more secrets.

She got as much mud out of her hair as she could and put it under a pretty hat, shaped like a turban with a little velvet bird on top. She put on dangling earrings that gave her a slightly gypsy look, and sprayed herself with Chanel No. 5.

Over branzino with lemon and capers at Papei, Michael explained that the Agency (he said "Ford," but she knew what he meant) had authorized him to hire her. "It's called a contract wife position," he said. "It's just secretarial," he added. "Paperwork."

She leaned in close. "What do we know about Tenente Pisano?" she asked quietly.

Michael frowned. "Why?"

She told him that Robertino's disappearance might be connected to the disappearance of Pisano's horse Camelia.

Michael nodded. "I think it's best if we steer clear of Pisano, unfortunately," he said. "If I promise you I'll do what I can, will you please let me handle it?"

She nodded.

"I really need you in the office," he said. "I'm away a lot, and there's no one there to answer the phone. You're the only one I trust. Which reminds me, I'll need to administer the loyalty oath."

"Michael," she said, then paused to steady her voice.

"What is it?"

"When I married you, I let you . . . assume things. Things that weren't true. I'm not from a highbrow family. I'm not rich."

"I don't mind those things. I'm not either. You knew that and you still married me. I love you for that."

"That's just it. I —"

"What is it, darling?"

"Darling" made it worse.

"I — I got too close to Carlo. I —" She stopped.

He frowned, then put his hand over hers. "Whatever happened, it's because I left you alone too much. I should have defied orders, told you right from the start what I was doing here. It's my fault you were lonely."

Could he really be understanding her and forgiving her so quickly? "I — I just feel terrible. I —"

"Shhh. Don't say anything more. We're here, we're together. Whatever happened before this doesn't matter, does it?"

He leaned across the table to kiss her. He was ready to forgive her and move on. Her marriage could begin again, fresh and new. It could be the marriage she had hoped for, longed for. It was . . . incredible.

She put her hands up. "Wait."

He stared at her.

She put her face in her hands for a second, then gathered her courage. If they were to have a real marriage, he had to know everything.

2.

March 1956, Vassar College

Winds as penetrating as any x-ray whipped through Poughkeepsie. Scottie was summoned to a meeting with her religion professor. The creaking skeletal trees she passed as she crossed the campus seemed to be screaming in agony.

She made her way to the lower level of the fantastically Gothic Thompson Library, a cathedral-like vision of battlements, pinnacles, stained glass and buttresses, its lower levels a warren of shelves shrouded in cold and darkness. You had to start a timer to turn on the lights, and it was dim even when they were on. The librarian said it had something to do with preserving the oldest volumes, which were stored down here. Some girls brought flashlights with them when they had to hunt down books on this level, Nancy Drews in Shetland sweaters, plaid Bermuda shorts and wool kneesocks. It was also where her professor had his office, which turned out to be more of a carrel. She had put on a houndstooth skirt, shiny black loafers and a cashmere twinset, trying to look like an A student instead of a barely C. All the girls had crushes on Professor Redd, including Scottie. He was married to a former Vassar girl, and had two little boys his wife would sometimes bring to campus to show off in their little plaid coats with velvet collars.

"I wish they'd give me a real office," he apologized. He had wavy, thick salt-and-pepper hair, a short beard that was going gray and gray eyes behind tortoiseshell glasses. A tweed jacket with suede elbow patches and a pipe. "I guess this is better than a snowbank, right?"

She smiled, but she was anxious. It had been hard to get through the readings for the course, "The Genesis of Genesis: How the Old Testament Evolved." Religion was a requirement, and she needed to pass this class to graduate.

"I know I'm not one of the best students," she told her professor. "But I do love the subject, and I'm already working on my final paper for the class. It's on Noah, about

God's decision to save the animals but not the people."

"That's wonderful," he said. "I thought if we went over your midterm together, it might be helpful." He patted the chair next to his.

"Yes," she said eagerly. "I could really use some extra help. All those 'begats' — I will admit, I got a little lost."

"Happens to the best of us. Now here, where you talk about Bathsheba —"

She leaned forward, and their heads came close as he read her answer aloud. She felt a tingle of energy in the air, and then felt his hand on her back.

"Yes, I uh, see what you're saying," she said. His hand was warm through her soft sweater.

"Do you know the Song of Songs?" He moved his head one inch closer to hers, and she could smell pipe tobacco and tweed damp from snowflakes. "It's one of the most beautiful passages in the Old Testament. *Behold, you are comely, my beloved; behold, you are comely; your eyes are like doves.* Isn't that some really lovely writing?" She nodded. His hand was moving in circles on her back. In a friendly way? Or more? She wasn't sure whether to run out of the room or not. She didn't want to misunderstand

and seem dim, or silly.

"I really appreciate your help," she said. "I can probably figure it out now."

"Let me just read you a little more. It's so wonderful and sensuous. Not what most people think of as 'the Bible' at all. I wrote my PhD thesis on this. It's my own translation. *Feed me with flagons of wine, spread my bed with red ripe apples, for I am lovesick. His left hand strayed beneath my head, and his right hand encircled me. I warn you, O daughters of Jersusalem, by the gazelles or the deer of the meadow, that you neither awaken nor arouse the love unless you return it.*"

He leaned in and nuzzled her neck. "You smell so good," he said. "I hope you don't mind. I can't help myself."

His beard tickled her. He did smell good. Underneath her fear, she could feel a desire growing in her. *He likes me,* she thought.

"You're so unbelievably beautiful." He kissed her ear. His hand had strayed to her thigh, was rubbing the tweed of her skirt between his thumb and forefinger. "I've been watching you in class all semester. I can't take my eyes off you." He now had one hand around her back, and was rubbing his way toward her left breast, while his right hand was working its way under

389

her skirt. *Nor arouse the love unless you return it.*

She wanted to run, but also, she didn't. It seemed disrespectful somehow.

"I — should probably go," she said.

"You don't like me?"

"No, no, I do."

"I like you so much," he said. "I wish you liked me, too."

"I do."

"Please just kiss me once," he said. "One kiss and I'll let you go."

It seemed rude not to give him one kiss.

She stood up, surrounded by shelves of books, and went to peck his cheek, but he put his arms around her, leaned in and kissed her long and hard on the mouth, shoving his tongue in. His hands went under her sweater and up her belly, then were on her behind, pulling her close. She felt something give way inside her, and suddenly he was pressing her up against Botany A–G, his hand finding its way under her skirt and then under her underpants and she was ashamed because it was wet there. He stopped kissing her for a second. "That's the most wonderful thing I've ever felt," he said. "That makes a man feel like a man."

He kissed her again, and pressed his erection against her. She knew she was supposed to run away, to stop, but she had been told it was wrong to make a man feel this way and then deny him. It was her fault. She hadn't meant this to happen, was confused, but her body wasn't. She let him undo her bra and rub her breasts. If he were a boy, and this were a date, she would stop him there, but it seemed bad manners to run out on her professor, and what would she say when she saw him next? What grade would she get? She heard footsteps in the stairwell, and they froze. Part of her wanted to cry out, but another part liked the hiding, the secrecy. He likes *me.* Then the footsteps continued down to the next level. He turned her around and held her from behind, kissing her neck.

"Do you mind?" he said. "This way we don't have to lie on the dirty floor." He took her hands and put them on the shelf in front of her, and she was unsure of what he wanted. He pulled her hips back and now she was bending over, her face in Gray, Asa, *Manual of the Botany of the Northern United States, from New England to Wisconsin and South to Ohio and Pennsylvania Inclusive.* She stared at the gold lettering on the dark green spine, inhaled the old leather smell, the mustiness of the pages, and didn't understand what was happening, then thought of horses and realized. In a quick movement, he lifted her skirt and pulled her underwear down. She heard his zipper and then he pulled her hips back toward him and she felt a sharp pain and gasped, tears in her eyes.

"The flowers are blooming in the land, the time to sing has arrived, and the murmur of the turtledove is back again," he whispered.

He held on to her hips and pulled her hard against him. She felt him deep inside her.

"I opened the door and stood erect for my beloved, my hands dripping with myrrh, and my fingers flowing with sweet myrrh, my fingers upon the lock of the door."

Then he groaned, butted her hard like a ram with his hips, and it was over. He zipped up, gave her a pat on her behind. "Dear me," he said. "You got me very excited there, you naughty girl. You'd better go clean yourself up."

She stood, blushing, eyes on the ground, and awkwardly pulled up her underwear and her kneesocks and reached behind to fasten her bra.

"I'll see you in class," he said. He lifted her chin with his hand and stared into her eyes. "I know I can trust you to keep this our little secret."

"I got pregnant," she said.

The color was gone from Michael's face. The waiter, coming to take his plate, took one look at him and backed away. *My marriage is over,* she thought.

"That's . . . awful," he said.

"I'm so sorry." She felt cold all over.

"The man should be beaten within an inch of his life! He should — did he ever say anything to you? Offer to take care of you?"

"I never told him."

He stared at her, furious, not comprehending.

"It would have ruined his marriage. He would have lost his job."

"But what about you?"

She blinked. "I never told anyone until now. I — I felt like it was my fault."

People were laughing and chatting around them, strolling arm in arm through the piazza.

"He made it seem like it was your fault, but it wasn't. He seduced you! A virgin!"

She had never really seen it this way before. It made her angry now, to think of it this way.

"He should have . . . ." Michael paused. "Well, he should have helped you."

"I was afraid that I would be disgraced. I *would* have been disgraced if anyone had found out."

"Why didn't you tell me?"

She sighed. "I was afraid. I knew you wouldn't marry me, wouldn't even talk to me if you knew. No one would. I would end up . . ." She thought of Gina. "I had no money, no family. I would have lost my friends. Been kicked out of school. No one would have given me a job." It wasn't much of a choice, really, she thought. She had done what she had to do. "I'm so sorry," she said.

They sat for a moment in silence. She kept her eyes down, ashamed. She wasn't sure what would come next. He would send her back to America, probably. Divorce her. She didn't cry. She just felt numb. She had no right to ask anything of him.

The world continued around them, waiters moving, people talking, plates of food going to and fro, but they were two frozen figures.

"Hey," he said at last, and took her hands in his. "Hey. Look at me."

She looked up. He was smiling at her.

"From this moment on, it's our baby. Ours. Okay?"

"Really?" Again she was shocked.

"Yes. Yes."

"Oh, Michael," she said, and threw herself into his arms. "Let's never keep secrets from each other again."

He held her as she cried tears of relief and joy.

He made love to her that night. He asked her, as he always did, was he hurting her, and was he hurting the baby, and she always reassured him, but he seemed unwilling to put his weight on her. They had always followed the same pattern: some kissing, eyes tightly closed, then he eased up her night-dress and eased down his pajamas. He finished with a grunt, and then apologized. Afterward, he went to sleep.

Tonight, she closed her eyes, and just as he came, she felt a rising in her belly.

"Wait, wait," she said, opening her eyes, grabbing him tight around the waist, lifting her legs and pulling him deep inside her, willing him to stay erect a few seconds longer. He looked surprised. She came with a long shudder that made her teeth chatter.

"Oh," he said. "Oh. You're sure that doesn't hurt the baby?"

She pulled him close and kissed him tenderly. "No, it doesn't. Thank you," she said.

As they lay side by side in the darkness, he said, "You know Robertino well, wouldn't you say?"

"Yes, pretty well," she said.

"Do you think he likes Americans?"

"You mean do I think he's on our side?"

"Yes."

She thought for a moment. "Because of his parents, he's an outsider and an insider at the same time. I'm not sure he can afford to be on anyone's side but his own."

He put his arms around her and they fell asleep entwined.

4.

Pisano came to see him about the missing boy and the dead hooker, fortunately at a moment when Scottie was off at the post office, a Dantesque place of swirling crowds and no lines in which one could easily lose half a day. Brigante hovered outside the Ford office, trying to eavesdrop. Michael shut the door with a loud clang.

"He taught my wife a little Italian," he said.

"Did you ever visit the prostitute?"

"Never," he said.

"Many men did," said Pisano. "I am not accusing you of anything, but you are a Sicilian and an American. Perhaps you know more than you are saying."

Michael sighed. "I never even spoke to her. And I'm not in the Mafia."

"And you say you never had Robertino run errands for you?" Pisano pressed. "You never asked him to get women for you?"

"No," said Michael. "I did not."

Scottie had told him her secrets, and he had shown her that he could still love her. It felt so good to give her that gift, to see her fear and shame turn to surprise and joy. He didn't really mind that the child wasn't his — in some ways it was a relief. If he turned out to be a terrible father, he was still better than the one who had created the child. Besides, he thought, it was all too perfect before — the pretty, adoring, faithful wife dutifully carrying his child. This felt more like what he deserved.

5.

Being a spy, it turned out, was crushingly dull. Scottie spent a few days dutifully typing up boring summaries of articles in the local papers. Because of her struggles with reading and writing, she had to type very slowly and often made mistakes. It was heavy going, especially given the rather dry subject matter — automobile production numbers, wheat harvest, gas prices, labor unrest in the steel industry.

"Please can I include this one?" she asked Michael. " 'Traffic cop attacked by crazed bull.' Way more interesting than these olive oil production numbers."

Michael laughed. "They would assume it was code for something. I'd like to see what they deciphered it to be." He had explained to her that these financial reports were essential to their mission, which was largely to figure out where Italy was in terms of economy and politics, and where it was going. Other analysts took that info and added in a layer of what America's role in Italy's future should be, and where the Soviets fit into all that.

"That's the 'intelligence' part of Central Intelligence Agency," he said. "Not the kind of thing that shows up in the movies. We're really here to be the eyes and ears of the president and Congress, to help them make good foreign policy decisions." Michael did not tell her that this was in fact what former CIA director Walter Bedell Smith had wanted the CIA to limit its mission to. But Angleton had argued that the ruthlessness of the Soviets and the escalating Cold War demanded the newer, self-created missions of disinformation, counterintelligence, propaganda and coups. The Dark Arts. It was amazing to Michael how an entire foreign policy could be shaped by a battle between two men, how many millions of lives were affected by decisions more influenced by ego than facts.

She was looking for staples one day when she noticed one of the cabinets was locked.

"Where's the key for this?" she asked Michael.

"Oh, I'm sorry," he said. "That's for me only."

"What do you have in there?" she whispered. "Microcameras and exploding umbrellas? Pen guns?"

He rolled his eyes, and she laughed. "I never missed a single episode of *Foreign Intrigue,*" she said.

Despite Michael's love of numbers, Scottie began to slowly change the tone of her reports. When she wrote about wheat prices, she talked about the owner of the bakery and the importance of artisan-made bread in the community, about the culture of women. When she wrote about tourism, she talked about Tommaso, the waiter, and how he was spending his tips, his dreams of a beach vacation. When she talked about health care, she wrote about Signor Banchi, but also about poor dead Gina, and the women at the bakery, and Franca and her herbs and the pervasive trust in the old ways of healing. She talked about the legacy of war. She had no idea if anyone ever read them, but in her reports she strove to capture the essence of Italian culture as she understood it. "While I am at a loss to fully explain it," she often began her summations, "I can nonetheless speak with admiration of the Italian practice of . . ."

Scottie took to stopping in to see Signor Banchi on her ever-longer lunch breaks. He had moved out of the hospital, back to his little house down the hill from Porta San Marco in the olive grove. He was not improving, and kept asking for Robertino. It had been almost two weeks since he failed to show up at the *tratta.* It was heartbreaking. No one in town was talking about him anymore. She told Signor Banchi to not lose hope.

She found herself thinking less about Carlo. She felt grateful to him for having shown her what a romantic bond could be, though. He had taught her how to be a better wife.

I'm happy, she thought. *I have a handsome, heroic spy husband who's fighting communism, and I'm right here by his side.* Life felt full of excitement and possibility again, and she finally felt close to Michael, even though she knew there were things he couldn't tell her about his work, for her own safety. But she felt like he needed her — and he told her so. She loved that they were spreading the truth about America, the best country in the whole world.

Together they went to see a woman outside Greve who was making wine on her family's estate. Her husband and her brothers had died in the war. Her name was Angela, and she was stout, with ruddy cheeks.

She showed Michael and Scottie the old stone cave with huge oak barrels, handmade glass vessels on top with oil in them to allow the wine to expand and contract without touching the air.

"It's alive," explained Angela. "Every barrel is different. If I treated them all the same, it would be a disaster."

Michael talked to her about what a tractor could do for her, how it could save her money in the long run because she would have to hire fewer people.

Angela frowned and gestured toward the men and women hoeing weeds in the vineyard. "These people expect to work here their whole lives," she said.

"Things change. That's not your fault," said Michael. "You're running a business." He meant to be kind, but Scottie saw Angela stiffen.

"If you're able to farm more acres and make more wine, your business will expand and you'll have other work for them," said Scottie.

"No," said Angela. "I'm sorry. We are all responsible for each other."

In the car on the way back to Siena, Michael and Scottie puzzled over this resistance to change.

"She's being ridiculous," insisted Michael. "Tractors save people backbreaking labor. They can find other jobs, less exhausting ones. She's saying the feudal system is better."

"Maybe she's right and we're wrong. Maybe all of it — cars, tractors, factories — maybe they're not making our lives better."

"They're making our lives easier. I don't want to walk everywhere. Do you want to do the laundry in a stream? Cook over a fire? Watch me try to kill a deer for our dinner? I hope you're not too hungry."

"When we came here I thought we were right about all of it, and that they were wrong. But I do think some of the old ways are better," she said, thinking of Banchi.

"Go work in the fields for a few days and then tell me you don't want to ride a tractor instead."

"I bet the horse-drawn world was more fun."

"Not the manure. My parents talked about what it was like in New York when they arrived. Picture a blizzard of poop."

"I'm imagining your mother saying that." She laughed. "Do you miss them?"

He frowned. "Sometimes. I miss my mother's lasagna."

"I can try to make that."

He put his hand over hers. "Let's make it together."

"You know how to cook?"

Something flickered in his eyes. "Just a little. I mean, I sat at the kitchen table doing my homework and watched my mother."

"No Chef Boyardee?"

"Never." He shuddered.

"Then I guess all American conveniences aren't better," she said.

Michael's lasagna was in fact exquisite — he claimed the secret was that he whipped the ricotta by hand, gently folding in the egg and nutmeg. She took some down to Signor Banchi.

"Buonissimo," he declared, but poked at it

listlessly. She felt shy about telling him that it was Michael and not her who had made it, as if somehow he would think less of both of them.

Nonna Bea came down the path as Scottie was leaving Banchi's farm. Usually Nonna Bea wanted nothing to do with Scottie — she treated her like a Martian who might be carrying an interstellar virus, and who definitely did not speak any earthly language. Occasionally Nonna Bea made the sign of the cross when she saw her and spat on the ground when crossing paths with her, as if she were a black cat. But today, Nonna Bea not only looked at her, but reached out a claw and grabbed her arm.

"L'americano," she said with toothless urgency and a fair amount of spittle.

"My husband?" asked Scottie, awaiting some sort of lecture from Nonna Bea that she really hoped was not about how to please a man.

"No, no, l'altro," said Nonna Bea. *"Il diavolo."* The devil. *"Sta venendo qui. Venga, venga."*

The devil is coming? Scottie grappled with this. She nodded vaguely.

Nonna Bea spat a torrent of words that Scottie found hard to follow, all the while dragging her back toward Banchi's house. For a tiny old woman, she was very strong.

"Zitto!" called Nonna Bea to Banchi, telling him to keep silent, as she dragged Scottie through his living room into the kitchen. There was a pantry with a piece of fabric for a door. Nonna Bea pulled Scottie with her behind the curtain. Scottie pointed to their feet, which showed clearly beneath the curtain, Nonna Bea's rough old boots and Scottie's loafers. Scottie grabbed four large tins of tomatoes and stepped up onto two of them, helping Nonna Bea up onto the other two. It was slightly precarious, to say the least — one tilt and they would go headlong into a wicker bin of onions. Scottie could smell Nonna Bea's breath, a mix of bad teeth, garlic and cats. Did she eat them, Scottie wondered, or just lick them? Probably Nonna Bea's last bath had been sometime around Scottie's birth.

They waited in the heat for a few minutes. Scottie started to move, but Nonna Bea grabbed her hand again and gestured silence as they heard a knock at the door and a *"Permesso?"* from the other room.

She didn't recognize the man's voice. He greeted Signor Banchi and introduced another man, a *notaio,* or notary. She heard papers shuffling, and words of encouragement. American-accented encouragement.

"This is a very good deal," he said in English, then added to the other man impatiently, "Translate that."

"This is enough money to buy anything you need."

Signor Banchi was silent except for a soft moan.

After a long pause and an irritated sigh, "We can help you find your grandson if you help us," said the man.

Scottie's eyes widened and she nearly gasped. Nonna Bea put her finger to her lips.

"Leave the papers," coughed Signor Banchi. "Come back tomorrow. *Domani.*"

They waited until they heard the men leave, then went into the living room, where Signor Banchi was sitting.

Scottie snatched up the papers. "This is disgusting," she said. "*Schiffoso!* Preying on a sick old man. Do you think they kidnapped Robertino?"

Nonna Bea nodded and gave a small burp. "Bad men," she said. *"Diavoli. Americani di merda."* Shit Americans.

Scottie let that one slide. Best not to enter into a discussion of stereotyping just now. She grabbed the papers. "I'm going to take these, but I will keep them safe," she said.

"I don't want the money," stuttered Banchi, tears in his eyes. "I just want my grandson back."

Ital-Amer Hotel Corp. It was an address in Rome. Under the signature bar for the company was a name. Ben Lippincott, Representative.

Michael would want to look into this himself, but he was in Rome. This couldn't wait, she decided.

Scottie climbed up the steep hill to Piazza del Duomo, sweating and out of breath. She raced across the piazza, past the enormous black and white cathedral, the still-beating heart of the ancient city. She pushed through the front door of the Questura and asked for Tenente Pisano.

"We're closed until four thirty," said the officer at the desk.

"That's ridiculous. You're a police station. You're always open."

"Only for urgent matters. Otherwise we're closed from one to four thirty."

"And what do you do during your three-and-a-half-hour lunch break?"

The man stared at her, then smiled in a very disrespectful way.

"It is an urgent matter. I need to speak to Tenente Pisano immediately."

"Pisano!" called the man. "Your mistress is here."

Pisano emerged, angry, from a small office. His expression did not soften when he saw Scottie.

"Your car is stuck again?"

"I need to find out where an American is staying." He loomed over her, smelling of burned toast.

"I am not here to help you complete your bridge foursome."

"It's important that I find this man. I know you keep track of all of the foreigners. You know where they all sleep."

"Yes," he said knowingly. "But this is police business, not yours."

"This is perhaps a matter of importance to both of us."

"How so? Who is this man you're looking for?"

"An American hotel developer. Ben Lippincott."

"And why is Signor Lippincott so important to you?"

"Tell me where he is and I'll tell you."

"This is Italy, Mrs. Messina. I do not need a reason to throw you in jail, and I do not need a reason to keep you there."

She sighed. "Carlo Chigi Piccolomini said you would help me."

He looked surprised. "What does the marchese have to do with this?"

"It's private," she said. "You'll have to ask him."

"If it's a favor for the marchese, of course," said Pisano, opening a large book on his desk and scanning a list of entries. His manner had changed entirely upon hearing Carlo's name. She remembered that Carlo had said Pisano wanted to see Italy return to being a monarchy. Of course he would hold Carlo, as a member of the outlawed nobility, in high regard.

"Lippincott. Hotel Villa Scacciapensieri," he said after a moment. "Three nights. Leaves tomorrow. Born 11 June 1928. Springfield, Missouri."

"Thank you," she said.

"It is my pleasure," he said, and gave a slight bow.

"I heard your horse is missing," she said, turning back from the door. "I'm so sorry."

A shadow darkened his face. He came around the counter, removed his hat and whispered to her, his voice croaking. "I must tell you something," he said, placing a firm hand on her back and leading her outside.

Pigeons roosted on the ledges of the Duomo. They walked together in silence up a few steps and through the front entrance of the enormous cathedral. The interior was cool and dark, as if blanketed by six hundred years of whispered prayers. She looked up and the X's of the vaulting began to swim. On one wall hung hundreds of little tin arms and legs like cookie cutters, thank-yous to God for saving people's limbs and hearts and babies. It was all too much. She looked down and gasped — she was stand-ing on an image of a dead infant, one of a dozen or so scattered under the feet of a battling horde of men in armor with raised swords, about to stab unarmed women who were begging for mercy. The babies' eyes were closed. She stepped away and shud-dered.

"Perhaps you know where Robertino is —" he said.

"I don't."

"But in case you can get word to him, I want to tell you this. I was never going to sell her to the butcher," he said. "I said that in front of my father, when she threw me off, because he is my father and I cannot *fare brutta figura* in front of him, but I swear to you now here, in front of God" — here he turned toward the altar and made the sign of the cross — "I was going to give her to the boy. A surprise, for his fifteenth birthday. He's the only one who can ride her. I'm afraid that I have made him disappear. That he thinks that he needed to steal her to save her life. And now he is himself in danger. It's a tragedy," he said. "And I am afraid it's all my fault."

She put a hand on his crisp black sleeve. "We will find him," she said.

The Villa Scacciapensieri was fancier than Scottie expected, and she was glad she was wearing her Balenciaga. It was now a little tight around the midsection, a hand-me-down from Leona from two seasons ago, but no one here would know that. She had pictured a sleepy country hotel, but the place was busy — shiny cars pulling up the semicircular gravel drive, bellmen running about, elegantly dressed guests gathering in the lobby by an enormous fireplace.

She had planned on dining alone and making discreet inquiries about Ben Lippincott, but she saw the journalists Rodolfo and Fiammetta at a table outdoors on the terrace with another man. They waved her over.

"We've only just ordered a Campari and soda," Fiammetta said. She was wearing a red strapless cocktail dress with rhinestone buttons down the front. "Join us." Scottie realized the man at the table with them was

Ugo Rosini.

"Signora Messina," he said, standing up and kissing her hand. "How are you enjoying your stay in Siena?" She had forgotten how short he was, and how strong, and how very handsome. Had forgotten that behind his glasses were light brown eyes with absurdly long lashes. "I understand you have become friendly with the Chigi Piccolominis. Americans are always seduced by the idea of nobility."

"He's a friend, not a title." She felt a sharp spike of anger and a flush of embarrassment. "And aren't titles illegal anyway?"

"Yes — because of course all families are old families, aren't they? Just that some people had ancestors who were better at exploiting others, and passing on their wealth."

"You sound like a jealous man," parried Scottie.

"I am," said Ugo with a smile.

Ugo launched into a lengthy and very scholarly discussion of the novels of Faulkner, Fitzgerald and Hemingway, which he admitted he had read in translation, but still hoped she would permit him to comment on. She would. She relaxed and sipped her drink as he talked about the American South, and the Montgomery bus boycott,

412

and the steelworkers strike.

"You know a lot about America," said Scottie.

Fiammetta laughed and said, "Ugo knows a lot about everything." Rodolfo, too, seemed to know all about current affairs in America. Scottie was ashamed that she knew hardly anything about what was happening back home.

"These amazing people have been holding out for seven months, walking everywhere, giving each other rides when they can," said Rodolfo. "Never a sign of violence from them, but Dr. King's house was firebombed with his wife and little daughter inside."

"Is that true?" said Scottie. "I didn't read about that."

"There's no newspaper in America that's printing the truth," said Ugo. "They said it was King's own fault, that he's an extremist, or worse" — and here Ugo dropped his voice and pretended to be frightened — "a Communist!" The others laughed, and Scottie felt her face redden.

They were making her feel ashamed of herself and her country, which made her mad. "You don't understand," she said, frustrated. "You should go there. You'd see. It's wonderful. In New York, you can buy anything. And everything is open all night.

And you can hear any kind of music, eat any kind of food. People are happy."

"Six hundred thousand steelworkers are not so happy," Ugo said, and Rodolfo added, "Nat King Cole was attacked onstage in Alabama. Maybe everyone is not as happy as you think."

"Well, everyone's not happy here either," said Scottie. "It's not like Italians get along with each other so well."

Fiammetta and Rodolfo laughed, breaking the tension. "True," Ugo said. "It's our national pastime to dislike and distrust each other. We always think other countries have gotten it right and we haven't. The opposite of America. You have American exceptionalism, and we have an inferiority complex. We're very vulnerable that way. And the U.S. is very arrogant."

Before Scottie could rise to this latest challenge, Ugo was leaning across the table and looking into her eyes. "You have come to Americanize us, so you may as well know what being an American really means. You love your country, but true love, remember, is the flower of knowledge. If you don't really know something in its entirety, you can't really know if you love it or not, can you?"

■ ■ ■ ■

Scottie stood up as if she were going to the restroom and asked the waiter quietly if he would point out Signor Lippincott, who was staying at the hotel. She handed him a thousand-lire bill.

"The man at the corner table," the waiter whispered. She looked over and saw Sebastian Gordon sitting with another man, younger. Gordon looked up as she approached their table.

"My dear Mrs. Messina," he said, kissing her hand. "And in Balenciaga, what a treat. You make even last year's collection look good."

Scottie ignored the slight and turned to the other man. Sleek blond hair and a long face, somewhat blank eyes. If he were a horse, she'd put her spurs on and be ready for him to duck out before a fence and dump her on it.

"This is Mr. Lippincott, from Boston," said Gordon. "Sit down, won't you?" he said as Scottie was already pulling out a chair.

"Just for a moment," said Scottie. "I'm dining with friends."

"Yes, I saw you with dear old Ugo," said Gordon, with a raised eyebrow. "Tut-tut.

415

What would Senator McCarthy say?"

Scottie froze slightly. She hadn't thought about the implications of being seen with a Communist Party leader in public. She smiled, all wide-eyed innocence.

"Well, there's no law against that here," said Gordon. "Is there, Mr. Lippincott?"

"I'm not a lawyer," said Lippincott absently. Cold-blooded, she thought.

"Are you here on pleasure, Mr. Lippincott?" Scottie asked him, reminding herself to appear to be just a silly woman.

"Business," he said.

"Lippincott's going to solve our hotel shortage," said Gordon.

"I asked you to keep that quiet," snapped Lippincott.

"There are no secrets in Siena," said Gordon smoothly, pouring them all a glass of wine.

"I'm waiting for a deal to close," Lippincott said.

"There are so many lovely old buildings to put a hotel in," said Scottie.

"The city needs something modern. Good plumbing, air-conditioning." Lippincott was warming to his topic. "Lots of parking. The old stuff is nice, but come on. The water is a trickle, and it's hot as hell. The rooms are small and smell like mold. When you've been out walking around old churches all day, don't you want to come back to a room where things actually work?"

"Like in America?"

"Yes, exactly." He looked down at the remains of his tepid cocktail. "Where the employees aren't on strike at lunchtime, there's an elevator you can turn around in, and you can get ice in your drink, for God's sake."

"Boy's a genius, isn't he?" oozed Gordon.

She wondered what Gordon's agenda was. "I suppose you're right," she said to Lippincott. "That is what people want, isn't it? They want to bring America with them when they travel. Italian scenery and food with American convenience and comfort."

"You got it. No one here gets it. But they will. Once you have those things, you don't want to give them up."

"But you're meeting resistance?"

"Mostly from the town council. This city is a mess. They don't know what they want. I'm waiting out the next election. Hoping they wise up and elect a business-friendly mayor, get that expansion plan approved."

"You want to buy Signor Banchi's farm?"

Lippincott looked surprised, and a little wary. Sebastian practically grinned, as if he had known all along why Scottie was at his table.

"Yeah, he told you?" Lippincott said. "I wish that kid would reappear."

"We all do."

"He was the one who introduced me to his grandfather. Little operator, that one. Carried my bags into the hotel for me, and before we'd gotten to my room he had signed himself up as my guide, interpreter and representative agent."

"Robertino wanted his grandfather to sell?"

"Yeah, of course. He wants to own his own horse operation. Racing. Supply horses for the Palio. Ambitious kid. He had a property in mind and everything. Without him, Grandpa's not signing. I even asked the consulate in Florence today if they could help, but they said they can't interfere in a local matter."

"Robertino's disappearance seems to have inconvenienced many people," said Gordon. "I'm not sure anyone would notice if I popped off."

"Some might even be relieved," said Scottie.

6.

"Why didn't you tell me your cousin is buying up property in Siena?" Michael asked Duncan. When Scottie had telephoned him at his hotel in Rome about having met Ben Lippincott, he was surprised. "Oh. I know him. From Yale."

"Seems like every American in Italy went to Yale," she said.

Lippincott was a cousin of Duncan's. Michael had met him once at a party. He had the supercilious, heavy-lidded ease of the very wealthy, and didn't seem particularly bright. Michael remembered talk of Nantucket, and sailboats, and a cousin who had drowned while out on the water with him. It was odd that Duncan hadn't told him Ben was in Siena. But then he hadn't told him Julie was parading around Tuscany, either. There seemed to be a lot that Duncan wasn't telling him.

He had walked from his hotel down the Via Veneto to the embassy in Palazzo Margherita, a giant pink monstrosity, growing ever more angry. Duncan's office was on the top floor in the back. He showed his passport to the guard at the gate, was waved through. In the lobby was a crush of Italians applying for visas. Though the great swell of people leaving Italy had slowed

419

somewhat since the war, there were still thousands wanting to start a new life somewhere else. France and Germany were now popular destinations, allowing better economic opportunity and more trips home to see family left behind. Michael thought of his parents, eager and anxious in a similar crush of their compatriots forty years ago, leaving what they knew to start over in a place where they knew no one, and didn't speak the language. What must their lives have been like to take such a risk?

Duncan had been on his feet when Michael came through the door, shuffling papers and looking distracted. "I have a meeting with the ambassador in five minutes. You shouldn't have come," he said, glancing toward the secretary and closing the office door.

"I'm an American businessman. I can come to the embassy. Can we meet later? The bar at the Excelsior?"

"Julie and I are dining with the Colonnas and the Brandolinis." Michael recognized the names of Italian nobility.

"So what about Lippincott?"

"What about him? I am not my cousin's keeper." Duncan went on, "Did you place some more articles in the papers about Luce's visit? I didn't see any new ones mentioned in your last report."

"I've put feelers out."

"Put Scottie on it."

"I'm keeping her in the office."

"Are you? Who is this boy she's looking for?" Duncan asked.

"No one," he said quickly. "A kid she met. He's disappeared. Why was your cousin with Gordon?"

"Gordon knows everyone." It was an accusation.

Thank God Duncan hated confrontation. He would continue to kick him if Michael stayed down, but would back off if Michael fought back, so he snapped, "Am I getting a Catholic candidate elected to stop communism or to help your cousin open a chain of hotels?"

Except Duncan didn't back down, just stopped moving papers around and looked coolly across the desk at Michael. "I'm beginning to think you're too emotional for this job."

"Emotional? Half of what you tell me is lies. I'm living in a goddamn hall of mirrors."

"Scottie seems to be meeting everyone. She had drinks with Ugo Rosini, too."

"What?" Scottie hadn't mentioned that part.

"I like it. It's bold," said Duncan, shifting again, keeping Michael off balance. "Get the information right from the horse's mouth. Have her find out if Rosini is sympathetic to NATO. He could be a valuable back channel to national party leadership. If we can get some of these local guys to contradict the party line on getting American missile bases out of Italy, we might get the Socialists to split with the Commies on that issue. Then they can ally with the Catholics and form a center-left coalition. The ambassador thinks any kind of alliance with the left is anathema, but I think that's a better plan than trying to form a government with the Fascists and the Monarchists."

What was anathema, Michael thought, was the fact that they were plotting the future of another country's government. At least Duncan was now talking to him, sharing. "That makes sense," he said. "But splitting the Socialists and the Communists — how is that going to happen?"

"I know. Not easy. Right now they both want better working conditions, higher wages, and they think of the Soviet system as a good model for that. We had hoped that the Polish uprising would show them what getting in bed with the Soviets really means."

Michael nodded. "It was on the front pages, but now it's blown over."

"We need the Soviets to show their hand. Maybe it will happen in Hungary."

"What do you mean?"

"Don't worry about it. Not your mission. Tell Scottie to get close to Rosini. Feel him out on the NATO thing. If we can get a few key local guys to accept that having our bases on their soil keeps us all safer, we might be able to pull this thing off." Duncan smiled at him.

Michael felt a sense of relief, and smiled back. "What is 'this thing' anyway?" He made it sound like a joke, though he really wondered what the answer was.

"Avoiding World War III." Duncan slapped him on the back as if they were a couple of heterosexual lacrosse players. "Keep up the good work. And here." He pushed a large box of Benzedrines at Michael.

Through the glass Michael could see Clare Boothe Luce coming through the office area, smiling at everyone, wearing a striped full-skirted dress and a large pin in the shape of a dog. Her swanning presence, floating regally along, gave him an idea.

"Are you sure she can't come to the Palio?" he asked Duncan. "They're planning on showing her a very good time." He had been surprised by the excitement in the city about her visit — he had assumed that a city full of Reds would hate Luce on principle — but she was American royalty, and, if not a movie star, then like one, and the papers were filled with stories of how the *contrade* were planning extra-special displays for the eminent visitor. The Wave *contrada* planned to make a sculpture of her out of pecorino, the local sheep's-milk cheese, and parade it on their float on Palio Day. The Tower *contrada* had commisioned a local poet to write an "Ode to La Luce," which would be read in unison by a group of schoolchildren. The Snail *contrada* was building a giant papier-mâché sun, and the Caterpillers were choreographing an interpretive dance based on Luce's play *The Women.*

"Not a chance, I'm afraid. Niarchos is counting on her, and Pam Churchill's going to be there."

"Do you think we could get a movie star or someone in her place? Maybe Charlton Heston or Kim Novak or someone like that?"

"Why don't you ask Gordon? He runs in that crowd."

"Sebastian Gordon?"

"Yes, just give him a call. He'll know who you should talk to."

FOURTEEN:
IL NICCHIO, THE SHELL

"THE RED OF THE CORAL QUICKENS
MY HEART."

July 26, 1956

1.

"Good joke, inviting me to your party only to find my wife already there. Ha!" Gordon had had an agenda that night, and Michael wanted to know what it was. Gordon sounded jaunty on the phone, and when Michael suggested lunch in Florence, Gordon said he would come to the Ford showroom.

When he arrived, Gordon smiled impishly. "I'd been dying to have you two over. When she appeared on my doorstep looking so delicious, on the arm of a handsome marchese, it seemed too, too amusing not to stage a little Feydeau farce." He was unrepentant, Michael saw, ignoring the insinuation about the marchese. "I thought you'd find it amusing. And it really was a lovely party."

Michael thought of what Scottie had seen in the grotto. It made him angry that Gordon thought it was funny that a nice girl like Scottie should be exposed to things like that.

"I didn't find it funny," he said coldly. "I was surprised to see Julie there."

"Julie. Was she the minx who came with Giannelli? I don't know her, but she seems quite formidable." Sebastian was examining everything in the office, picking up staplers and peering at them as if they were rare Greek vases. "I worried that you might react that way. You Americans are a little stuffy about certain things. Perhaps I was a bit naughty and I owe you a good turn."

"Well," said Michael, thinking this was a stroke of luck. "We'll just put it behind us."

Sebastian tried the locked cabinet and smiled, leaning against it. "Now I *must* buy a tractor or else my *fattore* Piero is threatening to leave me and go off to the Guicciardinis, damn them, and I want to buy one of your lovely American models. Aren't they huge?" he said, walking down the row of gleaming gigantic machinery in the showroom.

"What are you growing?" Michael asked. Sebastian's chatty confidence made him nervous.

"Grapes. Your country's insatiable thirst for cheap Chianti is too good a chance to miss. I've planted three more hectares of Trebbiano and two more Sangiovese. I'm drowning in the stuff, so it better sell. I suppose I could have gone more high end. I hear there's talk of regulating Chianti growing, setting the percentages of grapes according to old Ricasoli's recipe. But for now, the more I can grow, the more I can sell. That villa costs an arm and a leg to run, I must say."

"You could sell it and live quite comfortably, I imagine."

"Never. I want to be buried there, after I die at age a hundred and ninety-seven surrounded by beautiful things. That property is in my blood. I can't bear the idea of it being turned into a luxury hotel."

"So this Lippincott wants your place, too?"

"He does, but I won't sell. He's no idiot — good time to be buying up properties," Sebastian said. "Farmers are fleeing in droves. Not so good for you, though, old man. Sorry about that."

Michael nodded. "I should switch to

scooters. Those are selling like crazy."

"Yes, I fear for my life sometimes, just walking down the *lungarno,* or here down Via di Città. The new urban plan for Siena should change that, though. They're talking about banning scooters and cars from certain streets."

"Yes, I'd heard that. And of course the highway will change everything."

"Never go through, old man. Fanfani won't hear of it."

Amintore Fanfani was a leading member of the Christian Democrats and a former prime minister who led a faction that was suspicious of raw capitalism and wished to promote the common good rather than free markets. He was the bane of Luce's existence, for a center-left alliance would put Communists in key ministerial posts.

"What do you mean?"

"The highway's not going through Siena. It's going through Arezzo."

"Arezzo?" While a lovely city that was home to a Roman amphitheater and some marvelous frescoes by Piero della Francesca, Arezzo was not on a direct line from Rome to Florence, and would necessitate a sharp and expensive jog to the east. "How did that happen?"

"Fanfani's hometown, of course. For all

429

his talk about the dangers of capitalism, he wasn't going to let it become a backwater. When that highway goes in, everyone in that province is going to be drowning in cash."

"And Siena?"

Gordon smiled. "Will remain a beautiful jewel, untroubled by factories, pollution and crowds."

"In other words it will be poor and backward."

"Well, it's still got Monte dei Paschi. And the Palio. You sound very loyal to your new home. I'm surprised they've won you over. The Sienese are not known for their warmth. Dante called them frivolous and vain."

Michael was hot and irritated by Gordon's barbs. "I must say, I'm annoyed by all of these generalizations. I'm just a person. I don't want the responsibility of representing an entire country, and if someone from Siena, or Bari, or Rome cuts me off in traffic, I don't immediately think 'Everyone from Bari is a bad driver.' "

Sebastian grinned and thumped him on the back. "Jolly good. Though everyone from Bari *is* a bad driver, as any Italian will tell you. Now let's go get some lunch and close this deal. I want the big red shiny one." He ran a hand over the tractor's wheel cover.

Michael wanted to tell the man to go to hell, but the sale would help supplement his rather meager government paycheck. For all the millions it funneled around the world, the CIA paid very badly. His personal account at Monte dei Paschi was overdrawn, and he was anxious about skimming any more out of the bribery fund. He locked up the shop and followed Sebastian in the Fairlane to a hotel outside the city walls with a good restaurant that Sebastian liked, the Villa Scacciapensieri.

They pulled up to the large yellow villa with its row of arched windows covered in brown shutters, looking like it, too, had secrets to hide. The squat, square building with its jaunty striped awning was surrounded by beautiful manicured gardens with lemon trees in huge pots and bright red geraniums in small rectangular planters.

A light breeze cooled the sweat on Michael's neck as they went out the back into the garden. A headwaiter showed them to a prime table with a pair of wrought-iron chairs in an elevated corner of the terrace, where they could see everyone else. A pergola of grapevines arched overhead, making the space feel leafy and secluded, and the view of hills, fields and castles was right out of Giotto. Sebastian ordered Campari and sodas without asking. He then took out his notebook and began sketching Michael's profile.

"You might ask first," said Michael, squirming.

"You're so testy," teased Sebastian. "So handsome and such a prick. Your wife must have her hands full."

Michael was suddenly deeply uncomfortable.

"The world is your oyster, my boy. You should suck it down in one gulp and be happy. A beautiful wife, a good job, and an Italian assignment. It's not the Belgian Congo, dear, for all its shortcomings. Life here is a party. Join the fun."

The waiter brought them each a plate of prosciutto and melon. The salty prosciutto melted into the perfectly ripe sweet melon, yet Michael hardly tasted it. Why had Gordon picked this place? And why was he needling him? It felt like a trap.

"*Ciao,* Pippo," said Sebastian to one of the waiters, a young man with olive skin and green eyes.

Pippo's *"Buongiorno, signori"* was weirdly high-pitched, like Mickey Mouse.

"Castrato," whispered Sebastian when the

man had moved off to another table. "Illegal since 1870, but it still goes on."

"Why would someone — ?"

"Opera. The pursuit of beauty can be a terrible thing."

Pippo smiled shyly as he returned with a bottle of champagne. "Compliments of the manager," he said.

Sebastian smiled grandly. "You see, if you're friendly to everyone, good things happen."

A pasta came, with the lightest imaginable lemon cream sauce, which melted on Michael's tongue.

"They make the tagliolini here," said Sebastian. "A woman named Maria with forearms like oak trees."

Michael had to admit it was the most delicious pasta he had ever tasted. And the champagne went right to his head. He badly needed a Benzedrine, but he had left them back at the office. Waiters with little metal rulers cleared crumbs as soon as they fell. Gordon seemed to know everyone, waving and *ciao*-ing and blowing kisses. The chef came out and made him taste something new he was trying. Sebastian pronounced it *squisito,* and the man beamed.

Michael supposed Sebastian was going to stick him with the bill for all this. He might as well get something useful out of it.

"Do you know any movie stars?" Michael asked.

"My dear boy. I do public relations for Italy's top luxury brands. I know scads of movie stars. Do you have a crush on Deborah Kerr?"

At the Farm they had told the Junior Officer Trainees that they needed to learn to hold their liquor, because the Soviets would drink you under the table. Though Michael had always been a bit of a lightweight, he figured it didn't matter since he was unlikely to go head to head in alcoholic combat with a Russian. He was now remembering his father's war stories about the Brits and their legendary drunks. His head swam as Pippo flashed those green eyes at him and poured him another glass of champagne, then brought out a bottle of red wine to go with their *bistecca,* a thinly sliced rare steak with rosemary and peppercorns.

"I'd like to get an American movie star to come to Italy for the August Palio," he said, trying to focus.

"I thought dear old Clare was coming."

"Just between us, I've gotten word that she can't make it. It would be nice to soften the blow with a big name."

"Of course," said Sebastian. "The Italians

seem to be addicted to the American cinema. I saw *Giant* last week at the Excelsior, and it was packed. I think the Italians are falling in love with your lot. Bit jealous, I must say, though of course we Brits had our day of empire building. I wish we'd thought of using Elizabeth Taylor's breasts to win *our* wars."

Michael chewed his steak, thinking it was the finest he had ever tasted. All would be well. Gordon would find him a star, introduce him around, solve his problems without even realizing it. He wondered if he should recruit him formally, as an asset, or just pretend they were friends.

"Tell me about yourself," said Sebastian. "What do you do when you're not selling tractors?"

Michael's caution was disappearing with the wine. He blinked and there was a grappa to go with the coffee. It was nice to be relaxed.

"I see a few close friends," he said.

"Not an easy boat we're in, is it?" Sebastian said quietly. "Always keeping our heads down, watching our backs." The joking tone was gone.

Michael said nothing.

"Why must they hate us, when all we want to do is live our lives? We're not hurting anyone. Your man McCarthy is the worst. And Hoover! I have friends in the States who ran screaming for their lives. It doesn't make you un-American to be homosexual."

He knew he should protest, protect himself, deny it, tell Sebastian that he hated all fags, but he couldn't. *In vino veritas,* he thought.

"I suppose it doesn't," said Michael awkwardly.

"What a man does behind closed doors is his own business."

Michael simply nodded and sipped his grappa, as if it were the most natural thing in the world to be talking about men having sex with each other. As if it were not a crime, grounds for being fired according to the U.S. government, cast out of decent society. The Catholic Church was willing to let you mull it over, Michael thought grimly, but God expected you to stop there. Any action was a sin.

"Finding the male body attractive — how can that be a crime when you look at what we've all just been through, bombings and holocausts? Art is not a crime. Love is not a crime."

Michael stared into his empty coffee cup. He wished Sebastian would stop saying these things, but he kept talking, and talk-

436

ing, and the waiter's eyes were so green . . .

Sebastian went on, his voice soothing, melodic, capable, reassuring, "The Italians, of course, have a much more liberal attitude, as they do about most things. They understand the subtlety of human behavior. As you said yourself, labels rarely fit."

Sebastian stood up. Michael tried to, but he felt woozy. God, he needed a Benzedrine.

"Looks like we'd better put you down for a quick *pisolino* before you get behind the wheel, old man."

When Michael started to protest, Sebastian said, "No problem at all. Whenever the top-floor suite is empty, the manager always lets me in for a quick lie-down. Just the thing. A little siesta. Yet another aspect of life the Italians have figured out."

Michael did not protest as the bellman took them up in a small metal elevator and opened the door of the suite at the far end of the hall. If the bellman had winked, or smiled or snickered, Michael would have run away, but the man's face was perfectly expressionless.

The suite was spacious and airy. The shutters were closed but the windows open, so that it was cool and dark inside. Under dark stenciled beams were beautiful antiques, a white sofa and an inlaid table.

"What beautiful roses," he said, admiring the bouquet in a silver vase.

"See? Just the thing. Two bedrooms. You take that one."

Michael staggered into a room with a black iron bedstead painted with lemons. A white damask coverlet was pulled back to reveal smooth white linen pillowcases. Michael almost cried with relief at how inviting it looked.

He took off his jacket, his shoes and socks, his shirt, unbuckled his trousers and let them drop to the floor.

"Take a cool shower and you'll sleep even better," Sebastian called from down the hall.

"They won't care?"

"No no, no one in here tonight."

Michael removed his undershirt and underpants, went into the adjoining white marble bathroom and stepped under the cool water. The soap smelled like lemons. He could have stayed under the water forever.

He padded back into the bedroom and lay facedown on the bed, his body sinking into the soft mattress.

"Isn't that better?" Sebastian's voice was in the doorway. Michael rolled over to see the man standing just out of the room in the hallway, wearing a white robe. His hair was wet and slicked back like a seal. Firm pale calves descended to beautiful feet.

Sebastian was a kind man, Michael thought. How had he not seen that before? Of course he had his defenses up, as they all had to, to survive, but Sebastian was clearly a man of great wisdom and compassion, and so very attractive.

Just one last time, he thought, *and then I will be a perfect husband, till death do us part.* He held out his hand.

2.

It was a hot, sticky morning. It would have been smart to hide out indoors until the inevitable afternoon rainstorm cooled the city off, but instead Scottie threw on her lightest casual summer dress and sunglasses, and leashed Ecco.

The Rome office wanted them to get closer to "Big Red," Ugo Rosini. She was thrilled when Michael asked her to handle it.

She called Ugo and arranged to meet him for lunch at a small place off the beaten track in Via Sant'Agata, a simple trattoria, since she knew they would never have privacy in Siena. All of the workmen having their *ribollita* at the adjoining tables greeted Rosini warmly, thumping him on the back.

As soon as they sat down, the waiter plunked bowls in front of them.

"You look beautiful," Ugo told her. "Italy suits you. Can we be lovers now?"

"I'm glad you don't hate all Americans," she said. "That's part of why I wanted to see you."

She felt his hand on her leg under the table.

"Come away with me. We'll go to Rome for the weekend."

"Tempting." She blushed, sipping her wine and ignoring the bean and cabbage soup.

"I've missed the taste of you."

"You've never tasted me."

"I have in my dreams."

It was so clichéd. She knew Ugo had no real attachment to her. He was playing a game. And so was she.

She removed her foot from its shoe and retaliated, stroking his thigh with it. He choked a little and had to sip his wine.

"How do you feel about NATO?" she asked, her toes brushing against the growing bulge in his trousers.

"I am not opposed to . . . NATO," he said gruffly. He was managing to eat his soup, which was impressive under the circumstances.

"Because NATO could be very good for the Italians," she said. "Very good."

His eyes closed a little. She felt like Mata Hari.

A plumber carrying a sack of wrenches clapped Ugo on the back and gave him a hearty greeting.

"I should probably go," he said reluctantly, downing a glass of water and dropping bills on the table. "I would very much like to take you somewhere and ravish you, but I have a campaign meeting in ten minutes. Damn it."

"I just want you to know that there's no reason for us to be enemies," she said. "Quite the opposite."

They walked together back toward the Campo. He was teasing, flirtatious, but also respectful, in a way that no American would ever master.

"I hope your meeting goes well," she said, as the piazza opened before them.

"Listen, *cara,* there is something I think you should know about the missing boy," he said, a hand on her arm.

"Robertino?"

"I believe he was the one who stole something from my office."

She frowned. "Robertino? A thief? I don't believe it," she said.

"I fear he may have fallen in with some very dangerous people." He paused, as if deciding how much to tell her.

"Who are these people?" she asked. "Mafia?"

"I think it is someone closer to you than you think," he said, then paused again. "I can't say more, except be careful," he said at last.

A shiver ran through her. Was he implying . . . Michael?

"Okay. Thank you again," she said abruptly, and walked away. She was unnerved by this. Was Rosini playing her? Or genuinely warning her?

She went back to the office, but Michael wasn't there. His note said he had gone to lunch. She thought about what Rosini had said. Would Michael have asked Robertino to steal something from Ugo? He would never have put the boy in such danger. Except . . . She thought about all the months that he had kept his true profession from her. Did she really not know him at all?

What secrets was he still keeping from her?

She stopped in front of the locked cabinet in the back part of the office. She looked at her watch. She had time before he got back from lunch.

FIFTEEN:
LA CIVETTA, THE OWL

"I SEE IN THE NIGHT"

1.

Michael went straight home. Scottie was strange when he arrived. He told himself she couldn't know about him and Sebastian, but it was like she did. She looked pale. This was worrisome. She was sitting on the pink couch in the living room. There was no book, no teacup, no magazine, nothing to suggest she'd been doing anything other than staring into space before he walked through the door.

"Are you ill?" he asked.

"Just tired," she said. "I have a headache. I might sleep in the guest room if you don't mind." She stood up, and he saw shadows under her eyes.

"Of course, darling. Are you sure you're all right? Is the baby — ?"

She put her hands on her belly and gave

him a smile that seemed falsely reassuring. "Yes," she said. "I'm fine. He or she is kicking me a lot, that's all. How was your lunch?"

He glanced up anxiously at the overhead light fixture, to remind her they might be overheard. "Ford's got new models coming out they're very excited about," he said. "There are some customs issues to get through, but I think we're going to have a bang-up fall."

She nodded. He had never seen her look this way. There was something else besides pain on her face. He put a hand on her arm and she pulled away.

"Sorry, hot," she said.

"What's the matter?" he whispered. "Are you really all right? How was Rosini?"

"Friendly. I just need to lie down." She went into the guest room and closed the door.

The dog looked up at Michael.

"What?" he said.

Ecco stared at him for a moment, then went to the guest room door and scratched at it. It opened a crack, he slipped in, and the door shut again.

He went to early mass and confession. What had happened with Sebastian was a mistake.

It would never happen again. He put a pebble in his shoe so that he would feel the pain of his sin all day. The door was still closed when he got back from mass, and still closed when he limped off to work. He would encourage Scottie to see a doctor, though he didn't trust Italian doctors. It was time they made arrangements for her to go back to America to deliver her baby. He didn't want his child born in an Italian hospital, or on Italian soil. He stopped at the office. Signor Brigante waved to him and intercepted him on his way into the Ford warehouse.

"I sold two yesterday," he crowed.

"Complimenti," said Michael, stepping around him.

"Things are looking up! We'll pull these rotten Tuscans out of the Middle Ages, yes? Not that they don't all deserve to be eaten alive by mosquitoes while tied to a tree."

Michael slipped into the cool, dark, tiled expanse of the warehouse. The tractors by now were old friends. He took off his jacket and ran a dust cloth over them. There was nothing decorative or stylish about them — everything had a purpose. They were honest. The good part of America. The part they did well.

His heart stopped. The cabinet had been

jimmied open. He peeked in. Everything was there — the printing press, the money, the comic books, the Minaccia Rossa posters and leaflets, the gun. It looked like whoever opened it had taken nothing.

Except . . . *oh God,* he thought. Who would take only *that?*

He drove up to Sebastian's villa. It seemed clear to him that Sebastian had kept him out of the office yesterday afternoon for a reason. He hated himself for falling for it. The villa looked less glamorous than it had at the party. The stucco was pitted, and tiles were hanging precariously.

He rang the bell several times, and finally shutters and a window upstairs were thrown open.

"Who the hell dares to appear at this hour?" Sebastian bellowed. "Oh, it's you. Come up."

Michael was a little nervous at seeing Sebastian again. He waited in the living room — Sebastian probably called it a salon. At last he appeared, wrapped in a Chinese silk dressing gown complete with tasseled tie. *Of course,* Michael thought. Then he noticed something on Sebastian's face.

"Why are you wearing makeup?"

Sebastian sighed. "I ran into some unpleasant fellows in an alley last night."

"Are you all right?" Michael was suddenly concerned and a little angry, too. And afraid. "They beat you up?" He had a vision of Sebastian, poor pompous Sebastian, his white linen suit stained with blood, being kicked in the stomach by a gang of thugs. Damn it, this was why you couldn't be flamboyant. You just couldn't.

"Pushed me around a little. I got much worse at boarding school. Now I'm making coffee, and you can't stop me." Sebastian waved him toward the kitchen at the back of the villa.

"I'd have thought you'd have had a house-boy or something for that."

"He's gone to the sea for the summer. That's the problem with Italians. They expect vacations."

"How ungrateful of them. Did you break into my office?"

Sebastian stared at him, seemingly as shocked as he. "No," he said. "But that sounds bad."

There was the sound of a truck outside, and within moments, a crew of workmen came filing past them and headed up the main staircase.

"The army is here, thank God," crowed Sebastian. "Upstairs, my dears, to work, to work!" He handed Michael a cappuccino and growled, "Some damn fine asses in that group, weren't there?"

"You want to get beaten up again? What are they here for?"

"I'm finally having the plumbing redone, the roof fixed and the electricity modernized. And I'm building myself a stunning walnut-paneled dressing room."

"Relative die?"

"You might say that. How are you fixed for cash, old boy?"

"That's a bit personal."

"Pretty wife, she shouldn't be wearing last season's clothes."

"She doesn't care."

"All women care. If I'm not wrong, you have a baby on the way, too. Those things are expensive."

"We're fine, thank you. I have a good job."

"Yes, of course. The great Ford Motor Company. Putting a nation on the road, fueled by gasoline from all the world's most interesting places."

Michael followed him outdoors, where Sebastian plunked down into a chair under a grape arbor. The table was full of half-filled glasses and candle wax. Michael moved an empty bottle of port away from his place and set his coffee down.

"Looks like it was a good party."

Sebastian nodded and looked thoughtful, which was unusual.

"I have friends who are very wealthy," he said at last.

"Nice for you. Better for them."

"Very nice for me. They paid for a copper roof on the *limonaia* last year."

"Well, at least the lemons will have a roof over their heads. Look," he said, "about yesterday. It's very important to me that Scottie not be hurt."

"Who would hurt her? She's utterly charming. I grew up with lots of horse-women, of course. She's much more *vispa* than most of them."

That was the word Rodolfo had used about her.

Sebastian went on. "She's bright. And sly, I think. She wants people to underestimate her."

"You won't tell her."

Sebastian smiled. "My friends would love to know you."

"I'm always happy to meet people."

"We would talk, and I would pass on your thoughts to them."

Michael paused.

"It would be well worth your while."

"They need tractors?"

449

Sebastian stood up. "Better. They only need information. Back in a jiff."

He disappeared into the villa.

Michael smiled to himself. He was being recruited for British intelligence. How funny. But of course Sebastian would be working for the Brits. The right background, the right schooling, the connections, living abroad . . . Though in theory the Agency and MI6 were allies, that happened at higher levels, and he wasn't allowed to admit anything about his own employers. But it was still funny.

Until he remembered what was missing from the safe.

Sebastian returned with a plate of small, dry cookies.

"Best I could find, I'm afraid. I ate these in the nursery as a child." He bit into one and grimaced. "Possibly this same package."

"Did you break into my office?"

"No, I didn't," said Gordon cheerfully.

"Are you MI6?"

Gordon smiled. "They approached me a few years back. I was resistant at first. Not my cup of tea at all. I had an older brother in the service, died parachuting into France. Secret codes, passwords, exploding pens, those ghastly trenchcoats — I wanted no part of it."

450

"Serving your country, though, isn't it?"

Sebastian smiled. "I thought about it. About what they were asking. Only for information, the kind of thing anyone could pick up if they spoke the lingo. If it wasn't me, it would be someone else, wouldn't it? Someone else would be collecting all that lovely lolly. But still I said no. And then the Beni Culturali came after me."

"The Culture Ministry?"

"Told me I had a legal obligation to maintain the villa. Historic site and all. I told them I *wanted* to maintain the villa, but it's bloody expensive. They told me certain repairs had to be made or I would lose the property. My own mother's house! They were going to take it away from me and make it into some ghastly museum, or worse, just shut it up. I love this place."

"I know."

"I want to die here."

"You said that."

"People don't understand. All they see is a building. But it's . . ."

"History?"

"Yes. Think of all the people who have laughed and loved and cried in this place. The ghosts! They don't want sour-faced schoolchildren and bloody Americans with cameras traipsing through. They want par-

451

ties, and drinking and sex. I can't fail them. People think because you're a lord you're rich, but they forget that the older brother gets it all in England. Usually they make at least an attempt to look after the siblings, but my brother's a first-rate rotter. Told me I wasn't to show my face in London or he'd run me out of there. So I went to work as a publicist, as you know, hawking Italian luxury goods. I'm good at it, it turns out — that bamboo-handled bag I gave to Liz Taylor just sold out. But, as so many have pointed out, an honest living is not enough."

"So you give your friends information?"

"I do, yes. Not much more than anyone could read in a newspaper, really. I mean, yes, maybe sometimes a bit more, but it's all quite innocent. You would like it, I think. You and I would just be friends, as we already are, and we'd chat, and the things we'd chat about I'd tell my friends. It's nothing more than that. It's a way to defuse tensions, I think."

"Not much tension between us and the Brits."

Sebastian reached over and turned on a radio. Doris Day was massacring "From This Moment On." *That's a bit loud,* Michael thought.

From this moment on, you and I, babe, we'll

be riding high, babe . . .

"Oh, I'm not talking about the Brits, dear." Sebastian smiled.

Michael's heart sank. "The Italians?" he asked weakly.

Sebastian shook his head.

"Oh Lord," said Michael. "I need to sit down."

"You are sitting down. Have a whisky."

"It's nine a.m."

"Then have two. Long day ahead." Sebastian upended the crystal decanter into Michael's coffee cup. The scent of the overflowing ashtray was making him gag.

Michael tossed back the whisky and closed his eyes. "You're a . . . you work for . . ." He whispered, "The Soviets?" He hoped that when he opened his eyes, Sebastian would be shaking his head and looking horrified.

He was smiling and nodding. "It's really quite a good thing when you step back and think about it," Sebastian said. "Back channels and all that. As I said, defuses tensions. When people really know what the other man is thinking, it can avoid misunderstandings."

"I have to go," said Michael.

"I wish you wouldn't."

"I can't see you again, I'm afraid."

"That's being rather hasty. Look, I know you're CIA and all, but once you're in bed with one of these chums, you may as well bed them all, don't you think?"

Michael stared at him.

"Well, it's true. They've all got designs on poor little Italia, when she's barely out of nappies. The Americans ride to the rescue with their millions to repair the damage they inflicted, in exchange for a few bases, of course. The Soviets fund and seduce the Reds, who already have momentum. Everyone wants to sell, sell, sell their products here. The best thing Italy can do is confuse them both."

"Confuse them?"

"Just let them think things are chaotic here."

"Things *are* chaotic here."

"Exactly. There is a certain stability in chaos, you know. At least that's the line I'm feeding my side."

"What makes you think I'm CIA?"

"What you are is a terrible liar."

Michael frowned.

"Look, this would be easy for you. I know your boyfriend is Dulles's nephew or something. I hear he's very chummy with the ambassadress. Very chummy."

Michael paled. "Did you . . ."

454

"No, for God's sake, don't ask me again if I broke into your office. I didn't, but you'd better find out who did. My friends are prepared to pay you ten thousand dollars a month," Sebastian said.

Sixteen:
Il Valdimontone, The Ram

"UNDER MY BLOWS FALLS THE WALL"

1.

Scottie sat on a bench in the park outside the Fortezza, her mind racing. It had been since the previous afternoon. Ecco, who would usually have been sniffing every bush and blade of grass and liberally sowing his scent, was sitting in front of her, staring at her, worried. Finally he barked, once.

She burst into tears and gathered him on her lap.

"What am I going to do?" She put her face in the dog's fur.

The Minaccia Rossa posters in the cabinet she'd busted open were confusing. So Michael was . . . a Communist? But for her, that was the least of it. The money was not surprising — as a CIA agent, he had to have access to cash. The American comic books. She would have found this charming, except

456

as she flipped through them she realized that they were the same comic books that Robertino had been reading. Batman. Superman. Lash Lightning. These comics weren't on sale here — the boy could only have gotten them from an American. And who brought comic books to Italy? It hadn't seemed strange to her at the time to see them in Robertino's kitchen.

It made sense. Michael had been getting information from Robertino. Robertino had access to the hotels; he talked to everyone. It was perfect spy logic, except for the fact that he was a child, and making him an asset made him a pawn in a global game of Battleship.

Ugo said Robertino had stolen something from his office. He had implied that Robertino was mixed up in something bad. Had he stolen it for Michael?

That made her angry. And a little sick, to think that Michael would do that, and that he would keep it from her, even after the boy disappeared.

Michael could have killed him to keep him quiet.

She tried to shake off the thought, tell herself that she knew her husband, that he wasn't capable of such a thing.

Except she was now realizing that she

didn't know him at all.

The only item she had removed from the cabinet was a pocket-sized magazine called *Physique Pictorial* that contained pictures of mostly naked men. Scottie was confused, then shocked, then curious, then shocked again. She thought of the grotto.

She wanted to reverse time, unlearn everything she had learned along the way. She wanted to think her father was an honest man and not a thief. That stolen money had not paid for her ponies and her tuition at the best schools. She wanted to think America was a great and good country that saved people in need and where all men were created equal and justice was served. She wanted to believe all people were basically good and would do good if given the chance, and she wanted to believe in God. Hell, she wanted to believe in Santa Claus. It was such a nice story.

Ecco licked the tears off her cheeks. She couldn't sit there any longer — people were starting to stare.

Mechanically, she walked Ecco back toward the apartment. She would read a magazine. Rearrange the furniture. She would make lunch for Michael. She would perhaps bake a pie. An apple pie.

2.

He was pale when he came through the door at lunchtime. She was trembling. They played a brittle, false scene with each other. Ecco was whining because of the weird tension in the room. She finally grabbed him by the collar and tossed him into the bedroom and shut the door.

She sat back down at the table. Her hair and makeup were perfect. His suit was crisp and his tie straight. They smiled at each other.

"Sad about the *Andrea Doria* sinking."

"And to think that was the ship we were on."

"We're awfully lucky to be alive."

But somewhere between the artichoke soup and the veal cutlet, tears began to drop into his plate.

She saw it all dissolving, everything, his tears washing away the colors of her life, the buildings, the clothing, the people, until she stood on a bare patch of dirt, naked and alone, her marriage going down with the *Andrea Doria.* Her anger rose in her throat, anger that she didn't know she had inside her, anger that seemed to light her on fire, make her levitate, flaming, like the burning wrapper of an amaretto cookie.

"What happened to Robertino?"

Ecco began barking in the other room.

He gave a short sob and covered his face with his hands. "I don't know."

"You put him in danger. You asked him to steal from Rosini."

He nodded, still not looking at her. Ecco's barking had become high-pitched, and he was scratching at the bedroom door.

"Did you kill him?"

Bark bark bark.

"No!" He remembered the orders. "They wanted me to," he said quietly.

"Who wanted you to?"

"It wasn't — they didn't say 'kill Robertino.' But if the mission were compromised, if an asset betrays our side . . ."

Now Ecco was howling, frantic.

"An asset? Our side? What the fuck is 'our side'?"

His face twisted in a self-hating smile. "The good guys."

She wanted to slap him. "You're a liar! You lied to me about *everything*!"

What could he say to that? "You're right. Robertino's disappearance is probably my fault. I — I've wanted to tell you everything, but I couldn't. I couldn't. I was so afraid. I'm afraid because —" He took a breath and the words caught in his throat.

"You're a homosexual. You have sex with

men." Her voice was cold, hard.

He nodded. The dog's barking was now deafening.

Michael stood and walked over and opened the bedroom door. Ecco came racing out, but Scottie was already on the move, out the door. The dog ran after her, still barking, desperate to defend her, loyal to the tip of his comma-shaped tail.

3.

An hour later, she turned the Ford into Carlo's driveway. The castle looked still, and dark. She hadn't noticed the bullet holes the first time. She wondered if German officers had been quartered here. Many had taken the nicer villas in the area, she knew.

Maybe he won't be home, she thought.

But she could see him. He was working a horse in the round pen. The horse was moving beautifully, arching its neck, using its back, its stride springy and compressed. It was poetry.

He waved to her and smiled. When the horse had slowed to a walk and finally a halt, he went over and patted it. The horse was pleased with him and with itself.

Carlo led the horse over to where she was standing.

"Ciao," he said.

She burst into tears. Carlo did not say anything. He put his hand through the bars of the round pen and laid it gently on her back, the way you would put it on the neck of a fussy horse. To transmit the calm from you to it.

Finally she stopped crying. Carlo led the horse out of the round pen and into the stable. She watched as he slowly untacked the horse, rubbed it down, gave it some grain and then turned it out into the field.

"Do you want to tell me what's happened?"

She stared at the ground. "Not yet," she said. "I shouldn't have come, but I didn't know where else to go."

"Are you all right?"

She gave a half smile. "I need a place to stay. To think. But not here," she added quickly. She knew what would happen if she did, and it was not the way she wanted things to be, not the way she wanted to make that decision.

"Why don't you use the house on the mountain?" He had mentioned the place — a cottage on Monte Amiata.

"Isn't Franca there? You said she uses it."

"She stops in there when she's collecting herbs, but she doesn't stay. It's pretty bare-bones. Can you start a wood fire?"

"Sure."

"I'll give you some supplies."

She stayed outside, and he returned with a loaf of bread, half a wheel of pecorino and a bottle of wine, all in a net sack. "There's a little store in Santa Fiora. You can restock there. The *signora* who runs it will be fierce at first, but if you compliment her poodle she'll melt and give you big hunks of her homemade *porchetta*. The poodle's name is Lila."

"Thank you," she said.

He stared at her for a moment, then nodded. She headed for the car. "Amiata," he called out, "is full of ancient magic. And ticks. Check your socks."

Scottie looked up at the enormous mountain, mysterious and forbidding, and then she got in the car.

4.

When Michael went to the warehouse, there was a man with a briefcase waiting for him. Signor Brigante was trying to steal the man away, making absurd offers for tractors.

"I give you two for price of one," he said. "Three! Three!" he wailed as Michael approached. "American tractors are shit."

Michael nodded to the man and unlocked his office. They shut the door on Signor

463

Brigante, and could hear his beautiful loafers stamping away down the concrete.

"I'm here to give you a polygraph," said the man.

"Why?"

"Routine. This door lock?"

"But . . . I've never had one. It's been a complicated day." He thought about the Benzedrine he had taken. Would that make him a better liar?

"I calibrate for that. Don't worry. Everyone in the Rome office got theirs earlier. Florence is tomorrow. Just routine. Goodness, it's a long road to get here."

"They were building a highway," said Michael. "But now they're not." He sat down opposite the man and watched him set up the machine. They called this "fluttering." He didn't believe for one second this was routine. This was Duncan. He couldn't know about Sebastian — unless he had someone watching Michael all the time. He might. More likely, their last conversation had set off alarm bells for Duncan, so he had turned to a machine for the truth.

The man put a band around Michael's arm, and another around his chest. A scroll of white paper was loaded in.

"Name?"

Michael's heart was racing. He stuttered

464

out his name.

The needle jumped and clicked and lurched and the inexorable roll of white paper tick-tick-ticked out of it. It did, in fact, flutter.

The man ran through a basic list of questions. Michael knew what was coming next.

"Have you ever had illicit contact with a foreign agent?"

"No." Michael watched the needle jump and the paper spew.

"Have you been recruited by a foreign power?"

That's what the man had been sent to ask. It's what they always asked. It was all that mattered to them. They would ask you to lie, betray and murder for them, while demanding absolute, verifiable loyalty. The defection of Burgess and Maclean had upended everything, thrown spy handlers on both sides of the Atlantic into a paranoid panic. The two had fooled everyone, seeming to be perfect upper-crust loyal Englishmen spying for jolly old England, queen and country, while actually maintaining a crazy, unfathomable loyalty to a nation they had never visited, to an ideal they had held on to since university. Angleton was a very close friend of Kim Philby, the suspected "third man" dismissed by MI6 but unprosecuted for lack of proof. The accusations against Philby had shaken Angleton to his core, sent him on a mad mole hunt.

Michael tried to keep his voice steady, his heart constant. He thought about his mother, crying for Marco, the men at the door delivering a gold star for their window. "No."

"So what's the best place to get a gelato around here? I can't get enough of that *limone*, but I like *stracciatella*, too."

After the man left, Michael sat for a long time just staring at the wall.

Then his random thoughts coalesced into a plan. Minaccia Rossa would strike, and strike hard. And all of them could go to hell together.

SEVENTEEN:
LA TORRE, THE TOWER

"BETTER THAN FORCE, POWER"

The mountain loomed before her, black against the starry night sky. The car began to climb up toward Arcidosso. There was no moon, and in this little-electrified area of Italy, the Milky Way was like a white tulle wedding arch. She dropped the car into a lower gear and slowed for some deer that had Ecco on high alert. She steered around a giant toad whose eyes glowed in the headlights. There was utter blackness all around her, and she was was glad of Ecco's company.

She drove through the ancient medieval centers of Castel del Piano and Arcidosso, then, after a sharp, nearly vertical right-hand turn, saw a battered handmade sign for Santa Fiora. It wasn't 1956 here; it was a place out of time, like in a fairy tale.

She gasped and slammed on the brakes as

a pair of eyes shone in her headlights. As she came to a stop, the silvery tan figure revealed itself.

A wolf. She couldn't believe her eyes.

Ecco gave a ridiculous growl as the wolf disappeared into the darkness. The roads got rougher as she drove on. She realized, the farther she got from him, that she was more worried about what would happen to Michael than what would happen to her. He was a homosexual. What a lonely life that must be, she thought. To have to keep a secret like that. She wanted to ask him, talk to him about what that had meant for him, what it had cost him.

The Ford bumped along the dirt road. Slowly, a house appeared in the darkness ahead. She found a flashlight in the glove box and got out. Ecco hopped out beside her and raced off into the darkness, barking. The crickets were so loud it sounded like they were inside her head. When she closed the car door, the darkness was profound.

She shone the flashlight around. She could smell woodsmoke in the distance. She saw three or four small outbuildings. It was a neat and tidy cottage, from what she could see in the darkness.

She caught a familiar scent — horse. It

must be just Franca's donkey she was smelling, she thought. But this would be a long way to bring the little guy.

Holding the string bag of supplies in one hand, Scottie shoved the flashlight under her arm as she struggled to open the heavy front door, warped by centuries of rain and snow. She leaned into it, and finally it gave. At that moment there was a rushing sound, and everything went black.

Scottie woke up in complete darkness. It was a strange sensation, to open her eyes, then close them again, and have there be no difference. She had a terrible headache and was lying flat on a bed. She listened. She could hear a slow drip of water. The smell was dank and cool, as if she were underground.

"Hello," she called out. It hurt to speak. She touched a knot on her head and winced.

She heard footsteps. A woman's voice demanded, crying, "Why have you come here? What do you want?"

"Franca?" she said, trying to keep her voice calm. "Franca, is that you?"

"I don't know you," said the woman. "Please go away."

Scottie could hear other movements around her. Her eyes began to adjust to the dark. She began to make out shapes — dried herbs hanging from the ceiling, demijohns of wine and olive oil.

"Franca? It's Scottie Messina." She tried to sit up, her head aching. "I came to your house near Siena. With Carlo." She paused, feeling guilty, then went on. "I'm sorry I didn't knock."

"I didn't mean to hit you. I was frightened."

Scottie wondered if that was true. Franca had every reason to want to hurt her. "Carlo said you wouldn't be here. He said it was all right for me to stay. I'm so sorry to have bothered you." She sat up, feeling sick to her stomach.

Franca put a mug of tea in her hands. "It will ease the pain," she said.

"Thank you."

"Just drink it and get out. I'll show you the way." Scottie heard a lamp being lit. Franca stood before her in one of Carlo's old monogrammed shirts and an incongruous pink flowered skirt. Black rubber boots, very clean. "Please leave."

"Yes. I will." Scottie tried to stand, but sat back on the bed. She looked up and realized she could just barely make out another figure in the darkness, across the room on a cot. "Who's there?" she called.

"No one," said Franca. "Get out of here."

Scottie realized she recognized the person on the cot. "Robertino? Is that you?"

"No," said Franca, in anguish. "You took my husband. You can't have my boy."

"Yes," said Robertino quietly. "I'm here."

"Are you all right?"

"I'm fine. But I broke my leg."

"She'll go to the police," said Franca, frantic. "You'll go to jail, for the horse."

"No. It's okay," said Scottie. "You won't go to jail. Franca, you know that. He won't go to jail."

Franca, weeping, lit another lantern. Across the room, Scottie saw Robertino clearly now, lying on his back, a cast on his leg. He was in a sort of makeshift traction.

"I stole the horse," he said. "I was coming here to ask her to hide the horse for me. But I fell off. I couldn't move. The pain was terrible. She found me, hid me from the police, took care of me, healed me. I told her not to tell anyone."

"I saved him," said Franca. She stared at Robertino for a long moment. "He looks so much like Raimondo." A sob caught in her throat.

It was wrong of Franca not to tell anyone that Robertino was here, was safe, but at the same time Scottie felt so terrible for her, to have lost a child. "I'm sorry. I know you and Carlo loved him very much." She paused. She only knew what Carlo had told her. Scottie felt she owed Franca more than that. She needed to know her side. "Were you there when it happened?"

Franca paced back and forth, agitated. Then she began to speak.

"It was my son's birthday. He was fourteen. Food was so scarce, and I just wanted to make him a nice lunch. That was all. I was lucky to find some flour. I picked the weevils out of it. Rolled it out on the kitchen table. Tortelli." Something in Franca's eyes shifted, as if she were transported back to that day. "They cook quickly. I have a little bit of butter I bought on the black market. A tiny hunk of cheese for my darling son. My husband is late. He's always late. Probably with his whore. Did he tell you that?" She turned on Scottie, fury in her eyes.

"No."

"A nurse. A German nurse. He was . . . with her. That's why he was late. I put the pasta on the table. I turn my back, to get the bread. Then I hear the planes. The Americans.

"There is no time to move. The bombs begin to rain down. The house shakes. I scream. I'm still holding the bread. I reach for my son, but he isn't there. The house disappears around me. There is a pause, a silence, I am deaf, then the sound comes back and I can hear screaming everywhere. Then I hear the sound of the planes again. I can't move. My leg is caught. I free it, but there are more bombs, more than the first time. It will never stop. Over and over and over, boom, boom, boom, dust and screaming and fire." Finally she was silent.

"I'm so sorry," Scottie said at last. "You have every right to hate America. To hate me."

Franca sat down on a chair. She picked up a jar of tomatoes, and Scottie wondered if she would hurl it at her, but then she set it down again. "I've been angry for twelve years," she said. "I'm tired." She looked at Robertino. "Then he arrived. His mother was dead, and he was hurt, like Raimondo. But he was alive. I could pretend I had my boy back." She began to cry. "I don't want him to leave."

"I know. But I need to get him to the hospital. He needs to go home. And Carlo is waiting for you."

"Carlo doesn't want me anymore. I'm broken."

"You're not broken," said Scottie. "He still loves you." She knew this was true.

A deeper quiet fell over the room. Franca put her hands over her face, her grief making her shake.

"I miss him so much," Franca cried, but she sounded different now. "I miss Raimondo."

"I know," said Robertino, pulling himself to his feet. He leaned over Franca, put his arms around her. "Thank you," he said. "Thank you for taking care of me. But I have to go now."

She nodded. Using Scottie as a crutch, Robertino hobbled out, leaving a silent Franca sitting alone.

Ecco was waiting by the car, a large chunk of horse manure in his mouth.

■ ■ ■ ■

PART FOUR:
LE CONTRADE SOPPRESSE

■ ■ ■ ■

The CIA's covert operations were conducted "on an autonomous and freewheeling basis in highly critical areas involving the conduct of foreign relations," said a follow-up report by the president's intelligence board in January 1957. "In some quarters this leads to situations which are almost unbelievable."

— Tim Weiner, *Legacy of Ashes:
The History of the CIA*

EIGHTEEN:
IL GALLO, THE ROOSTER

1.

Scottie was staring up at frescoes of the Black Death in the Ospedale Santa Maria della Scala when Tenente Pisano's face intruded into her field of vision.

"Buongiorno, signora," he said with his usual formality.

"Leave her alone," said Nonna Bea, who had been trying to spoon some horrible broth into Scottie's mouth.

"No, no, *va bene,*" said Scottie. Nonna Bea reluctantly withdrew.

"About this matter with the marchesa."

"She found Robertino, saved him," said Scottie. "He thought you were after him for stealing the horse. He fell off, broke his leg. She wasn't kidnapping him. She was healing him." Scottie had driven Robertino

477

down the mountain, brought him to the hospital. They insisted on examining Scottie, too, making sure she was all right as well, that the bump on her head was nothing more than a mild concussion.

The baby was fine.

"Yes, I have talked to Robertino," he said.

"How is he?"

"He's fine. The marchesa may be a little *pazza,* but she set the leg perfectly. He says she took very good care of him. He says he was there of his own free will. I have sent a truck for the horse."

"So she won't go to jail."

"No. She has returned to live with her husband."

It's so different here, she thought. *We haven't fought a war on American soil since the Civil War. We who stayed at home have no idea. The Italians seem so childlike, with their love of style and wine and laughter. But that's because they've been through hell, all of them, on all sides, who survived that. American tourists come here and they see only the happy, beautiful Italy they want to see, and that the Italians want them to see. The party. They don't see the scars. The ongoing struggles. Why would they? They don't see them at home, either.*

"My husband," she said. Had Pisano arrested Michael? Was he languishing in some jail somewhere?

"He was here earlier, while you were asleep. He will be back."

"Oh," she said, relieved.

"There is paperwork," he said, dropping a file folder on her nightstand. "All of which must be properly stamped and signed."

"Of course," she said.

He turned to go, then said, *"Grazie, signora."*

2.

Pisano did not tell the American woman that the night before, as she was driving up Monte Amiata, he had found her husband in the Ford office, a gun to his head. Pisano had begun talking softly as he pulled up a chair and sat down in front of the man, talking, talking, talking. Finally, the American put the gun down, and Pisano took it. Then they had continued talking.

The American began to cry, which was unpleasant, because it also made Pisano want to cry, which he could not do, except for a few very small, masculine tears that could be passed off as sweat.

"Did you kill the prostitute and Robertino Banchi?" Pisano demanded.

"No. But I think it's all my fault."

"I don't think it is. I happen to know that the prostitute got her drugs from Brigante."

Michael swiveled around to point in the direction of Brigante's warehouse. "That guy?"

"Yes. He has Mafia ties. He helped establish a network of prostitutes here, and he was trying to introduce heroin as well. And you. Apparently no one is 'only' a tractor salesman around here."

Michael looked at the gun Pisano had taken from him. "If you leave, I will end this here, right now."

"No. I need you alive. I know you are Minaccia Rossa."

Michael sighed. "I know you won't believe me, but it's a trick. To make the Communists look bad."

Pisano frowned. "Of course I believe you. Do you think I am stupid? I also know you are CIA. And that you asked Robertino to steal papers for you from Communist Party headquarters."

Michael nodded. "And then he disappeared. It is all my fault."

"I don't think so," said Pisano. "I have infiltrated every group in Siena. I do not think his disappearance is political."

"So where is he?"

"I don't know." He slapped his fist on the

desk and made Michael jump. "And this makes me angry."

Now Pisano knew the answers to these questions, and that was good. All was in order again. He thought of what the American man had said after that. How he had frowned, and rubbed his hand over his face, and said, "You said you needed me. How?"

"To keep using Minaccia Rossa to discredit the Communists."

Michael had smiled then. "I have a plan," he said. "But I could use some help."

3.

Scottie dressed behind a screen while Michael waited with Ecco.

"We were both worried," he said, nodding at the dog, who put his paws on Scottie's knees and wagged his tail.

They walked home from the hospital in silence. When the heavy front door closed behind them, Michael told her he had rented a small apartment near the Ford warehouse.

"You and Ecco can stay here for as long as you like," he said.

She did not ask him what came next.

"What can I get you?" he asked. "Cold drink? I could bring up a pizza."

"Nothing," she said. Michael sat down

next to her on the sofa.

"I'm fine," she said. "Perfectly fine. You can stop looking worried. I got a bump on the head is all." He reached for her hand. He kept his eyes down.

"I'm sorry," he whispered. "So, so sorry."

"How long have you known you . . . preferred men?"

"I don't know." His eyes were down again. He looked like he wanted to disappear into thin air.

Scottie offered, "I had a crush on a tennis pro when I was five. I remember pressing up against the fence while he played, desperate for him to notice me."

Michael sighed. "Five. That sounds about right."

"You must have been frightened."

"I don't want to be this way," he said quietly.

"Do you think you can change?"

He was silent for a moment, then shook his head. He began to tremble a little, and she reached over and took his hand.

"I'm sorry I thought you had done something to Robertino."

"I would never hurt him."

"I know that." She thought of the Minaccia Rossa flyers in the cabinet. "Are you a Communist?"

"No." He gave a short laugh, glanced around, then whispered, "That's part of . . . an operation I'm involved with.

"Oh," she said. "How are things . . . at work?"

He thought of Gordon, the polygraph, the way he had fucked everything up. "Okay," he said. "I'm busy with the reports. The election is only a few weeks away."

"You're good at this, you know," she said.

He looked up briefly, smiled. "I enjoy it, mostly." He paused, then said, "I love you very much."

She opened her mouth to respond, but he stopped her. "Don't. I know you don't love me back. It's fine. But I want you to know that you are the most extraordinary person I've ever met. You're smart, you're kind, you're courageous in ways I can't even fathom. I love you, and I will take care of you, no matter what."

He was gone, and she was alone.

She put her hands on her growing belly. Not alone for long, she thought. The baby would come at Christmastime. Before then she would have to decide what came next.

Nineteen:
Il Leone, The Lion

WHITE SHIELD WITH A BLACK STRIPE

1.

All along Scottie had thought that finding Robertino would solve everything, but it had only uprooted her and left her with nothing to do. Her need to dig, to know, to unbury secrets had led her to discover that her husband was a spy and a homosexual. She could not erase these things, no matter how much she wanted to. He had promised to take care of her. What did that mean? What did one do in these cases? She had no one to ask. Besides, she couldn't tell anyone — Michael's job was at risk, and more.

She realized there was one person she could talk to.

"I quite enjoyed meeting you," said Scottie on the telephone, "and I wondered if you'd like to come for a visit. My husband is away," she added.

She and Ecco met Julie at the Siena train station. Despite being visibly pregnant, Julie was straight out of the pages of *Vogue* in a tailored yellow Hermès suit with a hobble skirt, plus a frilled hat. The skirt was so tight that Scottie wondered for a second how she was going to actually descend from the first-class train car.

Julie reminded her of Leona in many ways. They were cut from the same upper-crust slice of life, and the name-dropping began immediately, the "do you know so-and-so," "my cousin at Hotchkiss," "our place in Maine" . . . This was a way of establishing status that Scottie was perfectly familiar with, after her years at boarding school and Vassar. She could play this game, but she was in no mood to.

"I believe your husband and my husband have a special friendship," said Scottie as they sat in the olive grove outside Sant'Antimo after hearing the monks intone Gregorian chants. Scottie had proposed a tour of Tuscan hill towns, Montalcino and Sant'Angelo in Colle and San Quirico, and this picnic in sight of the ancient abbey. It would give them time alone to talk, away from prying eyes and ears. She brought a loaf of bread, a half wheel of pecorino and a bottle of wine, remembering the way Carlo

485

had packed these same items for her, the last time she saw him. There was no point in thinking of Carlo as the man she should have married. There would no doubt be other men who would seem equally perfect, she imagined. The problem was what to do with the man she was already married to.

For today's picnic she had added a jar of olives and some slices of prosciutto, though the latter was attracting bees that had Julie swatting the air and emitting small shrieks.

"They're lovers," said Scottie, tossing a napkin over the prosciutto.

Julie stopped her frantic motions and looked away across the valley toward Monte Amiata. She lit a cigarette. "I've never said that out loud," she said, the smoke drifting away on the breeze. "Lovers."

Scottie waited.

"I've screamed at him about it," resumed Julie at last, her voice steady. "Cried and yelled and threatened. Doesn't do any good. He buys me things, but nothing changes." She examined her hat and tossed it aside.

"Well," said Scottie, "it's almost romantic, when you think about it."

Julie turned and looked at her sharply. "It is not. It is disgusting. How are you not angry? I've been furious for *years.*"

Scottie thought for a moment. "I'm not a

perfect wife either."

"But you're not a . . . *freak.*"

"They can't change."

"How do you know that? They could try. They could at least restrain themselves. I was livid when Michael appeared in Rome. Livid. Stalking us."

Scottie nodded. "Yes. I was upset, too, when I found out."

"The occasional dalliance I could stand. That happens, no matter who the man is. One turns a blind eye to that sort of thing. But this sickness . . ."

"Love."

"Stop calling it that."

"But isn't it better to think of it that way?"

"No. I mean, for God's sake, we're both pregnant. They have no respect."

"Do you think that Duncan loves both of you, you and Michael?"

"What a disgusting question!" Julie got up, walked away into the olive trees. Scottie waited a few moments, then stood and followed her.

"I hate you," said Julie. "If you were a better wife, maybe your husband would leave Duncan alone."

Scottie knew she shouldn't, but she laughed. "I did think that, too," she said.

"It's not funny."

"Oh God, Julie, I didn't invite you here to torment you. You're the only one who understands. The only one who knows what this is like."

Julie nodded, brushed away a tear. "Us. Mrs. Cole Porter. Maybe the Duchess of Windsor. There are rumors."

"The question is, why do you stay?" Scottie asked it in as kind a tone as she could.

Julie wandered back to the picnic blanket, poured herself another glass of Vernaccia. "My parents would never speak to me if I got a divorce."

"Is that the only reason? He has a good job, you enjoy living abroad? He's a good father, good to you in his own way?"

Julie shrugged.

"What I'm thinking," Scottie said, her voice rising, "is that there are no rules for this. The rules are effectively off. They don't live by them, and we don't have to."

"You mean lovers?" Julie said, finishing her glass of wine. "I've tried that. I thought it would make him jealous, make him pay more attention to me. He didn't care at all."

"So you're trapped."

"Yes."

Scottie let it go at that, and drove Julie around the countryside, sticking to safe topics like where to find the best ceramics, lace and handmade shoes. Buying things seemed to calm Julie, to put her back at ease. Scottie doubted her own emotions could be tempered by a pair of gorgeous leather boots, though she bought a pair, just in case.

Scottie drove Julie back to the station and kissed her on the cheek, waving good-bye as the train pulled out of the station. She looked down at Ecco and sighed.

"We need some pasta," she said.

TWENTY:
LA VIPERA, THE VIPER

YELLOW SHIELD WITH RED
AND GREEN STRIPES

1.

Michael found Sebastian at his usual table in the corner of the terrace at the Villa Scacciapensieri, reading a newspaper. He sat down and signaled the waiter for a Campari and soda.

"You never thanked me for my gift," said Sebastian.

"What gift was that?"

"*Physique Pictorial.* They're hard to come by."

Michael's eyes widened. "You sent that?"

"Discreetly wrapped in brown paper. I trust the boy didn't open it."

Michael sighed. "You didn't even know me then."

"No. But your reputation preceded you."

"Do you know everything about everyone

in Italy?"

Sebastian smiled. "Have you given any thought to my offer?"

"I can't accept it."

Sebastian tossed back his drink and called to Pippo to bring him another. "I will admit I am distressed. I can't bear to see your wife in those old dresses. At least let me give her a discount at Schiaparelli."

"She'll need maternity clothes soon, not high fashion."

"Is she terribly heartbroken over a certain tragic marchese's return to his wife?"

Michael was silent. Pippo brought them a *pinzimonio*. Sebastian grabbed a large piece of celery and wielded it like a weapon.

"And your boyfriend Duncan? How is he?"

"Is that Moscow asking?"

"Just me. Scout's honor."

"Like I would trust you."

"Oh, come on. It's precisely because I am untrustworthy that you can trust me."

Michael sighed. "He's still in Rome. There's nothing to say, really."

Sebastian studied him with narrowed eyes while crunching on the celery. "You're far and away his better in every sense, you know."

Michael selected a red pepper slice and

dunked it in the olive oil. "He's just invited me to Capri after the election." Michael had been surprised by the invitation. Duncan had waxed rhapsodic about what the trip would entail — azure water, a rowboat full of books, glasses of icy limoncello. Julie would be in Paris for the couture shows, Duncan said, and they would have two whole weeks alone.

"Yes, the election. A lot riding on that. Your friends' investments in the city. My friends' investment in the Italian market for foreign oil. Everyone but us is rich, it seems."

"So it seems," said Michael.

Sebastian dropped a sheaf of typewritten papers on the table.

"What's this?"

"The membership rolls of Siena's Communist Party."

Michael did not pick them up. "How did you get them? From Robertino?"

Sebastian smiled enigmatically. "I bought them, of course. Hadn't you noticed that everything in Italy is for sale these days? Let's just say my delivering them to you is a gesture of goodwill. I thought we might work together now and then on frustrating both sides in the pursuit of chaotic stability."

Michael did not say that he was one step ahead of him in that very mission.

Sebastian picked up the newspaper and frowned at the headline. "I thought Clare said she wasn't coming to the Palio," he said. "When is she going to let these poor people down?"

"She is coming after all," said Michael. "I'll be with her in the window at the Palazzo Comunale. It's all in place."

2.

It was the night of the *prova di notte,* when anyone could bring a horse to the piazza and test the Palio course. Scottie and Ecco were inside the apartment, watching boys and young men go rocketing around the curves on sturdy farm horses, shouting and hooting. She was envious. Finally, the last horse clattered out of the piazza and all was silent. She heard the clock strike midnight. She sighed and turned away from the window.

She was about to get into bed when she heard a knock at the door. Ecco whined instead of barked.

"It's me," called Michael. Surprised, she opened the door.

"Is everything okay? Come in," she said, but he stood in the doorway, grinning.

493

"I have a surprise for you," he said. "Get dressed. Pants."

"Why? Where are we going?"

"I told you, it's a surprise."

She changed her clothes and followed him down the stairs and through the big wooden front door. Robertino was there, grinning, holding the reins of a fat gray horse.

"You were upset when I said women couldn't ride in the Palio," said Michael. "It's a stupid rule. But no one can stop you from riding tonight."

She laughed out loud. "You two cooked up this idea?"

They both nodded bashfully.

"I told him not to bring a fast one," said Michael. "I don't want you to get hurt." He looked worried.

"This is Alisso," said Robertino. "He's a good boy." Robertino's cast was off.

"Should you be walking around on that leg?" she asked. "It's only been what — six weeks? — since you broke it."

"Nearly seven," said Robertino dismissively.

Scottie ran her hand over the neck of the gelding, put her nose against his fur and breathed in his scent. Heaven.

"You don't have to," said Michael. "Maybe this was a bad idea."

She grinned. "Give me a leg up."

"Watch that curve at San Martino," Robertino said, pointing across the piazza. "But after that, let him out."

The little gray gelding jigged anxiously underneath her, and Scottie patted his neck.

"Three times around slowly," said Michael.

"Three times around."

Scottie trotted out onto the track. The sensible thing would have been to gently canter the horse around the undulating, terrifyingly tight course. Instead Scottie let the gelding have his head. They shot toward the first curve. She tried to slow the horse, but had to settle for leaning back and aiming him high into the curve, so that she would have time and space to keep her legs under her and make it around.

The horse's stride shortened, jarring for a moment, and then lengthened again as he shot out of the curve like a slingshot. They galloped flat-out along the straightaway past the Torre del Mangia, and then had to slow for the sharp uphill turn that marked the transition to the long curve of the fan-top of the piazza. They raced up the hill, then crested and began the dangerous downhill gallop again. With every stride Scottie's joy grew.

Michael and Robertino were cheering as she galloped past them.

TWENTY-ONE:
L'ORSO, THE BEAR

BLUE SHIELD WITH A GOLD LION

August 16, 1956

1.

Scottie looked down at the gathering crowds, filling up the bleachers and the vast central part of the piazza.

The sound of drums came from everywhere as she leaned out the window and watched the *Corteo Storico* wend its way around the piazza. Huge floats depicting the symbols of the *contrade* were followed by archers, drummers and flag bearers in full action. The jockeys — *fantini* — were in ridiculous medieval costumes atop draft horses, looking hot and crabby, she thought. She waved to Robertino, who was riding for Istrice, but he seemed lost in his own world.

She looked across the piazza to the tall windows of the Palazzo Comunale, where

Michael would watch the race with the American ambassador, Clare Boothe Luce. "As Ford's local representative," he had reminded her. "I'd love to invite you, but there are only enough chairs for the dignitaries, so you wouldn't see the Palio at all," he said.

There was a knock at the front door, and she found Signor Banchi on her doorstep, having been helped up the stairs by Nonna Bea.

"Come in," she said. "VIP seating right this way."

She set chairs in the windows for them, and brought chilled white wine. Banchi announced that he had decided not to sell his farm to the American developer. Robertino could do whatever he wanted after the old man was gone, but Banchi was determined to die in his own bed. "And not any time soon," he added, vigorously tossing back his glass of wine. Together they watched the *Corteo Storico* finish its procession.

Scottie knew that Robertino and Gaudenzia were now safely inside the courtyard of the Palazzo Comunale, waiting for the signal to mount up. The gray mare and the other nine contenders would be tied to the wrought-iron circles on the columns.

"You see those whips?" said Nonna Bea,

pointing to a man walking toward where the riders were gathered. He was carrying an armful of strange curled sticks. "They're made from a dried bull's penis."

"From a bull's *what?*"

Nonna Bea laughed so hard Scottie thought she would have a stroke.

"It's true," said Banchi. "The jockeys beat each other with them."

Leave it to the Italians, she thought.

2.

Michael packed his briefcase very, very carefully with C-3 explosives. He had driven up the mountain and practiced setting off some smaller charges to test his skills, terrified out of his mind. But it turned out he was good at this. It required neatness, and precision, and color coding, all of which he was excellent at, and which pleased him. Still, it was nerve-wracking to think he was going to carry a bomb across a crowded piazza and into a government building.

A few hours later, Michael stood in a pale yellow room with tall ceilings next to the woman in gold, watching her wave to the crowds in the piazza. She did look almost exactly like Luce, he thought. It was Pisano who had found her. Pisano, who longed to oust the Reds as much as he did, though Pisano's goal was not democracy but the return of the Italian king from his exile in Portugal. He strode back and forth in his office while lecturing Michael about how a monarchy confers stability, values, a connection to history. "It eliminates corruption and upheaval. It is the only answer for a place like Italy," he thundered, his black boots shining in the light. Michael had nodded, both exhilarated to have found an ally and unsettled by Pisano's intense loyalty to Umberto II, who had ruled for exactly one month in 1946, and who Michael thought had all the leadership qualities of a head of cabbage.

The woman who would pretend to be Luce was an American Pisano had met in Naples during the war, a nurse. Michael suspected they had had an affair. She was from Louisiana, she had whispered to Michael. Pisano had lined up a black limo, and Michael had added small American flags to it. Pisano provided security guards, who were not in on the ruse. Only he and Michael and the woman knew what was happening, and Luce herself, who was safely on Niarchos's yacht in the Aegean. He hadn't told Duncan. He wanted it to be a surprise, the triumph of his Siena mission, the daring move that would once and for all sway the Sienese away from the Communists. A Communist attempt on the life of the American ambassador herself.

"No one will be hurt?" Pisano had asked when Michael explained the plan to him.

"No one," said Michael. But in truth, there would be one victim.

3.

Banchi gave a yell and clambered to his feet as the horses and jockeys exited from the hidden courtyard. The crowd began to scream. Nonna Bea jumped up and down.

Loyalty, thought Scottie. She felt she would never really understand it. Team sports, politics, patriotism and religion — she felt left out of these passions that electrified people. She was a party of one.

Scottie could see Robertino in the Istrice colors, his thin legs hanging down Gaudenzia's sides. The *contrada* had given him the nickname Mezz'etto, which roughly translated to Half Pint.

They rode uphill to a spot in front of Scottie's favorite ceramic shop. There, they stopped. Two ropes were raised, one in front of the horses and one behind. The horses were restless. Gaudenzia spun once, but

Robertino put a hand on her neck and she calmed.

"Don't waste your energy, mare," Scottie whispered. The entire crowd held its breath.

There were two false starts when nervous horses broke through the rope. Scottie felt faint. She was worried Banchi would have a heart attack.

"Give him a grappa," called Nonna Bea, fanning herself with a copy of *Vogue* she grabbed off a side table.

Finally, with the boom of a cannon, the rope dropped and the horses sprang forward.

4.

The nurse posing as Luce, caught up in the excitement of the race, was startled when Michael grabbed her arm firmly.

"Go. Now," he said.

She strode quickly across the empty yellow room and slipped out the door to where the *carabinieri* were waiting outside. They would escort her down to the waiting limo that would speed away, out of the city. "La Luce" would have narrowly escaped death at the hands of a Communist fringe group.

Pisano had told him to make sure he was well clear. But this way was better. An American death would make it a real event.

And he would die a hero, if only in his own mind. It wasn't as good as his brother's death, but it was dramatic, and it had a purpose.

Michael looked at his watch. He set the briefcase down in the window and waited. The cheering from the piazza was tremendous. It seemed to make the building itself shake.

There would be a bang, some smoke, and the *carabinieri* would rush in and find him. "Luce" would be seen as the intended target, safely escaped, the Reds blamed, the honor of the Palio insulted, and the Catholics embraced for their sense of safety and security and tradition. Vestri would win the election, and Italy would not go Communist. World War III would be averted. Scottie would get his life insurance, and a fresh start. He hoped she would understand.

I hope she names the baby after me, he thought. A nice funeral, maybe at Arlington . . . lilies . . . some white roses . . .

5.

Pantera and Onda broke first, but collided on the first San Martino, and both jockeys hit the ground and rolled to safety, arms over their heads like potato bugs. The riderless horses bolted forward.

"They can still win, those two horses," said Nonna Bea. Scottie nodded.

"Istrice!" shouted Banchi. Robertino and Gaudenzia were in sixth position. It would be a tough road to victory from there. They made it safely through the Casato turn, and finished the first lap.

"Two to go," muttered Scottie.

"Twenty-one years we haven't won!" shouted Nonna Bea. "Come on, you scoundrel!"

They rounded San Martino for the second time. Robertino slipped past the Ram and the Owl, putting him in fourth. The track sloped sharply down, then up again. Scottie remembered every bone-jarring foot of it from her wild ride the other night.

Bruco fell at the Casato turn, and the horse swerved, letting Robertino and Gaudenzia slip past into third.

"One more!" she shouted.

Gaudenzia masterfully negotiated the third San Martino, and slipped past the Eagle. Istrice was now in second, behind Snail.

Scottie shifted her binoculars up away from the race, saw Michael alone in the window. The one person who knew everything about her, who loved her despite all of her flaws, who had committed his life to her, was Michael.

I have to tell him, she thought. *Right now.*

"Go go go!" shouted Banchi at the horses as Scottie slipped out of the apartment. She made her way down the stairs but could hardly get out of the building, the crowds were so thick. She pushed her way through.

Scottie paused before she ducked into the building where Michael was. She saw Robertino's helmet fly off. He ducked his head and kicked Gaudenzia forward, and the mare leapt past Tanaquilla.

Scottie slipped past the security guard, who was too intent on the race to notice, and ran up the stairs.

"Michael," she said as she threw open the door of the yellow room. "Michael, I love you."

Michael paled as he saw her, shouted, "Scottie! Get out!"

6.

Banchi and Nonna Bea cheered as Robertino raised his whip in victory. His *contrada* members poured onto the track and surrounded him, and he was raised up to the sky. After twenty-one years, Istrice was victorious. It no longer mattered who his parents were. Robertino was reborn, a son

505

of Siena, a hero to his people.

And that was when the bomb went off.

Twenty-Two:
La Quercia, The Oak Tree

BLUE SHIELD WITH BLACK AND WHITE STRIPES, OAK GARLAND

1.

Pisano hoped the papers would call him a hero. He had been the first to rush into the bombed-out room, followed quickly by firemen. To his horror, there were two people lying inert on the floor. No one was supposed to be here! And what was worse was that he saw the person on top was the American. He went to him, rolled him gently over. Michael's body was shielding that of . . . *"Dio mio!"* he shouted. "Get a doctor!"

It is all my fault, he thought, while at the same time coming up with many ways to deny his involvement should it ever come to light.

He thought the Americans were dead, but to his infinite relief the woman sat up as

507

they kneeled over her.

"Michael," she said, reaching for her husband, grabbing his hand.

For what seemed like a thousand years, he didn't move.

And then, thanks to the infinite grace of the Madonna, whose name Pisano swore he would never take in vain again, the stupid American's eyes opened.

2.

Once again resting under the frescoed gaze of the sufferers of the Black Death, Scottie made Michael tell her the whole plan. Everything. He told her all about the Dark Arts, that he was sent to sway the election, that he was supposed to arm a militia in case of a Communist victory, and that he had planned to be the only casualty of the false flag attack by Minaccia Rossa.

"So you were leaving me to raise our child alone?"

"I hoped you would remarry. One of those Social Register types."

"Eew," she said.

They were checked over, and found to be miraculously unhurt, with the exception of some tiny pieces of window glass in Michael's back.

Ugo Rosini denounced Minaccia Rossa as

a violent fringe group, and was photographed bringing flowers to Michael and Scottie in the hospital.

Michael had mixed feelings when he received flowers from Ambassador Luce addressed "to a true American."

3.

"I thought life would be easier for you without me," Michael told Scottie when she asked him to move back into the apartment with her and Ecco.

"We're going to have to figure this out day by day," she said. "Today, I want you here."

"But don't you want to return to the U.S. to have the baby?"

"There's time," she said, and left it at that. He moved into the guest room. He was surprised the first day she came to his room in the morning with the newspapers and a basket of rolls and butter and got in bed with him, but after that it became their new morning routine, to lie next to each other, Ecco on their feet, and go over the news, the gossip and the movie listings.

"Gina Lollobrigida's in a new version of *The Hunchback of Notre Dame,*" she said.

"You could be in that one," he said, patting her tummy. "You could play Quasimodo, except the tragedy is that the hump is on your front."

She swatted him with the paper.

They went back to work together at the Ford office. It made sense that she be the one to get out and talk to people, get a feel for what was happening with the election. She was just better at it. She also helped him draw moral lines. No more Dark Arts. Michael focused on the bureaucratic aspects of the job that gave him a sense of making order from chaos. He had taken the cash that Duncan sent from Rome for Vestri and other shadowy purposes and stashed it. He told himself it wasn't theft — it was just safekeeping. He knew the Agency did not — could not — keep track of where it went.

He had promised to give Pisano the map that indicated where the arms cache was hidden, but after talking to Scottie he burned it. Pisano was angry, but what could he do? They were both operating outside of all laws.

Scottie talked to everyone. She had a real feel for the job, he had to admit. Her reports made you feel like you were on the ground, living in the culture. She was an excellent intelligence officer, if without any counterintelligence instincts. Michael liked it that way.

They were a good team.

4.

A heavy envelope with the crest of the Chigi Piccolomini family arrived, addressed to Scottie. She held it for a moment, not opening it, just feeling its weight. She had caught a glimpse of Carlo and Franca one day coming out of San Domenico with Ilaria, but she had stepped into a doorway, unwilling to intrude. They looked happy, she thought. Finally she opened the envelope, and there was a short note from Carlo: *Franca and I are going overseas for an extended trip. To show our gratitude we have left a small gift for you with Signor Banchi. Do keep an eye out for porcupines and wild boars . . .*

Curious, Scottie wandered down to Banchi's with Ecco. There, standing between the two enormous oxen, she found the small black mare she had ridden at Carlo's. The mare nickered at her, and Scottie put her face against the horse's neck.

"Thank you," she whispered.

5.

Her days now began with a ride. Michael was anxious about her falling off, but Scottie reassured him that she and the little mare took leisurely strolls that allowed her to meet and chat with country people, who often invited her in for a coffee, a glass of wine or, in the case of a shepherdess, a wedge of freshly made pecorino. Being atop a horse gave her a different perspective on the landscape and the people who lived in harmony with it. She dismounted to join the *vendemmia,* or grape harvest, greeted mushroom hunters under the oaks, and chatted with old women gathering chestnuts in the forests. The horse-crazy little girl who had fought for blue ribbons and acceptance was still inside her, but was now just one part of a different Scottie who saw the mare as a way to connect with the world rather than conquer it.

6.

Michael finally made good on his promise to teach her to cook. They began one Saturday morning with his *sfogliatelle* recipe. He described the laborious process of creating fine pastry, layer by layer. "Your turn," he said, pushing the sack of flour toward her.

"Not even going to try," she said, pouring some grappa into his orange juice.

"What are you doing?"

"Evening the score. If you make pastry like that, I'm never going to measure up. Plus, I've never seen you drunk."

"I don't like to lose control."

"I noticed. Maybe you should, once."

"Why?"

She poured a hefty splash of liquor into his coffee as well. He made a face, but downed the coffee. "What about you?"

"One of us should stay alert," she said. "To defend us in case of invasion. And I think it should be the pregnant lady." She struck a karate-chop pose.

"That *is* terrifying."

He showed her how to roll out sheets of fresh pasta as she poured him champagne, and then he demonstrated how to sear a steak while she poured him red wine.

"Hey, the meat's not gray inside," she said. "And so tender. Who knew?" She pushed her plate back. "Why should I learn all this if you're already so good at it?"

"Everyone should know how to cook."

"Well, I think everyone should know how to dance." She put on a Duke Ellington record and they danced in their bare feet. He was drunk, loose, laughing in a way she hadn't seen before. His face was finally relaxed. She taught him to Lindy hop, swing, jitterbug and boogie-woogie. They whirled around the room until they fell onto the sofa, dizzy and panting.

"You're good. The first man who didn't crush my toes," she said.

"It's because of my feet. Are these not the loveliest feet you've ever seen?" He lifted his feet for her to admire.

"They look like feet to me."

"No, no. Look closer. Look at the curve of the arch, the shape of that toe."

She was laughing. "I'm sorry, but feet are pretty much feet. They keep us upright, but they're not really much to look at."

"Are you kidding me?" he said, weaving over to the bookcase and returning, mock serious, with a volume on Michelangelo. He opened to the Pietà. "Do you not see the resemblance?"

She made a show of studying the photo of the marble statue and then his feet, using a cocktail stirrer as a lorgnette. "I suppose they are a little Christlike, now that you point it out."

"Right?!"

"Quite possibly your feet are prettier than Miss America."

"Let's not exaggerate," he said. "Let's just agree they're perfect."

"Hey, want to go see the new Sophia Loren tonight?" she asked the next morning as he was getting dressed. "*La fortuna di essere donna*. The luck to be a woman? Lucky woman?"

514

"Actually, I have to go to Rome." He had been feeling slightly hungover as he attempted to tie his tie in the mirror on the door of the armoire, but now he was suddenly sober. He went over and sat on the bed next to her. He had been putting it off, but there were reports he had to deliver. He wasn't even sure if Duncan was free that night, but he knew what the word "Rome" would mean to Scottie. He was anxious, unsure of what she would say.

She stared at him for a long beat, her face frozen, then forced a smile. "Have fun," she said.

"You don't . . . mind?"

"It's not what I expected when I said 'I do.' But at least I know." She got out of the bed. "I'll miss you. But I mean it, have fun."

He felt terrible. "What will you do tonight? Go to the movies without me?"

She stopped in the doorway, the emerald green silk pajamas he had bought her glowing in the morning sun.

"I might call Ugo Rosini."

Alarm shot through him, and yes, jealousy. "We're trying to defeat him in the election, remember?"

"All the more reason to get close to him."

Michael was silent.

"This isn't easy," she said at last.

"No," he said. "I'm sorry."

"Don't be sorry. Wear the blue suit. You look really handsome in that one."

She padded away, the dog trailing behind her.

Twenty-Three:
La Spadaforte, The Sword

RED SHIELD WITH A BLACK AND WHITE
LADDER FLANKED BY TWO SWORDS

November 1956

1.

It rained on Election Day. In the Ford office Michael had one of the new TVs now on sale in Siena tuned to the RAI news, and a radio on as well, also tuned to the RAI, and another radio tuned to Voice of America. Scottie came in, closing her umbrella. She slipped out of her raincoat. Her belly was growing large. She sat down and put her feet up on the desk, and Ecco curled up beneath her.

"Any election results yet?" she asked.

"No — the news is all about Hungary." From student protests in July, and the hijacking of a plane, the rebellion in Hungary against communism had swelled into a full-scale revolution. Everyone talked constantly about loyalty — to Hungary, to ideals of communism, to their ancestors and to their unborn children. Ten days ago, government buildings were seized and a new prime minister was declared.

The Soviets, it appeared, were content to let Hungary self-govern. Hungarian independence from Moscow was a reality.

They sat side by side, staring at the blurry black-and-white images.

"Did you talk to Rome?"

He nodded. "I could hear champagne corks popping in the background. Duncan was crowing about the uprising, but also admitted the Agency had been caught by surprise and that they have no one on the ground in Budapest. They're getting all of their information from the radio, like us."

"They've thrown off the Soviet yoke," Scottie said, as Michael poured them each a cup of tea. "I guess that's good."

"The CIA hired planes to drop leaflets telling Hungarians to rebel," Michael said, amazed. "And they did."

Michael and Scottie waited for Siena's election results, but they were not optimistic. Despite the vicious attack by Minaccia Rossa on Ambassador Luce, Ugo Rosini's left coalition was poised for victory.

The phone rang. Michael picked it up. "Rosini won," he heard Pisano say with a heavy sigh. He hung up.

Michael was crushed. He had almost inadvertently killed Scottie, had tried to kill himself to sway the election, and it wasn't enough. "Are you happy Ugo won?"

"No. But he was never going to lose," said Scottie. "Vestri was just too corrupt, even for Italians. You know that." In the weeks before the election Vestri had been caught taking a kickback from Lippincott, though interestingly enough, a judge had let Lippincott's deals and zoning waivers stand. Having tried Vestri's capitalism for a summer, Rosini's brand of "soft" communism was clearly what the working people of Siena wanted. Strong unions, good schools, pensions, health care, minimum wages, mandated vacation time. A humane lifestyle for everyone, employee and boss alike.

Their side had lost the election, and thus Michael had failed at his mission. And the truth was, despite everything, he was frankly not all that sorry about it. Vestri was a hard man to love, and Rosini was smart and had the city's best interests at heart. If Scottie liked him, he couldn't be all bad.

Michael took some papers out of the new safe, set a trashcan in the middle of the room, then burned the papers.

"What's that?"

"The membership rolls of the Communist Party."

Scottie raised her eyebrows.

"They won. It's over. A list of names does not tell you people's stories," he said. Was this treason? He wondered, watching the pages turn to ash. None of it was as clear as it had seemed when he was growing up, reciting the Pledge of Allegiance.

Michael was tamping down the ashes when Scottie sat forward and turned up the volume.

"Oh my God," she said. "Tanks."

Michael sat next to her. Even Ecco sat up.

For the next few hours, they watched in horrified silence as journalists shouted into the camera, ran and began to film again. Bloody faces passed in front of the screen, and sometimes the transmission was lost and the TV went black. Then they switched to the radio, and back again.

As the world watched and listened, Soviet tanks moved into Budapest and quickly and viciously crushed the rebellion. People were loaded onto cattle cars to be taken presumably to Siberia. The Hungarians sent out distress call after distress call to the West, begging the U.S. to take action.

"Help us, America!" shouted a frantic woman as gunfire could be heard in the background.

"Why aren't we sending troops?" demanded Scottie the next day, as the violence continued. "Isn't Eisenhower seeing this?"

"Britain and France are tied up in the Suez, and Eisenhower is adamant that America will not act alone," said Michael after talking to Duncan.

They watched as refugees poured across the border into Austria, and communications from the capital went dark.

"Call him again," said Scottie.

Michael called Duncan on the secure line. "You set them up for this," he said. "You led them to believe that the West would back them up."

"I never said that personally to anyone," said Duncan, though he sounded shaken.

Michael understood then what the mission had been. He hung up, sat down next to Scottie again, took her hand.

"They knew this would happen," he said. On TV there were images of the Soviets lining up protesters and shooting them. Scottie flinched, turned away.

"That," Michael said, pointing a shaky finger at the TV. "That — what we're all seeing — this is the best argument for

American-style democracy that can be made."

Scottie turned to him. "What are you saying?"

"When they dropped those leaflets. This was the mission. This." He pointed to the screen again. "Either the revolution would succeed, or it wouldn't. But it would be on television, so it was a win-win for America either way."

2.

He felt sympathy when, in the days that followed the Soviet crack-down, the Italian Communists tried to cope with and eventually split over the brutality unleashed on the unarmed Hungarians. This was not the happy workers' paradise they had been sold on those visits to Moscow. This was an oligarchy. An occupation. A nightmare. Totalitarianism. They did not want to be next.

The Italian Communist Party's national leader, Togliatti, caught between a hard place and Moscow, expressed support for the invasion. This provoked Ugo Rosini, along with a hundred other leading Italian Communists, to sign the Manifesto of 101, which called for discussion within the Party about its ties to the Soviets. As a result he was publicly branded a traitor by Togliatti. Rosini called a press conference and, weeping, tore up his membership card and resigned from the Party. "I can no longer see in the actions of the Soviet Union a desire for the common good," he said, "only for a familiar kind of oppressive empire."

On a national level, the Socialists dissolved their alliance with the Communists, and joined the centrist bloc of the Catholics in support of NATO and American bases on Italian soil.

"It's Duncan's dream come true," Michael told Scottie. "And Luce is learning to love it, too. She now says a center-left alliance was what she wanted all along."

Luce resigned her post and left Italy in triumph. At her last press conference, in a white mink stole and long white evening gloves, diamonds glittering around her neck, she waved good-bye from the Trevi Fountain.

"Arrivederci, Italia!" she called to the crowds. *"Grazie!"*

3.

By mid-November, the election was behind them and the power of the Communists in Italy deeply diminished. On a cool evening with hints of winter in the air, Michael and

Scottie walked across Piazza del Campo. Scottie stopped before they got to the front door, the huge oak arch under which their life in Siena had begun.

"What happens next?" she asked, standing beside the Fontana Gaia in a pair of gray flannel trousers and a houndstooth jacket. She had that "swallowed a basketball" look now — she would deliver for New Year's. 1957. What would that year bring, other than a new baby? He could not see in her the girl he had met at a party at Vassar seven months earlier. He had so vastly misunderstood and underestimated her, and every other force in his life. He had always seen her as a burden, but she was a friend, the best friend he had ever had. He really did love her.

"I don't know," he said, cautious. The two of them had not talked about the future.

"Will Duncan let you stay here, or send you somewhere else?"

"I don't know."

"Do you still believe in all of it?"

Though he had much time to think, Michael did not waste time debating the ethics of the double lives he led, as a gay man and as a spy. Like Scottie, with her Vassar-dance entrapment of him, he had simply done what he needed to survive.

He thought for a moment. "I do. Hungary proved we can't stop, because they're not going to stop. I don't want to see a world run by Moscow." He paused, then said, "They're talking about making Luce the ambassador to Brazil. But it could just as easily be Bangkok, or Bali, or Beirut."

"Will Duncan go, too?"

"I think he might. Scottie —" He paused. "Maybe you want to go back to America and never see me again. I'll give you a divorce, support you and the child."

She had thought a lot about what it would be like to be divorced and raising a child alone. She didn't have family to help. She knew if she had to, she could do it, but the idea sounded terribly lonely to her, at least right now.

Michael continued, searching her face with his eyes. "But if you need — if you want me to still be your husband, and a father, I will be a good one."

It was not the kind of love story she had read about in books or seen in the movies, not the kind of picture that sold cake frosting or cars or lipstick. And yet they were not playing roles, at least not to each other. It was a very different kind of marriage. She did not have to be anything other than herself. They had no secrets from each other, but many from the rest of the world. They liked each other, enjoyed each other's company. She had to tolerate his lover, and there would probably be more, but there would never be other women. She could have lovers of her own. It was what was politely called a marriage of convenience. But there were so many women trapped in inconvenient marriages to men they couldn't stand that it seemed exciting to contemplate continuing to be married to someone who genuinely loved her, and always would. And then there was the lasagna.

She thought of Julie. She hoped she would have the courage to leave if she ever felt like that. She was pretty sure she would.

She felt more ambivalent about the work they did. But it was better to be on the inside, she thought, being a voice of reason, than to abandon the Agency to people who saw anyone who didn't look like them or speak their language as something less than human beings. She thought of what Carlo had said about the cost of being on the wrong side of history. She loved her country, and what it stood for, and because she knew its secrets and did not always trust its leaders to do the right thing, she would keep the promise she had made herself to not just love America, but to know it, to see how others saw it, to recognize its flaws and injustices, and try to make it better.

If the CIA would ship a car around the world, then likely they would ship a horse.

A huge flock of starlings danced and swooped over their heads, forming strange cloudlike patterns. Michael looked up. "A murmuration," he said as the birds whirled in silent billowing shapes. "No one understands how it works, who's in charge."

Together they stared up, awed by the unexpected, inexplicable perfection of it.

"Brazil," she said, as if it were neither a question nor an answer.

ACKNOWLEDGMENTS

Many people contributed expertise, moral support, feedback and life-sustaining amounts of mortadella to make this novel happen. John and Jennifer Brancato deserve some kind of very large and shiny trophy for listening to me talk endlessly about this book *for years on end,* for coming along for the research, for reading draft after draft, all the while sharing exquisite food and drink. I am deeply grateful to Ranieri Polese and Helene Cadario (Ranieri: I promise I will send your books back now); Sarah, Giugi and Elisa Sesti; Charlotte Sommer; Keri Hardwick; Kathleen McCleary; Lisa Bannon; Art Streiber; Glynis Costin; Lacy Crawford; Lynette Cortez; Joanna Lipari; John Paulett; Eileen Daspin; Logan Robertson; Jessica Marshall; Sandy Schuler; John Ziaukas; Loren Segan — *grazie*! Elisabeth Dyssegaard: You are wonderful in every way. Claudia Cross: You are a great friend as well as a great agent. My colleagues, my students and especially my fellow writers at College of the Sequoias: Thank you for being so supportive. A special thanks for early kind words from Patricia Hampl, Robert Hellenga, Julia Claiborne Johnson, Chris Pavone, Diane Leslie and John Kwiatkowski. To the real Camelia: I'm toasting you up there in horse heaven, and thanking all of those who put up with you on earth: Andrea, Silvia, Pier Giorgio, Maura. A special thank you to Mark Ganem. *Salute!*

Every writer stands on the shoulders of many others. I relied upon these and other works to help me ground this novel in actual history: *1956: L'anno spartiacque,* by Luciano Canfora; *Advertising America: The United States Information Service in Italy (1945–1956),* by Simona Tobia; *The Brothers: John Foster Dulles, Allen Dulles and Their Secret World War,* by Stephen Kinzer; *The Good Spy: The Life and Death of Robert Ames,* by Kai Bird; *La Ragazza del Palio,* directed by Luigi Zampa; *Legacy of Ashes: The History of the CIA,* by Tim Weiner; *L'Italia in Movimento: Storia Sociale degli Anni Cinquanta,* by Luca Gorgolini; *Price of Fame: The Honorable Clare Boothe Luce,* by Sylvia Jukes Morris.

ABOUT THE AUTHOR

Christina Lynch's picaresque journey includes chapters in Chicago and at Harvard, where she was an editor on the *Harvard Lampoon.* She was the Milan correspondent for *W* magazine and *Women's Wear Daily,* and disappeared for four years in Tuscany. In L.A. she was on the writing staff of *Unhappily Ever After; Encore, Encore; The Dead Zone* and *Wildfire.* She now lives in the foothills of the Sierra Nevada. She is the co-author of two novels under the pen name Magnus Flyte. She teaches at College of the Sequoias. *The Italian Party* is her debut novel under her own name.